Praise for

*Sinners & Saints*

"Murray and Billingsley keep things lively and fun."

—*Juicy* magazine

"Double the fun, with a message of faith, *Sinners & Saints* will delight readers with two of their favorite characters from two of their favorite authors. It's a match made in heaven!"

—*Grace* magazine

Praise for

*The Deal, the Dance, and the Devil*

"Murray's story has the kind of momentum that prompts you to elbow disbelief aside and flip the pages in horrified enjoyment."

—*The Washington Post*

Praise for

*Sins of the Mother*

"*Sins of the Mother* shows that when the going gets tough, it's best to make an effort and rely on God's strength. It gives the message that there is hope no matter what, and that people must have faith."

—FictionAddict.com

"Ha[s] a great blend of faith, reality, conflict, and just enough heartbreaking scenes to keep you enthralled."

—HelloBeautiful.com

"Final word: Christian fiction with a powerful kick."

—Afro.com

Praise for
*Lady Jasmine*

"She's back! Jasmine has wreaked havoc in three VCM novels, including last year's *Too Little, Too Late*. In *Lady Jasmine* the schemer everyone loves to loathe breaks several commandments by the third chapter."

—*Essence*

"Jasmine is the kind of character who doesn't sit comfortably on a page. She's the kind who jumps inside a reader's head, runs around and stirs up trouble—the kind who stays with the reader long after the last page is turned."

—*The Huntsville Times* (Alabama)

Praise for
*Too Little, Too Late*

"[In this book] there are so many hidden messages about love, life, faith, and forgiveness. Murray's vividness of faith is inspirational."

—*The Clarion-Ledger* (Jackson, Mississippi)

"An excellent entry in the Jasmine Larson Bush Christian Lit saga; perhaps the best so far. . . . Fans will appreciate this fine tale. . . . A well-written, intense drama."

—*Midwest Book Review*

# Destiny's Divas

## VICTORIA CHRISTOPHER MURRAY

A TOUCHSTONE BOOK

PUBLISHED BY SIMON & SCHUSTER

NEW YORK   LONDON   TORONTO   SYDNEY   NEW DELHI

Touchstone
A Division of Simon & Schuster, Inc.
1230 Avenue of the Americas
New York, NY 10020

First Touchstone trade paperback edition June 2012

TOUCHSTONE and colophon are registered trademarks of Simon & Schuster, Inc.

For information about special discounts for bulk purchases, please contact Simon & Schuster Special Sales at 1-866-506-1949 or business@simonandschuster.com.

The Simon & Schuster Speakers Bureau can bring authors to your live event. For more information or to book an event contact the Simon & Schuster Speakers Bureau at 1-866-248-3049 or visit our website at www.simonspeakers.com.

Designed by Akasha Archer

Manufactured in the United States of America

10  9  8  7  6  5  4  3  2  1

Library of Congress Cataloging-in-Publication Data
   Murray, Victoria Christopher.
      Destiny's Divas / Victoria Christopher Murray.—1st Touchstone trade
   paperback ed.
         p. cm.
      1. African American gospel singers—Fiction. 2. Christian women—Fiction.
   I. Title.
   PS3563.U795D47 2012
   813'.54—dc23

                                                           2012011869

ISBN 978-1-4516-5046-4
ISBN 978-1-4516-5047-1 (ebook)

# Destiny's Divas

# Prologue

The Toyota Center rocked with thunderous applause as Destiny's Divas, swathed in purple, sauntered onto the stage. They paused, held hands, raised their arms into the air, then strolled away from one another, each to her own mark. Liza, with the elegance of royalty, moved stage left; Raine's sister locks, wrapped high upon her head, bounced as she edged toward stage right. And the young one, the beautiful one, as Sierra was so often called, held court at center stage.

As the deafening ovation continued, the three singing evangelists peered into the darkened arena, seeing no one. But, of course, they were there—twenty thousand Texans had come to worship, praise, and celebrate with Destiny's Divas.

With a concerted, majestic raise of their hands, the Divas quieted the capacity crowd and the air thickened with anticipation.

Three chords on the keyboard, and then the first three notes of their signature song. . . .

"Love the Lord . . ."

That was all their fans needed. The men and the women who'd paid fifty, one hundred, up to two hundred dollars for a ticket rose to their feet and roared their approval. The audience sang and swayed with the melody of the song that had stayed at the top of the gospel and R & B charts for five weeks.

After the first stanza, Raine and Liza pivoted, and with their sequined gowns flowing behind them they sashayed to the center, joining Sierra.

The people stayed with them, all those thousands of backup singers, worshipping and praising with one accord. At the end of the song, the lights on the stage slowly dimmed and the three posed, creating a *Charlie's Angels*–esque silhouette as they held that last note for seconds that nearly turned into a minute.

The thunderous cheering returned, vibrating the walls. The audience clapped, they stomped, they cheered. As the lights came up once again, Sierra, Raine, and Liza bowed to the ovation, soaking in the adoration that came to them from this: their first night, in their first city of their first tour. For minutes, they let the crowd adore them, then Raine and Liza eased back and rested on the high stools behind them on the stage.

"All right, Houston," Sierra said. "How's everyone tonight?" Her tenor tone reverberated through the arena.

"Great," "Wonderful," "Terrific," blended together and floated back to the stage, sounding like a new song.

"It is so good to be here, deep in the heart of Texas!" Sierra shouted as she sashayed to the left.

More applause.

"So, y'all ready for some real talk?" she asked, this time swinging to her right.

Laughter mixed with their applause—the crowd loved to

hear the Divas sing, but they'd also come to hear their motivating testimonies. This was the first time the Divas were speaking in person and this crowd couldn't wait.

Sierra strolled past the stool that had been placed in the center of the stage for her, but she never planned to sit. She would strut through her ten-minute testimony, hoping that would make her a little less nervous.

"Let's get down to it, right now," Sierra said. She paused, and even though just about everyone in the arena knew what she was going to say, they leaned forward with expectancy. "I'm saved . . . I'm single . . . and I'm celibate!"

"And you're fine," a guy yelled out from one of the front rows.

Laughter rose from those who were close enough to hear.

Sierra laughed, too; she was used to the compliments. "Thank you," she said. "But, I'm not here to talk about how I look on the outside; I'm here to talk about who's living with me on the inside. And inside of me, right here"—she pressed her index finger on her chest, then raised her hand in the air—"is Jesus!"

The audience was on their feet once again, and behind Sierra, the other two in the trio applauded as well. As the crowd quieted, Raine reached for Liza's hand. This was the beginning of their twenty-city tour, and they were all fueled by the adrenaline that came with success. Two number one singles, their first CD that had just dropped today, and now this. Did it get any better?

"Let me tell you how Jesus saved me," Sierra began as Raine and Liza settled back, both waiting for their turn to share.

And they would share, but not one of them would have any clue that their testimonies would end tonight. No one in the arena would have been able to predict that this would be the first and final show. Because in just hours, every lie they'd ever spoken would be revealed, every secret they ever held would be exposed, and every one of their lives would be changed.

After all, that's what happens with murder—it changes everything.

## CHAPTER 1

# *Sierra*

*F*ive had become her lucky number!

That was Sierra's thought as she climbed into the back of the taxi. She slammed the door shut before she said, "One Hundred Twenty-third and Morningside."

The turbaned gentleman gave her a cautious glance, and Sierra knew what he was thinking—she hadn't given an address and she was going up to Harlem, so she must be a jumper. Just because she was young and she was black, he thought she was gonna jump out without paying.

She wanted to roll her eyes when his glance stayed on her through the rearview mirror, but she smiled instead. He sighed as if it was too late to get rid of her, and edged the car away from the curb in front of Madison Square Garden where she'd just had lunch at The Afternoon Martini.

From the way the man mumbled, Sierra wondered if he was praying or if he was cursing her out. Well, he didn't have to worry about her jumping; she had way too much class *and* she was in a spectacular mood.

It was the number five that had her feeling this way.

"You ladies are still at the top of the gospel charts," Yvonne, Destiny's Divas' manager, had told her, Raine, and Liza over a celebratory lunch. " 'Love Unlimited' is hanging tough. Still number one."

"That's five weeks now, right?" Raine had asked.

"Yup," Yvonne had nodded and then raised her martini glass in a toast to the women. "And I've just confirmed your tour schedule. Another city was added—Winston-Salem—so twenty cities, five weeks. We'll start in Houston and end it right here in the Garden."

For Sierra, that part was both exciting and disconcerting. She was looking forward to the pampering that came with staying in upscale hotels and being whisked from one place to the next in limousines. But on the downside, she would be away from Andre for a long time.

As the cab rolled up Eighth Avenue, Sierra pulled out her phone to check to see if she had any messages from him. Nothing, so she clicked over to her Twitter timeline. But as she scrolled through the updates that she'd missed in the last ten minutes, her mind was on the love of her life.

This wasn't the best time to be leaving. Not with her birthday coming up in a week. She was going to be twenty-five five days after Valentine's Day and Andre was about to propose to her, though Sierra wasn't sure if he was going to do it on Valentine's Day or wait for her actual birthday. He hadn't exactly shared his plans, but he had given her a boatload of clues letting her know what was coming.

Like the hint he gave her a few weeks back. The two of them were bumping arms and shoulders and legs while they jockeyed for position inside her bathroom, which had only enough square footage for one and a half people at a time.

"Baby, we need a house!" he'd said as he smiled at her through the cracked vanity mirror.

"Really? We?" she'd repeated, wanting to make sure she'd heard him right.

He nodded. "Uh-huh. With lots of bedrooms and bathrooms." He laughed.

Sierra's heart had almost stopped beating. The only time a man talked about a house was when he was ready for a wife—that's what her mother had told her.

Hint number two came a couple of days later when she was at his apartment and she'd noticed that the pictures were down. Finally! The pictures that had been the bane of their relationship. The pictures of his ex-fiancée who'd broken off their engagement just a few days before Sierra and Andre had met.

How many fights had they had about the photographs that Andre still had on the living room mantel? Whatever the number, the conversation was always the same.

"Why do you still have pictures of *her*?" Sierra would ask.

"I already told you; I'm not taking down pictures of my mother."

Okay, true—Andre's mother was in all the pictures with that girl, but there had to be a way to handle this. Sierra wanted Andre to either get new pictures of his mother or grab a pair of scissors and get to cutting out Ole Girl—a project she would happily take on if he wouldn't.

Her nagging hadn't done much, though. At least not until the day she'd met him at his 14th Street apartment for an afternoon delight. They were only going to be there for an hour or so, and as they made love on the sofa, Sierra had rolled her head to the

side. Her eyes fluttered open and she noticed the empty mantel—every picture frame gone.

She had an instant orgasm.

Andre hadn't said a word and she hadn't asked. But no words
were needed. Sierra knew what this meant—Andre was making
room for her.

Then there was the biggest clue of all—Andre's credit card
bill. She'd just been wandering around his apartment wrapped
in one of his sheets last Sunday morning while he'd run to the
corner liquor store for a bottle of champagne so they could
make mimosas. She'd gone into his office and there it was—a
credit card bill was sitting right there, in plain view. Well, maybe
not in plain view; she'd had to jimmy the lock on his desk to get
the drawer open and then . . . it was right there for her to see. A
credit card bill with a charge for twenty-two thousand dollars!
To a store that was famous for their engagement rings—Tiffany's.

Sierra hadn't been looking for anything in particular, but
she'd found a treasure. Tiffany's. Twenty-two thousand dollars.
She wasn't sure how he was going to pay for that on his salary as
a staff writer for the *National Intruder,* but whatever, however, she
was about to be united in matrimony with her soul mate; she
was about to become Mrs. Andre Stevens.

This was her first done-right relationship. With Andre, she'd
done everything her mother had taught her—she'd always made
it about him, she told him he was always right (whenever he
was), and she always had an orgasm—at least that's what he
thought.

All of the above had helped her keep Andre, but then she'd
added insurance. Something that guaranteed that he would never
leave her. Something that her mother didn't know a thing about.

Thinking about that now, Sierra scrolled through the pictures on her phone until she found the one she'd taken about an hour ago in the bathroom. These were the shots Andre loved the most—the ones she took in public and then sent to him. Not that the stall in The Afternoon Martini was public, but she knew this photo would get Andre going for real.

Finding the picture, she typed the message: *This will be waiting 4 u when u get home. I'm not going to work 2day so come early. xoxo.* Then she pressed Send and imagined the smile this would bring to her man's face.

Yup, her mother didn't know a thing about this. Sexting was the bomb.com, as her favorite reality star always said. Sending shots of her various body parts was what kept Andre. He couldn't get enough of her. Whenever she sent one of these pictures to him during the day, she was sure to have a fabulous night.

Sierra sighed with pleasure. Finally, she had her happily-ever-after. She'd kissed more frogs than the law should've allowed. But now she had a prince. Having Andre in her life was worth every lie she'd been told, every wife she'd discovered, every tear she'd shed. Their relationship was so different from all the others she'd had since she'd moved to the city over six years ago. Except for his ex's pictures, they had no drama. No strange phone calls, no disappearing acts, no females showing up in the middle of the night. She hadn't gone off once in all the months she'd known him, proving that her other boyfriends who'd called her crazy didn't know what they were talking about.

The cab stopped at the corner of her block, just as she'd directed, and Sierra gave the driver a twenty and a five, then scooted across the seat toward the door.

"Thank you," the cabbie said, giving her his first clear words and first smile.

Yeah, he was happy now. Not only was she not a jumper, but she had tipped his racist behind well, so the next time he was asked to go to Harlem, he'd make the trip without making assumptions.

Sierra slipped out of the car, pulled the faux fur collar of her coat tighter, but when the wind whipped up Morningside Drive, she almost turned back to the cab so that he could take her straight to her front door. But this was a rule that she'd lived by—another something that her mother had taught her before Sierra had left Brooklyn and crossed the bridge to live in the big city.

"Don't be letting just anybody know where you live"—she could hear her mother's voice even now. "Not even a cabdriver. They're the worst. They'll memorize your address and come back in the middle of the night to rob you or rape you."

It was that vivid picture that had Sierra trudging down the street in her stiletto boots past week-old, waist-high snow piles.

"Hey!"

Sierra heard a man call out, but she didn't turn around.

"Hey!"

She was so over these catcalls. Men shouted out to her all the time, as if that was really the way to get her attention.

"Aren't you with that new girl group?"

Oh, wait . . . it was a fan! She paused, turned around, and saw the gray-haired man standing in the cut of one of the buildings. He was bundled up against the cold, his hands stuffed deep inside his pockets.

He didn't look anything like she imagined her fans to be, but neither did he look like a robber or a rapist. So she answered him—"Yes"—and smiled.

He gave her a toothless grin back. "I saw y'all on TV. One of those video channels. Y'all girls are something else. Keep up the good work."

"Thank you," she said before she turned back to her path. That was only the third time that she'd been recognized. It happened all the time when she was with Raine and Liza—primarily because of Raine, of course.

Raine. It was still hard for Sierra to believe that not only did she know Raine, not only was she a friend, but she was actually singing onstage next to her. Raine—or Rainebow, as she was known when she blew up in the nineties—was the reason for this being the best time in Sierra's life. She wouldn't have a career if she hadn't met Raine a few weeks after she joined one of the biggest churches in New York City.

"I'm putting together a new group," Raine had told Sierra after she pulled her aside one Wednesday night after choir practice. "Not only do you have an amazing voice, but I was so impressed with your testimony."

Sierra had tried not to be too starstruck as she stood in front of the R & B icon. As casually as she could, she responded, "You mean what I talked about last Sunday? About being celibate?"

"Yes! You're an amazing young woman. And more than singing, I want the women in the group I'm putting together to be examples of how to handle the challenges women face today. You would be quite a mentor."

There was no way for Sierra to tell Raine the truth. No way to explain that when Pastor Bush had stood at the altar and asked if anyone had any special testimony to share, Sierra had almost raced to the front. That was the moment she'd been waiting for ever since she'd joined the church.

The idea for what she'd said that day had come from Candy, one of the sales staff at the bookstore where Sierra worked.

"Guys are always trying to get with me because I'm a virgin," Candy had told her.

Sierra didn't even try to hide her shock when she asked, "You're kidding, right?"

"Nope. Guys are always . . ."

"I mean, you're kidding about being a virgin?" Sierra had been so intrigued that anyone over twenty could still be a virgin, and her first thought was, *What a man magnet!*

Eric had just left her and she was so ready to find The One. After a week of thought and research, she'd joined City of Lights, the church with the highest number of single men in the city because they were inspired by Pastor Hosea Bush.

So when she was given the chance, Sierra had stood before the congregation and told her story of being a twenty-two-year-old virgin because she was living life God's way, she was waiting for the man that He'd chosen for her.

Then she'd returned to her seat, knowing that in the next week, or two or three, the men would flock to her because she was such a virtuous woman and would make a wonderful wife.

She hadn't found a husband, but her lie had led to her big break, and now her lie had become her life. That was fine; it was easy enough to make her lie the truth. Sierra lived as two women—the virtuous one and then the other, who wasn't so righteous. But that was all about to change. She'd be able to live completely honorably now that she was about to be Andre's Mrs.

Finally reaching her brownstone, she rushed into the building and out of the 20-degree cold. She grabbed her mail from her box before she tackled the stairs. Seventy-two steps to her fifth-floor walk-up. Seventy-two steps that saved her a gym membership.

Turning the corner on the top landing, Sierra frowned when

she saw her door a bit ajar, and thoughts of a robber and/or a rapist jumped back into her mind. But quickly, she pushed those thoughts away. It was probably just the super busting into her apartment under the guise of fixing something. That seemed to be the little man's favorite hobby—always up in her apartment for one made-up reason or another. He was probably sneaking peeks in her underwear drawer—at least that's what her mother told her.

Still, she was cautious and stepped slowly, quietly on the wooden planks. She pressed her hand on the door, pushed it back, peeked inside, and then sighed.

"Andre!"

He jumped and turned around with wide eyes.

"You scared me," she said.

"That makes two of us."

She dropped the mail onto the front table and then wrapped her arms around her boyfriend's neck. "What are you doing here, baby?"

"I thought you said you had a business lunch."

She nodded. "I did, but it was quick. All Yvonne wanted to do was tell us about the tour and lecture me about the importance of staying . . . moral." She laughed. "And Liza had some first lady event she had to get to." Sierra stepped back. "I sent you a text," she said, changing her tone. "Did you get it?" she purred.

"Uh . . . I haven't checked."

"Take a look," she whispered as she shrugged her coat from her shoulders. "I wasn't wearing any panties." She giggled as she watched Andre's Adam's apple rise then fall in his throat.

"Uh . . . what about work? You're not going in to the bookstore?" he asked.

She shook her head. "I told you this morning that I was off." Turning toward the closet, she asked, "What's up with you? I thought you'd be at work digging up some dirt on that new player for the Knicks."

When Andre stayed silent, Sierra spun around to face him, and for the first time she really noticed him. She noticed his blank stare as if he had no words to say. She noticed that he was dressed in an old jogging suit, as if he was about to do manual labor. And she noticed what was in his hands—the plug to the TV.

Sierra squinted, confused by the picture in front of her. "Something's wrong with the TV?"

"Ah . . . nothing. The TV's fine." He lowered his eyes. "Look, Sierra, I might as well just come out and say this—I'm leaving."

Sierra stood there, not moving, just blinking.

He dropped the television cord and took a step closer to her. "I didn't want to tell you because I didn't want to hurt you."

"You're leaving—as in breaking up with me?" It was the shock that put the tremor in her voice.

He nodded.

All kinds of visions danced in her head—of the day they'd met, of the hours they'd spent making love, of the wedding she'd already planned—the wedding, the ring! No, this was not over!

"So, you were gonna just walk out of here with your TV and not tell me, not try to work out whatever is wrong?"

"Ah, come on, Sierra. You can't tell me you haven't noticed that things haven't been flowing between us."

"I *can* tell you that 'cause I thought everything was fine."

He looked at her as if he couldn't decide if she was joking. "I mean, you're all right and everything, but we never meant for this to be long-term."

His words made her cross her arms.

He cleared his throat. "Well, look, that's why I came by this afternoon. I didn't want to go back and forth about this."

"No, you came by this afternoon 'cause you thought I was out and you're a coward."

He was silent for a moment, as if he was contemplating her words. Then he shrugged. "I just didn't want to hurt you."

He'd said that twice now and it was those words that hurt her the most. How could he not hurt her? He was taking away her future, her chance to be his wife.

She needed to fix this. She needed to back up and think about the best way to handle the situation. She didn't have the skills to win any kind of debate with Andre; her high school diploma was no matchup for his bachelor's and master's degrees. But she could certainly use the gifts that God had given her— and with her looks, she was always the winner.

So she tossed her bronze-colored curls over her shoulders and sucked in her cheeks. "Baby, please," she whined. There was little space between them, but in the five or so steps that it took to reach him, she put more sway into her stroll.

The sudden switch of her approach startled Andre.

"I love you." She pressed up against him so that he would feel what he'd be missing if he left. "Whatever it is, we can work it out." Then she kissed him. But though she could feel the hard beat of his heart, he didn't part his lips. "You really don't want to give up on us, do you?"

Andre took a couple of steps away from her. "I thought we were in the same place with this. I didn't know there was any 'us.'"

The trembling started in her soles and was quickly rising. But she fought hard to press her anger down. She couldn't revert to past tactics. "I just don't understand." Her voice was soft. She had to stay calm. She had to stay sultry. Motioning toward the couch, she said, "Let's talk." She settled onto the sofa and crossed her legs, making sure that the hem of her skirt rose high enough for him to see the top of her sheer thigh-high stockings.

She watched Andre watch her and the way his eyes glazed as he stared at her legs. Inside, she smiled, but she kept the sorrow on her face.

Andre's Adam's apple shifted again, but then he shook his head as if freeing himself from a trance. "Talking won't do anything."

"Why won't you even give me, give us, a chance?"

"Because there's no chance that needs to be given!" he exclaimed as if he couldn't believe that she didn't get it. "We're not in a relationship."

Sierra shook her head. "What would you call it?"

"I'd call it a good time."

She uncrossed her legs, then leaned to the left and crossed her legs the other way. Again, she watched him, pleased when he took an extra breath. "That's all I was to you? A good time?"

He lifted his eyes from her legs to her face, but she didn't mind. Her face was just as captivating. He said, "Sierra, you knew the deal when we met. I'd just broken up with Tamara."

She cringed at the mention of Ole Girl's name.

He said, "I told you that I wasn't ready to get involved with anyone."

"You told me that you couldn't wait to get me in bed."

"Yeah, well, look at you. Who wouldn't want to sleep with you?"

She was trying, trying hard to keep it together.

Trying hard to stay sane.

"Look, you found me at a bad time, Sierra, you know that. What else would you call meeting a man at a bar crying? I was crying over Tamara."

That name was making her blood boil. "You weren't hardly crying."

"I didn't mean it literally, but you know what I'm saying. I thought we'd just hang out for a few nights."

"That turned into *five months*."

"Longer than I expected."

"Well, do you know what I expected?" She didn't wait for him to answer. "I expected a ring. I thought we were going to get married."

This time he took giant steps away from her. "Whoa! I never said anything about marrying you."

"You didn't have to. I know that you bought me a ring. From Tiffany's."

He frowned for a moment, as if he was confused. Then his eyes widened with understanding. "How did you know about that?"

"Does it matter?"

"Yeah, 'cause if you know about that then you need to be a reporter. But that necklace had nothing to do with you."

Sierra blinked. "Necklace?"

He nodded. "For an exposé we're doing."

"Not a ring? Not my ring?"

"No! I can't marry you."

"Why not?"

"Because I don't even know you like that. And anyway, it wouldn't be good for me to get into a relationship. I need to put a little time and space between me and Tamara."

There was that name again. "You've had five months," she shouted, her voice rising as fast as her blood pressure. "You weren't saying anything about needing space every time you jumped into my bed."

"Well . . . you know . . ."

Sierra wanted to crack him upside his head, but she was not going to lose it and she was not going to lose him. So she inhaled deeply, then released it. Over and over, just like her best friend Denise, a psychologist who specialized in anger management, often advised.

She felt herself calming, and Andre must've felt it, too, because he sat down next to her.

"I'm sorry, Sierra," he said softly. "I thought you knew what this was for me and I thought it was the same for you. I mean, how're you really going to be in a relationship with me and then be in Destiny's Divas talking about being celibate?"

He was asking her that question now? After all the mornings, noons, and nights that they'd sexed it up? After all the pictures she'd sent him? After all the video recordings they'd made? "All I ever say on the radio and all I'm gonna say onstage is that celibacy is good."

"Yeah, but those folks think you're actually celibate. That's why I didn't think you'd want to make this long-term. I'd figured by the time your tour began, you'd be turning your back on me and living your life real."

"Our relationship is real."

"Come on, Sierra. Stop calling it a relationship when we were just kicking it. When you were just my good-time girl."

*Good. Time. Girl!* Those words exploded in her head. "Are you calling me a ho?"

"No . . . wha . . ."

Before the word was out of his mouth, Sierra grabbed the

red porcelain vase on the table with the single (just about dead) rose that Andre had given her last week and did exactly what she'd been thinking just minutes before. In one swoop, she crashed the vase upside his head.

"What the hell?" He jumped up, pressing his hand against his temple. "Girl, are you crazy?"

She leapt from the couch and stood inches from him. "Oh, you ain't seen crazy yet! You just called me a ho!"

He stared at her as if he'd never seen her before, then shook his head. "I'm out." He pushed by her, but then turned around and almost moonwalked out of her apartment, as if he was afraid to turn his back on her.

Before he got to the door, she said, "Don't forget your TV. Isn't that why you came by?"

His fingertips were still pressed to his head, and Sierra saw a trickle of blood. *Good!*

He paused for a second, then said, "Nah, you keep it," as if he didn't trust getting anywhere near her.

"I don't want your stupid TV," she shouted. "I don't want anything from you."

But he walked out the door, saying nothing more. As if he hadn't heard her, as if he didn't care.

He was just gonna leave like that?

*Oh, no!*

She grabbed the thirty-two-inch flat screen with a strength that she only had at moments like this. Racing through the door, she watched Andre's face stretch with shock, but he kept backing away toward the staircase. She waited until he had taken three steps down, then hoisted the TV over the railing, aiming at his head.

Andre jumped back, barely escaping the crashing metal,

crushing plastic, and splattering glass as the TV bounced, then tumbled down the stairs. When it finally landed on the floor below, Andre looked up at Sierra with wide, shocked eyes.

She said, "I told you I didn't want your sorry TV."

He shook his head. His hand was down now and she could see the gash on his forehead. *Good!* Something to remember her by.

"You are one crazy ass."

She shrugged. "And now you know."

Pivoting, she turned her back on him, even as he yelled, "Crazy, crazy, crazy!"

As if those words would bother her. Please, she'd been called much worse than crazy before.

The moment she stepped back into her apartment, she had another thought. Sierra dashed into the bathroom, grabbed what she'd come looking for, then ran back into the hallway.

"Hey, Andre," she yelled, though he was on the second floor by now. Still, she tossed his toothbrush down the stairs and watched it tumble until it landed on top of the mangled steel mess that used to be his TV. Now she was rid of everything that he'd left behind.

Everything, except for her heart inside that had been cut wide open, once again. Maybe five wasn't such a lucky number. Because Andre was the fifth man who had cut into her soul in as many years.

# CHAPTER 2

## *Raine*

The streets of Manhattan were her gym and Raine took full advantage of her membership. Even now, as the biting February wind swirled around her, she plodded down Eighth Avenue, chuckling as she remembered the horrified looks on Sierra, Liza, and Yvonne's faces when she hugged them good-bye in the restaurant's vestibule.

"You're not going to grab a cab?" Sierra had asked her.

"You know I don't cab it unless I have to. I have time to walk."

"In this weather?" the three of them had sung together.

"It's just a little over a mile," she'd chuckled. "I'll get some exercise and do my part to reduce my carbon footprint."

This time her three friends rolled their eyes in unison.

"Sometimes you take that all-natural, save-our-planet stuff too seriously," Sierra had said.

Raine's response had just been a wave. She couldn't figure out why they always acted so surprised. Surely her girls knew her by now. She was a walker when she wasn't jogging, and today was the best of days to walk. The thermometer hovered right at 20 degrees, and that's what made it so wonderful. The cold made her keep up the pace; it forced a serious workout.

With the long strap of her vegan satchel draped across her body, Raine pumped her arms as she pushed across town, then flexed her legs as she forged downtown. She wasn't oblivious to the number of New Yorkers who did double takes when she passed by, but she kept her head down. Not that she didn't love her fans. It was just that there were days when she didn't want to be Rainebow, the R & B superstar. And this was one of those days, especially after three girls had followed her into the restaurant's bathroom to get her autograph. With that incident, she'd met her daily quota of fan engagement.

The cold shrouded her on the outside, but the recycled fleece and microfiber ankle-length coat kept the wind exactly where it was supposed to be. Heat rose on her skin as her heart beat in sync with her steps, and by the time she arrived at the East Side Towers, she was in full cardio mode.

The doorman pulled the door open when she was still a few steps away and she strode past him, not slowing down until she was wrapped inside the warmth of the lobby.

"Thank you, Stanley."

"My pleasure," he said, and then turned right back to the door to welcome the next highbrow New Yorker who called these high-rise luxury apartments home.

Inside the mirrored elevator, Raine pressed the PH button, then snatched the skully hat off her head and shook out her shoulder-length sister locks.

The walk had been invigorating, but it wasn't just the exercise that had her heart pumping. It was the excitement of what was happening with her career. So many had said that she was finished when she walked away from the R & B gold mine that Babyface had cultivated for her since she was nineteen. Rainebow had risen high on the charts and shared popularity over the years with the likes of TLC, Mariah Carey, and had even been called (to the chagrin of Whitney Houston) the New Voice. But when the news hit the press that Rainebow had a vision from God and was walking away from her thirteen-year career, the critics had asked what she was smoking.

Though the skeptics had predicted that she would have a rapid demise, Raine hadn't allowed anyone's voice to be louder than God's. She'd followed her heart, raised her necklines, lowered her hemlines, and crossed to the other side. The industry waited for her to fail, to fall, to disappear from pop culture. But God had given her this idea of singing evangelists—three women, three decades, three testimonies. It would be their music that would attract a following, but what Raine wanted to do most was touch hearts, remove strongholds, and witness for God with their stories.

It had been easy for Raine to call Liza Washington. She'd met the first lady years before when one of Raine's foster mothers had taken her to Ridgewood Macedonia where Liza's husband was the pastor. Although she hadn't been taken to the church often, she never forgot the pastor's wife, who always had a kind smile, a gentle spirit, and a voice that could only belong to one of God's angels. She would be the perfect one to testify about having a long love, a wonderful marriage.

While Liza had been the obvious choice for the Diva in her forties, Raine didn't have a clue where she would find her twentysomething singer. Sure, there were thousands with voices that could raise the roof, but could they stand? Were they living for God?

Then Sierra had given her testimony and Raine knew she was the one. She'd seen the young woman a couple of times at choir practice, and though she hadn't heard her sing, her story was amazing. Sierra was living the way Raine wished that she had, and if she had to, she'd pay for her to have singing lessons.

And so Destiny's Divas was born.

Now, three years later, Raine was back on top of the charts, and soon to be on her first gospel tour where she'd be singing *and* testifying for the Lord.

"Ha!" She laughed to herself as she stepped off the elevator.

She wished she had every telephone number for all those doubters. She had only one question: How'd they like her now?

But there was no need to focus on the negative when today was all about celebration. Five weeks at number one! Wow!

Their first single, "Vision," had made it to number two on the gospel charts. But "Love Unlimited" had shot straight to number one and was even rising on the R & B billboard.

She'd had lots of top sellers in her past life and had made a boatload of money. But this—what she was doing for God—was much more gratifying. It was all about walking in her purpose.

She pressed her key into the door marked PH1, and even after fourteen years, she smiled. This apartment had been such a smart investment for a twenty-two-year-old back in '96—not only financially, but because it was a large enough space that she was able to turn the bachelorette pad into a home for her and Dayo when they married two years later, and then for both them and Nadia when she'd given birth to their daughter.

Pushing the door open, her face glowed with her smile. She couldn't wait to share her news; after all, Dayo and Nadia were part of her testimony. As the middle member of Destiny's Divas, she told the world how she and her family shared a love that was completely unconditional.

Then . . .

A scream from inside the apartment smothered those thoughts.

"It's not fair!" she heard her daughter shrill.

"Calm down." That was the baritone of her husband, whose bedroom voice sounded the same in every room of the house.

Raine frowned. What had her normally composed twelve-year-old so upset? She shrugged off her coat, took quick steps down the hall, then slowed when she heard her husband again.

"Respect, Nadia," Dayo said, his volume just a bit louder.

There was only one reason why her husband would make that demand. And once Raine stepped into the grand room of their penthouse, she saw that she was right.

"Mom!" Nadia jumped up from the dining room table where she'd sat across from her grandmother. She was all long arms and longer legs as she barreled toward Raine. "Mom! You said that I could hang out with Shaquanda."

Raine's eyes moved from Dayo, who stood stern and strong like the African prince that he was, to his mother, who sat with shoulders squared and hands folded as if she was perched on some kind of throne.

Since neither adult gave Raine any hints, she asked her daughter, "What happened?"

"You said that I could go to Shaquanda's house after I finished my chores," Nadia whined.

"Yes"—Raine nodded—"and after you read two chapters of the book I gave you."

"I read three chapters!" she cried. "But she still won't let me go!"

Raine heard her daughter say "She," but she directed her words to her husband.

"I gave her permission," she said. "What's the problem?"

"The problem is that I said she could not go."

Raine inhaled before she turned toward the voice. "Why would you tell her that when I told her that she could go?" she asked her mother-in-law.

Her mother-in-law pressed her palms flat on the table and leaned forward as if she were ready for battle. "I've told you before that those are not the kind of people we should be associating with."

Heat and her hair rose on the back of Raine's neck. "If when you say *those* people you mean people who live in the projects, then you're talking about me. *Those* people, Lulu, are my people. I grew up in the projects."

Beerlulu spoke no words, but passed a look to her son that could only be interpreted as "Exactly!" As if she finally agreed with something that Raine was saying.

"Nadia," Raine said, "can you go to your room for a moment?"

"But, Mom. Shaquanda is waiting for me. Her sister is going to pick me up."

"She can wait just a little bit longer."

Nadia dragged herself down the hall, as if the ninety pounds she carried on her five-foot-five frame were too heavy to bear.

Raine waited until she heard her daughter's bedroom door close before she turned back to her husband and mother-in-law. She didn't have to say a word. Her attitude was in her stance—all of her weight back on one leg, arms folded, eyes squinted, neck ready to roll. "So, do you want to tell me why you're telling my daughter she can't when I say she can?"

Beerlulu bowed her head slightly. "I apologize if that's how you see it," she said, though Raine didn't hear any regret in her tone. "But my granddaughter is in her formative years. I don't want her catching bad habits from that girl, like the language that she uses."

*Oh, no,* Raine thought. Had Shaquanda cursed or something in Beerlulu's presence? "What did Shaquanda say?" Raine looked to her husband, hoping for some sign. But as always when it came to Nadia, he deferred to his mother.

Beerlulu said, "She called here asking for my granddaughter, calling her"—she paused for a moment as if it took effort to say the next words—"*Baby Mack.*"

Raine frowned. "And?"

"My granddaughter's name is *not* Baby Mack."

It took Raine a moment to respond because surely there had to be more to Beerlulu's objection. "You're kidding, right? That's the reason why you decided Nadia shouldn't go to her friend's house?" Raine couldn't help but laugh. "That's just some silly nickname they made up. Shaquanda calls Nadia Baby Mack, and Nadia calls her Biggie Mack. Those names don't mean anything."

"And that's why she needs to be called by her given name. Because her name does mean something. That Baby Mack stuff makes her sound like one of those music people."

Raine raised an eyebrow.

Beerlulu smiled as if she had made her point, but then she added, "That name makes her sound like one of those rappers you have here in this country."

"See, that's the first point," Raine said, her voice rising just a bit. "You need to remember that we're in *this* country."

For the first time, her husband spoke. "Respect, *mchumba,*" he said softly, speaking in English and in his native tongue. He stepped to her side and took her hand.

Calling her "sweetheart" in Swahili, coming closer to her, holding her hand—it was all a plea for peace. But inside, Raine growled. Dayo was always talking about respect for his mother.

But it was a difficult concept when the woman had so little respect for anyone else.

To his mother, he said, *"Hooyo,"* calling her by the name he'd
learned from a Somalian boy when he was just a child in Kenya.
"There is nothing wrong with that name. It's a nickname. It's just
fun."

This time Raine was the one to say "Exactly" without moving her lips.

But his words meant nothing to his mother. Beerlulu said, "I
don't know why you fight me. I'm working hard to grow Nadia
into a proper young lady."

"That's my second point," said Raine, jumping in. She felt
Dayo's eyes boring into her, screaming his favorite word. But
Raine had no patience left for her husband, his mother—nor
respect. "You don't need to raise *our* child. That's *our* responsibility."

"As the elder, it is my responsibility to step in if mistakes are
being made. I do it with my nieces in Brooklyn," she said, referring to her extended family who had come to New York years
before. "And I will most certainly do it with my granddaughter
if she's not being raised right."

Raine tossed her hands in the air and faced Dayo. Her lips
barely moved when she said, "Handle this."

Beerlulu stood, paused for a moment, and then with her
hands folded at her waist, she glided past her son and daughter-
in-law as if she was royalty. As if she had no further need for this
discussion. As if *her* point had been made and her wishes would
be carried out. She moved toward her bedroom without another
word. Her son and daughter-in-law had been dismissed.

Raine's eyes were wide when she said to Dayo, "How could
you just stand there and let her tell Nadia that she couldn't go?"

He held up his hands. "I walked in about two minutes before you; I was trying to figure it out myself."

Raine blew out a short breath. "You know this isn't about any nickname. This is about your mother undermining me, as always."

"You have to understand, Raine, where my mother comes from it's the responsibility of the village, especially the older women, to raise the child. She's just doing what she knows."

He sat down as if he wanted to discuss this, but Raine stayed standing strong. "That's the problem. She can't behave that way here. Not in this country and not in this house."

"I know, we just have to work with her."

"No, we don't, and here's the thing," Raine said. "I could handle it when your mother just came after me, criticizing me as your wife, as a singer, the way I dressed or whatever. I didn't care if she liked me or not."

"What're you talking about? My mother loves you."

She ignored his lie, treated it as if he hadn't spoken. "But what I can't handle is the way she's taken her disdain for me out on my daughter. I won't stand for that."

"She's my daughter, too."

"Well, then, we both need to protect Nadia."

"You know that's crazy, right?" Dayo said as if he hadn't just witnessed what had gone down. "You're saying that our daughter needs protection from her grandmother?"

With a sigh, Raine said, "Come on, babe. You've got to see that what I'm saying is true. Your mother would love her grandchild if you'd married a Kenyan woman. But you married some American rock star, and she hates it. Just like the rest of your family. No one is happy that you're with me. And that means no one is happy with Nadia."

Dayo shook his head. "You're wrong, but I'll talk to my mother."

"Do you know how long you've been saying that?" She paused, giving him time to think about that. "Two years. Since she got off the plane and walked through that door."

"I'll handle it this time."

"Dayo, I'm not about to have Nadia upset like this every other day. It's not healthy for her, and frankly, this isn't good for your mother, either." Raine paused. "We need to talk to your mother . . . about moving."

He was already shaking his head, the way he did whenever Raine brought up this subject. But unlike the other times, she was not going to be denied.

"I'm not saying that she has to move far away. She can be close, but she needs her own place so that we can all live in peace." Raine gave him a moment to digest her words, then added, "I'm calling Mary," referring to the Realtor she and Dayo had worked with a few years before, when he'd moved his store to Second Avenue. "She told me she's doing residential properties now, and I'm gonna ask her to find something for your mother."

She didn't give Dayo a chance to agree or disagree; she turned and marched out of the dining room the same way her mother-in-law had done. It was amazing how a grand afternoon had morphed so quickly into a battle. But she was going to win this fight because she would protect her daughter at all cost. Protect Nadia the way she had never been protected. And everyone in this house, including Dayo, needed to understand that.

If you messed with Nadia, you were messing with Raine.

That was just a fact.

# CHAPTER 3

## *Liza*

*L*iza eased her Navigator inside the garage, switched off the ignition, and then leaned back into the comfort of the leather seat. Exhaustion burned inside her bones; she hardly had enough energy to move. Between breakfast with her assistant, then lunch with Yvonne and the girls, followed by the dinner she'd had with the mothers of the girls who were part of the Deliver Our Daughters ministry that she ran with her husband, Liza felt as if she hadn't had a moment to breathe. All she wanted to do was climb up the stairs and crawl into bed.

But as tired as she was, Liza was hoping for some special time with Mann tonight. Not that there was anything wrong. When she spoke as the matriarch of Destiny's Divas and told about the honor of and the gifts received from being a submissive wife, she was telling the truth. These young girls didn't know a thing about not only keeping a man, but having one in your life who loved and adored you for twenty-eight years. Oh, she definitely had a thing or three to share with young women, and some old ones, too. To reach and teach, that was her mission.

But with experience came wisdom. And five weeks was a long time for a husband and wife to be separated, even for a couple as solid as they were. Especially since recently, Liza had been feeling that their marriage was a bit off-kilter. Mann was still loving and adoring; it was just that he'd been acting a little differently, a bit distant. As if he had a lot on his mind. That she could understand. It wasn't easy leading a movement.

Mann Washington had been called to bring God's Word forth to young women, and he was changing lives. Just the pressure of that responsibility had to be exhausting.

Grabbing her bag, Liza jumped from the SUV, and the moment she pushed open the door, she was engulfed by the massiveness of her 4,500-square-foot home that felt twice its size since her children had left.

Her children.

Every time a thought, a song, or a word came to her that reminded her of her children, her heart ached. First, there was their daughter, Ingrid. Her perfect-until-she-was-thirteen-then-turned-into-a-rebellious-monster child, who now flew in only once a year from LA on the red-eye for Christmas but always left before the sun went down.

Liza could never figure out when their world went wrong with Ingrid. She and her daughter had always been close, and Mann had doted on Ingrid as if she was his second wife.

But once Ingrid left home when she turned eighteen, she only kept in touch with her mother, and she spoke as few words as possible to her father during her annual nine-hour holiday visit.

As bad as it was with their daughter, it was even worse with their son. Charlie began his quest to escape when he was just six, running away after getting a whipping from his father. That time, Charlie had traveled only as far as the park one block over. But after more attempts, he finally succeeded. On the day after his eighteenth birthday, he put an ocean between himself and his father, moving to London, and carving a hole into his mother's heart at the same time.

*I'm not leaving you, Mom,* was what his note said even though that was exactly what he'd done.

Of course, Liza knew that the relationship between father and son was nothing like the adoration Mann had for Ingrid. But it was just that Mann wanted his son to stand tall on his shoulders.

"I'm just trying to teach you to be a man because I love you," was what Mann always said to Charlie, even as he held a belt in his hand.

Liza had tried to explain it to their son. "Your father is the pastor; people are watching him. That's why he's so hard on you."

"But isn't that the reason why he's supposed to love me?" Charlie had asked. "I mean, he loves Ingrid. Maybe he hates me because I'm a boy and he wanted a girl."

"That's ridiculous," she'd told him.

But her words gave her son no comfort. He moved away and, unlike his sister, he never returned. In the five years that he'd been gone, Charlie called home once a year, on Liza's birthday, and he only spoke to his mother.

Liza sighed as she traveled back from that memory. Mann was always telling her to live in the present. Her children had made their choices, and while Mann might not have been the best father, he was a world-class-champion husband. He lived by Jesus's command—he loved his wife the way Christ loved him.

With those thoughts in her mind, she stepped into their living room. Only the light from the streetlamps and the moon peeking through the living room drapes illuminated the downstairs space, but that was all Liza needed to move within the walls that had been her home for almost twenty-eight years. She headed toward the curved staircase and her boots sank into the thick carpet as if she was stepping into quicksand.

On the second landing, she faced the golden glow coming from their bedroom. The light inside their room was never bright, just soft and sexy because of the bulbs that Mann specially ordered.

Her smile was back as she stood at the bedroom doorway and watched her husband. His eyes were intense as he rested on their bed and studied the screen of his laptop.

"Hey, baby." She'd whispered those words, but Mann jumped, slammed the laptop shut, and placed it on the nightstand.

She said, "I'm sorry; I scared you."

His lips spread into a slow smile. "If being startled for a second is the price for having you home, I'm willing to pay."

He stood up, opened his arms, and she melted inside his words and his embrace.

"You're home early," he said as he backed away.

"If you can call nine o'clock early." She laughed softly.

"Well, normally, you're not home till nearly midnight after one of those dinners."

"I know, but I left Portia to handle closing up everything." She slipped out of her fur and tossed the heavy coat onto the chaise. "I wanted to be with you."

"I'm so glad."

She kissed him, then moved toward her walk-in closet. "What were you working on?" She glanced over her shoulder at his laptop. "Your sermon?"

"Yes, ma'am. You know I've got to come correct this Sunday."

Indeed! This was the second Sunday, Reclamation Sunday, where all of the adult members of Ridgewood Macedonia were asked to bring one young girl to church to hear the message of the Reverend Mann Washington.

This was his mission, what God had put on his heart. A movement that she and Mann had begun over twenty years ago to build up youth in the community. It was a two-part ministry: Deliver Our Daughters and Save Our Sons.

Liza came out of the closet dressed for bed, and when Mann eyed her fitted satin pajamas, she spun around a couple of times so that her husband could get a full 360-degree view.

"You like?" she asked.

"You bet," he said softly, seductively as he walked toward her.

Liza shivered at the sound of his voice, at the lust that she was sure she saw in his eyes. The last time had been a long time ago, and she hoped that maybe tonight he would want to do more than just hold her.

He took her hands into his for a second, then gave her a quick kiss on her forehead. "So tell me: How did the dinner go?" he asked as he turned away from her and that intimate moment at the same time.

Inside, she cried for him to come back, but all she said was, "It was good, though we had a little problem."

He frowned as he climbed into their bed.

She explained, "Qianna Tucker's mother stood up and said that she was concerned with the amount of time Qianna was spending with you and the other pastors."

"What? She's not spending any more time than any of the other girls."

Liza shrugged. "That's what I told her, even when she kept insisting that something was going on. The way she was talking, I began to wonder if Qianna was telling her that she was at the church when she was really hanging out somewhere else."

"Good point. You know how these teenagers are."

Liza nodded. "Right? Anyway, Portia shut her down. Took her outside, and when Mrs. Tucker came back, she didn't have another word to say."

"Well, that's good. But let's not talk about work anymore. Let's talk about my favorite subject—us."

She grinned. "Sounds good to me, but first, I have to send a quick email to Yvonne. I just thought about something she needs to know."

"You have to send it tonight?"

Liza nodded. "She gave us our tour schedule today. Five weeks, twenty cities."

"Wow! That's great!"

"Yeah, but I realized afterward that I'll be away for your birthday and I wanted to see if that was one of our days off."

He shrugged. "Well, whether it is or not, I'll work something out and come to you."

"Really?"

"Of course. To spend time with my beautiful bride"—he kissed the palm of her hand—"I'd swim the Atlantic Ocean if I had to."

She hugged him; his words were more proof that a spouse didn't get much better than Mann Washington.

He said, "I might try to meet you in a couple of cities."

"This night just keeps getting better and better." She kissed his cheek. "But I still want to send that email, just to let her know, because by morning, I'll have forgotten all about it." She reached for his laptop, but he grabbed her wrist as if he thought she was about to steal something. Frowning, she said, "I was just gonna use your computer for a minute. It won't take me long to send the email."

"Uh . . . I was just gonna add something to the sermon I was working on and I don't want to lose this thought." He placed the computer on his lap. "Can you send from your BlackBerry?"

She shook her head. "You know that thing is so slow." After a moment, she added, "Okay, I'll use the desktop."

"Make it quick; I'll be waiting for you."

He winked and Liza wondered if that was an invitation. If it was, forget about sending an email—she was going to stay right there in bed with her husband.

But then he opened his laptop, and his attention was back on the screen. She scurried out of the bedroom so that she could get back quickly.

Her bare feet were as silent as her boots had been just minutes before as she rushed down to the opposite end of the long hallway. The home office they shared was a massive space created when Mann had a contractor knock out the wall that stood between their children's bedrooms.

Second to her children leaving and hardly ever (never) coming back, that had been the most difficult day for Liza. Her hope had been to keep the children's rooms exactly the way they'd left them, filled with memories that she could soak up whenever she needed to feel closer to them. But now, except for the few photographs that adorned the living room mantel, there was little evidence that children had ever been a part of their lives.

Liza clicked on the light switch, sat at the grand cherrywood desk, then let her hand graze the mouse. The computer sprang to life and Liza shook her head. How many times had she told Mann to power down? She wasn't into the save-our-planet movement the way Raine was, but she and Mann could at least make the effort to save electricity.

She clicked on the email icon, typed a quick note to Yvonne, then pressed Send. She wiggled the mouse to shut down the computer, but just as quickly, she moved it up to open the Web.

She hadn't had a moment to call Mann today and tell him the news about Destiny's Divas still holding the number one spot on the charts. Mann was waiting for her, but wouldn't it be exciting to print out some great blog or positive review that she could show him? All she needed was two minutes on Google.

In the browser, she typed *www* but before she could type another letter, *www.females4men* popped up. She frowned, then before she could think, she clicked on the link and the front page of the website slowly fanned across the screen.

*Females4Men—Discreet Connections—For Your Pleasure.*

There was a place to enter a login name and password, but Liza quickly moved the cursor to close the site, then she shut down the computer.

As icons on the desktop faded one by one, Liza sat with her eyes as wide open as her mouth. What had she just seen?

Females4Men?

What the hell was that? How did that site end up in the search engine of their computer?

The answer came quick since there was only one other person in their home.

Mann.

But that made no sense. Not Mann Washington. With complete certainty she knew that her husband was absolutely faithful.

Still.

Her breathing was quick and shallow as she searched her mind for other explanations, but she kept coming back to one.

Mann.

Maybe this had something to do with his upcoming sermon. After all, many of the girls he was trying to save were young women who needed deliverance from all kinds of sins: truancy, drugs, promiscuity. Maybe he was going to talk to them about the dangers of the Internet.

Yes, that was it. This was about Sunday's sermon. That made perfect sense.

Satisfied, she pushed herself from the chair, but when she got to the door, she turned and stared at the computer. Then, with a flick of the light switch, she sent the room into total darkness.

# CHAPTER 4

## *Raine*

*R*aine's eyes weren't even fully open when she shot straight up. Her breathing was rapid as her eyes darted from one corner of the darkened bedroom to the next.

She sat, not moving, perched on the edge of the bed. And then she heard it again. Jumping up, she grabbed her bathrobe and dashed down the hallway. With each step, the moaning became louder, until she burst through Nadia's bedroom door.

Her daughter was totally hidden by the duvet, covered from head to toe. But Raine could see the outline of Nadia's body, thrashing beneath the covers. Raine rushed to her bedside, knelt down, and shook Nadia gently, careful not to wake her too quickly. "Nadia," she whispered. "Wake up. Wake up." She folded back the duvet. Even in the dark, she could see her daughter's face—her eyes shut tight, her mouth wide open. "Nadia."

It took a few seconds for the squirming to stop and then another moment for her eyes to flutter open and settle on her mother.

"Mom!" she exclaimed as she leapt across the bed. She wrapped her arms around Raine's neck. "You're here."

"Of course, sweetheart." Raine frowned as she felt Nadia's

trembles. "It was just a dream, honey," she assured her over and over, still holding her as tightly as she could.

Nadia hugged her mother for a bit longer before she leaned back and shook her head. "It wasn't a dream. It was a nightmare and it was real."

Raine turned on the lamp on the nightstand before she climbed into the double bed and wrapped her arms around her daughter. It had been years since she'd had to comfort her child after a bad dream, though the way she quivered now, it seemed that the bogeyman had returned.

Raine stayed quiet, and just held Nadia until her shaking subsided. "Are you feeling better?"

"A little bit." Nadia's voice was so small.

"Do you want to talk about your dream?"

Her daughter shuddered. "It wasn't a dream, Mom. I told you, it was a nightmare." She squeezed Raine even tighter and curled up into her chest.

For minutes, Raine asked no questions; she just held her and rocked her. There were so many times when she wished for these moments—when she could just hold her daughter, as she had when she was an infant. But though she missed those days, she didn't want them back this way. She never wanted to see her daughter trembling and groaning with fear.

"Mom," Nadia whispered, finally breaking the silence, "the next time you go away, I wanna go with you."

Raine paused, thinking about how today she'd come home with this great news about her tour. But though she'd been excited about it earlier, this wasn't the time to tell Nadia that she'd be leaving in just a few weeks. So all she said was, "You know you can't go with me, sweetheart. What're you trying to do? Get out of a big test or something?" She chuckled to keep it light.

Nadia stared into her mother's eyes. "I'm not trying to get out of anything. I *have* to go with you."

The intensity of her stare, of her tone made Raine's heart beat a little harder. "Honey," she began as she pushed a long braid away from her daughter's face. "You know that's not possible. Plus, I thought you loved school."

"I do, but I can still go to school. People can teach me while we're on the road. They do it all the time for the kids on *American Idol*."

"But if you go with me, you'll miss your friends. And what about your dad? He'll be all by himself if you go."

"No he won't." Nadia shook her head. "Grandmother will be here with him."

Raine frowned. "Did something happen . . . between you and your dad?"

"No."

"Is this about what happened with your grandmother today?"

She shook her head. "It's about nothing. I just want to go with you so that I won't miss you so much."

It was the gift of being a mother that let Raine know there was more to her daughter's story. "Nadia, talk to me," she said softly. "You can tell me anything."

Her daughter lowered her eyes and bit her lip as if she wasn't sure if she should speak what was on her mind. Then: "I'm afraid that one day you're going to go away, and when you come back, I won't be here. And then you won't be able to find me."

Gently, Raine placed two fingers beneath her daughter's chin and made her look straight at her. She said nothing for a moment; she just searched her daughter's eyes, and the fear that Raine saw surged from Nadia straight to her. Now her heart pressed even harder against her chest. "What do you mean you won't be here?"

Nadia tried to lower her head again, but Raine held her in place. She said, "That's what my dream was about . . . about Grandmother. I think she's going to take me away." She crossed her arms, holding herself as if she was suddenly cold. "She's trying to turn me into an African and she's gonna take me to Kenya."

"Baby, she's not gonna do that."

Nadia shook her head as if Raine didn't know what she was talking about. "You should hear her sometimes, Mom. She wishes she was there instead of here. That's what she tells Dad. And today, before you got home, she said that I needed to be brought up there where girls are raised to be proper women." Then she added with a whisper, "And yesterday she said that she wished that I had a different mother."

"She said that to you?"

"No, to Dad. But I heard them. I didn't mean to. They didn't know I was home. But she said it, Mom. She wants to take me away from you because she doesn't like me and she doesn't like you, and I'm scared."

"Oh, sweetheart." Raine grabbed her daughter and held her close once again. "She's just talking, she doesn't mean any of those things."

"Yes she does!" She looked up at her mother again, her eyes now filled with tears. "Mom, if you don't take me with you, when you come back I'll be gone," she wailed. "And then I won't ever see you again."

Raine drew her daughter back into her arms. "You don't have to worry; I would never let that happen and neither will your father."

"I don't think you can stop her," Nadia cried into her mother's chest.

"I can," she said as she rocked Nadia. "And I will. No one

will ever hurt you, sweetheart. No one will ever take you away from me. I promise."

As she held her daughter, a forgotten feeling began to simmer inside. It had been a long time since she'd held any kind of hate in her heart. Raine thought she'd expunged it all on the day she'd been emancipated from the foster care system. It had taken serious effort to rid herself of the hatred she'd felt for the men and women who'd only taken her into their homes for the money, the people who'd fed her little, beaten her a lot, and made her so aware that no one in the world had ever wanted her.

She'd triumphed over all of that negativity and had walked in love from the day she'd set out on her own. With the help of City of Lights, the church she joined when she was eighteen, she'd left her past behind, focused on her future, and because of that, tremendous blessings had come her way.

But the churning inside let her know that those buried-deep feelings were still with her.

"I promise you," Raine whispered, "you're not going anywhere."

She comforted Nadia and held her until her crying stopped. Still, she didn't let her go, and even when she felt Nadia settle into her sleep breathing, she held her.

As the minutes ticked to an hour and then as each hour turned to another, Raine kept her daughter in her arms. Her plan was never to close her eyes, never to let her daughter go.

But soon Raine slept, holding Nadia throughout the rest of the night.

# CHAPTER 5

## Raine

The cup felt warm, very soothing in her hands, even though the tea inside had long ago cooled. Raine sat at the head of the dining room table with her fingers curled around the ceramic and her eyes straight ahead on the spectacular view of the grand dame that sat right outside her window, the Brooklyn Bridge.

This was how she loved to begin her weekend mornings—in the silence of her apartment after Nadia had left for her piano lessons and Dayo and his mother had left for The African Sun, their African art and artifacts store on Second Avenue.

But though this had always been such a peaceful place, today Raine felt no peace, and though today was Valentine's Day, she had no joy. It had been difficult to find peace or joy in the last two days with Nadia's dream so heavy on her mind.

She hadn't told Dayo about what Nadia had said, sure that he would just wave their daughter's words away as nothing more than a young girl's angst.

*She's almost a teenager,* was what he would say.

But she was her mother and Raine knew Nadia was not melodramatic. No, her feelings were real, and Dayo would know that, too, if he'd been there to look into their daughter's eyes.

Maybe she should have shared everything with him when she'd returned to their bedroom yesterday morning after spending the night with Nadia. . . .

"You're up early," Dayo said as Raine tiptoed back into their bedroom just a little before six.

She paused for just a moment, then said, "I couldn't sleep." Another beat and then: "I'm going to definitely call Mary this morning," she'd said.

Dayo's eyes were wide as he pushed himself up in the bed. "You're really going to do this? You're really going to call the Realtor and put my mother out."

She crossed her arms, pressed her lips together, and tried hard not to respond when all she wanted to do was snap back and tell him that his words were ridiculous. But she wasn't going to let this turn into a fight.

Dayo swung his legs over the side of the bed, his back to his wife. For a moment, Raine the peacemaker had risen inside of her, trying to convince her to acquiesce once again, to just let his mother stay. But her own mother love had been stronger. She couldn't give in . . . because of Nadia.

Raine had eased around their oversized bed and settled next to Dayo. They'd sat for a moment in shoulder-to-shoulder silence, both of their eyes straight ahead.

"I love you," he said, reaching for her hand.

"I know that."

"And I love my mother, too."

Those were words that Raine had longed to say about her mother-in-law, but they were not in her heart. That saddened her to her core. All those years ago, when Dayo had told her that his mother was coming to America, Raine had been thrilled.

With her husband, her daughter, and now with his mother, she'd have the extended family that she always longed for.

But from the day Beerlulu arrived, it was clear the woman did not approve of the wife her son had chosen. From the way she turned up her nose at Raine's cooking to the disdain she had for Raine's career, it was clear Beerlulu was not interested in finding common ground.

Their division was greatest when it came to Nadia. Beerlulu was horrified at the way Nadia spoke, at the clothes she wore, at the friends she chose.

It was her reaction to Nadia that made it impossible for Raine to have any love for her mother-in-law. Not loving her child was worse than not loving her.

Raine said to Dayo, "I know you love your mother, but that doesn't mean she has to live with you."

"She doesn't know this country."

"I'm sure we'll be able to find her something close, maybe even within walking distance."

At first, Dayo nodded, as if he agreed, but his words told Raine that he didn't. "It won't matter how close she is; anywhere but here and she'll be alone."

"She'll hardly be alone. Not with your aunts and all of your other relatives."

It was true, Dayo and his mother had an entire community of family who had migrated through the years to America. It was only because of all who waited for her here that Beerlulu had finally agreed to leave her beloved homeland and come to America to be with her only child.

Raine added, "Maybe one of your aunts can move in with her."

He shook his head. "My mother is the oldest. It would be a

disgrace for her to have to do that, to have to depend on one of the youngest."

Raine frowned. Wasn't she living with them? That didn't seem to bother her. But Raine wasn't about to challenge Dayo on ways that were foreign to her. So, she'd just said, "I'm going to do everything that I can to make this easy for her." She had squeezed his hand. "Between the two of us and your aunts, your mother will be fine."

Though he still held her hand, his eyes were on the window that framed the same view of the East River that could be seen from most rooms in their penthouse. But though she couldn't see his expression, Raine knew her husband so well she could almost see his thoughts and she braced herself for his next words.

"I understand why you want to do this, but we haven't given my mother a chance. We've never talked to her about how you feel . . . *exactly* how you feel . . ."

Raine shook her head. There was no need to have a talk. Beerlulu knew what she was doing; she knew what her words meant. Still, Dayo was not going to let his mother leave without a fight, and it was only because she loved her husband so much that she had agreed to one final talk.

It was supposed to have been this morning, over breakfast. But when Raine had awakened, instead of her husband, she found a note on Dayo's pillow saying that he was going to their store for an hour and he and Beerlulu would be back.

The store didn't even open up until ten, but Raine knew what this early morning excursion was about. He had taken his mother away to coach her, to get her to understand the stakes of this game.

*So please don't go anywhere. I really want us all to talk.*

Raine shook her head as she remembered the last words of

Dayo's note. She was sure he really believed this little tête-à-tête would resolve their issues. She could tell by the hope in his eyes when she'd agreed to the meeting, and the gratitude in the hug as he'd held her. But her decision was already made.

When she heard the sound of the key twisting in the door, Raine inhaled, preparing for battle, and within moments, her husband stood beneath the arch in the hallway. A few steps behind him was his mother.

"Good morning," Raine said as Dayo strode toward her with his hands behind his back.

Beerlulu simply bowed her head.

With a kiss on her cheek, Dayo presented her with a bouquet of roses. "Happy Valentine's Day, *mchumba*," he said.

She inhaled the fragrance of his gift. "Thank you." Though Dayo always bought her flowers on Valentine's Day, she had a feeling this gift was more of an offering. In past years, he'd professed his love with a dozen roses; today there were twenty-four flowers in the bouquet.

She sniffed the flowers again. "I love these."

He smiled as if he had a plan—double the bouquet, double his chances of success. His smile widened as if his plan was working. "Did you get my note?"

Raine nodded and placed the flowers on the buffet table. "Is everything okay at the store?"

"Yeah . . . I just wanted to . . . you know . . . check on a shipment coming in," he stammered.

Raine returned to her chair and brought the cup of cooled tea back to her lips. As if she was supposed to believe that.

"*Hooyo*," Dayo said as he held out the chair next to Raine.

Raine was surprised that her husband hadn't taken more of a

referee stance and sat in the chair between them. Instead, Raine was in the middle, at the head of the table, while Dayo sat across from his mother.

Silent seconds went by, and though Raine wanted to be the first to speak, to just blurt out, "Beerlulu, you've got to go," she waited for her husband.

Dayo began, "Besides God, you two are the ones I love most on this earth." His glance moved between his wife and his mother. "And if I came from you"—he looked at Beerlulu— "and I chose you"—his eyes moved to Raine—"there has to be common ground between the two of you."

Raine nodded, wanting Dayo to know that she was on his side now, even though she wouldn't be on his side later. But Beerlulu didn't move. Her gaze was straight on her son, her shoulders stiff, her face unsmiling, unyielding already.

Dayo continued, "*Hooyo,* we really want you here, but . . ."

Now Beerlulu moved . . . well, her eyebrows rose. "But? Is there any question about me being here?"

Beerlulu's eyes were still on Dayo, but Raine spoke anyway. "It's not a question," she said, jumping in, "it's a fact. We think you should move—not far away, but to your own apartment."

For a couple of seconds, Raine thought she was going to have to get her mother-in-law a brown paper bag for her to breathe into. Her smooth, radiant, charcoal complexion, which Raine had admired from the moment she first saw her in person, seemed to drain of blood, losing it's glow.

"You . . . you . . . you . . ."

For the two years that Beerlulu had been in this country up until this moment, she had always been clear, articulate, almost professorial in her delivery. But now Beerlulu stuttered as if she didn't know how to speak English.

Beerlulu took a breath and started over. "You never said any-thing about moving." Her stare was hard, but directed only to Dayo. "You want me to move?" She spoke as if Raine was not in the room.

Raine said, "This was my idea . . . something that I think would be best for all of us."

Beerlulu's gaze stayed right on Dayo, and then, with just the tiniest of movements, she finally faced Raine with eyes that bore hard into her. "Why would you want to rip me away from my family?"

Her words were over the top, but Raine kept her voice soft. "Lulu . . ."

Beerlulu squared her shoulders and sat up even taller when she said, "My name is Beerlulu."

It was interactions like this that made Raine want to get up and walk away. How many times had she shortened Beer-lulu's name? But now, suddenly, it was a problem? So she took a breath. "Beerlulu, we're not trying to rip you from anything. We just want you to be more comfortable."

"I am very comfortable here." Her statement was so strong, it sounded like a demand.

"But this is not what's best."

"How can you speak about what's best for me?" she hissed. "You're trying to say that you're doing this for me, but this is all about you. Why don't you speak the truth? Why don't you say that you don't want me here?"

Another deep inhale and then Raine replied, "Because that alone is not the truth. I'm really thinking about all of us."

"How can you be thinking about everyone if my son doesn't agree?" She turned her eyes back to Dayo. "You don't agree, do you?"

Dayo was silent as his eyes volleyed between the two women. Then: "I love you, *Hooyo*." He reached over and covered Raine's hand with his. "But she is my wife and this is our home, and she has to be happy."

Raine squeezed her husband's hand, grateful. She knew how tough it had to be for him to say those words, to take her side against his mother.

Beerlulu glared at her with eyes that bore emotions so strong, Raine pushed her chair back to get a few inches away from the heat.

"My husband's dead and now you want to take my son away from me?"

"It's not like that," Dayo protested. "*Hooyo,* you will never lose me."

The pain in his voice broke her heart, and Raine felt herself losing it—losing her memory of the reasons why this had to be. Then she remembered the night before . . . and her trembling daughter.

"Beerlulu," she began, coming back to where she needed to be, "I would never want to take you away from Dayo and I couldn't even if I tried. That's not what this is about. We want you here, we want you in our lives. That's why we're going to find something close, right here in Manhattan."

The older woman stared as if Raine's words made no sense.

Staying soft but strong, Raine added, "I want all of us to be happy."

"I am happy here. With my son. With my granddaughter."

Raine hesitated, giving Beerlulu a chance to add her to that list. When she didn't, she said, "Nothing's going to change when you move. You can come here every day. You can have dinner with us, you'll see Dayo and Nadia whenever you want."

"Then why should I move?"

"Because . . . your being here . . . is not good . . . especially not for Nadia."

Beerlulu bounced back in her chair, shocked by those words. "How can I not be good for my granddaughter?"

"She thinks you don't like her."

Beerlulu pressed her hand against her chest as if she was pushing her heart back inside. "How can you say that to me? You're putting that into her head!"

Raine had to take another moment, another breath. "I haven't said anything to her. This is what *she* told *me*."

Beerlulu shook her head. "I love my granddaughter with all of my heart." She blinked rapidly as if she was fighting off tears. "Everything that I say, everything that I do is because I love her so much."

"I know . . ."

"I'm just trying to protect her," Beerlulu continued. "Are you paying attention to the television programs she watches, the music that she listens to, the friends that she has?"

"We pay attention to all of that, and while that bothers you, Dayo and I are fine with it."

Even though Dayo nodded in agreement with Raine's words, Beerlulu shook her head. "You must not be seeing what I see. On TV, I see grown women acting like children and I see children acting like animals. I listen to your music and I hear words that disrespect and denigrate. I hear the talk among Nadia and her friends about boys and I'm horrified." She paused before she added, "No! I don't want my granddaughter influenced by these American children, these American ways."

"Listen to what you're saying! Nadia is an American child. Do you think she's an animal?"

"Of course she's not, but I don't want her to become like these other children. Did you know that her friend, that girl, *Shaquanda*"— she turned up her nose as she spoke the name—"her older sister is having sex!" Her voice was filled with her astonishment.

Raine and Dayo frowned together. "How do you know that?" she asked.

"I hear the children talking. They should never be talking about that kind of thing."

"We can't stop that talk," Raine said. "We've spoken to Nadia about sex and what it means and how it's a gift from God to be shared between a husband and wife."

"And there is nothing in your culture that teaches that. Everything around my granddaughter encourages sex with anybody and at any time. That's why she needs to be taken . . ."

"Mother!" Dayo exclaimed, and Beerlulu slammed her mouth shut.

Now there was total silence.

*What just happened?* Raine's eyes moved from her husband to his mother. She couldn't recall a time when Dayo had addressed Beerlulu that way. What happened to *Hooyo*? Why had he stopped her? What had she been going to say?

"Take . . . Nadia . . . where?" Raine's eyes were thin slits as the memory of Nadia's fears rushed back.

The mother and the son exchanged a glance before Beerlulu said, "Take her to spend more time with her relatives in Brooklyn," she said proudly, as if that was the solution to all of the problems. "She doesn't know her aunts or their husbands. She doesn't know her cousins."

Raine watched the two for seconds longer, looking for a clue to the truth. "No one," Raine began slowly, "is taking Nadia anywhere. Not unless I'm with her. Or Dayo."

"Of course," Beerlulu said.

Raine waited a second more before she continued, "Plus, taking her to Brooklyn isn't going to change anything. Her cousins are teenagers, too. They're listening to the same kinds of music and watching the same kinds of movies. Trust me on that."

"Oh, no." Beerlulu shook her head. "The girls are nothing like Nadia. Those girls are being raised by our women, they are being raised by the rites of our culture. They are being raised right."

Raine inhaled deeply.

"And that's all I'm trying to do." Though Beerlulu's words were insulting, her tone was filled with sincerity. "I just want to make sure my granddaughter is raised correctly."

"See," Raine started, then lowered her voice, "that's my biggest challenge, Beerlulu. Raising my child is my responsibility. You need to leave this to me."

"How can I when you don't know how? How can I when you're not very good at raising her because of where you come from?" Beerlulu sat proudly, almost smiling as if that insult was the final word.

And it was.

There was silence as Raine turned her whole body to face Dayo; he shook his head and lowered his eyes, knowing the battle was over and he was on the losing side.

After a moment, he looked directly at his mother. "Let's take a look at some of the apartments the Realtor has before we decide exactly what to do."

Beerlulu's lips parted and formed into the shape of a perfect O. "After what I just explained, you still want me to move?"

Raine nodded.

Beerlulu said, "I'd rather return home than live anywhere else in this country."

She wanted so badly to tell her mother-in-law to get to fly-ing, but Raine sat silently; it was best if Dayo handled it from here.

"*Hooyo,* you're not going back to Kenya, so don't say that. Like Raine said, you're going to be very close to us. We'll let the Realtor know what we're looking for."

Beerlulu pressed her lips together and glared at her son as if that look alone would change his mind. When she got nothing back, her eyes hardened, defiant once again. She pushed back her chair, and without a glance or a word, she stomped away as if she was marching off to war.

Their eyes followed Beerlulu before they faced each other. The pain was evident in Dayo's eyes and Raine searched for words to comfort him. But she had nothing, so she just squeezed her husband's hand.

He looked down to where their fingers were entwined, and with the gentlest of movements, he pulled away, stood, and moved in the opposite direction of his mother. Seconds later, Raine heard the door to their bedroom close.

*Happy Valentine's Day.*

# CHAPTER 6

## Sierra

This was not the way Sierra was supposed to be spending Valentine's Day. She was supposed to be in a romantic restaurant, not at the local bar. She was supposed to be sitting across from the man who'd just proposed marriage, not staring into the face of her best friend, who stared back with nothing but pity.

Denise shook her head. "You know you need to get it together, right?"

Sierra took a sip of her third mojito.

"You look pitiful."

Sierra wanted to smack Denise for saying that, but her friend spoke the truth. She did look pitiful and that was another thing that was so wrong about tonight. She was supposed to be wearing a fierce dress that would've shown Andre (and every other man) why she was such a prize. But instead, she'd just tossed on a pair of skinny jeans, a cashmere sweater that she'd paid too much for, and then stuffed her hair beneath a Yankees baseball cap.

No, this was not the atmosphere, not the company, not the attire that she was due on what was supposed to be her best Valentine's Day ever.

"So, are you going to tell me what happened?" Denise asked in her psychologist's voice, which Sierra hated.

Sierra's eyes roamed around the dimly lit bar. The Chocolate Tavern, Harlem's latest hot spot, was packed with moving-on-up black urban professionals—mostly men—standing around, profiling, bobbing their heads to the beat of old-school music. The looks on their faces were the same—they were searching for that special Valentine's Day hookup. The chance to get the goodies without having to buy a gift. What disgusted Sierra was that this strategy would probably work. As long as the man was breathing and smelled halfway decent, there were enough women here doing their own profiling, looking for their own hookups.

As the Ohio Players crooned about heaven being like this, Denise continued her interrogation. "Are you going to answer me?"

The flickering teacup candle's flame shined a dim light on the worry lines etched on Denise's forehead. Of course her friend was concerned. Since third grade, the two had talked about everything, but this time Sierra hadn't planned to—because to her this wasn't a breakup—at least not a permanent one. She'd decided that Andre was the one and she would get him back, no matter what she had to do.

Sierra had planned to spend this night at home doing what she'd been doing—crying and strategizing. But then Denise had come and dragged her out of her apartment, and Sierra knew that her friend, who was trained in the study of people, was going to push and prod until Sierra gave in and gave up the story. So instead of stalling any further, she began to tell what happened.

"Did you go off on him?" Denise asked once she finished.

"Why would you ask me that?"

"'Cause that's how you roll," her friend stated as if it was a fact. "But if you didn't, then I'll know that the advice I've been giving you is working and I can send you my bill."

Sierra laughed. Of course, she didn't tell Denise the whole story; she decided to just say the words that her friend would want to hear. "Girl, I learned long ago not to try to keep a man when he doesn't want to stay."

Denise leaned her head back and laughed so hard Sierra wanted to smack her again. But how could she when her friend knew all her secrets? Denise had been there when she'd flushed Eric's keys down the toilet (before she begged him to stay) and when she'd slashed all four of Ray's tires (before she begged him to stay) and when she told William that she was dying of cancer (before she begged him to stay). Then there was Morris; she pretended to be pregnant, then pretended to have a miscarriage. When she had begged him to stay, Morris did exactly what all the other men had done—he ran like hell, never even giving her the proverbial "I hope we can be friends" spiel.

Sierra said, "What I *should've* said was I've learned my lesson." She twisted her neck with attitude. "When Andre said he wanted out, I told him to get to stepping."

Denise peered at her with unbelieving eyes, and Sierra squirmed. It was as if Denise was searching for the truth inside Sierra's soul, but thank God, He hadn't yet passed out that gift. So all Denise could do was imagine. She wouldn't know about the vase and the TV and the toothbrush. And she really wouldn't know how Sierra had spent all of these hours crying over her lost love, trying to figure out how to get him back. Because one thing she was sure of—Andre was hers!

"Well, a lesson learned is a great lesson," Denise said, her voice rising over Sierra's thoughts and the music. "And truthfully, it's good that you and Andre broke up."

Sierra's eyebrows rose. "I thought you liked him."

"He was okay, not that I really knew him like that; you guys were only together for what—five minutes?"

Sierra rolled her eyes.

Denise added, "I'm teasing, but you know it's close to the truth. You didn't even give yourself two weeks between your breakup with Morris and your hookup with Andre. Now, you can have some time and space to think about what's really important to you, like Destiny's Divas."

"Nothing for me to think about with Destiny's Divas; that's the best part of my life. Yvonne told us that we're still hanging in there at number one."

Denise smiled. "I hear 'Love Unlimited' all over the radio."

At least Sierra had that going for her. All the promises that Raine had made to her about Destiny's Divas were coming true. According to Yvonne, they were knocking at the door of breakthrough success.

Leaning forward, Denise said, "What you're doing with Destiny's Divas really concerns me."

"What?"

"The single, celibate testimony you got going on."

Sierra rolled her eyes. "Why is everybody always bringing that up?"

"Everybody?"

"Yeah, Andre said something about it, and now you. What's the big deal?"

"You're lying."

"Do you think women will really care if they find out I'm not really celibate?" Sierra waved her hand in the air. "Please. I don't think so."

"Then you're really naive."

"Well, if anything were to happen, it wouldn't be my fault." Sierra shrugged. "Raine's the one who invited me to be a part of the group."

"After you lied to her."

"I didn't lie *to* her. She made some assumptions after she heard my testimony."

"She assumed you were telling the truth, Sierra! I'm serious, you really need to check yourself."

Sierra would never say it out loud, but there were times when she'd been in bed with one man or another and felt a tinge of guilt. But the thing was, even though it was a lie, wasn't it a lie that truthfully needed to be told? Celibacy was a good thing—for some people.

"I don't think it's a big deal," she said. "And anyway, what I say is really how I want to live. I just need to get back with Andre."

"What . . . did . . . you . . . say?" Denise asked. She turned her head slightly as if she needed to adjust her hearing.

How had Sierra let the truth slip through her lips? "I just have to find the right man first," Sierra corrected.

"My opinion," Denise began, "forget about Andre and let the right man . . ."

Sierra held up her hand. "Do you know how many times you've given me this lecture?"

"Apparently not enough. You're still out there looking when it's . . ."

". . . the man who finds a good woman," Sierra finished for Denise. "But that isn't working because I haven't been found yet. And tell me, how does that make sense because"—she scooted her chair back, though there was little room since the tables were stuffed together—"look at me." Sierra wanted her friend to really see her because even in her busted outfit, she was probably the best-looking woman in the place. "I should've been found a long time ago."

Denise laughed. "I'll never have you in my office trying to build your self-esteem."

"What? Am I supposed to ignore the fact that I'm beautiful?"

With a chuckle, Denise shook her head.

"I'm just stating a fact. I know I didn't have anything to do with my looks. It was just God paying me back for being the biggest loser in the parental sweepstakes. You think it was easy growing up with a mother who drank herself into the grave?"

"You know you have a lot of mother issues, right? One minute you're quoting a million Beth truisms. And then in the next minute you're calling her a drunk."

"Because Beth was both," Sierra said. "She was a wise drunk."

Denise raised her eyebrows. "Is that a medical condition?"

"Seriously, being a drunk didn't negate what my mother knew. She drank herself to death because of the problems she had with men. But that didn't stop her from teaching the lessons she'd learned. At least whenever she was sober."

"See what I mean? Issues."

Sierra shook her head. "My only issues are with my sperm donor. Do you know what it's like having a father who I could pass on the street and not even know it?"

"Sierra, this is what I'm talking about. You had a mother who you say was a drunk but had wisdom. And a father who never cared, but you missed him. That's a heavy load." Denise continued, "I think you want a man in your life to give you the family structure that you never had."

"Please don't give me that psycho mumbo jumbo."

"I'm just telling you what I know." Denise raised her voice

over the O'Jays crooning about money. "I think you have some real issues to work out. You need to speak to someone."

Sierra laughed out loud. "Why? I have you. We don't even need a couch or an office. You can psychoanalyze me anywhere," she said, glancing around the club.

"Make fun all you want, but I'm really worried about you."

"I'm fine," she said, taking another sip of her mojito.

"Is that why you look at every man you know for more than two hours as your husband?"

Sierra gulped down the rest of her drink as if it was Kool-Aid. "That's mean."

"If the truth is mean, let it hurt. Every guy you meet is the one! Before you know anything about him. Before you have a chance to see if you even like him, you love him and you're ready to walk down the aisle."

"I've never talked to any of them about marriage."

"You don't have to. It's written all over your face. You're needy, you're clingy. The word *desperate* is etched right there." She pointed to Sierra's forehead.

"Ouch!" Sierra raised her empty glass, motioning for the waiter to return. She needed another one, quick. Before she stood up and really smacked Denise.

As she searched for the waiter, she stopped when her eyes met those of the standout in the crowd—he was the tallest man in the place, surrounded by several other guys who stood by him as if they were bodyguards. With an assessment that had become her expertise, she took inventory of the stranger. Even from feet away, even in the dim light, she could see the intensity of his dark eyes, the squareness of his strong jaw, the perfection of his physique that had to come from a love affair with the gym.

He raised his glass as if he was giving her a salute, and she twisted in her chair before he could see her smile.

"I know you don't want to hear all of this," Denise said when Sierra turned her attention back to her, "but you don't even give these guys a chance to fight for you. Let a man work a little. Let him earn the gift of being with you."

"Okay."

Denise looked at Sierra out of the corner of her eye. " 'Okay, like you agree?"

" 'Okay' like I agree and I hear you. For real."

Denise squinted as if she was trying to get a closer look at Sierra. "I hope so." A pause, and then: "You know, not everyone could take what I just said."

"And not everyone could say what you said and walk away without a busted lip."

They laughed together.

Denise said, "I only want the best for you."

Sierra nodded, knowing Denise was speaking the truth. Over the years, her friend had always encouraged her. From pushing her to study for test after test to trying to talk her into attending college with her at New York University. Sierra had never taken her friend's advice. Her grades were decent, but not because she studied. And she'd never applied to college because she had dreams beyond four more years in a classroom. But maybe now would be a good time to listen to her friend who seemed to know all things.

"I just want you to take this time to put yourself in a good place so you can enjoy the success that's coming your way."

Sierra nodded as her eyes wandered again to the bar, to the stranger whose eyes were still on her. This time her gaze lingered and she took in the smooth baldness of his head and the hair

that framed his chin. The man seemed familiar, and Sierra wondered if they'd met. He raised his glass in another salute, and this
time she didn't turn away. She gave her smile straight to him.

"Listen, we really should be getting out of here," Denise said.
"I want to make the early service tomorrow." She placed her
credit card on the edge of the table. "You going to church in the
morning?"

Sierra looked at the man again, and this time her eyes stayed
on him. She studied him as he studied her. "I'm not sure," she
said, finally answering Denise, even though her eyes were still on
the man.

"That's another thing you need to be doing—you need to
start attending church on the regular," Denise said as one of the
waiters scooped up her credit card.

"Yeah." Sierra tore away from the delicious sight and turned
back to her friend. "But the good thing is that no one knows
that I'm not going to church. When I'm not there, my pastor
thinks that I'm over there at Abyssinian with you, and when I'm
not with you, your pastor thinks I'm at home at City of Lights."

Shaking her head, Denise said, "You're gonna burn in hell."

Sierra snickered and twisted in her seat under the guise of
getting her purse off the back of her chair. But she wanted to
give the stranger more of her to see.

Denise announced, "You ready?"

Sierra nodded, and stood up quickly, moving forward so that
her friend would have to follow her.

"Hey," Denise yelled out. "This way is quicker."

But Sierra pretended that she didn't hear Denise above the
Isley Brothers singing "Hello, It's Me." She didn't care if Denise
followed her or not.

Sierra pressed through the crowd, taking the path where

she'd have to pass the stranger. She already had her plan: If he spoke, she would stop. If he didn't, this night would be his loss.

As she shoved against the bodies that were squeezed together, she ignored the "Hey, baby" and the "What's up, sweetheart?" There was only one man on her radar, and when she looked up, he was still there. Still staring, still smiling, even wider now that she was coming his way.

When she was just feet away, he mumbled something to the guy next to him, then took a couple of steps toward her until they were face-to-face. He greeted her with "Hello, it's me . . . it's me, baby. I've thought about us for a long, long time," he sang along with the Isley Brothers.

Sierra laughed. "I bet you use that line on all the ladies."

The man chuckled with her. "No, I haven't. It's been laying low in my heart just waiting for you."

Sierra was thinking that was one of the sweetest lines she'd ever heard when behind her Denise coughed, as if that was a classy way to get someone's attention. That fast, Sierra had forgotten about her friend, and now she wished she'd made up some lie like she'd had to go to the bathroom so Denise would have been on her way. She shot a look over her shoulder, hoping her friend would catch the clue and leave.

But whether she caught it or not, Denise just stood there glaring. "We need to get out of here." It was a demand, as if she was Sierra's mother.

Sierra widened her eyes a bit, trying to send another signal.

But Denise wasn't having it.

Finally, Sierra hissed, "You can go on."

"I'm not leaving without you."

Sierra sighed; Denise was blocking for real.

The man said, "Listen, it seems like you were on your way

out, so let me give you this." He flicked a white card from inside his jacket, but before he handed it to her, he jotted something on the back. "This is my personal cell phone number. I hope you'll use it, and use it often."

Sierra took the card without looking at it. "Maybe I will, maybe I won't. We'll see."

He nodded, as if he was impressed. "Confidence. One of the most endearing qualities I find in a woman." He stepped back a bit and assessed her. "A very attractive woman."

For a moment, Sierra wished that she'd worn something more catching, but then she wondered why. Dressed like this, she was the standout in this crowd, and he'd just proven it.

When Denise tugged her arm, Sierra said, "Good night," and let her friend drag her past the bar, past the bouncer, past the red velvet rope, and finally onto the street.

"You know you're acting like you've lost it," Sierra said the moment they stepped outside into the midnight wind.

"You need to *lose* that card."

"Why?"

"Because."

"That doesn't sound like a professional answer."

"Just because."

"Oh, that's better." Sierra laughed. "I didn't plan to keep it anyway."

Denise shook her head, not believing her friend, but she hugged her anyway. "I pray for you."

"Thank you; I need every one of those prayers."

Denise held up her hand and a gypsy cab rolled right up. "You want us to drop you off?"

"Girl, you know my mama's rule. I'm just gonna walk up the street and around the corner."

Denise blew her a kiss and hopped in the car, and Sierra stepped quickly across Lenox Avenue. It may have been a cold winter's night, but Harlem was still aglow; 125th Street was filled with pedestrians rushing and cars rambling down the street.

But neither the street nor the cold was on Sierra's mind. All she could think about was the card she held between her fingers, stuffed inside her pocket.

She bit the corner of her lip as she thought about the brief meeting with the stranger. It was short, but it'd given her enough time to know that she liked what she saw. He was handsome, she was beautiful. Forget about making music together, they would be a world-class symphony!

But then . . . *screech!*

Sierra brought her thoughts to a halt. What about Andre? He was the one she wanted.

At the corner of 123rd and Morningside, Sierra walked over to the trash bin to toss the card away. Taking it out of her pocket, she glanced at it for the first time.

Jarrod Cannon.

"Jarrod Cannon?" she whispered. "O-M-G! I knew he looked familiar." She stared at the card, not sure what to do.

Andre Stevens or Jarrod Cannon? What a choice!

After another moment, she tossed the card into the trash. Yeah, being with Jarrod Cannon, the newly elected congressman for the good people of Harlem, could have been interesting, but she was choosing what was in her heart.

Andre was who it was going to be.

# CHAPTER 7

# Liza

*R*everend Mann Washington's voice ricocheted off the walls, louder than anyone else's in the sanctuary. His tenor was crisp, clear. He could have easily been a top-charted singer like his wife if he hadn't been called to save souls.

"I just want to praise you, through the good and the bad. . . . I'll praise you whether happy or sad."

With his head back, his eyes closed, and his hands raised, the reverend looked just like most of the five thousand parishioners who filled every seat. But while men, women, and children worshipped around her, Liza kept her eyes open and on her husband.

The way she had for the last three days. Ever since she'd seen that website: Females4Men.

That website had stayed with her for every one of the sixty or so hours that had passed since, though she hadn't said a word to Mann. At least not directly.

When she'd awoken on Friday morning, the explanation that she'd come up with for why the site had popped up on her computer did not stand up under the light of day. She needed a better answer. But when she rolled over and discovered that she was alone in bed, she'd wrapped herself in her robe and had gone downstairs.

Mann had greeted her in the kitchen with a kiss, a cup of coffee, and a dozen Krispy Kreme donuts that had just been delivered by Buddy, Mann's armor bearer. Mann sat at the kitchen table with the newspaper in front of his face like it was just an ordinary morning.

As she'd sipped her coffee, Liza watched and wondered what was the best way to ask her husband if he was having an affair with some woman he'd met on the Internet.

Finally, she'd asked, "So, is your sermon set for Sunday?"

His face was still hidden behind the newspaper. "Yup."

She'd waited for more before she asked, "Anything you want to share?"

This time he dipped the newspaper and peered at his wife over the top. "Why would you ask me that?"

Another sip of coffee gave her time to come up with an answer. In all the years of their marriage, Mann had never shared his sermons with her or anyone. He said it was all about being fresh in the pulpit. It was about not being persuaded by anyone other than God.

He'd told her that the first week of their marriage and so she'd never asked. Until now. Today she had to know because she needed him to corroborate the explanation that she'd made up in her mind.

"I was just thinking," she said finally, "that it might be good for us to start sharing. I mean, on tour I'll be standing onstage giving my testimony." She'd shrugged. "It'll be like a little sermon, so it makes sense for us to talk about that kind of stuff now."

He'd folded the newspaper, tucked it under his arm, and

stood. "I'll always be here for you, my beautiful bride. I'll help with anything you need. But as for me and my sermons, you know how I do." He'd chuckled before he kissed her cheek. Then he'd left her in the kitchen, alone, to do nothing except think.

Thinking was all she'd been doing—thinking and arriving at the same conclusion.

*That website was just for research and he'll talk about it in his sermon.*

"Let's praise Him, church."

The sound of her husband's voice snapped her from her thoughts and she clapped like those around her.

"I am so glad to be here in the house of the Lord," the reverend said. "What about you?"

A hum of "Amen" and "Yes" resonated through the church.

He said, "Giving glory to God, who is the head of my life." He paused. "And next, giving honor to my bride, the lovely first lady, Liza Washington."

The congregation applauded as they always did. The reverend smiled and Liza did her best to pass a smile back to him, but she was ready to get past all of this so that she could hear the message.

"Y'all know I love that woman, right?" The reverend laughed.

Everyone joined him—except Liza.

"Yes, God blessed me the day he brought Lady Liza into my life. She's the love of my life and my partner in our ministry."

"Amen."

"She's also the mother of our two beautiful children."

Liza cringed as more amens rang even louder through the church, but then the reverend paused, placed his hand over his heart, and tapped three times.

This time Liza couldn't help but smile. Three taps—I love

you—the silent signal they shared when they couldn't say the words aloud.

Reverend Washington continued, "It is because of my bride, my children, my love for my brothers and sisters in Christ, and above all, my love for the Lord that I speak today to the young women. Because young women are the ones who hold our futures in their hands."

"Amen!" rang out.

"Our future lies within you, young ladies," he said, beginning his message the same way he did every second Sunday.

"Preach!"

"Oh, y'all are not hearing me." He paused. "Can I see the number of young women who have never been here before? If this is your first time visiting Ridgewood Macedonia, can you please stand?"

As the congregants applauded, Liza took a quick glance around the main sanctuary and the balcony. There were a good number, probably close to one hundred teenage girls standing.

Mann's smile was broad when she faced her husband again.

"That's what I'm talking about," Mann said as he motioned for everyone to sit and get settled again. "I'm talking to the young ladies today. Anybody under twenty. The rest of the folks in here can go right on to sleep."

Chuckles rose in the sanctuary.

The reverend said, "I'm here to talk to you because you are the most important part of our society. I bet no one has ever told you that before, huh?"

Liza imagined that behind her heads were shaking. But she didn't turn around; her eyes stayed on her husband. She was waiting for him to get to the part where he explained why he was on that website, the part that would remove all of her thoughts that her husband might be having an affair.

An affair.

Really, truly, that was just not possible. If there was anything that she could say about her husband, it was that not only was he a man of the Word, he was a man of his word. Twenty-eight years of marriage and she'd never suspected another woman. How could she when she knew where her husband was every hour of the day? He never disappeared, never had any mysterious emergencies, never received phone calls that he had to take privately—nothing.

Even when Mann traveled to conferences and other speaking engagements, he was always with Buddy, his armor bearer, whom Liza totally trusted. And just like when Mann was at home, when he was away he called her constantly, letting her know his every move. And he never hung up without telling her just how beautiful she was. It didn't matter that middle age had snuck up and added quite a middle to her frame. "My beautiful bride" was what he called her all the time.

Sure, they weren't heating up the sheets the way they'd been when they first married. At that time, Mann couldn't get enough of her. For four years straight, they'd made love almost every day. But then life happened—she gave birth to their first child *and* his Deliver Our Daughters ministry was born. Two years after that, she'd talked him into a similar ministry for young men, though Save Our Sons never thrived the way the girls' ministry did.

From the beginning, their youth movement had been demanding and taxing, so she understood Mann coming home too tired to do anything more than hold her in his arms. But that was enough because it had never been about sex with the two of them. Liza was in love with their intimacy, the way he held her, the way he sang to her almost every night.

It was his singing that had always held her heart. Maybe it was because he was singing the first time she'd laid her fifteen-year-old eyes on him, back in 1982, back in Corinth, Mississippi . . .

It was gonna be one of those dog-hot August days.

"That's right," the weatherman said on the TV that blasted in the living room, "it's already ninety-three degrees at ten o'clock and we expect it to hit one hundred by noon."

Liza blew out a long breath when she heard that. What was she gonna do? Her mother had her in this high-collar lace-trimmed dress that scratched and choked her at the same time. It was bad enough that the floral pattern was going to attract every mosquito in Mississippi. And what was she supposed to do with this big ole mop of a mess on top of her head?

With her brush in her hand, all she could do was stare at her reflection in her mirror. She was going to be one sweaty, bit-up, choking, crazy-looking fool by the time she got to church.

"Liza Mae, are you ready?"

"No, Mama," she yelled out.

She heard her mother's grunt, then her steps, getting heavier and heavier as she marched across the loose wooden planks. Liza counted in her head—one, two, three, four, five, and there she was in the mirror's reflection. Her mother's hands were on her ample hips and her bright red lips were pressed together. "You know we have to be on time today. What is that big-city preacher gonna think of us coming up in that church late like we don't have any kind of class."

"I'm sorry, Mama, but this dress is choking me. I'm gonna die. And I can't get my hair . . ."

"Oh, give me that," her mother said, grabbing the brush.

Liza tried not to smile—this was exactly what she wanted. Millicent Devine was the only one who could tame Liza's thick, wild mane.

In fifteen minutes, Liza had one long French braid that hung down the center of her back. But by the time she and her mother climbed into the rusty black 1964 Chevy Impala, and her father backed the clunker out of the driveway, they were already five minutes late, and the church was fifteen minutes away.

The weekly announcements were just about over when Liza and her parents scooted down the center aisle of the church, which was filled with wooden backless benches. The Devines grunted their apologies and stepped over Beulah Lee Hicks and her two daughters, who rolled their eyes, sucked their teeth, and mumbled and grumbled that only sinners came into the Lord's house so late.

By the time they settled down, Liza's dress was sticking to her skin, her braid was unraveling, and mosquitos had feasted on her ankles.

She blew out such a long breath that Millicent looked at her sideways. But Liza didn't care. She needed to hurry and be grown because when she could make her own decisions, she wouldn't be coming anywhere near a little church house that didn't have air-conditioning, but was still packed with fifty black folks. There should've been a law—all black churches should've been closed when the temperature rose above 80 degrees.

But all she could do was complain in her head because if she had said a word to her mother, Millicent would have told her, "We gotta be here to see the big-city preacher."

Humph. That's all anybody had been talking about. She didn't know why she was supposed to care about some old pastor. Shoot, he was probably as boring and as annoying as Pastor Jackson, whose false teeth clicked every time he said a word that began with an *S*.

"It's my great pleasure . . ."

Liza didn't even notice that Reverend Jackson had stood up.

"On this Sunday"—he clicked, then paused to give his teeth time to line up again—"I want to introduce to you, straight," click, another pause, "from New York . . . Reverend Mann Washington."

*Mann? What kind of name is Mann?*

As the congregation applauded politely, Liza stretched in her seat to see which old man up at the front with Reverend Jackson would get up. But Reverend Jackson held up his hand.

"Wait a minute," he said. "Y'all didn't let me finish, saints." Click and pause.

Snickers floated through the congregation and Liza rolled her eyes.

"Reverend Washington just happens to be Miss Bessie's grandson."

Now the applause was a bit louder as everyone cranked their necks to see Miss Bessie's beaming face.

"Reverend Washington, I turn it over to you."

The man who was sitting next to Miss Bessie kissed her on the cheek, then strutted to the center of the church. When he took the microphone from Reverend Jackson, Liza almost fell off the bench.

*That's Reverend Washington?*

It couldn't be. This guy didn't have any gray hair and he was dressed in a real cool green suit with a matching pocket handkerchief and even matching shoes. He didn't look anything like the preachers Liza knew.

"Thank you, Reverend Jackson," the man said in a voice that sounded like he was singing.

Then, before Liza could have another thought, he did just that—he started singing.

The man just leaned his head back, lifted his hands, opened his mouth, and started singing.

"If you want to know . . . where I'm going . . . where I'm going, soon."

Without saying anything more than thank you, he broke out in his song!

For the second time, Liza almost fell off the bench. Of course, she'd heard "Going Up Yonder" many times before; it was a favorite of the Corinth Baptist choir with Miss Bessie singing the lead. But every time Miss Bessie opened her mouth, all Liza wanted to do was cover her ears.

It wasn't like that with her grandson, though. Liza didn't want to cover up anything! All she wanted to do was sit and stare and hear this man who sounded just like that singer on the radio—Luther Vandross. By the time Reverend Washington got to the end of the song, Liza was in love.

After the service, a shy Liza stood with her parents in the reception line at the meet-and-greet in the church's backyard. They edged up in the line slowly as every mother in the church tried to give their daughters time with the young, single big-city preacher.

When it was their turn, Liza's mother spoke first. "It's so nice to meet you and have you here with us, Reverend Washington," she said, shaking his hand.

Then Liza's father said, "That was some message. Thank you for bringing forth the Word in such a powerful way."

"You're welcome. And who am I having the pleasure of speaking with?"

"I'm Milton Devine and this is my wife, Millicent. And our daughter, Liza."

She'd been hiding behind her father, kind of. But now Liza stepped into the big-city preacher's view.

He took one look at Liza, and that's where his eyes stayed. Reaching for her hand, he said, "Devine. Did you say your name was Devine?" He smiled, a kind of crooked smile with only the left half of his mouth.

She shook her head. "My name is Liza Mae Devine."

"It's the perfect name for such a beautiful young lady."

He was still holding her hand, but Liza didn't mind. The longer he held it, the longer he would talk, and the longer she could hear that voice. "Thank you, sir," she whispered.

"You're the prettiest girl in the church," he said, still holding on to her.

"Thank you, sir," she repeated.

He chuckled. "You don't have to call me 'sir.'" Finally, he let her fingers go. "I'm sure I'm not that much older than you."

He stared at her hand, making her shift from one foot to the other.

"Oh, Reverend, she has to call you 'sir' 'cause she's a good Christian girl. We raised her right."

"That you did," the reverend said to Millicent even though his eyes were still on her fifteen-year-old daughter.

They moved along, but only because Beulah and her two daughters were behind them, embarrassing everyone by the way they were rolling their eyes, sucking their teeth, and muttering about how some people were so rude, taking up all the good preacher's time.

But as Liza mulled around the backyard, following her parents as they chatted with other members of Corinth Baptist, she watched the reverend, who was watching her. All she wanted was for him to break away and come talk to her in that voice.

"It's time for us to go," her mother said soon after.

*Dang!* Liza lost all hope. She'd never see the big-city preacher again.

But then: "Reverend Washington accepted our invitation," her father said as he led Millicent and Liza to the car.

"What invitation, Daddy?"

"Your daddy and I invited Reverend Washington, Miss Bessie, and Reverend Jackson to dinner tonight."

That news put a smile on Liza's face and she grinned all the way home. . . .

"I want you young ladies to really get this last point."

Liza had to blink to bring herself back from all those years ago.

Mann was walking down her side of the aisle. He paused in front of her and tapped his hand three times against his chest again. Then he continued his journey through the congregation. "You, as young women," he said, "are the center of all relationships. You weren't made from dust, you were made from a part of the man. That's where relationships began. You weren't put on earth to work the way God commanded man. You were put here to be a helper—a relationship role.

"This is why Deliver Our Daughters is so important," he said, continuing to snake through the church. He marched up one aisle, then down the other, passing as many of the four thousand congregants who sat on the main level as he could. "When you become part of this alliance, you will receive support for every part of your life so that you can learn how to build and nurture relationships. We have counselors who will help you and from this day forward, no matter what's going on, you will never be alone. Our alliance will always be here—from your home-work to your health. From college to career. We will stand by you and with you from this day forward."

He picked up his pace as he headed back to the front. "So, I'll close with this: I hope you will join our ever-growing team designed to help you become the best women you can be."

Taking the two steps up to the altar, Mann faced the congre-gation. "The future lies within you, so please join us!" He held out his hand, beckoning the young women to come to the altar. "Come up here now, so that I can meet you and pray for you."

No one moved. And then the organ began to play. Mann opened his mouth. "Come forth," he sang. "Join us," he encour-aged, in song.

It was as if he was the Pied Piper—the young women began to rise. At first, it was just a trickling, but then more and more until the young women stood in front of him three rows deep. Mann greeted each one, though he still sang.

The girls kept coming, some crying—and those were the ones Mann took special time to greet. He held them—for just a moment—assuring them that no matter what had happened in their lives, it would be better now. He shook hands with the other girls and hugged any who offered a hug to him first.

From her seat, Liza soaked in Mann's compassion. Her remi-niscent journey back to their beginning made her miss most of her husband's sermon. But just watching him now told her all she needed to know. The way he handled these young women—with kindness and gentleness—there was not a deceitful bone within him.

It was the devil's trickery that had led her to that site and made her believe her husband was having an affair. It was a lie!

There was such surety in her heart now. She was going to toss away those thoughts and never allow them into her consciousness again.

With that decision, she stood and joined her husband at the altar. Now that her head was clear, there was much work to do. She had to help her husband save this next generation of girls.

After all, that's what they'd been doing for twenty years. This was their calling.

# CHAPTER 8

## *Raine*

Raine smoothed down her dress, shook out her locks, then headed toward Nadia's bedroom. Knocking on the door once, she peeked inside. "You okay?"

Nadia sat in the middle of her bed with only one earbud from her MP3 stuffed into her ear. She looked up from her laptop. "Yeah. I'm just doing my homework. Are you and Daddy still going to the museum?"

"Of course, sweetie," Raine said, stepping into the bedroom. "I'd do anything for you."

"You're not doing it for me," Nadia smirked. "It's a fundraiser for the school."

"Well," Raine began as she stroked her hand over Nadia's braids, "anything I do for the school is for you, but let's talk about your homework." She jiggled the cord from Nadia's earbuds.

"I need the music to help me concentrate, Mom!"

Raine smiled; another mother would not believe that, but she understood. Nadia was definitely her child.

"What time are you and Daddy coming home?"

Raine peered at her daughter before she answered, studying

her, seeing the lines of concern in her forehead. "Just a couple of hours." She sat on the edge of the bed so that she could look straight into Nadia's eyes. "You know you can always call me whenever. If you need me or your dad."

"I know," Nadia said, her voice quivering the way it used to when, as a toddler, she cried whenever her parents left her with her nanny.

"You're gonna be okay," Raine told her daughter. She hadn't shared with Nadia the news about Beerlulu moving out. She added, "I'll let you know when your dad and I are leaving, okay?"

Nadia nodded and Raine closed the door, standing there for just a moment. She knew what Nadia's questions were about; she never wanted to be left alone with Beerlulu, which was exactly why Raine was doing what had to be done. Once her mother-in-law was in her own place, Raine would call any number of sitters who could stay with Nadia whenever she and Dayo went out. This would never be a concern for her daughter again.

But when she stepped down the hall and stopped in front of their library, Raine got a glimpse of the other side of this emotional situation. Dayo sat at the desk, holding his head as if his heartache throbbed through every part of his body.

His heartache was fresh, now that he'd have to let his mother go. But her sorrow had started a long time ago—the day Beerlulu stepped off the airplane. From the way she'd hugged Dayo and only shook Raine's hand to the way she constantly chatted about the heartbroken Kenyan girls that Dayo had left behind.

Dayo had tried to quiet his mother when she talked about the women still waiting for him. "The only woman on earth for me is Raine," he'd said as they'd driven home from the airport. He had glanced at Raine through the rearview mirror and winked.

She'd been grateful for her husband, but still hurt by his mother. Especially when Beerlulu had even taken a jab at Nadia.

At first, Beerlulu had beamed with pride when Nadia came bouncing out of the room.

"You look just like your *babu,*" Beerlulu said as she hugged and kissed Nadia until the girl couldn't stop giggling.

"Grandmother," Nadia had said. "What's a babu?"

"Not what, sweetheart, who. I was telling you in my language that you look just like your grandfather. God rest his soul."

"Really?" Nadia said, grinning like she was pleased.

But then Beerlulu had stepped back and looked Nadia up and down and frowned. "Those pants you're wearing—why are they so short, *Mjukuu?*"

Nadia had laughed, not recognizing the question as criticism. "They're called shorts, Grandmother," she said, as if she just knew that her grandmother had to be kidding.

The saddest part about that first day was that it was the best day.

"I didn't see you standing there," came a voice through her reminiscence.

"I . . . I was just coming. . . ." She paused and looked at her husband, still dressed in the sweater and pants that he'd worn to work. "You're not ready."

He shook his head. "I don't think we should go."

Raine frowned. "What are you talking about? I have to be there. I'm on the committee."

"Then you go."

She pinched her lips together, stepped into the library, and closed the door behind her. But Dayo held up his hand, stopping her from speaking.

"I'm not going, Raine. My mother is not feeling well."

"What's wrong with her?"

"She's upset about this move and I need to be here for her."

"So let me get this straight. You don't want to go to the fund-raiser for your daughter's school because you want to hold your mother's hand."

"You think this is a joke?"

"No, but it would be if it wasn't so sad."

"Glad that you can be so dismissive of my mother."

"Your mother is upset about nothing. Grown women live alone all over this country."

"My mother is not like other women."

*You got that right.* "I know that, but our lives can't stop because of your mother. We made this commitment to the school months ago."

"All right," he shouted, stunning Raine. She wasn't sure if she'd ever heard her husband raise his voice. He pushed back the chair. "I'll be ready in fifteen minutes."

She shook her head as he stomped past her. Twenty minutes later, she kissed Nadia good-bye with promises to be back home before she was asleep.

"Can I call Shaquanda?"

"You finished your homework?"

"Yes." She held up her laptop.

"Okay, but remember, be off the phone and in bed by ten."

Nadia nodded, pushed her earbuds back in place, and lay across her bed.

Raine waited in the living room while Dayo checked on Beerlulu. Then, when he came out already wearing his coat, Raine followed him to the front door. She said a quick prayer when they entered the elevator and Dayo didn't hold her hand as he always did. And when the elevator doors parted in the

parking garage, he walked so fast that she wondered if he'd forgotten she was with him.

His silence continued as he sped uptown, and Dayo still had
not said a word when they finally turned onto Fifth Avenue,
then slowed to a stop. Still a few blocks away from the Guggen-
heim Museum, they waited in the long line of cars leading to
the valet.

As their car edged forward, the silence grew louder until
Raine couldn't take it anymore. "You know this is ridiculous,
right? This is not us."

Dayo kept his eyes forward, saying nothing.

Raine crossed her arms. "So you're mad at me? Why?"

"I'm not mad, I just don't have anything to say."

She blew out a long breath.

He said, "You don't understand. I walked into my mother's
room and she was crying. She's sad, she's afraid, and it's as if you
don't care."

"I care, Dayo. It's because I care that she's still there and I
didn't kick her out of my home a long time ago."

For the first time he looked at her. His fingers squeezed the
steering wheel as he said, "Kick her out? Is that what you want
to do with my mother?"

Inside, she growled. "No, but . . ."

"And out of *your* home?"

"You know what I mean. I'm just tired of fighting about
this."

"There would be no fight if my mother wasn't being . . .
kicked out."

"Okay, maybe I used the wrong words, but you can't tell me
that you don't understand why I want to do this. You can't say
that you haven't seen how she treats me."

"I've seen it and I understand what you're saying. But you're not hearing me. The things my mother says and how she says it—none of it means anything. That's just how she is, how she was raised."

"And I'm supposed to sit in *our* home and take it. Just be miserable?"

"So now I make you miserable?"

She laughed only because she didn't want to scream. There would be no end to this fight—at least not for the next few hours. Dayo would sulk and twist every word she said. Did she really want this to play out in public? "You know what? Maybe you were right. Maybe we should forget the fund-raiser and just go home. I'll give the school our check tomorrow."

It was as if he'd been waiting for her to speak those words. Dayo nodded, then swerved the car to the left so fast the tires screeched. He drove past the line, past the museum, and stayed on Fifth Avenue, hitting every green light as he sped downtown toward their apartment. Now Raine was as upset as Dayo, her chest heaving in and out as she seethed.

Why wasn't Dayo hearing her?

Silence stayed with them from the museum to their home, from the car to their elevator. Both of their steps were heavy with anger as they marched to the penthouse door.

Dayo turned the key in the lock, and as they stepped inside, they both stopped, frozen.

"You're behaving like an animal."

"Grandmother!"

"Why did you lie to me? You were talking to that boy."

"I wasn't!"

"Don't you know that if you continue this way you will have no honor. You will be like a piece of spoiled meat. You will bring disgrace upon our family!"

Raine tried to push past Dayo, but he rushed into the living room ahead of her.

"What is going on?" he demanded to know.

Beerlulu's and Nadia's eyes shot up at the same time, both of them turning toward Raine and Dayo.

Nadia jumped up from the chair. "Daddy!" she yelled. Then she shuffled toward them, taking small steps.

It took a moment for the scene in front of her to register, and then Raine cried out, "What the hell is going on?" She took giant steps toward Nadia, knelt down, and in five seconds released her from the rope that was wrapped around her ankles.

Nadia's cries were bordering on hysteria, and when she was free, she ran into her father's arms.

*"Hooyo . . ."*

Beerlulu's eyes darted from Raine to Dayo. "She was on her phone, talking to a boy. Saying that she would see him later."

"I said that I would see him in school," Nadia sobbed. "It was Shaquanda's brother."

As if Nadia hadn't spoken, Beerlulu said, "And when I asked her about it, she lied."

"And so you tied her up?" Raine screamed.

"I wanted her to sit still so that she would listen to what I had to say. She never listens to me."

"You weren't talking to her. You were berating her!"

"I was trying to make her understand."

"You tied her up!"

"Not to hurt her," Beerlulu said. "Just to get her to listen and to understand and to see how wrong . . ."

"You're the one who's wrong, Beerlulu."

Beerlulu looked to Dayo as if her son would save her. "I was . . . I was just trying . . . Dayo, I did that to you when you were young." Turning to Raine, she said, "She wasn't hurt, I would never hurt her."

"*Hooyo*," Dayo began as he held on to Nadia, "you are never to speak to my child that way again."

She placed her hand over her heart. "I swear, I was only trying . . . surely you remember, you understand how we raise our girls."

Dayo shook his head.

"*Mwana*," she said, calling him "Son" in her language. "Please. You know. You remember. You understand."

His voice was low when he said, "I will never understand." His tone was sad when he added, "Not this. Not this way. Not here."

He gave his mother no more chances to explain. He turned away with Nadia in his arms and took his sobbing child from the room.

Raine waited until she and Beerlulu were alone. There was so much she wanted to say, but Dayo had said it all—almost.

She said, "I'm calling the Realtor in the morning and we will be going to look for apartments sometime this week. You can come or you can stay home, but get this straight." Raine took a step closer. "You *will* be moving out."

Then she turned and marched away, leaving Beerlulu standing in the middle of the living room alone and now trembling with her own sorrow.

# CHAPTER 9

*≈*

## *Sierra*

Sierra had tried it all—phone calls, emails, texts, Facebook messages, and about a thousand DM tweets. That's what she'd done all day yesterday. Instead of going to church, instead of calling Denise to go to brunch, Sierra had stayed inside and used every techie tactic to reach Andre.

Nothing worked.

So this was her last shot—literally!

Slipping into her purple pumps, Sierra took in her reflection in the full-length mirror, fluffed out her hair, shifted her weight from one side to the other to figure out the best pose. Then she wondered again if she needed any makeup. It didn't take more than an instant for her to decide that today she would be au naturel—completely.

She sucked in her stomach, making her twenty-four-inch waist even smaller, then grabbed her cell phone from the nightstand. She held the phone up, carefully framed her image, glanced in the mirror. *Click!*

"This is good," she whispered as she studied the picture she'd taken. If she had been into that kind of thing, she would've been ready for her *Playboy* closeup. But her exhibitionism was reserved for her man.

She typed the message: *Come home,* then paused and wondered if Andre would get the double entendre. She laughed. This was a naked photo—of course he would.

She pressed Send before she kicked off her shoes and slipped into her bathrobe. After a minute or two, Andre would be on the other end of her phone line. He might have been able to ignore all of the calls she'd made and all of the messages she'd left in the past few days, but he'd never be able to resist a naked picture of her. He'd be at her door for a nooner.

That meant she had to stay home.

Ugh! She hadn't thought about that. She didn't have any sick days left at the bookstore, but there was no way she could go to work. Picking up her cell again, she punched in the number, and as it rang, she scrolled through the excuses she'd already used.

"Hey, Earl," she said to the salesperson who answered. "Is Marva there?"

"Nah, not yet," he said.

Sierra breathed, relieved. At least she wasn't going to have to lie to the owner of the Hue-Man Bookstore. Marva Allen had given her a job when she'd first come to the city six years ago. Because of Marva, she never needed a nine-to-five and could pursue her modeling/acting/singing career. Even though she'd been a flake more times than she hadn't, Marva still believed in her, always trying to convince her to use her brains instead of her beauty.

"Uh . . . listen," Sierra began, thinking about what she was about to say, "can you tell Marva I won't be in?"

"Okay." He chuckled, as if he knew some kind of story was coming. "What do you want me to tell her *this* time?"

"Tell her," Sierra began with an attitude, "that . . ." She paused. She would need more time than just today. Probably two or three days to get Andre to really forgive her for knocking him upside his head. "Tell her that my grandfather died."

"Again?" he asked, sounding as if he was about to bust out laughing.

"Look, Earl . . ."

"Hey, don't get mad at me. I'm just trying to help you out. You've used that before."

"I had more than one grandfather," she snapped.

"Yeah, you had about five or six, but all right. I'll tell her." He hung up as if he knew that if he stayed on for one more second she would curse him out. Sierra almost wanted to go down to the store and tell him what she thought of him in person. He was always in her business. As if the store belonged to him or something.

But then she asked herself, why was she wasting a single brain cell on Earl when this day was all about Andre?

Checking her phone, she frowned. At least five minutes had passed since she'd sent the picture; she should've heard back from him by now. A text, or something to say that he couldn't wait to see her. When ten more minutes passed, Sierra began to pace.

Phone calls, texts, tweets—why wasn't he responding? What had happened between them the other day was the first time they'd had any kind of serious conflict. The entire five months they'd been together, she'd been able to keep all of her anger inside. So why was he so mad at this one time? Surely Andre understood forgiveness and second chances.

*Maybe I need to apologize.*

She clicked back to the photo and typed a new message: *Really sorry. Let me make it up 2 U.*

*That's gonna do it,* she thought as she lay back on her bed to wait. As she flipped through the TV channels, Sierra planned Andre's homecoming. First, she would tell him how much she loved him and that there was nothing better than their fist-clenching, toe-curling, body-quivering sex that made her brain freeze. He needed to know that he was her soul mate, her sex mate, her love mate.

She'd played it wrong and would never do that again.

Picking up her cell phone again, she checked—still no message.

That was okay. He was going to call, text, or something. She knew for sure that she and Andre were not finished.

And the thought of that made her smile.

# CHAPTER 10

## *Liza*

*Liza* slowly rolled past the black Escalade, eyed the tinted windows, then turned her car into the driveway. What was Buddy doing at their home on a Monday?

The one thing about her husband was that he was consistent. Part of that consistency was that he was home every Monday to rejuvenate after the two services he preached on Sunday and prepare himself for the week ahead. Not even his armor bearer disturbed this time.

Liza sighed as she grabbed her messenger bag. Whatever was going on, she prayed that it wasn't going to keep Buddy at their home too late. While Mann had the privilege of staying home on Mondays, weekends were her only days off.

Mondays were her busiest days at church. Between all the youth she had to register for the Save Our Sons or Deliver Our Daughters ministry after the second and fourth Sundays and her position as a contributing editor for *Life as a First Lady* magazine, where she wrote the featured article every week, Mondays were just exhausting.

Today was no different. It had been a day that had begun before the morning rush hour started, and now, almost twelve hours later, she was just getting home, tired but with all of her work complete. She and her assistant, Portia, had worked non-stop, even through lunch, so that she could be home by six and share the evening with her husband. After all the thoughts that had been on her mind about websites and other women, she wanted an intimate night to sweep away any residual doubts.

So whatever brought Buddy to their home had better be close to over. She had big plans for her husband and she wasn't going to be denied.

The moment she stepped inside the house, Liza heard the voices—low and serious. They were in the living room, which was surprising. Whenever Mann and Buddy met in their home, Mann preferred to talk in the office, with the computer, copy machine, and fax within arm's reach.

As she moved closer, the words became clearer.

"We need to settle again. This is not the time to fight."

She frowned as she made her way toward the voices. That wasn't Buddy speaking and it certainly wasn't Mann.

"I agree." This time it was Buddy. "People are tired of pastors getting caught up, and a scandal like this could break us. Trust me, let's settle. We don't need this."

The urgency in Buddy's voice frightened her and she quickened her steps. At the arch entrance of the living room, she paused. The men were sitting together—Mann and Buddy on the sofa, two other men sitting in the chairs across from them. They were all leaning forward, their heads bowed, their eyes intense, so focused that no one noticed her.

"We don't need what?" Liza said. The question was meant for all of them, but her eyes were on Mann. "What scandal? What's going on?" The questions toppled out, one over the other.

The men sat stiff and startled for a moment. Their mouths

were halfway open, but they were silent, as if their words were stuck inside.

"Sweetheart," Mann said as he sprang off the sofa and over to her in a single bound. "What're you doing home?"

"I live here," she kidded, though the lines in her face showed no humor. She looked past her husband to Buddy, and then to the other men. She'd met them before—one black, the other white—though she couldn't recall their names. But she remembered their reputations—they were a team, celebrity attorneys who handled some of the biggest legal scandals in the country. Their most notorious case was the football player who murdered his wife. They'd lost that case—the football player went to prison for life—but they'd garnered so much publicity that after that they were hired by the biggest stars in Hollywood and New York.

So what were they doing sitting in her living room?

But all she said was, "Gentlemen," and then waited for someone to give her an explanation.

"Liza, you remember Tom Brody and Stan Weitzman. They were at our last men's forum."

"I remember." She nodded as all the men shot up and stood straight, as if they suddenly remembered their manners. Then she said hello to Buddy before she turned back to her husband. "What's going on?" She repeated the question with a bit more intensity.

He shook his head. "Ah, it's nothing; just some church business."

She waited for him to say more, and when he didn't she said, "It sounds like more than that." Then she turned to Buddy. "You said something about a scandal?"

Buddy lowered his eyes and didn't part his lips. The other

men did the same. Mann spoke, as if he was the only one who had permission. "Look, sweetheart, we're just about finished. Let me handle this and then I'll explain it all to you."

Her glance roamed from man to man, all still standing, all still silent. She waited for one of them to step up and tell her what she wanted to know, but when no one moved, she said, "Okay." Her eyes continued to dart back and forth, though. "I have the girls' applications from yesterday's service right here." She tapped the bag that was strapped to her shoulder. "I'll put them on your desk."

As Mann nodded, the others shifted, exchanged glances.

Her frown deepened until Mann said, "Great, sweetheart," and he kissed her cheek. "Give me a few minutes. I'll be right up."

She said good-bye to the men, then paused, waiting again for one of them to give her something.

But when there was nothing else, she turned and slowly ascended the stairs. At the top, she paused, listening. Their murmurs were so low now, she heard nothing.

All kinds of thoughts rushed her, but as she walked into their office and pulled the Deliver Our Daughters folders from her bag, there was one word that stood out.

*Scandal!*

That's what Buddy had said. What kind of scandal? What did it have to do with their church? With Mann?

She slipped the files onto the desk, right next to the computer monitor. Now new thoughts took over—of the last time she'd sat in this chair, in front of this computer.

Did the scandal that Mann and those men were speaking about have anything to do with the website she'd found?

She shook her head. This was ridiculous. She was connecting

dots that weren't even there. She needed to stop with the specu-
lation, but the only way she could do that was if she had some
answers.

She stomped across the office ready to go back downstairs.
Somebody was going to tell her something. Stepping into the
hallway, she bumped right into Mann.

"My beautiful bride," he said, wrapping his arms around her.

She stood with her arms at her side until he backed up. "Did
they leave?"

He nodded. "It's just you and me, babe." Then he gave her
that smile. That smile that was meant to distract and disarm.

But she wasn't going to let him do that to her. Not this time.
She crossed her arms. "What's going on?"

"I told you, nothing."

"A scandal is not nothing."

"I don't know what you think you heard, but there's no scandal."

Really? He was going for *that* Jedi mind trick? Really? "I
know what I heard, Mann. But let's just say my ears did lie to
me—did my eyes lie, too? Are you telling me that I didn't see
those two attorneys sitting in the middle of our living room?"

He held up his hands and walked away. "I can't believe you're
trippin' about this."

She marched right behind him into their bedroom. "I'm just
asking questions after walking in and finding my husband in ca-
hoots with two high-powered attorneys talking about scandals.
Help me make sense of that."

He sighed as if Liza held the world and was pushing it down
on his shoulders. "All right." He faced her. "I didn't want to say
anything because I made a promise, but you won't let it go."

He paused as if his words were supposed to change her mind.

She stood there with her arms crossed and the toe of her boot tapping silently against the carpet.

Mann dropped onto the bed. "It's Buddy."

"Buddy?" Her tapping stopped and the lines were back on her forehead again.

"Buddy may be in some trouble," he said. "But I don't want you to worry 'cause we know it's not true. He didn't do anything."

"What was he supposed to have done?"

Again, he gave her a weighted sigh. "We all promised not to say a word, especially since it's not true and within a day or two this will all go away."

Slowly, she sat down next to him. "Buddy." His name settled in her mind. "So," she continued as if Mann hadn't spoken, "is some woman claiming to be pregnant?"

His eyes opened wide. "Sweetheart, I don't want to talk about it! It's going to be handled."

But his expression had given him away, had told her that some part of what she said was close to the truth. "I'm right; I just know it. He's gotten someone pregnant." She took a breath. "Is the woman married?"

"What? No! Sweetheart, it's nothing like that," he said. "I promise everything is gonna be fine." He gently pressed his lips against hers. "Let's not waste any more time talking about this. There're so many other things we can be doing." Wrapping his arm around her waist, as he tickled her ear with his lips, he said, "Like talking about you and me. And me telling you that I'm so happy you're home early."

"It's not that early," Liza said with one side of her mind while the other side was still on Buddy. "I wanted to be home in time for dinner so that I could cook . . ."

"No, no cooking for you. Not after the day I'm sure you've had. Let's go out."

She shook her head. "I'm too tired."

"Then we'll order in." He stood up. "Chinese?"

"Yeah, yeah, that's fine," she said without looking up.

"Okay, I'll call it in. There's a menu in the office." He paused at the door. "The applications for the girls . . ."

She waved her hand. "On your desk."

"Are the photos attached to the applications?"

"Most of them," she said, her thoughts still on Buddy.

"Great. I'll be right back, my beautiful bride." He winked before he strutted out of the room as if nothing had happened.

She was pissed, felt dismissed. As if his wink and his smile were a magic wand that would make what she'd seen and heard go away. Did he think that she was that naive? That same girl from Mississippi? Did he really think that his wink and his smile could control her as he was able to do all those years ago. . . .

Liza had no idea how her mother and father had wangled that big-city preacher into accepting an invitation to *their* house for dinner, but it didn't matter.

The moment her father stopped the car in the driveway, Liza jumped out, dashed through the front door, and charged to her bedroom. Her hope was that he would sing again, because when he did that, she could hardly move. Oooh-weee! She couldn't wait.

"Liza Mae?" By the time her mother ambled into the house shouting her name, Liza had all six dresses that she owned tossed across her bed. "I don't know what you're doing in there," her mother shouted, "but make sure you don't do anything to mess up your dress. I want you to look fresh for dinner."

"Don't worry, Mama," she called out. "I'm gonna change

right now." She paced back and forth, eyeing her dresses. Nothing she had was worthy of such special company, but anything was better than what she had on.

"What do you mean you're gonna change?" Now Millicent was right outside her bedroom. "I bought that dress just for you."

"But, Mama, it makes me look like a baby."

"What you talking 'bout, girl?" Millicent stomped into her room.

"That's why they call these sleeves baby-doll sleeves, Mama." She tugged at the material that bit into her skin. "I look like a baby."

Millicent sucked her teeth. "You don't look like no baby. Don't you think I know how to dress my own daughter?"

If Liza had answered that question, she would've told her mother no. And then she would've had to face the big-city preacher wearing this ugly dress *and* a big-ole busted lip because Millicent didn't take any kind of back talk from Liza or any of the other kids in Corinth.

So Liza just let her mother go on.

"You're gonna wear that dress 'cause it's cute. Humph. Trying to tell me that I *don't* know what I'm talking about." She marched out of the room. "I *know* what I'm talking about."

Millicent was still huffing as she made her way into the kitchen and Liza slowly hung each dress back in her closet.

For the rest of the afternoon, her lips were poked out. Every time Liza passed a mirror or saw her reflection in one of the shining pots as she helped her mother with dinner, she felt like she was in the middle of some cabbage patch with all the flowers on her dress. She looked like a silly ten-year-old instead of a sophisticated fifteen-year-old.

Then Reverend Washington walked in. He had changed suits—this time he wore a gray one with matching gray patent-leather shoes that glowed as if they had been spit-shined.

After he escorted his grandmother into their home, Reverend Washington greeted her father with one of those half handshake, half pat-on-the-back hellos, and then he hugged her mother.

*Then* he turned all of his attention to Liza. He lifted her hand and kissed the tips of her fingers. "Liza Mae, you sure are a pretty little thing in that dress."

Millicent beamed and Liza blushed. Inside, Liza felt warm and fuzzylike. Maybe her mother did know what she was talking about.

Milton and Millicent prided themselves on how they'd raised up Liza Mae, so their only child was allowed to sit in the front room with the grown folks as Reverend Washington entertained them with stories of the big city.

"One day I hope to get to New York," Milton said. "When I was a little boy, my grandfather told me New York streets were paved with gold, and ever since then, I've been dreaming about walking down those streets."

They all laughed—except for Liza. She was in the corner, seen but not heard, sitting in one of the ladder-back chairs that had been dragged in from the dining room. Leaning forward with her elbows resting on her legs and her chin cupped inside her hands, she absorbed every word the reverend said.

"Paved with gold?" Reverend Washington was still laughing. "I'm afraid that's a gross exaggeration. The only gold-paved ones that I know of are the streets that are awaiting those of us who call Him the Christ."

Just listening to him made Liza sigh. He wasn't singing as she had hoped, but his talking sounded like music. Even the words he chose were like notes in a perfect song—*gross exaggeration* and *those of us who call Him the Christ*.

But like any good song, his music came in two parts. His voice was the melody, and everything else about him was the harmony: his suit and matching shoes, his wavy hair, his hands that moved to the beat of his words.

Yup, he was music. He was a choir all by himself.

When Reverend Jackson finally showed up, they moved into the dining room, where her mother had laid out a Sunday soul food spread.

"Miss Devine, everything here sure looks good," Reverend Washington said. They all knew he was talking about the food, even though he was looking at Liza. "I haven't eaten like this since the last time I visited my grandmama."

Miss Bessie slapped his arm. "And how many years ago was that?"

He kissed his grandmother's cheek, apologized for not coming to see her more often, and added, "But I have a feeling I'll be here a lot more from now on." Again, his eyes were on Liza.

Milton sat at one end of the table and Reverend Washington sat at the other, but not before he pulled out the chair for Liza to sit right next to him.

After they blessed the food, the feast began. Around the table, the serving tray with the fried catfish went in one direction while the fried chicken went in the other. Then they grabbed the macaroni and cheese, brown rice and gravy, candied yams, string-bean casserole, corn on the cob. No one stopped until the plates were piled high.

While the adults talked and laughed, Liza stayed quiet, eyeing the reverend every time she had the chance—which was often because he talked to her more than he did the others.

"Liza Mae is such a pretty name," he said. "Where did you get it?"

"From my mama and my daddy," she said.

He laughed at her innocence and then asked Millicent the same question.

"Well, to be honest, her name was supposed to be Lisa Mae after that painting—I love the *Mona Lisa*—but one of the nurses made a mistake on her birth certificate," Millicent explained. "Changed the *s* to a *z*."

"We didn't notice it for a week," Milton continued. "But we took it as a sign from God."

"And she's been Liza Mae ever since," Millicent finished.

Then the reverend asked Liza about school, and her friends. "I bet you have a boyfriend," he whispered as the adults talked at the other end of the table.

She shook her head.

"No!" He leaned back as if he was surprised. "A pretty little thing like you?"

She shrugged. "I don't have a boyfriend or any girlfriends. The girls say that I think I'm cute and the boys are just silly."

"Do you know what the girls really mean when they say you think you're cute?"

She shook her head and then watched his juicy lips move.

He said, "They really mean that *they* think you're cute."

She giggled. "Really?"

"Trust me. I know these things. And you know what?"

She shook her head again.

"Those girls are right."

There it was again, that warm, warm feeling inside.

"So you don't have any friends at all?" he asked.

She shrugged. "I used to hang out with my cousin all the time, but he moved and I don't see him as much anymore."

"Your cousin?" He paused. "Your kissing cousin?" He laughed.

He gave her that crooked smile again, but though she loved the way he did that, this time she frowned. *Kissing cousins?* She loved her cousin, but nobody would ever find her kissing him. She lowered her eyes and stuffed her mouth with a fork filled with black-eyed peas.

When Milton stood up and said, "Reverend Washington, Reverend Jackson, please join me in the living room while we let the women clean up," Liza wanted to tell her father to just take Reverend Jackson and leave the cute reverend with her. No one had ever said the things that he said and no one had ever looked at her the way he did.

The only sad part about Sunday was when it was time for their company to leave. That night, Liza went to bed with visions in her head and a song in her ears. Her dreams were all about the big-city preacher.

When she woke up, her dreams continued. Because the next morning, right as she was running out the front door to catch the school bus, there he was. She swung open the door and he was standing there with his fist in the air as if he was ready to knock.

"Good morning, beautiful angel," Reverend Washington said.

She squeezed her eyes shut, then slowly opened them again just to make sure that her dreams hadn't followed her to the front door.

"Is your father home?" he asked after a while when Liza had said nothing.

She nodded and stepped back so that he could come inside.

Behind her, Milton greeted the reverend. "So good to see you again," he said as they shook hands.

Liza stood at the door until Milton said, "Liza, you better get moving so you can catch your bus."

"Okay, Daddy" were the first words she'd said since she'd opened the door. She glanced at the reverend; he smiled that crooked smile. Then he winked. She was in heaven. . . .

That wink and that smile had made her fifteen-year-old heart skip a million beats. And he'd been doing that to her ever since. There was no doubt that she loved him, but she also loved who they were and what they'd built together.

That's why Mann's explanation wasn't good enough. There was more to it and she knew just the person who would tell her what she needed to know.

And she would get to him tomorrow.

# CHAPTER 11

## *Sierra*

Just as Sierra was about to say "I do," her eyes popped open!

*Girl, don't you know . . . You're so beautiful . . . I wanna give all my love to you, girl . . .*

It took a moment for the music to register—her cell phone! Frantically, she patted through the comforter on her bed as the song continued to play.

This had to be Andre. She had just been dreaming about him, about them, about their wedding.

Finally, she grabbed the phone from under the pillow and pressed Accept Call, turning off Musiq Soulchild.

"Andre!"

"No," the woman said slowly. "This is Yvonne."

Sierra plopped down on the bed. If she had checked the screen, she wouldn't have even picked up. "What's up, Yvonne?" she said, focusing her eyes on the clock. *Seven forty-three?*

"Just wanted to remind you of the meeting this morning." *Meeting?* "Uh . . ."

Yvonne sighed. "We're meeting this morning to go over some details for the tour."

"Yeah, yeah," she said.

"Be here at nine, Sierra," Yvonne said in a tone that sounded like she was talking to a child. "We're having it so early because you said you had to get to work, remember?"

"I'll be there, Yvonne," Sierra said, and then clicked off her phone. She tossed her cell across her bed. She would bet anything that Yvonne wasn't calling Raine or Liza, jerking their chain this way.

*Just a hater,* Sierra thought as she rolled over.

But once she sat up, her thoughts weren't on Yvonne or the other Divas. It was all about Andre and he had not called.

It was unbelievable, inconceivable. Every man she'd ever been with had come back—at least once. All she had to do was lie, cry, and beg, then make promises never to go off again. She'd done all of that in every message she'd left for Andre.

Swinging her legs over the side of the bed, Sierra scrolled through her phone, just to make sure she hadn't slept through a call or a text. There was nothing.

Something had to be wrong. Maybe he was on a big story. She clicked on her Facebook icon and shuffled through the postings on her page.

Nothing from Andre.

*He has to be on some big story if he's too busy to be on Facebook.*

But on his page, she saw that she was wrong. Fifteen minutes before, he'd updated his status: *Crazy leaves clues!!!*

Already seventeen people had responded with: *LOL, ROFL-MAO,* and *PREACH!*

And he had commented on his own status: *Yeah, I've been hanging around crazy for months. I'm just glad I got out with my life. LOL.*

*Is he talking about me?* Sierra wondered.

She closed Facebook, opened Twitter, and scrolled through

her timeline. But there was nothing from the man who just seconds before she'd opened her eyes had been about to place that ring on her finger.

She raised her cell above her head, wanting to sling it across the room, ready to see it crash against the wall and shatter into a thousand pieces. But in the next moment she changed her mind. With only two checks so far from the recording company, she didn't have money like that. If she broke this phone, she'd be without a one for the foreseeable future.

So, as gently as she could, she tossed her phone onto the nightstand, then lay back in bed. It wasn't until her head hit the pillow that she felt the first tear traveling down her cheek. Her cries were usually from anger, but this was worse than being mad—this hurt. Because Andre wasn't coming back.

And now she had to go to this stupid meeting with Yvonne and Raine and Liza? If she'd had any lies left, she would've called Yvonne back, but what reason did she have to miss this? It wasn't as if she was going to be in bed with her legs wrapped around the man she loved.

She dragged herself into the shower, then back to her bedroom. She only had enough energy to slip into the same clothes she'd worn Saturday night—same jeans, same sweater, same cap. With only ten minutes to the start of the meeting, she dashed down the five flights of stairs.

The air hadn't warmed, not one bit, since she'd last been out over the weekend, but the fact that spring was nowhere near was not on Sierra's mind.

She did have a few options with Andre. She could show up at his apartment since he worked from home. Or she could wait outside his building for him where he wouldn't make a scene in front of his neighbors.

That's what she would do—right after this meeting—head straight to his apartment.

Outside of Yvonne's seventh-floor office, she paused, wishing now that she'd taken a little more care in how she looked. Her appearance was another thing that Yvonne always jumped on, something Sierra couldn't figure out. As cute as Raine was, as sophisticated as Liza was, neither one of them came close to her shine. But that never stopped Yvonne from lecturing her.

"You never know who's going to see you or which tabloid is going to be out snapping pictures. You have to be ready."

Sierra had never told any of them that her boyfriend worked for the biggest tabloid out there—not that they even knew she had a boyfriend. But Sierra was sure that if anyone ever submitted an unflattering picture of her, Andre would make that picture disappear. It didn't matter that they were no longer together. He'd loved her enough not to let anyone hurt her—even if it was just a photograph that didn't show her in the best light.

Sierra pushed the door open, said "Hello" to Yvonne's assistant, and then strutted into the office like she meant to look this way. "Hey," she said, putting a little extra singsong into her voice as she sauntered to the conference table where Yvonne, Raine, and Liza sat.

"Good morning." Yvonne's eyes roamed over Sierra and then she glanced at her watch.

Sierra slipped into the chair next to Raine, across from Liza and Yvonne. She glanced at Raine, who kind of growled a hello, and Liza simply waved her hand.

*Uh-oh, something must've happened.* She couldn't remember a time when Raine wasn't smiling or when Liza's greeting didn't come with a hug. But today her fellow divas sat slumped in their chairs and Sierra braced for the bad news.

"Now that you're here"—Yvonne paused as she looked at Sierra, and Sierra did her best not to roll her eyes—"let's get started."Yvonne stopped as her eyes lingered on Raine and then she turned to Liza.

Sierra's glance followed Yvonne's; she twisted to get a good look at her singing sisters. It didn't take but a second to figure out what had made Yvonne pause. Truly, it was a bit shocking because Raine always looked like a rock star and Liza never stepped out without looking like a proper first lady.

But today her partners were dressed almost as she was. Raine had on a sweat suit, as if she'd just come from running, and Liza had on jeans, which was a huge surprise since Sierra never imagined that Liza even owned a pair.

"Anyway,"Yvonne continued, "I want to go over the schedule and then talk about your testimonies,"Yvonne said, looking from one to the other. "This is going to be much different than the radio tour. Onstage, you'll be talking about ten minutes each."

"Ten minutes?" Liza said. "That's actually a long time."

"That's why I want to make sure that all of us are on the same page. But before we even get started with that . . ." She stopped again and placed her palms flat on the conference table. . . . "I need to talk to you guys."

The three singers' eyes stayed on her.

"We've talked about this before, but I have to sign some papers with Kevin, the tour promoter, so I just want to be sure." Yvonne glanced around the table, then stopped when she looked at Sierra.

"What?" Sierra asked.

"This is for all of you," Yvonne said, even though her eyes stayed on Sierra. "Is there anything that I need to know as your manager?"

"Anything like what?" Sierra asked.

"Anything like anything that could later be a problem. Anything like someone later on being able to say that you're not practicing what you preach. Anything that could have the promoter suing us if something were to come out."

She looked at Sierra for an extra moment, but Sierra stared right back at her, even though beneath the conference table her legs trembled. Inside, she released a sigh of relief when Yvonne turned to Liza and Raine. "You know I'm a publicist by trade. You know I can spin anything, but I have to know what I'm dealing with."

There was a moment of silence before Raine said, "I've lived my entire adult life in the spotlight and everyone knows everything about me."

Yvonne nodded and looked at Liza. "It's just a formality for you, too, First Lady, but I have to ask."

Liza twisted from one side of her seat to the other. "I don't have anything," she said, though she lowered her eyes as she spoke.

Yvonne let a few beats go by before she turned back to Sierra. "Everyone's really looking at you because you're talking about celibacy."

*Oh my God! She's talking about Andre.* But with a confidence she really didn't have, Sierra said, "And?"

"And there are some people who don't believe that anyone over eighteen can be celibate. You know this. You know how many people called into the radio stations challenging you."

"I'll say it again . . . and?" Sierra pushed herself up in the chair. "People can challenge me all they want, but no one can challenge the truth."

"Okay," Yvonne said, looking at each of the women. "Well, there you have it." Her smile told them that the subject was closed. "Let's get down to business." She handed a folder to Liza, then scooted two folders across the table to Sierra and Raine.

Sierra glanced at the contents: the itinerary for the tour with their days off highlighted. It was the days off that she'd been looking forward to, but now there was no need to think about Andre sneaking into whatever city they were in.

"The calendar is pretty straightforward. The first show is April first, the same day the CD drops." She paused and turned to Liza. "I got your email about Mann's birthday."

Liza said nothing.

"It's not an off day, but I may be able to get the promoter to fly him in." Yvonne paused, as if she was waiting for some words of gratitude.

But Liza didn't utter one syllable.

Yvonne frowned. "O-kay. Let's move on to your testimonies because they're going to be as important as the songs."

Sierra asked, "So we won't just be saying what we've been talking about on the radio?"

"It'll be the same subjects, but you'll have more time to give your testimonies. Plus, the way it will be set up on the stage, one of you will be speaking while the other two will sit back. So the focus will be on whoever is speaking, and I just want to make sure that there'll be substance in your teachings. Like, for you, Sierra—you're going to be talking about how love waits. I really want you to delve into what life is like being in your twenties and having made the decision to wait for your husband."

Sierra crossed then uncrossed her legs.

Yvonne continued, "I want you to give scriptures to support how and why you're living your life this way." She paused. "Share your favorite scriptures. The ones you stand on every day."

Sierra had to lick her lips, then swallow, before she said, "I have a lot . . . of scriptures . . . that I like, but I just talk about being celibate because that's what we're supposed to do as Christians."

"And what you've been saying has been great, but I want more," Yvonne said to Sierra, then motioned to Raine and Liza, too. "All of you are going to have to talk about *how* you do it. Sierra, you have to reach these young women where they're at, talk to them about how you fight the same temptations they face."

Sierra nodded with confidence even though she didn't know one single scripture. But wasn't that what Google was for? "Christians" and "celibacy"—once she typed that into her smart phone, she'd come back with a testimony that would be fit for any preacher's pulpit.

"And Raine," Yvonne said, turning to the star, "you always include scripture, but now I want you to talk beyond your testimony of becoming a Christian. You're going to talk about love that's unconditional. Put the focus on your family and the love that you get from your husband, your daughter, and your mother-in-law." Again, Yvonne paused, waiting for affirmation from Raine. "Especially talk about your mother-in-law because people need to understand that unconditional love extends beyond your immediate family." Again, Yvonne was met with silence.

Yvonne's shoulders slumped, as if this meeting was making her weary. She turned to Liza. "First Lady, yours is pretty simple—love everlasting. Just continue to talk about the fact that when you wait on the right man, God will bless you with a long union. I know you haven't talked about it before, but I think it would be great if you discussed how you got married at a young age. You were married at, what . . . nineteen, right?"

A beat, and then Liza nodded.

"You can tell them that God has been in the mix of your marriage from the beginning."

"Okay."

"And you already give a lot of scripture; you're the pro." Yvonne laughed as if she hoped that would lighten the heavy mood. But when no one shared her glee, she released a long, frustrated sigh. "Ladies! Can someone tell me what's going on? Why are you all so distant today?"

No one said a word.

Yvonne said, "Look, y'all know that I'm here to help, right?"

Only nods, no words.

"Well, then"—Yvonne shrugged—"we're going to have a few run-throughs—not only the songs, but the testimonies as well. We're going to do our first miniconcert in two weeks." She paused as if she had an announcement that would put a smile on all of their faces. "At City of Lights!"

"Huh?" the three said together.

Yvonne frowned and repeated what she said. "It was Lady Jasmine's idea. I just mentioned that we would be doing one or two full run-throughs before we hit the road and she suggested a concert at church."

"A Sunday concert?" Raine asked.

"No. This'll be a Friday night. A full-fledged concert, where they will charge admission and everything. Maybe even a private reception for special guests. Pastor Bush expects to sell out the moment it's announced."

"Are we getting any of that money?" Sierra asked.

"Yes. It won't be much because they can only have eight thousand people in the sanctuary. But you'll each get a little something; I'm still working that out." She waited, but the smiles that she expected didn't come. "O-kay," she said slowly. "So the last thing I have are the sketches of the gowns that you'll be wearing." She slid the drawings across the table to each of them. "Three different

styles that I think fit your personalities. But same color—purple—
same material that I got from your contact, Raine."

Yvonne's eyes traveled along the table, from Sierra to Raine.
It wasn't until she settled on Liza that the first lady said, "These
look nice."

Yvonne held her hands in the air as if she was surrendering.
"That's all I got. I'll call you, guys. I'd like to get together at the
end of this week to review your testimonies, so if you can work
on those that would be great."

"Okay," the three sang together.

Yvonne was almost shivering with frustration, and for the
first time ever, Sierra felt sorry for their manager. Clearly, there
was something going on with Raine and Liza, but there was
nothing she could do to help; she had her own problems.

Sierra jumped out of the chair. "Well, if we're done, I'm out,"
she said. When Yvonne squinted her eyes, Sierra said, "Work,
remember?"

Yvonne nodded, but before Sierra could hit the door, Raine
said, "Wait, I'll take the elevator down with you."

"Me too," Liza added.

*Okay, this really is different,* Sierra thought. Usually Raine and
Liza hung around afterward with Yvonne, just chitchatting about
whatever—Sierra never knew because she never stayed. But
today the three barged out of the door as if they were racing to
see who could escape first.

Inside the elevator, Sierra scrolled through her phone, part
searching for a message from Andre, part not wanting to look at
Raine or Liza. She didn't want to say a word—she couldn't risk
them turning the tables and asking what was going on with her.

So the three rode in silence, stepped off the elevator in silence, and walked out of the building in silence, pausing only

long enough to wave good-bye, and then they split, fanning out in three different directions.

Sierra's steps were quick as she tried to stay ahead of the wind. She surged past other pedestrians all eager to find shelter from the biting cold. But this weather wasn't going to stop her, she was on her way to Andre. She was going to let him know that her heart was breaking. She was going to tell him that he just had to come back!

As she stood at the corner, waiting to cross the street, a sleek, shiny Town Car eased to the curb in front of her. The back door opened before one man slipped out, followed by another. Their heads were down; they were deep in conversation.

But Sierra caught a good glimpse of one of them.

Jarrod Cannon.

She wanted to stop him, say hello, remind him that they had met. But right before she called out his name, she paused. She was wearing the same outfit she had the other night. He would see her, remember her, then wonder what her story was.

So she just watched him strut into the building with a swagger that reminded her of President Obama and she felt her smile slowly coming back. She needed to call that man and she would, since she had his personal number.

Then Sierra remembered.

She'd thrown away his card, betting on Andre instead! What a fool move that had been! But how hard would it be to find the number for Congressman Jarrod Cannon?

Sierra pivoted and headed in the direction of her apartment. Forget Andre. She had something better to do. She needed to get home and make a call.

Suddenly, her heart felt so much better.

# CHAPTER 12

# Raine

Raine busted through the apartment door.

"Dayo!" she shouted as she tossed her keys onto the console by the door. Dashing through the apartment, she called out again, "Dayo!" She checked every room until she was sure that neither her husband nor his mother was there.

"Damn!"

She knew she shouldn't have gone to the meeting with Yvonne. She had a feeling that once she left home this morning, Dayo and Beerlulu would flee, finding some excuse for why they couldn't look at apartments.

Well, Mary had called, told her that she had seven listings for them to see, and that she would meet them at twelve thirty. It was only noon. Dayo and his mother still had plenty of time to get home, but whether they came back or not, Raine was going to find an apartment today.

Shrugging off her coat, she dialed Dayo's cell again. Just like the last ten times she'd called on her way home, her call went straight to voice mail. She tossed her cell onto the sofa and paced.

After the horror of what she and Dayo had witnessed Sunday

night, even Dayo agreed that Beerlulu had to go. Raine just hoped that time hadn't changed his mind.

But how could it after the way Nadia had cried in his arms?

"I told Mom she hated me," Nadia had sobbed when Raine had followed her and Dayo into their daughter's bedroom.

"Your grandmother doesn't hate you," Dayo had tried to assure her. But even as he comforted Nadia, Raine saw Dayo's own pain. He'd been hurt by what he'd just walked in on as much as Nadia.

Raine had stayed with Nadia for the rest of the night, while Dayo had gone into Beerlulu's bedroom to talk to her. And then, yesterday, Raine had kept her traumatized daughter home from school, while Dayo and his mother left the penthouse before most New Yorkers had even risen.

When Dayo returned last night without Beerlulu, Raine hoped that he had dropped his mother off at the airport. But after dinner Dayo had explained.

"My mother is going to spend the night with her sister," he'd said, as if Raine would care. "That's best for tonight."

Raine nodded, only because she was being polite.

He said, "My mother cried all day."

Raine had crossed her arms and done her best to keep her "so what" inside.

"She is very sorry," he added. "And she wants to apologize to Nadia."

She pressed her lips together and willed her brain to keep her silent. There was no need to go off. She'd won this war.

But Dayo continued, as if he felt a great need to explain. "You have to understand, it's very different for the women in my country."

Raine had really tried, but she couldn't keep her words

inside. "I don't care how different things are for your mother. She should have known never to have done that to Nadia."

"I agree; I just want you to understand that what my mother did really came from a place of love."

She had twisted her lips. He could try to pass that explanation off to his daughter, but it wasn't going to work with his wife.

"No matter where you come from, Dayo, that's not love. And if that's what your mother calls it, not only is she moving, but Nadia will never again be alone with her."

Dayo had looked at his wife as if he was trying to find more words, but there were none. He bowed his head in defeat. "Did you call Mary today?"

"She'll be here tomorrow. At twelve thirty."

Now Raine glanced at the clock once again. Dayo and Beerlulu had ten minutes. But Raine wasn't going to trip; she had her plan—she was going to keep it moving.

Just as she had that thought, Dayo entered through the front door with Beerlulu just a couple of steps behind. Beerlulu stood close to her son, as if she thought she might need protection from his wife.

"Did we miss Mary?" Dayo asked.

Raine glanced at her watch. "No, she's probably downstairs right now." She didn't miss the exchange between Dayo and his mother.

He sighed before he said, "Good." His voice was low when he added, "We can all ride down together."

Raine grabbed her coat, then marched through the door. Inside the elevator, Beerlulu uttered the first words that Raine had heard from her since Sunday.

"Before we meet the Realtor," Beerlulu began, facing her

son, "I want you to know that I will be making the decision about the apartment since this is where I will be living . . . by myself." She held her head high. "It will be my choice."

"That's fine, *Hooyo*," Dayo said.

It was fine with Raine, too.

An hour of looking at apartments passed. By the time the second hour had gone by, Raine recognized that Beerlulu wasn't about to make a decision.

As Raine had instructed, Mary had led them from apartment to apartment in some of the city's best neighborhoods. First, there was the unit in the new condos on Ninth Street in the Village.

Beerlulu had turned up her nose. "Too urban."

Raine had no idea what that meant, but she said nothing as Mary took them to the next place—an apartment on Fourteenth at First in Stuyvesant Town.

"Too small," Beerlulu said before she'd even stepped both feet inside.

The classy high-rise near Lincoln Center had "Too many windows," and the brownstone on the Upper West Side had "Too much space."

Beerlulu's game was clear—if she was never satisfied, she would never have to move.

After the seventh showing, Mary said, "That's all I have for today," as they stood in front of another brownstone that had "a bizarre smell," though Beerlulu's nostrils were the only ones sensitive enough to pick up the scent. "I guess I'll have to find a few other places."

"That's what you're going to have to do, young lady," Beerlulu said before she marched in front of all of them toward the car.

Dayo shrugged and Raine lagged behind her husband as she walked next to Mary.

"Wow, your mother-in-law is hard to please," said Mary.

"Yeah." Raine's eyes followed Beerlulu as she scurried to the car, eager to get out of the cold.

Mary lowered her head. "You know there is that apartment . . ."

"No!" Raine hissed in a whisper. "I told you, we're not doing that. We'll keep looking," she said, sure that soon Dayo would pick up on his mother's game.

"Okay," Mary said as the two stepped to the car. "I thought this was urgent."

"It is," she said. *But not urgent enough for that,* Raine thought.

Raine sat in the passenger seat, while Dayo joined his mother in the back. Beerlulu and Dayo chatted as the car rolled downtown, but Raine stayed silent, thoughtful, wondering if she should say something to Dayo about his mother now or just wait it out until the next trip.

As Mary eased her SUV around the circular driveway to the East Side Towers, she said, "I'll get back to you in a couple of days." Looking in her rearview mirror at Beerlulu, she added, "I promise I'll find something that you'll like."

"Thank you," Beerlulu said. "Remember, it can't be too small, but I don't want it to be so big. And I want it in a quiet neighborhood, but I want to feel like I'm still in the city. And . . . not too many children."

Raine cringed, waiting for Beerlulu to add something about how she hated American children, but all she said was, "But, I don't want to feel like I'm in a senior citizen's home, either."

Raine and Mary sighed together.

Mary said, "I'll do my best," before she edged the SUV to a stop. While Dayo helped his mother from the car, Mary jumped from the driver's seat and hurried around to the other side. "Are you sure?" she whispered to Raine.

"Yes," she responded, barely moving her lips. "Don't even think about that apartment. Just keep looking and we can go back out in a couple of days. She'll settle on something; she'll have to."

"Okay, I'll give you a call," Mary said to the three.

Beerlulu bowed her head as if she was grateful. "I hope I'm not being too difficult, but I'm really looking for an apartment where I can be most comfortable—"

"Excuse me," the doorman interrupted. "I didn't mean to eavesdrop, but you said you're looking for an apartment?"

Raine's eyes widened. "No," she said.

But at the same time, Dayo said, "Yes. Something for my mother."

Stanley said, "Did you know there's an apartment in this building? I have the key for any Realtors who stop by."

Raine didn't even try to hide her moan.

Dayo turned to Mary. "An apartment? In this building?"

Looking between Raine and Dayo, she said, "Yes, there's one in here, but it's so small." Turning to Beerlulu, she added, "I knew it wouldn't be something that you'd be interested in."

Beerlulu said, "I'd like to see this apartment."

Mary's eyes were filled with apology when she looked at Raine, then she exchanged her SUV keys for the key to the apartment.

Inside the elevator, Beerlulu asked Raine, "What do you know about this apartment?"

"Nothing," she lied, keeping her eyes straight ahead. There was no way she was going to admit to knowing about this apartment from her very first SOS to Mary.

Beerlulu chuckled under her breath as if she knew the truth.

As they stepped off on the eighth floor, Mary explained,

"This is one of the smaller units. It's even smaller than the apartment we saw in Stuyvesant Town."

"That's fine," Beerlulu said with a slight smile.

They moved together like a military unit as they marched down the hall, then halted in front of apartment 8F. Mary fumbled a bit with the lock, and Raine prayed that God would grant her peace—a peace that would only happen if Beerlulu lived far away.

Mary entered, then Raine, and before Beerlulu stepped over the threshold, she said, "I'll take it."

"What?" Dayo asked as he followed his mother inside.

"I'll take it," she repeated.

Raine knew there was nothing she could say to stop Beerlulu, but still she told her, "You need to really take a look at it." She pointed to the window. "You don't have a view."

Without glancing toward to the window, Beerlulu shrugged. "That's fine."

Following up on Raine's attempt, Mary added, "And it's a junior one-bedroom." She held her arms out as she stepped across the 360 square feet of space. "This is it—your living room, dining room, and kitchen in one open space." Pointing toward the bedroom, she added, "And it's not very big in there."

Beerlulu shrugged again. "I don't need much room to sleep."

Raine sighed. "And look at this kitchen. It's really small."

Now Beerlulu looked at Raine. "I won't need a kitchen, isn't that true? You said that I could have dinner with you every night." Turning to Dayo, she said, "This is the place that I want."

"Don't you want to at least walk around, take a look at the bathroom?" he asked.

She shook her head. "We've been out all afternoon and I don't want to cause any more problems for this young lady who's been kind enough to take us all over the city."

*Yeah, right!* Raine thought.

"That's my job." Mary glanced at Raine before she said to Beerlulu, "I really think you should give me some time to find something better for you."

"Nothing will be more perfect than this."

"Okay, then," Raine said, thinking of another approach. "This is good, but we can still have Mary find you a few other places so you can compare."

"No need to compare when this is perfect for me. Besides, if I don't say yes, this could be gone by the time we come back"— she turned to Mary—"right?"

Mary's apology was in her eyes again when she looked at Raine. But when she glanced at Beerlulu, Mary told her the truth. "Yes, it could be gone."

Beerlulu nodded, satisfied. "Then this is the one I want."

While relief swept over Dayo, Raine was filled with dread. But as Mary told them that she would get the papers from the leasing office, Raine tried to talk herself down. At least Beerlulu would be out of their apartment. And she wasn't next door; she'd at least have to take the elevator.

Back in the hallway, Raine felt Beerlulu's eyes on her and she let Dayo and Mary walk ahead so that she could face her mother-in-law. Neither one parted their lips, but they spoke nonetheless.

Beerlulu told Raine that she had won.

Raine replied that it might seem that way, but if anything ever went down like what had gone down on Sunday, Beerlulu would regret knowing her.

Beerlulu chuckled.

Raine rolled her eyes.

# CHAPTER 13

## Liza

Liza felt bad that she hadn't stepped up.

It was clear that something was wrong with her girls, and in the past, if anything felt off-center, she would have stopped them all and prayed. But even though Sierra and Raine acted as if they needed some serious spiritual guidance today, Liza didn't have a single prayer inside of her for them.

She shook her head as she rolled through the crosstown traffic heading for the bridge. What kind of first lady was she? Her friends could've really needed her.

Well, not so much Sierra; Liza wasn't that concerned about the flighty, flaky young one who always seemed to live in the middle of drama. But Rainebow, she was the steady center of their trio; a mother earth, always filled with joy.

But that wasn't the Raine who'd sat across from her this morning.

Any other day, Liza would have taken her out for a cup of tea, given her a listening ear, an open heart, and they would've prayed. But it's hard to help someone with their spiritual oxygen mask when yours isn't properly in place.

Liza flowed with the traffic as she drove over the George

Washington Bridge and left her regrets on the New York side of the Hudson River.

As her SUV rattled over the bridge, her thoughts flipped to the dreams she'd had last night; dreams filled with ghosts, not from her past, but from the days that were to come. The images had played in her mind like a movie: scene 1—breaking news that told the world what Buddy had done and how Mann had covered it up. Mann fought hard to save his church, but in the end, he lost and resigned in shame. Cut to . . . she and Mann fleeing the city because of the outrage in the Christian community, finally settling in and hiding out in Corinth, Mississippi. Fade to . . . the two living their last days as outcasts, dying old, alone, and in disgrace.

All because of *The Scandal*.

She'd awakened in a sweat and with not much time to drive into the city for her meeting. But as she rushed through the morning, she hadn't been able to shake her nightmares.

Mann had said nothing more last night, even as they shared their Chinese dinner. Then she'd gone to bed while Mann retreated back to the library to perfect a speech that he would be giving at the Ridgewood City Council meeting today. This morning, he was up and gone by the time she'd awakened.

So, all these hours later, she still had nothing . . . except for a dread inside of her spirit. She couldn't believe this was actually happening to them. While pastor after pastor across the nation had to step down from the pulpit because of one transgression or another, Mann had been a straight-up guy whom many admired.

But if this scandal was as big as she was beginning to suspect, she and Mann would find themselves in the middle of her nightmares. And if Mann took this fall for Buddy, it would be because of her. Because Mann had come to Corinth and met her. . . .

Thoughts of the reverend were in her mind as Liza took her time walking to the bus stop. What was he doing at her house this morning? Maybe he was planning on staying in Corinth and he wanted to know what her daddy thought about that.

Liza had no thoughts of reading, writing, or arithmetic on that day. Only Reverend Washington was on her mind, and she prayed that he would still be at her house when she returned from school.

When she ran home from the bus stop, the house was empty—well, except for her parents. But it felt like the house was empty because Reverend Washington wasn't there.

She wanted to know why the reverend had come by this morning, but she was smart enough to know that this was grown folks' business. So all she did was keep her mouth closed and her ears open. But there was nothing to be seen or heard.

Then, after dinner, while she was washing the dishes, the phone rang. Her father picked it up, grunted a few times, hung up, then whispered to her mother, "Reverend Washington."

Liza's ears perked right up.

"Liza Mae, you finish up in there," her mother called out to her before her parents disappeared behind closed doors.

Hardly sixty seconds ticked by before Liza tiptoed through the living room, down the hallway to the bathroom. She locked the door, then climbed onto the side of the tub, pushed herself up on her toes until she was just inches from the vent. Balancing as if she was on a tightrope, she jiggled the cover gingerly, quickly, quietly, until . . .

"That's what he said?" Her mother's voice came through the

hole, making Liza feel like she was sitting right in their bedroom on the other side of the bathroom wall.

"Yup," Milton replied, though his voice was still a whisper. "He said that he received word from the Lord the moment we walked into the church. He said, he hadn't even seen Liza yet, but that God had described her to him."

Liza frowned. God had been talking about her? To Reverend Washington? She knew that God talked to some people, though He hadn't ever said a word to her. She just figured that God only talked to adults and she never much thought about what God said when He did speak. She never would've figured that He talked about people, especially not about her.

Milton said, "Reverend Washington's sure that Liza is the one who's called to be his wife."

Those words made Liza rock on her toes, lose her balance, and crash right onto the floor. She wasn't sure how she did it, but she held her screech inside and cowered in the corner. Surely her parents would be banging on the bathroom door at any moment, with promises to ground her forever.

But they must've been so caught up that they hadn't heard a thing. So Liza climbed back up and balanced herself once again.

"His wife?" Millicent said over and over. "How can she be his wife?"

That was the same question Liza was asking. She couldn't get married. Didn't you have to be, like, twenty to do that?

"Look, Millicent, I don't know. I don't have all the answers. But I know one thing. I will never question God or a good right reverend like Reverend Washington."

"She's so young," Millicent said, and in the bathroom Liza agreed.

"I know, but really, she's not that much younger than when we got married."

"She's a young fifteen, Milton. She's not as sophisticated as I was. And even if she was, there's still a big difference between fifteen and eighteen. Is Reverend Washington gonna wait three years?"

With the way the next words came out, Liza could imagine her father shaking his head. "He wants to marry her now. Look, Millie, our daughter will get chances that we never had. She'll get to leave Corinth and be married to a pastor who's making a lot of money. Her life will be so much better there than here."

"What about college? We've been saving up for her college since she was born. She's supposed to be the first."

"Why do kids go to college? So that they can have better opportunities, right? What opportunity is going to come to Liza that's going to be better than this? She won't need college if she's Reverend Washington's wife." There was a moment of silence before her father added, "This is what we're supposed to do as parents, give our kids the best shot. Millie, with where we live, with the little we have, this is as good as it's gonna get for our little girl."

Liza knew that she had already stayed too long and heard too much. She pushed the cover over the vent. Right before the cover clicked into place, she heard her mother say, "And anyway, isn't Reverend Washington just a little too old for our little girl?"

She almost wanted to jiggle the cover so that she could hear the answer. But if she stayed any longer, she'd be caught. She tiptoed out of the bathroom, thankful that the floorboards didn't scream beneath her feet.

Inside her own bedroom, she closed the door, jumped into the middle of her bed, then crossed her legs one over the other the way she saw those girls on *Three's Company* do it.

Had she just heard what she heard? Reverend Washington, the man who was music to her eyes and ears wanted to marry her? What was she supposed to think about that? There was a lot going on in her head, but there were a few things that she knew for sure. One was that living here in Mississippi was making her miss out on a lot. Every time she watched TV she could see that.

There were no tall buildings in Corinth, no glamorous women who wore dresses that glittered, and no sophisticated men who drove cars that shined so bright you could see your face in the hood.

There was nothing in Corinth except church and school. And those obnoxious Hicks sisters who picked on her every day.

Liza's eyes drifted from the left side of her bedroom, where the big old dresser that had belonged to her grandmother was pushed in front of the window, to the right side, where her desk, which had been given to her by one of her father's tow company customers, sat. At least her bed matched the bookcases that her parents had bought at Mitchell's Value Furniture.

Just like Corinth, there was nothing special about this bedroom or this house. Her mother did everything she could, but Millicent couldn't make a two-bedroom shack look anything like those big ole pretty houses on *Dallas* and *Dynasty*. This house wasn't even as nice as George and Louise's apartment on *The Jeffersons*.

The more she thought about it, the better it seemed. Leaving Mississippi would be a good thing—as long as her parents came along. Her mother could teach her how to be a wife and she'd go around New York every day with her father walking on those streets made of gold.

She went to bed a happy girl, dreaming about what life was gonna be like once she got to the big city. . . .

The tap on her SUV window startled her.

"What you doing in there, Liza?"

She held her hand against her pounding heart. "Buddy, you scared me!"

"I've been standing there on the steps waving to you." She could see the white cloud of his breath as he shivered. "You didn't see me?"

She shook her head. The truth was, she hadn't seen Buddy or anybody or anything since she crossed the bridge. Her mind was so deep in the past she hadn't even realized she'd driven twenty miles into the suburban community where she'd lived from the moment she moved to New York. It was New Jersey, really, but with its proximity to the city, most residents claimed New York as home.

"Well, are you coming in?" Buddy asked.

She nodded, then motioned for him to get out of the cold.

He trotted up the steps that led to the side door of Ridgewood Macedonia, but Liza didn't make a move. She sat and took in the view. The church was a massive structure that still had the architectural details of the original church—the stained-glass windows and even a front porch. Over the years, Mann and the board had built out the church twice, buying the real estate on either side of the property and expanding from a structure that at first held two hundred congregants to the one that now had five thousand seats, was the home of an award-winning choir, and was ground zero for their youth ministry, which received accolades from all over the country.

Which was why there was no way she could just stand by.

She jumped out of her SUV, then dashed up the steps and through the door. She was going to get some answers.

⮞

She had checked Mann's office first, and his secretary, Elaine, confirmed what Liza already knew—Mann was at the luncheon for the Ridgewood City Council. Buddy's office was connected to Mann's, but instead of using the small hallway that led to his office, she went to his front door, tapped, and peeked inside.

The telephone was pressed to his ear, but Buddy waved her inside.

"Okay, I'll get back to you," he said before he hung up. With a grin, he stood up, walked past Liza, and checked to make sure that his door was closed. Then he faced her with opened arms and love shining on his face.

"How ya doing, Cuz?" he asked as they embraced.

"Wow. You haven't called me that in a long time."

"You haven't called me that, either." He motioned toward the sofa against the far wall of his office. "You know how your husband likes it."

Yes, she did. Everything was formal with Mann. He was only called Reverend—even by her when they were in front of people. He'd had her drop the Mae from her name when she'd moved to New York because Liza Mae was too country, and he insisted that no one know that Buddy and Liza were cousins, cut from the same Mississippi cloth.

It was that last thought that took away Liza's smile.

"Buddy, I need to talk to you." She shrugged off her fur.

The light on his face dimmed, too, as he sat next to her.

She said, "I know that you're in trouble."

He looked into her eyes for only a moment before he turned away. "Is that what Rev told you?"

She nodded. "He didn't tell me much, I think because he knew I'd be so concerned." She reached for his hand. "Did you get some woman pregnant?"

His head snapped back and he faced her once again. She was surprised when his lips curled into just a wisp of a smile. "Is that what Rev told you?" he repeated.

"Yes. I mean no. Well, really he didn't say too much, but it doesn't take a genius to figure this out." She paused to study her cousin's face. To see if his expression would tell her what he wouldn't. "Is the woman married, Buddy?"

He laughed, though there was not a bit of humor in his tone. "I know Rev didn't tell you that."

"I told you, he didn't say anything except that the allegations were false, and that it was all going to go away."

"Well, if that's what he said, then we don't need to be talking about it."

"But he only said that to protect you."

Buddy shook his head. "It's not just me he's trying to protect. It's the church, it's everybody. And it's what the attorneys told us to do."

"But it's just you and me right here, so talk to me." When he stayed silent, she added, "We've always talked about everything."

He shook his head. "I'm not going to say anything else, Cuz. I gotta go with the reverend's program."

She sighed. "How am I supposed to help if I don't know what's going on?"

He pushed himself up from the sofa and made his way back to his desk. "What you need to do, Liza Mae," he said as he grabbed a folder from his desk, "is go on down the hall to your office or go home. You don't need to help anything. That's why your husband has me and the attorneys. This is all going to be taken care of. Trust me."

She stared at her cousin, trying to figure out why he was being so difficult. It had never been this way before; he would tell her all kinds of things that were going on in the church that Mann decided she didn't need to know.

So why the evasiveness now? If Buddy would just open up to her, she knew she could help in some way. "Buddy, Mann has worked hard to build this ministry," she said, needing him to understand her point.

He tossed the folder back onto the desk and looked straight at her. "Don't you think I know that? I've been right here by his side . . . and yours."

"Well, if you've done something that could cost Mann what he's built, maybe it would be better if you would just—" She stopped, hoping he would get it without her having to say it.

"Just what? Go on, Cuz. Finish it!" he demanded.

"Maybe it would just be better if you stepped aside."

He shook his head and chuckled at the same time.

"Just for a little while," Liza said. "Until this is fixed. So that no one will think Mann is covering up anything."

"You know what's so funny?"

"Nothing's funny."

He spoke as if she hadn't. "It's that you don't even know what you're talking about."

"Then tell me, Buddy!"

He turned his back, as if he was dismissing her.

She jumped up from the couch. "All I know is that I don't want anything to happen to Mann's ministry because of you."

When he spun around, Liza had to take two steps back. The love that had been in his eyes had hardened into rage. "Trust me, Liza Mae. This has nothing to do with . . ." He stopped, held up his hands. "You know what? You need to leave. Or better yet, let me get out of here. I have to pick up Rev in a little while anyway."

He grabbed his coat, then tried to rush past her. But Liza reached for him, grabbed him. One second, they stared at each other. Next second, he snatched his arm away. Then he stomped out, slamming the door for good measure.

She'd ignited her cousin's rage with just a few questions and now she knew for sure, this was exactly what she thought. Some woman in the church was claiming to be involved with Buddy. Claiming that she was pregnant.

Though not the best of circumstances, the only reason it would be a major deal was if the woman was married. Liza tried to imagine who it was. Was it a deacon's wife? Or maybe it was the spouse of one of the assistant pastors, who would use this to get Buddy thrown out of the church so that her husband could take over.

This was precisely the sort of thing that caused so many ministries to fall. And if it wasn't enough to take Mann's title from him, it would surely be enough to split the church. Either way, this scandal came with a price that she and Mann shouldn't have to pay.

Liza stood alone in Buddy's office with only these thoughts before she grabbed her coat, swung it over her shoulder, and accidentally swiped the framed photograph on the corner of Buddy's desk, knocking it to the floor. She knelt down, and before she even had the picture in her hand, she was smiling.

No matter how old they'd gotten, this was the Buddy she remembered, the Michael Jackson look-alike, standing between his parents, Uncle Bubba and Aunt Billie, her mother's sister. She laughed out loud as she studied the photo—Buddy, only ten years old, trying his best to look like Michael, with his Afro, flowered vest, and bell-bottomed pants.

Growing up, she and Buddy had been as close as siblings since neither one of them had any. Born one year, one month, and one day before her, he was her big brother/cousin, friend, protector, and confidant, who lived just three blocks away until Buddy's father found a better job over in Tupelo.

Her ten-year-old heart felt like it had been mashed like her mother's potatoes on the day she'd watched her aunt and uncle carry her best friend away. Buddy had been on his knees in the station wagon, waving out the back window, as she ran behind the car until her knees ached and she couldn't keep up anymore.

The move took Buddy and his parents just sixty miles up the highway, but Liza knew she was going to die. How was she supposed to live without Buddy? Who was going to laugh at her jokes, watch all the great TV shows, or play the new Atari games with her?

Even though they didn't see each other often, they'd stayed close, through long telephone calls and holiday visits. As close as they'd been, their relationship became even stronger when Buddy sat next to her on the same airplane the day she left Corinth, Mississippi, for good. . . .

After she had snuck into the bathroom and heard her parents' conversation, Liza expected Milton and Millicent to come into her bedroom and tell her all that they'd been discussing. But they said nothing that night, nor the next morning, nor the next evening. Days passed, and there was not a word about Reverend Washington. After a while, Liza began to wonder if she'd imagined the whole thing.

But then on Sunday, Reverend Washington was back in church, singing and wearing a royal blue suit with matching shoes. She sat as mesmerized as she had been the week before, and her smile was still stuck in place when he came up to her after the service. As last time, he kissed her hand, and when she saw the Hicks girls glaring at her, she knew they would harass her the next day. But she wasn't gonna worry about tomorrow when Reverend Mann was standing right in front of her today.

This time he came to their home straight from church, and when her father said, "Liza Mae, why don't you go out on the porch with Reverend Washington," she was thrilled. She hoped that he was gonna sing for her.

The only thing was that she saw the tears in her mother's eyes, and at first, it confused her. But then she decided that her mother was just sad because soon they just might all be leaving Corinth.

She sat next to the reverend on the wicker love seat that didn't really have enough room for two people. But still, Liza and Reverend Washington squeezed onto the cushion together, and when she sat with her knee pressed up against his leg, she felt okay. As if she was supposed to be here.

"So," the reverend began, "did your parents tell you that I talked to them?"

She shook her head. "No, sir."

"We're going to have to fix that."

"Fix what?" She frowned.

"If we're going to be dating, you can't be calling me 'sir.'"

She smiled. Just a little. Dating? Her mother had told her that she wouldn't be able to date until she was sixteen. Not that there was anyone in Corinth that she wanted to go out with. All the guys she wanted to date were on TV. Like Chachi on *Happy Days,* and Lionel on *The Jeffersons.* She even liked that guy on *Trapper John, M.D.* But he was too old for her.

Thinking of old, she wondered now about Reverend Washington. How old was he? He had to be older, since he lived in the big city, and he was a reverend, and he traveled by himself.

He said, "So, do you think we can work on that? Do you think I can get you to stop calling me 'sir'?"

She nodded. "What should I call you then?"

"Well, when we're in front of other people, just call me Reverend Washington. But when we're by ourselves"—he paused and took her hand—"I want you to call me Mann."

She stared down to her hand. "I don't know anyone else with that name."

"And I don't know another girl who's as pretty as you."

There it was . . . that warm feeling again. Only, it was even warmer this time. "Can I ask you something?"

He moved closer, so close that his lips were almost on top of hers. Now she wasn't warm, she was hot. But she asked him anyway. "How old are you?"

The question surprised him. Made him back up just a little. "Does it matter?"

She shrugged. "I don't know."

"Well," he said, "I'm twenty-eight."

In her head, she counted the years between fifteen and twenty-eight.

"What do you think of that?" he asked.

Sometimes it was easier for her to talk with her body. So she shrugged again.

"Well, I know enough for the both of us, and I say it's okay. So is that all right with you?"

When she shrugged again, Reverend Washington laughed and pulled her back so that she was leaning against him. They sat that way for a little more than an hour, watching cars roll by, some more slowly than others, as many tried to get a peek at the couple sitting on Milton Devine's porch. They sat that way until Millicent called them for dinner, but then her mother told them to enjoy the food because she was going into her bedroom to rest.

That night, Reverend Washington said good-bye to her father, then asked Liza to walk him to the door. When they were alone, Liza had her first kiss. A gentle one, all lips. And the heat traveled to the deepest parts of her.

Liza slept with her arms wrapped around her pillow, and imagined that it was Reverend Washington she was holding.

The next weeks passed at sonic speed. Every weekend Reverend Washington returned on Sunday, met Liza and her parents in church, then went back to their home, where she and the reverend sat on the porch and talked, and he sang to her. He sang all kinds of songs—mostly religious ones. But one day he asked her to pick something for him to sing.

"Do you know anything by Michael Jackson?" she asked.

His eyebrows had stretched almost to the top of his forehead. "You like Michael Jackson?"

"Yeah, a little. But my cousin Buddy loves him."

"Okay. Well, let me see." A couple of ticks of the clock and then he pulled her into his arms and sang "Rock with You" over and over.

That was the night she knew that she would go anywhere with this man. That was when she began to wonder when their family would be moving to New York.

The Sunday visits continued until three months went by. On the day before her sixteenth birthday, a Wednesday, Liza moseyed into her home after school, but just inside at the door, she stopped, shocked.

"Reverend Washington!" Liza exclaimed, remembering to use his formal name since they were in front of her parents. "What're you doing here?"

"Waiting for you." The reverend jumped up from his chair, then, without saying another word, he slipped a ring from his pocket and onto her finger in such a smooth motion, Liza didn't even realize what had happened.

"Liza, I have come to love you, exactly the way God told me I would," the reverend said. "And now"—he faced Milton and Millicent—"it's time for us to be man and wife. It's time for you to be my beautiful bride."

Liza glanced over Reverend Washington's shoulder and looked at her parents, who sat shoulder to shoulder on the sofa. She waited for one of them to tell her what to do since Reverend Washington hadn't even asked her. But her father just sat there with a big ole grin on his face, while her mother dabbed at her eyes with one of her Sunday handkerchiefs.

Since neither one of them said anything, Liza just shrugged.

Reverend Washington laughed and pulled her into his arms.

"Does this mean we're all going to New York now?" she asked.

"Yes, sweetheart," Reverend Washington said. "We'll be going down to the courthouse tomorrow with your parents because even though you'll be sixteen, they still have to sign some papers. . . ."

Now Millicent sobbed, but when her father didn't say anything, neither did Liza.

Reverend Washington continued, "You and I will be married and we'll leave for New York tomorrow night."

Liza frowned. "Mama," she said, looking over the reverend's

shoulder once again, "you're going to get everything packed that fast? How we all gonna leave tomorrow?"

"They're not coming with us, sweetheart," Reverend Washington said. "It'll just be you and me."

Now Millicent wailed and Liza wanted to cry with her. "You're not going with me, Daddy?" Liza's voice quivered.

Her father shook his head as he stood up. "No, baby. You're gonna be a married lady and your place is with your husband."

"By myself? In New York?"

"You won't be by yourself," Reverend Washington said. "You'll be with me."

The thought of being anywhere without her parents almost made her faint. How was she supposed to live without her father? How was she supposed to breathe without her mother?

She shook her head. "I . . . can't."

"It'll be all right, sweetheart," Reverend Washington and her father said at the same time.

Liza looked from one man to the other and she burst into tears.

She had never cried so hard and for so long. She sat next to her mother and cried as they held each other. She cried when Reverend Washington asked her to walk him to the door to say good-bye.

"I'll see you tomorrow, my beautiful bride," he said as he kissed the tears that streamed down her face.

She cried when she and her mother went into her bedroom and packed her bags as if she was never going to return.

"Mama, why aren't you and Daddy coming with me?"

"We can't, baby," her mother sobbed. "You're gonna be a married woman."

She cried through the night, and by the time the morning sun rose on her wedding day, her tears had made her sick.

As Liza rocked on her knees with her face over the toilet bowl, her mother said to her father, "I think we may need to take her to the doctor."

"Are you sure?" Milton peered down at Liza. "What's wrong, baby?"

Liza held her head up long enough to wail, "I want you and Mama to go with me!"

Then she'd crawled back into her bed, still sick, still crying, as her mother paced and wrung her hands. And her father paced and watched the clock. And he muttered, "We're gonna be so late," over and over.

Around ten in the morning, her father found the right medicine.

Buddy. Her cousin. He was on his way and he would go with Liza Mae and her new husband to New York.

"Buddy's gonna really come with me?" she stopped crying long enough to ask.

"Yes, sweetheart. Your Auntie Billie is helping him pack and your Uncle Bubba's gonna drive him right over. Buddy will be here in a couple of hours."

"Reverend Washington said it was okay for him to come?"

This time it was her mother who answered with a nod. "We talked to the reverend and he thinks this is a good idea."

With a final sniff, Liza rolled out of bed and slipped into the white lace dress that Reverend Washington had brought with him for her to wear to their wedding. . . .

Those memories made Liza sigh as she picked up the frame from the floor. She'd been so scared at first—to do anything without her mother and father. But with Buddy by her side, she'd gone to New York and made a life that she truly loved.

Now Buddy was putting that life in jeopardy. And it was all

her fault because Buddy would never have been in New York if it wasn't for her.

She loved her cousin, but she loved her husband more.

As Liza slipped into her coat, she was even more convinced that the best thing was for Buddy to step aside. No one needed to know why—he could just be sent on a vacation back to Mississippi. Then, when the woman was proven to be a liar, he could come back. But if the scandal broke, it would be lessened by the fact that they'd been proactive.

The more she thought about it, the more she was sure.

Buddy had to go.

# CHAPTER 14

## *Sierra*

*I*t was five days after Valentine's Day—Sierra's twenty-fifth birthday. And five didn't feel like such a lucky number right now. This day wasn't playing out anywhere near the visions she'd had in her mind for months.

First, her phone only rang once—before dawn, when Denise had called her with birthday wishes. But that was it. She hadn't told Raine or Liza about her birthday, and even though she'd signed some papers with Yvonne, she wasn't surprised that their manager had such personal failings that she hadn't remembered her birthday.

What got her the most, though, was that Andre hadn't picked up the phone to call. After all she'd meant to him, he didn't even bother to scroll through his phone and click on her name to reach out to her.

Not that she cared. Not anymore. If Andre was willing to forfeit the prize he'd been given when they'd met, then he needed to get what was coming to him. Sierra could see him now, begging for forgiveness in a year after he watched her meteoric rise to fame and fortune. She would ignore him, act like she'd never known him, though she needed to thank him for making room in her life for Jarrod Cannon.

From the moment she'd left the Harlem State Office Building on Tuesday until now, Mr. Cannon had been on her mind. She'd raced home and spent hours on Google. Finding Jarrod Cannon had been simple. Even getting his number was easy enough. The challenge came with his people. He had people who kept people away from him.

For the last forty-eight hours, she'd been calling, and calling, and calling, trying to convince his assistant that she wasn't just another constituent. She'd already dialed his number three times today, and as she held on to the phone now as it rang, she already had her Plan B in place.

"Congressman Cannon's office; this is Keisha speaking. How may I help you?"

Sierra rolled her eyes. If she had known that it was going to take this many times to get through to him, she would've made friends with his assistant on the first call. But by the third call, they were enemies, so now Sierra didn't waste time on pleasantries.

"This is Ms. Dixon. May I speak with Mr. Cannon, please?"

The young woman sighed. "He's not in, may I take a message?"

"I've left my number for him at least twenty times; I don't think he's getting my messages."

"Actually, you've called about fifty times and I've given him every single one."

"Well, something is wrong and Mr. Cannon isn't going to be happy when he hears that I haven't been able to get through."

"I don't know what to tell you, Ms. Dixon," the woman said with a bit of an edge in her tone. "You've called, he has your messages, he hasn't called you back, so . . ."

Sierra clicked off her cell, not sure if Keisha was still talking or not. Time for Plan B.

Inside her bathroom, Sierra checked the soles of the pumps that she'd bought at Payless. With the tip of her finger, she tested to see if the red spray paint had dried. Yup! Now she had her own pair of Louboutins—Sierra style.

In less than five minutes, she was dressed, standing in front of the mirror, twisting from left to right. She'd been so disappointed when she didn't get to wear this dress on Valentine's Day, but now she realized the blessing. Not everyone could pull off this shocking white in winter, and when Jarrod saw her again, he'd know right away how special she was.

She was completely covered, from the high turtleneck collar, to the long sleeves that extended past her wrists, to the mid-calf length. But the knit left nothing to a man's imagination. This was one of those what-you-see-is-what-you-get dresses—exactly the way she wanted it.

Slipping into her shoes, she checked the bottoms in the mirror—perfect! Nothing was better than this—she had a pair of thirty-four-dollar red-soled pumps.

She threw on her coat and was out the door, down the stairs, and already two blocks away on 125th Street within ten minutes. Even though the whipping wind sent loose trash swirling around her, she took careful steps. A scuff on the soles of these shoes would give away her secret. So even though she shivered, she slow-strolled, thinking the whole time of the dossier she'd put together.

Jarrod Cannon had just been elected into office in 2010 when across the country Democratic candidates were being slaughtered in local and statewide races. Jarrod, though, had won by a landslide with over 90 percent of his congressional district.

He'd just been sworn in as a junior member of the 112th Congress, and already there was talk of his political future as possibly the second African American president.

That was when Sierra received clarity on this whole situation. Andre had just been a place holder for Jarrod.

It wasn't until she was in the lobby of the Harlem State Office Building that Sierra thought about Yvonne. The last thing she needed was to have to explain her presence to her manager. But she was in the elevator and in front of the congressman's office without having seen a soul.

The office was quieter and much sparser than she expected. A young woman sat behind a metal desk with the phone pressed to her ear. She gave Sierra a welcoming smile, though she did that thing that all women do—she gave her a quick once-over in three seconds flat. Her smile was not as bright when she met Sierra's stare now, but the girl held up her finger, asking Sierra to give her a moment.

Sierra nodded and did her own assessment: the woman was about her age, but that was where their similarities ended. This woman was one of those thick sista-girls, with her hair pulled back into one huge Afro puff. She wore a top made from kente cloth, and Sierra just hoped she wasn't wearing a matching skirt or pants.

As the woman jotted notes onto a pad, Sierra strolled along the perimeter, checking out the pictures and plaques that adorned the walls. Before Valentine's Day, she'd only seen Jarrod Cannon on television. She knew he was running for some kind of office—it was hard to be a part of Harlem and not know that. But there wasn't anything about him that interested her then. Sure, he was fine, but she was so in love with Morris . . . and then Andre. There was no room in her brain to process Jarrod.

But now, after due diligence, she'd discovered fascinating facts about this third-generation Yale law school graduate who was the youngest of a political mini-dynasty. His father and grand-father had both been state senators in North Carolina. Jarrod, though, had brought his political skills (and dreams) north.

His ambition was going to be her good fortune.

"May I help you?"

Sierra turned around; when she walked in, she'd been sure this was Keisha, and now her certainty was absolute.

"I'm here to see Mr. Cannon."

The woman squinted, as if Sierra looked or sounded familiar. She glanced down at the calendar spread open on her desk. "I'm sorry; I don't have you on his schedule." Looking up, she said, "What's your name?"

Sierra wasn't fooled by her sweetness. The smirk she wore gave her away. "I'm Sierra Dixon."

"I thought so," Keisha said with her saccharine tone still intact. "Like I told you before, I've given the congressman your messages and." She stopped as if that was a full explanation.

"Is he in now?"

"No."

"Then I'll wait." Before Keisha could say another word, Sierra slipped off her coat and watched the young woman's eyes roll over her. When she completed her assessment and looked into Sierra's eyes, Sierra could see her envy.

Sierra shrugged. It was always like this with women. They hated her on so many levels.

She lowered herself onto one of the cushioned chairs and crossed her legs. From the corner of her eye, she watched Keisha check out her shoes. She tipped up the toe just a bit so that the assistant could get a good view.

*Yeah, baby. These are red-bottoms.*

She made a show out of laying her coat across the chair and then pulling her cell from her Louis Vuitton purse, which Keisha had to now (because of her shoes) believe was real. Keisha's eyes hadn't left Sierra, and finally Sierra glanced her way as if she just remembered that Keisha was there.

When their eyes met, Keisha said, "I don't know what time . . ."

Before she finished, the door opened and the congressman and the gentleman that he had been with the other day walked in. As before, their heads were bowed as they chatted until Jarrod looked up and stopped, his finger in midair as if he was about to make a point. His partner took two steps more, and then he noticed Sierra, too.

Sierra knew that every move she made counted, and so she stood slowly, sensually, her eyes locked with Jarrod's the whole time. "Hello," she said, pulling her voice from deep in her throat.

"Uh . . ."

Jarrod squinted and a slow panic began to rise within her. Did he not recognize, not remember her?

"I'm Sierra," she said, praying that her voice would jog his memory. She couldn't stand here like this. Not with the way she'd called his office, not with the way she'd just about threatened Keisha's job.

Probably not more than a second ticked by, but it felt like half a lifetime as Sierra stood, waiting, maintaining her smile, her stance, her facade of confidence.

"Sierra!" Jarrod said. "Good to see you." Stepping closer, he took her hand. "This is a surprise."

"I'm sorry to just drop by." She looked from Jarrod to the man with him. "I was in the neighborhood."

His gaze roamed over her, up, then down, then back to her eyes. "In the neighborhood? Dressed like that?"

"I just came from a photo shoot."

"Ahh . . ." the men said together.

Jarrod added, "You model?"

"Not often. I did something for a friend."

His partner said to him, "Listen, let's finish this up later."

"Oh, no," Sierra said, "I don't want to disturb you. It's just that I'd left a couple of messages and when I didn't hear back from you . . ." She glanced at Keisha.

"Messages?"

Before he could ask, Keisha said, "I gave you all of them. There were about fifty."

Jarrod laughed. "Well, I would never see you in that pile. I thought I gave you my cell."

"You did." She waved her hand. "Long story."

"Listen, Pete, give me a sec . . ."

"Nah, I'll come back this afternoon." He smiled and nodded at Sierra. "Nice meeting you," he said, even though they hadn't been introduced.

"Come into my office," Jarrod told Sierra. Before she had a chance to agree, his hand was on the small of her back and he led her past a rolling-eyed Keisha.

Inside, Jarrod began, "Like I said"—he took her coat from her arms—"I'm surprised to see you."

"Really? It wasn't surprise I saw in your eyes. It was more like 'Who the hell is she.'"

"Are you kidding me? You think I don't remember you?" He laughed as he motioned toward the sofa. When they sat together, he continued, "Let me see." He unbuttoned his jacket before he sat back. "Uh: dark blue jeans, pink sweater, Yankees cap. Even in the dark, I was mesmerized by your light brown eyes and the tinge of gold in your complexion, and your hair—though you had it tucked beneath your hat, I imagined it"—he reached out and gently stroked her curls for a moment—"just like this."

Inside, Sierra sighed. *Dang!*

He said, "You were sitting across the room with your body-guard."

She laughed. "Denise's not my bodyguard."

"She's not?" He frowned as if he was confused. "It seemed that way because she dragged you away"—he leaned closer to her—"before I had the chance to drag you away myself. So"— the tip of his tongue took a slow trip across his lips—"are you convinced now?"

Sierra wasn't sure what she was supposed to be convinced of; she'd forgotten what they were talking about. His tongue . . . and his lips had distracted her.

He laughed as if he knew his lips had hypnotic powers. Leaning away, he said, "So, did I pass your test?"

It took a moment for her to be able to speak again. "It wasn't a test. But if it had been, you would've passed."

"Great. So, let's go to dinner."

With everything in her, she wanted to say yes. This was her birthday and the best gift would be to spend the rest of the day—and night—with him. But that's what she'd done with Andre, and Morris and William and Ray and Eric. This time she wanted different results.

So her plan had been to come here, make contact, and pretend she wasn't too interested.

"That's not why I came by," she said as if she was surprised he would ask her out. "I was hoping that you could help me with something."

"Oh." His disappointment was apparent. "This is a business meeting."

"Well, kind of. I did try to call you."

"I gave you my cell so that you wouldn't be caught up with all the other calls."

"Yes you did, but . . ." Her words trailed off as if she couldn't remember what in the world she'd done with his card.

"Okay, I got it. How can I help?"

"Well, I don't know a lot of people in New York . . ."

"You just moved here?"

"Kinda. And I really need an entertainment attorney and thought that you might know a great one."

He chuckled. "Great, huh? Not just good?"

"I only believe in greatness."

"I like that."

"So, do you know of one?"

"I might." Then he said nothing else.

"Well . . . would you mind giving me his . . . or her . . . name?" she asked, wondering what was going to happen once he did. How was she going to keep him interested?

He said, "Sure. Have dinner with me and I'll give you his name, his number, his email, his website, his Facebook page, his Linked-In account. Anything else?"

She laughed. "You're a funny dude."

"See, you appreciate me already. So, when are we going to get together?"

"I'm sorry," she said as if she almost pitied him, "but like I said, that's not why I came by."

"So, why are you here, Golden Lady? All dressed up like this?"

"I told you—I was on a photo shoot and I don't live too far from here. . . ."

"Are you involved with someone?"

She leaned back, as if surprised by that question, but then she surprised herself with, "Are you?" She asked before she could think about it, but she was glad she did. This way, she could look at his face, see into his eyes. Determine if he had a relationship with truth and honesty.

Without letting a beat go by, he said, "Would I be asking about you if I was involved with anyone?"

She searched for a twitch of his eyebrow, a quiver of his lip. There was nothing. "I don't know," she said. "I don't know you like that, so you could tell me anything."

"But you know me well enough to have dinner with me— since we're both unattached."

His cell phone rang, stopping her from saying yes, and when he glanced at the screen, he held up his finger. Sierra nodded, and decided to use the moment to make her move. As much as she was dying to stay, she had to leave.

As she slipped into her coat, he shook his head—"Don't go" was what his gesture meant. She bobbed her head up and down—telling him that she had to.

When he hung up, he said, "So, I guess this means we're not going to dinner?"

She shrugged. "This means that we're both busy."

He leaned against the edge of his desk, folded his arms, and peered at her as if he wasn't used to being denied. "Well, if not tonight, when?"

"Can I get back to you on that?"

He nodded slowly. "Okay. But just think about how many days, how many minutes, how many seconds we're both missing out on because of you."

She laughed.

He said, "But in the meantime, I'll check with my attorney to see if one of his partners handles entertainment."

"Thank you. Just remember, he has to be great."

"Absolutely. Give me your number and I'll shoot you the information as soon as I have it."

She jotted her cell onto a notepad on his desk. He picked up the pad and held it against his chest. "I'll treasure this. I won't toss it away the way you tossed mine."

There was no reason to tell him that he was wrong.

"Let's try this again." He pulled a card from his business card holder and wrote his number on the back. "I hope you'll hold on to it this time."

She smiled as she took his card but said nothing. Then she held out her hand to shake his. At first, he just stared at her hand, dangling in the air. But then he took hers into his. "You really are something, Golden Lady."

"I'll take that as a compliment."

"It is. I'm intrigued and I'll be waiting impatiently for you to call and tell me that not going out with me tonight was the biggest mistake you've ever made."

She could have stood there and held his hand all day, but she'd accomplished what she came to do. There was no doubt she'd be on the congressman's mind for the rest of the day and, she hoped, the night. Pivoting, she sashayed her way out of his office.

"See ya," she said to his assistant as she passed her, as if they were the best of friends.

Slipping her coat back on, she carried her smile into the hallway, onto the elevator, onto the street. She smiled through the wind and through the catcalls that came her way.

*Oh, yeah!* Five was still her lucky number.

True, she was going to spend her birthday alone, but her prize was going to be beyond one date, one birthday dinner. She wanted the whole life that this man had to offer. And she had no doubt that she would have it—if she played the game right this time.

# CHAPTER 15

## *Raine*

Raine was sure that Beerlulu thought she'd won by choosing the apartment just an elevator ride away. But Raine wondered how victorious Beerlulu would feel when she found out that she'd be living in that apartment before seven days had passed.

From the moment Beerlulu decided that apartment 8F was where she wanted to be, Raine went into action.

She began on Wednesday. . . .

Dayo kissed Raine good-bye, then left for the store with his mother. Once the door closed, not even two seconds ticked by before Raine jumped up from the dining room table, leaving her teacup still half full on the place mat. She had to move quickly; Dayo and Beerlulu had left almost thirty minutes later than usual and her appointment was at nine. Glancing at the clock, she was already late. Good thing she didn't have to go far.

It was nine ten when she stepped into the Sales and Leasing Office on the second floor of her building. The manager was standing at the door, waiting for her.

"Good to see you, Mrs. Omari," he greeted her.

Nothing but business was on her mind, but still she forced a smile.

"I have to tell you I love your new song," he gushed.

"Thank you," she said, then went right to the reason why she'd asked to see him. "The apartment . . ."

"Ah, yes. The Realtor called and said you were interested in eight F for your mother-in-law."

"Yes. I need it right away."

"That won't be a problem." He directed her to have a seat in front of the desk piled high with papers. "That's one of our corporate-owned spaces, so we don't have to contact anyone. We'll just do the normal application, then the credit and referral check on your mother-in-law."

"She's only been in the country for two years. I'm not sure how much credit she has."

"That's okay," he said. "It's just a formality, really. Something we have to do with each potential resident. I'm sure with your mother-in-law it will be fine."

"How long will that take?"

"Not long," he assured her. "Usually about a week."

Raine shook her head. "Not good enough." She unzipped her purse and grabbed her checkbook. "How much is the rent?"

With a frown, he sorted through a bunch of folders before he grabbed one and glanced inside. "Thirty-one hundred, but because you own one of the apartments"—he waved his hand as if he was shooing away her checkbook—"we won't be needing a deposit." He smiled as if he was sure she'd be pleased with that.

But she ignored his words, did a quick calculation, scribbled onto the check, then handed the man the check for $37,200. "Here's the first year's rent."

"But—"

"Do what you have to do," she interrupted, not wanting

to hear anything that would deter her plan. "I need her in that apartment by next Tuesday."

He glanced at his calendar. "In six days. It's usually a four-teen-day process, at least to do the credit and reference checks and then to have the apartment completely assessed and ready."

"Well, I need it to be less than a week this time." She slid the check across his desk.

The man took the check into his hands, then nodded as if he was used to dealing with people who made things happen with their checkbooks. "I can set up the lease immediately, if you're willing to have your name on it."

"Whatever. Just do what you have to do." Standing up was the way she told him that they were done. "Oh, and can I pick up the keys tomorrow? I'll need three sets." She marched away before he could protest, and back in the elevator, she checked off the first item from her mental "to do" list.

Day one was done.

Then yesterday, day two. . . .

Raine once again waited until she was alone before she jumped into action. The moment Dayo and his mother closed the door behind them, she grabbed her coat, purse, and keys, and five minutes after Dayo, she was in the lobby.

"Mrs. Omari, you just missed—"

"I know." She cut him off. "Can you please call me a cab?"

His eyebrows rose just a bit; he was used to seeing Raine barging around the city on foot or in their own hybrid SUV. But today she had no thoughts of her carbon footprint. Today efficiency was king.

At 24th Street, she traded the cab for a Zipcar, and as she eased into the Prius she thought this was the perfect name for what she had to do today—zip from store to store, filling the car with new apartment essentials: kitchen appliances and utensils, plates, pots, pans. Linen and pillows and towels—the list went on. It was a day that started at nine, and even when she returned the car at five, she was only half done. But this was only the second day; she had time.

Now it was day three in Raine's seven-day plan, and this was going to be the most challenging so far. Today Dayo had to become actively involved in her quest to get rid of his mother.

She could have easily talked to Dayo in their home, but The African Sun was better. At his store, Dayo could make a quick decision; he wouldn't have time to figure out a way around her request.

The February cold was consuming, but outdoors she could breathe, think, and strategize. That was why she was looking forward to the mile-and-a-half trek from the apartment to the store. She'd have time to find the right words, gentle words to get Dayo to cooperate.

She couldn't believe it had come to this. When had she ever needed to plan her words to speak to her husband—the man who could finish her sentences, the man who knew her thoughts. Their communication had always been so free, so easy. From their first meeting, they had flowed together as if they had always been meant to be. . . .

Raine was only twenty and had just purchased the penthouse—the first place she'd ever called home. She wanted her apartment to reflect all that she was, all that she'd achieved. Her accomplishments were throughout the 3,000-square-foot space: the two Grammys that she'd won for her first single were on the mantel and photographs of her with her famous peers were in each room. What was missing, though, was the essence of her—who she was.

She knew nothing about her beginnings since she'd been put up for adoption at birth, but had spent her life in foster care. But though she had no desire to find birth parents who didn't find her worthy enough to love, she wanted to connect to someone, something, and she chose the motherland. Surely she was just a few generations removed from the continent of Africa.

But her interior designer hadn't been able to deliver on that level, and when she'd mentioned her frustration to her mentor, Babyface had told her, "You need to hook up with my man, Dayo Omari. He's African, so he's got pieces that no one else has; and his specialty is one-of-a-kind African art so you won't feel like your place looks like everyone else's."

Babyface had guided her the right way in every other part of her life, so she'd given Dayo a call. He showed up the next day, and was not at all as Raine expected. He'd been dressed in a very well-tailored suit, though she was impressed beyond his attire. It was his mere presence, his sophistication. He had the stride of royalty, held his head high with dignity, and his deep voice carried the strength of his confidence as if he knew just about everything.

His knowledge of African art and artifacts went beyond books and the Internet. He spoke as if this was his life, as if he was Africa.

Raine had difficulty keeping her eyes off him as she gave him a tour of her penthouse and pointed out places where she wanted to hang pieces and he showed her where the art would have the most impact. He took notes along the way, telling her that he wanted to capture her personality in every piece he found for her.

Less than an hour passed before he said, "I'm going to bring some pieces for you within the next week," he said. Opening his notebook one more time, he added, "Let me get your full name."

From the moment he walked in the door, she suspected that he didn't recognize her. It was the way he treated her, glancing at her as if she was just another client, speaking her name—Raine—as if he was saying "Sally" or "Jane." But now the moment had come—where she would say her name and the raving would begin.

"Raine," she said. "Actually, I'm known as Rainebow." Then she waited.

He stayed silent as if he was waiting for her to say more. Then: "And your last name?"

She frowned. It wasn't that she was conceited; it was just that she'd come to expect the gushing. It was hard for her not to be recognized. Her CD was in rotation on all the major stations, she was the new face of Revlon, and she'd just been contracted to be in an I Love New York campaign where she was featured in a giant billboard in Times Square. Though she was sure that it was her performance on *Oprah* last year that had shot her into the stratosphere.

She'd given up pretending that she could hide behind oversized sunglasses and baseball caps. So as she stood in front of Dayo, she was shocked and delighted that he really didn't know who she was.

"I just go by Raine," she said. "That's my legal name."

He nodded as if he approved. "That's cool," he said, putting away his notebook. "Is that the name your parents gave you?"

She shook her head. "I never knew my mother or my father." She stopped there, leaving out the rest of her sob story. She'd given up feeling bad for herself a long time ago.

"I'm sorry," he said.

"Don't be. I had a decent life growing up and I've been blessed to have made it even better."

He grinned. "Blessed, huh?"

"Always blessed," she said. "Never lucky."

"You got that right. There's nothing lucky about the blessings of the Lord. Christ made sure of that."

*Christ?* She thought Babyface had told her he was from Kenya. And even if he hadn't said that, she would've known he was African. His features bore the pride of his continent. His skin was the smooth color of rich chocolate, his nose was broad, his lips were luscious. This man was the manifestation of tall, dark, and handsome; he could easily pass for that fine African brother who'd been in Janet Jackson's *Love Will Never Do* video a few years back.

He was African for sure, but his talk of Christ confused her.

She said, "Babyface said that you were Kenyan."

His shoulders stiffened and he lost a bit of his smile. "I am," he said, his tone a bit defensive.

"I'm sorry," she said, sensing his shift. "I wasn't trying to get into your business," she said. "It was just that you said 'Christ' . . ."

"That surprised you? Why?"

She shuffled her feet a bit. "I just . . . thought . . . you were African . . . and assumed you were Muslim."

He nodded, as if he was not a bit surprised. "I'm Christian."

"I'm sorry."

He released a soft laugh. "You're sorry that I'm Christian?"

"No, not that. I mean, I'm sorry for my assumption. I'm sorry for even asking." She held up her hands. "Look, I'm just plain sorry."

Now he laughed. "Don't be. I just didn't know where you were going with your questions and you're certainly not the only one who thinks that all Africans are Muslims."

She released a breath. "Well, at least I learned something today."

He bowed slightly. "Glad I could be of help," he kidded before he turned toward the door.

She wanted to stop him, to get a little more time, so she said, "Maybe you can help me with something else since I'm in a nosy mood."

He grinned. "I don't think you're nosy. Just curious."

"Okay. Your name. Dayo. I like it."

"Thank you."

"Does it have any special meaning?"

"It meant much to my mother. The name means 'joy arrives.'"

She hoped that he wasn't kidding because to her that was the truth. Dayo had walked through her door and joy had come into her morning.

When he turned back toward the door, she tried to think of another excuse to extend his stay. It was refreshing to talk to someone about something other than her life and her career.

But nothing came to mind, and right as his hand touched the doorknob, she said, "Would you like to go out to dinner sometime?"

She hadn't meant to blurt it out that way—it shocked her as much as it surprised him. It wasn't as if she'd had any practice doing this. She'd never had to ask anyone out before, so this was the best she could do.

His hand was still on the knob as he pondered her question for a long moment, long enough for Raine to regret having asked.

But then he twisted his torso to face her and those luscious lips spread into a smile brighter than the summer sun. "I'd like that. I don't know the city that well. Maybe you can show me around."

"And you can tell me more about Africa," she said. "I hope to go there one day."

One date turned into two, four, six, eight, and then not a day went by when they weren't together. They bonded over their mutual love of family (her desire coming from her longing to have what she'd never had and his coming from being part of a strong, sturdy, successful family in Kenya), their love of music (even though Raine had to cover her ears whenever Dayo sang), and their unconditional love for God.

Thirteen months later, they were engaged, to no one's surprise since pop stars always made moves like that for publicity. But then Raine and Dayo shocked the world when they actually eloped just a couple of weeks later. Without family or friends, they'd flown to Vegas and had done that Little White Wedding Chapel ceremony.

"You're way too young to get married," her agent said.

"This is going to ruin your career," her manager told her.

"He probably just wants your money," her accountant cautioned her.

"Is he in this country legally?" her lawyer questioned her.

Only Babyface cheered her; the rest of the folks she ignored. She never even bothered to give her management team any explanation. They would never be able to understand anyway. They'd all been raised by at least one loving parent—how were they supposed to understand that she was just seeking what had been given to them as a birthright?

Plus, Dayo loved her completely because she was Raine, the woman God had chosen for him. The woman he could talk to, laugh with, learn from. It was the same for her. . . .

It had been that way all of these years. That's why this place where she and Dayo were now was so foreign to her. Having to choose her words, having to care about the way every sentence came out—this was not them.

But the memories of their beginning made her remember their connection. All she had to do was talk. It was the love Dayo had for her that would help him to understand.

So as she strolled into The African Spot, she was ready. She waved to Scott, the manager, as he cashed out a customer. Throughout the store, people browsed and mingled and Raine absorbed the scene. With no signs of Dayo or her mother-in-law, she headed toward the back, past the musical display of African drums and harps, rainsticks, and calabashes. Inside the hallway, she slowed her steps when she heard the voices, even though the two were speaking softly.

"Making me move away will not change anything, *Mwana*," Raine heard Beerlulu say. "No matter where your wife sends me, my granddaughter is still not properly prepared to become a woman."

"*Hooyo,* you speak of things from a different country, a different time."

Raine eased against the wall and edged closer to the half-open door.

"How can you say that?" Beerlulu questioned Dayo. "You have not been away from your country for so long that you do not remember. Don't you want your daughter to become a proper woman?"

Raine frowned at the distress in Beerlulu's voice. As if something was wrong with Nadia.

Dayo replied softly, "I just don't know."

"You don't need to know. This is woman's business. I am the one who's responsible for making sure that all of the daughters, the nieces, and the granddaughters are prepared for womanhood and marriage."

"Marriage," Dayo stated. "Nadia is twelve. In this country she's at least a decade away from being married."

"Still, she has to be ready. And this . . . this will prepare her, this will stop her from being influenced by all this garbage in this country."

It took everything inside of Raine to remain in her hiding place when all she wanted to do was barge in and tell Beerlulu that there were plenty of planes leaving from JFK every day.

But she stayed, not moving, just listening. Trying to figure out the words that weren't being spoken.

"I don't know," Dayo said. "I need to talk to Raine."

"No!" Beerlulu said, her tone letting Dayo—and Raine—know that would be a mistake. "She will not understand."

"Well, it's not going to happen without Raine."

*What?*

"Then I will talk to her," Beerlulu said. "My sisters and I will talk to her."

Dayo's chuckle sounded empty, like there was no humor, no joy inside. "*Hooyo,* my wife asked you to move. Do you think she's going to listen to you about anything?"

"I will handle it," Beerlulu said, her tone filled with confidence. "I will get her on my side, we will become friends, and then she will listen, and she will see." She paused. "In time your wife will agree."

In the silent seconds that followed, Raine realized that her mother-in-law was preparing to leave the office. It took her only a millisecond to jump two feet back and duck into the bathroom. She pressed her body against the door and listened for the footsteps. She heard Beerlulu's determined gait—heavy steps that always announced she had arrived.

When the sound of Beerlulu's steps faded, Raine did her own march to her husband's office.

The phone was pressed to Dayo's ear and his eyes widened a bit, but his smile was welcoming.

"Okay, great," Dayo spoke into the telephone. "I have a customer who will pay top dollar for that." He motioned for Raine to sit in the chair across from him.

She sat, but had to work hard to keep the ends of her lips turned upward while her mind replayed the conversation. What had Beerlulu been talking about?

When Dayo hung up, he said, "So how did I get so blessed?" He circled his desk. "To have you brighten my day." He kissed her cheek.

She needed to talk to Dayo about Beerlulu's move, but she had to take this detour first.

"I saw Beerlulu leaving," she said, and watched his expression.

"Yeah, yeah." His smile faded as he retreated to the other side of the desk. "She's on her way to Brooklyn."

"To see her sisters."

He nodded. "My cousin is picking her up." He glanced down for a moment, and when he raised his eyes, his smile was back. "A new shipment just came in—some great pieces. You wanna take a walk out back?"

She shook her head. She didn't want to see anything—she only wanted answers. "I overheard a little—you were talking about Nadia?"

He nodded, but spoke no words.

"What about Nadia?" she probed.

"My mother just wants the best for her."

*And so do I,* she wanted to scream. But she wanted the information, not an argument, so she kept her anger inside. "I know that, but what does she mean by preparing Nadia? Preparing her for marriage? She's twelve."

"That's what I told her," he said. "*Mchumba,* you have to understand. My mother is still entrenched in the ways of our people."

Raine frowned and shrugged at the same time. "What does that mean?"

He held his head down so long that Raine wondered for a moment if he were praying. "Americans talk about old-school," he said when he finally looked up at her. "But you don't know anything about old-school. My mother, my people—we have rites and rituals that go back thousands of years." He stopped as if he had said enough, or maybe too much.

"What does this have to do with Nadia?"

"Nothing," he said, too quickly.

She squinted, trying to see Dayo's thoughts on his face. "Your mother," she began, "she's not thinking about"—Raine started shaking her head—"some kind of arranged marriage?"

"What?" Dayo was shocked. "No! Nothing like that. *Hooyo* just wants Nadia to know some of the ways of her African side of the family. That's all she was talking about. Listen." He stood up. "It's all good. Let's go out to lunch."

It was a quick switch of lanes and Raine waited a moment before she decided to let it go. "I can't do lunch today. I just came by to tell you that everything is almost ready for your mother's move."

He frowned. "Already? What about the lease? We haven't signed anything."

"I took care of that," she said, deciding that if Dayo had his secrets, she would have her own; she'd tell him about the check later. "I knew you really wouldn't want to be involved." She added, "Beerlulu will be able to move in by Tuesday."

"This coming Tuesday?" He face was stiff with shock. "You mean, like, in four days?"

She nodded.

Dayo's shoulders slumped a bit.

"I know it seems so soon, but there's a reason I want to do it this quickly."

He glanced up.

"I'll be leaving on tour in just a little over a month, and I wanted to make sure your mother is really settled before I go."

Dayo pondered her expression, her words, and she could tell that he wondered if she spoke the truth.

It was a truth that she'd come up with. It was a truth he'd never be able to debate.

Still, he said, "I thought we'd have more time for my mother to get adjusted to the idea."

"Well, she wants that apartment, and if we don't take it right away, someone else will get it."

"But how are we going to furnish it and get everything else we need by Tuesday?"

"That's why I'm here. I wanted to see if you had any furniture in stock. And whatever you don't have . . . I'll go shopping for the rest."

"I have some, but still"—he shook his head—"I don't think you're gonna be able to do so much so fast."

*Trust me.* She smiled. *Watch me.* She said, "Well, let's just see what I can do." When he looked at her as if he was studying her, she added, "And if we don't make it by Tuesday"—she shrugged—"it's okay. As long as we let the leasing office know, we should be cool."

Dayo nodded, satisfied now. "Okay," he said, coming back around his desk. "Let me show you a new living room set that just came in from Kenya. *Hooyo* was just saying how much she liked it."

She kept her smile small, though inside her heart danced as she checked off the biggest item on her mental "to do" list.

Dayo was on her side.

# CHAPTER 16

## *Liza*

*I*t was a nightmare.

Liza was running as fast as she could, but her legs weren't moving. She had to get away from the newspapers with their devastating headlines: *Breaking news! Reverend Washington resigns! New Jersey reverend crawls out of city in shame!*

She was thrashing, her hands were flailing, her head whipped from side to side. But she was getting nowhere. The headlines were getting closer, closer, closer.

*Run, Liza, run!* She heard her husband's voice in the distance. "Liza! Liza! Liza!"

Her legs began to move, but she wasn't running. She was on her knees, crawling forward slowly toward consciousness.

"Liza!"

Her eyes fluttered open. "Mann!" She peered up into her husband's stern face. "What happened?"

He stepped back from the bed and stared down at her. "You were dreaming . . . or something."

"Oh." She rubbed her eyes, remembering. It was the dream that she'd had for the last few nights. Never in her life had she had the same dream before; this had to be prophetic or something. "Are you just getting home?" She glanced at the clock, surprised that it was close to midnight. "Were you at church all this time?"

His answer was, "You talked to Buddy!" It was a question, yet at the same time, it was a demand.

It took a moment for all of her senses to work with her brain. All she could manage was, "What?" with squinted eyes.

"Buddy," he said as he paced in front of her. "You talked to Buddy!"

Pushing herself halfway up, she said, "Yes. I did. Three days ago."

Before the last word was out of her mouth, he snapped, "Why did you do that? Why did you go to him? Why did you say something when I told you not to?"

The volume of his voice made her sit up straight. She leaned back against the headboard, crossed her arms. "Oh, so he went running to you."

"No, apparently his loyalty is still to you. We were meeting with the attorneys, tonight, and when they talked again about making sure that all of this stayed within this circle, Buddy told them about you. He hadn't said a word to me."

Liza wasn't sure which made her husband angrier—the fact that she'd said something or the fact that Buddy had not.

"I only talked to him because I wanted to know the whole truth."

"I told you everything you needed to know," he said, his voice still raised. "Do you know how I looked in front of the attorneys? As if I don't even know what's going on in my own home, with my own wife?"

"I'm sorry about that, Mann, but I didn't know what else to do." She planted her feet on the floor. "I'm really worried about what a scandal could do to our church. And it doesn't help that I'm about to go out on the road."

"Oh, so that's it. You're more worried about what it could do to that Divas group."

She pressed her lips together to hold back the first words that she wanted to say. After a moment, she said, "You know it's not like that. You know I care about you."

He stopped moving and stood like a soldier in front of her. "Well, if you care, don't go behind my back."

"Then you shouldn't stand in front of my face and tell me nothing's wrong."

"What's gotten into you, Liza? Why can't you just trust me? You have all these years, why are you changing now?"

She held up her hands, exasperated. "I haven't changed at all. I'm still the same wife who's looking out for her husband. That's been my role for twenty-eight years."

"No, your role as my wife is to do what I tell you to do."

His words made her lean back a little. "That was a long time ago, Mann. I'm not even close to being that little girl anymore."

He shook his head, glared at her, huffed and puffed.

She picked up a pillow, held it in her arms and pretended that she was holding her husband. Her voice was softer when she asked, "Why are you so angry when all I want to do is help?"

"You'll help by staying out of this, not going behind my back, and not telling my armor bearer that he has to quit."

Still wishing that the pillow was Mann, she tossed it to the side. "After everything that's been going on in all these churches across the country, I think Buddy should at least take a leave of absence. For God's sake, he's my cousin; you know I don't want to do anything to hurt him—but I don't want him to do anything that would hurt us, either. I'm just saying, get him out of the picture until . . ." She didn't get a chance to finish her thought.

"Liza, just stay out of . . ." He stopped.

Her eyes narrowed. "What were you going to say, Mann? Were you going to tell me to stay out of grown folks' business?"

He shook his head. "No."

"I'm grown," she said as if she had to remind him.

"You don't have to tell me that," he snapped as his eyes roamed over her body. "But, this is not about being grown. This is about letting me take care of my ministry."

"I thought it was ours." When he didn't respond, she held up her hands. "Fine! Your ministry. Do whatever you want!"

He stared her down for a moment longer before he left her alone. It took everything inside of her not to pick up the pillow and throw it after him.

She knew what was coming; he would lock himself inside their office for hours. That was his MO whenever he got upset. The only saving grace was that she could count on one hand the number of blowouts that they'd had over the years.

She grabbed the pillow and punched it. Why was he being like this? And why so protective of Buddy? Sure, their relationship had lasted as long as her marriage. Mann was Buddy's mentor and Buddy was always there for Mann. But there was too much at stake now. She didn't care what Mann said.

She had no intention of leaving anything alone.

# CHAPTER 17

~ஓ~

*Sierra*

Sierra was beginning to feel that number five again.

It had been difficult, but she'd let five days go by before she picked up the phone and called Jarrod yesterday morning, casually asking if he had the information she needed.

"I certainly do," he'd said. "But like I promised, I was just waiting for you to come to your senses and call me."

"I would've called sooner if I knew you had already found an attorney for me," she lied, all the time smiling, all the time pleased that this man had been waiting for her.

"Well, let's not waste any more time," Jarrod had said. "I'm in DC right now, but I'll be home tomorrow night."

Sierra hadn't thought about that. Did he spend most of his time in Washington? How was that supposed to work with them?

"Tomorrow will be perfect," she'd said, knowing she couldn't play any more games.

"Great," he'd said, letting her hear his smile. "I won't be landing until about six, and I'll come straight to you."

After she gave him her address, he said, "So, you're one of my peeps." He laughed. "I hope I got your vote." And then: "Wait, don't answer that. I don't want you to think this is any kind of business dinner. So, I'll pick you up at seven tomorrow?"

"Seven it is."

And seven it was.

Sierra had come downstairs just a few minutes before and now she waited in the vestibule with expectation. At exactly seven, a black Town Car slowed, then stopped in front of her building.

Her lips widened into a smile when the back window slid down slowly and Jarrod peeked out, looking just like Mr. Big on *Sex and the City.* She stepped out of her brownstone and he slid out of the car.

Even though she wanted to look directly into his eyes to make sure that Jarrod appreciated her entrance, she wasn't about to look like a fool, tripping down these steps. So she kept her eyes lowered and held on to the railing as she maneuvered down in her red-bottom stilettos.

Today, her thick, bronze curls cascaded over the padded shoulders of her black coat with its faux-mink collar. It wasn't her warmest coat, but it was her most tailored one. Before she even took it off, Jarrod would be reminded of what she was working with.

At the foot of the stairs, he was waiting with outstretched arms. "Hello, Golden Lady," he said as he gave her a quick hug. Then he held her hand and helped her to step over the small pile of snow on the curb.

She slid into the backseat, butt-first, and then slowly she swung her long legs inside. His sigh was faint, but she heard it and was pleased.

Once they were both in the warmth of the car, Jarrod said to the driver, "Okay, Harold," then he pressed a button that closed the privacy window between the front and the back.

As Sierra snuggled into the softness of the seat, she wondered if Jarrod rolled like this all the time, since this looked like the same car she'd seen him getting out of last week. Did congressmen have it like that? Not that money was her objective, since she'd be making her own soon enough. She just wanted to truly understand this man's potential because it was his potential that she wanted.

In the silence, she searched for a way to begin their conversation.

*Men need to feel needed. Men need to be feel wanted. Men need to feel important.*

Her mother's wisdom rang in her ears.

"When you said you were going to pick me up, I didn't expect all of this."

He nodded slightly, and his face was stretched with such seriousness that Sierra wondered if she'd said something wrong.

He said, "So, you like the way I do it?"

Sierra laughed. "Yeah, this is a good start."

He leaned toward her slightly, as if he was about to whisper in her ear. "Well, before tonight is over I hope that my grade will be better than good."

She'd never had a challenge pulling the finest of men, but Jarrod was at the very top of the fineness list. *Stupid-fine*, she thought as she studied his perfection: the flawlessness of his complexion, his thick but shaped eyebrows, and his lashes that would have been a gift to any woman.

She sighed, but only on the inside. In the old days, she would have already been all over him. But now she had wisdom and a plan.

"We'll see," was all she said. Then, with a smile that was as sexy as she could make it, she turned away and peered out the window as if riding in the back of a Town Car with a congressman was all so regular to her.

But her heart was pumping as fast as the car was speeding down Central Park West. She could feel it already. She was winning!

"Excuse me a second," he said when his cell phone rang.

She nodded, but stiffened, and kept her eyes on the window.

"Yeah," he said. "Yeah," he repeated.

Sierra did her best to lean closer to him without appearing obvious. She needed to know—was he talking to a woman?

"Uh-huh. Sure. What about later tonight?"

Was he making arrangements to meet up with someone after being with her?

"Okay. I'm out." He snapped his cell shut.

His phone was still in his hand when she tilted her head. "Who was that?" When his eyebrows rose high on his forehead, she rushed to give an explanation that didn't sound crazy, "I mean, it sounded important and I just wanted to make sure that everything was okay . . . you know . . . because you're a congressman and everything. . . ."

He gave her a half smile. "It's just business." Then he pressed a button and spoke through an intercom. "Harold, after you drop me off, I'll need you to double back and give those papers to Pete. He needs to get them out tonight."

Exhaling, her heartbeat was back on track, but she had to be careful. She couldn't lose it with Jarrod. She had to remind herself that he wasn't Eric or Ray or William or Morris—and he definitely wasn't Andre.

They rounded the monument in the center of Columbus Circle before the driver stopped, then double-parked in front of the Time Warner Center. Sierra reached for the door handle on her side of the car, but gently Jarrod rested his hand on her lap, stopping her. On his side, the door opened and then Jarrod stepped out, reaching back to take her hand. He led her through the maze of cars that blocked the curb and within moments they were inside the warmth and the hustle and bustle of the tourist-filled crowd that packed the Center.

Jarrod led Sierra up the escalators, past the retail outlets, then stopped in front of two oversized doors. When they stepped inside, Sierra felt like she'd been transported to another world. Behind her, the music that was New York City still played, but inside this space, the lights were dim and the serenity was stirred only by the soft gurgling of waterfalls.

A man who looked like a Secret Service agent with his dark suit and earpiece, nodded at Jarrod. "Congressman," he said before he pulled open a glass door.

Inside this new space, there was a bit more light, mostly from the bar that seemed to glow as if it were the restaurant's stage, but the sounds were still soft, Zen-like compared to what was beyond these walls.

"Welcome to Masa, Mr. Cannon." A petite Japanese woman scurried toward them, her steps small because of the red and gold kimono that draped her body. She lowered her eyes, bowed slightly, and then held out her hands.

Jarrod shrugged his overcoat from his shoulders. "She's going to check our coats," he told Sierra.

Since the woman was already holding Jarrod's, Sierra moved quickly, unbelting her coat, then slipping it off. Her plan had been to take her time, but it didn't matter—Jarrod was still about to get the show of his life.

She handed her coat to the woman, who turned away at the precise moment another woman approached.

"How are you, Mr. Cannon?"

"I'm fine, Amaya," he said before he planted his hand at the base of Sierra's back, guiding her forward to follow the woman.

Again, Sierra wished she could see into Jarrod's eyes. He was behind her, so that was impossible and totally unnecessary since she knew where his eyes had settled.

She'd chosen the crisscross-pleated, curve-hugging bronze dress that was fashioned so that she looked just as good going as she did coming. It had carried a five-hundred-dollar price tag that had made her cringe. But there were two factors that made her relax just a bit: first, Yvonne had told her that she'd be receiving another royalty check soon, and second, this was an investment in her future with Jarrod.

As she strolled, she wished that the light in the restaurant was brighter, but even in the dimness, she knew what Jarrod saw was good enough. When the woman stopped and pulled out the chair, Sierra slid in, and the woman bowed as Jarrod sat.

Once they were alone, he said, "You are beautiful."

She smiled through the candlelight that flickered in the center of their table. "Thank you."

Before she could say anything more, they were joined by another member of the waitstaff, this time a young man who, like the women before him, addressed Jarrod by name and asked about their drink selection.

"Do you like sake?" Jarrod asked, taking the menu from the waiter's hand.

Her mind moved fast. She had to prove herself worthy to be with this man with his Ivy League degree who was moving on up. Should she say that she did like sake? Or should she tell him the truth—that she had no idea what sake was?

She decided to settle in the middle when she nodded. "But I'll let you order for me."

"We'll have the Masa Dry—a carafe, please," Jarrod told the waiter.

The young man bowed, then disappeared.

Sierra took that moment to glance around; the restaurant wasn't very small, but there weren't even ten tables in the space. She asked, "Is this kind of like a semi-private room?"

Jarrod shook his head. "They have two rooms, but only twenty-six seats. There's one seating every night and you have to wait weeks to get a table."

"So how did you . . ."

With his arms pressed down on the table crisscrossed in front of him, he leaned forward. "I'm friends with the owner, and after I saw you on Thursday, I called him and told him to save a table for me."

She frowned. "You knew we were gonna go out tonight?"

He nodded. "This is the only night this week that I'm in the city."

"Wow, lucky for you that I called you last night."

He laughed. "Yup, lucky for me," he said in a tone that made her know that he felt she was lucky, too.

She loved his self-confidence, but she didn't want him to be so cocky so soon. "You know, I came close to not calling you back."

"Why?"

"'Cause you're Jarrod Cannon. A newly elected congressman."

"And you're Sierra Dixon. A member of that hot group, Destiny's Divas."

Her face stretched with surprise. "How . . . did you know?"

He flipped his napkin from the table to his lap. "I'm a newly elected congressman, remember? I'm trying to go places, and the company I keep is very important to me."

She nodded.

"Plus, don't tell me you didn't spend a couple of hours on Google researching me."

She laughed. "You got me."

"Well, in the world today and the access we all have, I would've thought it strange if you didn't check me out."

"I'm glad I did and I'm glad I called."

"I'm glad you did, too, 'cause I was about to find your address, drop this attorney's information in the mail, and delete your number from my phone."

He laughed, but Sierra knew he was serious. She was sure that there was no short supply of women sniffing behind him.

"But," he continued, "none of that matters because we're here together."

She held up her glass of water as if she was toasting him, took a sip, then asked, "You come here a lot, huh?"

He nodded. "This is one of the best places in the city." He paused. "You know what? I didn't ask if you were allergic to anything. Do you like sushi?"

"I haven't had it a lot. Only once, really. I was on a radio tour in Los Angeles a few weeks ago and Rainebow took us to a Thai restaurant. I liked it, but I might like something else on the menu, too."

"No menus here. Masa adjusts what he serves daily based upon how he feels. So, just one menu—he serves everyone the same meal."

"I've never heard of a restaurant like this before."

"Don't worry, I promise you're in for a treat." The waiter returned with a carafe of sake and another young man was right behind him with tuna tartare.

Sierra picked up her fork, but Jarrod reached across the table, rested his hand on hers, bowed his head, and blessed the food.

He said, "Amen," then took a sip of his sake. "So, I'm having dinner with one of Destiny's Divas. How about that."

"It's no more special than having dinner with a congressman. I've never been out with a politician before."

"I guess we're just two special people," he said. "So, how long have you been singing?"

"All my life," she said before she tasted the tartare. She moaned. "This is so good."

"And we're just getting started," he said, pointing to her dish with his fork. Then: "Destiny's Divas is an interesting concept; you're the youngest in the trio?"

She nodded. "Yup, there's me, Liza, and Rainebow."

"Ah, yes. Raine. I met her a long time ago."

"Really?" Sierra put down her fork. "Were you guys friends?"

"No. She came down to North Carolina and a group of us hung out while she was on tour. It was years ago."

She didn't know why it bothered her, but Jarrod knowing Rainebow made her feel unsettled. Yeah, Raine was married now, but she'd been wild back in the day. Had she been wild with Jarrod?

"So . . . are you friends?"

"Me and Raine? Nah." He grinned. "Unless I would be more interesting to you if I said that we *were* friends."

She shook her head. "That wouldn't earn you any points, trust me."

He laughed. "No, I never saw her again. But I have to say that I've always been impressed with her story, and not just how she was raised. I'm talking about what she did with her life. How she pursued a dream, handled it, made the paper, and kept it. She needs to give a class to a bunch of these celebrities on how to surround yourself with folks who are smarter than you." He shook his head as if he had someone in mind. "That's why her world is so tight now. I'd heard that she started a new group."

Sierra nodded, just as the waiter brought their second dish—aji mackerel sashimi. "Yeah, she handpicked me and Liza."

He dabbed the corners of his mouth with his napkin. "The concept is brilliant: testimonies and talent from women in three different decades of their lives. Brilliant," he repeated. "But, how do y'all sing and testify?"

"We're about to go on tour for the first time so we'll see. But the plan is that we sing a few songs, then we talk, then sing more songs . . ." She waved her fork in the air. "You get the picture."

"Sounds exhausting."

"I'm betting that it will be exhausting *and* exhilarating. But, I don't want to talk about Destiny's Divas anymore," she said. "I wanna know what you like to do when you're not out solving all of America's problems."

He laughed out loud and Sierra liked that. Before he could answer, Sierra leaned a bit forward and let her eyes roam over the parts of him that she could see. "Wait, don't tell me," she said, grateful for the excuse to let her eyes linger. "You like to play basketball."

"And you came up with that how?"

Sitting back in her chair, she said, "You're obviously in really good shape. So either you work out in a gym—and I can't imagine you being locked inside too often—or you like to run up and down the court."

"You're a connoisseur of men, huh?"

"Just special men."

He held up his sake cup in a toast to her. "Thank you for the compliment. And for the record, I'm a runner and a basketball player."

She clicked her cup against his.

Over their next courses of uni risotto, Kobe beef sukiyaki, and the best dish—shabu-shabu, composed of fresh lobster and lobes of foie gras—Sierra and Jarrod chatted easily.

Sierra learned that he was raised in North Carolina by so-cially conscious parents who believed education was the great equalizer and the path to all success. His father had been a pro-fessor of African American studies at Duke before he ran for office, while his mother was a high school science teacher, but their millions came from a chain of launderettes that they situ-ated near college campuses. Jarrod spent his summers working in the family business before he attended Hampton University. Four years later, he followed his father and grandfather at Yale Law School.

His story and his being impressed with Raine's history made her adjust her own past just a little when he asked about her.

"I was accepted into Columbia," she said, knowing that wasn't something that could be checked on the Internet. "But then my mother got sick and I had to take care of her. So, I dropped out before I even finished a semester."

That wiped the smile right off his face. "I'm so sorry," he said.

She continued her fairy tale with the story that was part of her official bio: "My mother was very sick. Breast cancer," she said. Every time she repeated this story, she thought about how she was doing her mother a favor by giving her a much more heroic death compared to the one she suffered—her liver shut-ting down because of her years of alcohol abuse. "It was really hard," she continued, "because at the end, my mother could not take care of herself."

Jarrod reached across the table and squeezed her hand. "How long has it been?"

"Six years."

"I'm so sorry, Sierra," he whispered. "You're so young to have lost your mother." He paused as if he wondered if he should ask the next question. "Your father?"

This was the part of her bio where she stuck to the truth, even though she hated having to say that she didn't know her father. She wanted to lie about him, too. She wanted to tell the world that both of her parents had suffered painful but courageous deaths.

The problem with that, though, was that she was afraid that one day her father would pop up. Because isn't that what always happened when a person became famous? Didn't long-lost daddies come crawling out of whatever hole they'd hidden in until they smelled money?

So, she told Jarrod what she told everyone else and prayed that this part of her history didn't make her less valuable to a man like him. "I never knew my father. I don't know if he's dead or alive."

He nodded as if he understood. "What about brothers? Sisters?"

She shook her head. "I'm pretty much on my own."

As the waiter cleared away their plates, Jarrod said, "To be so young, you've been through a lot."

She nodded, wondering if he knew just how old she was. But he'd already said he'd done research on the group, so he probably could give a good guess. "Yeah, I miss having my mom here to see what I'm doing," she said, truthfully. "But, I have a few good friends."

He leaned forward. "I'm hoping you'll let me be one of those friends."

She smiled. "Of course! We're friends already, right?"

He shook his head.

She frowned. That was not the reaction she expected. "What's wrong?"

"I cannot believe some man hasn't swept you up already."

She blinked when an image of Andre flashed through her mind. "I could say that about you. You've got to be the most eligible bachelor in New York."

"Then I guess we're both blessed to have found each other."

That's exactly what she'd been thinking.

"I have something to ask you," he said. Again, he leaned forward, but this time he slid the candle in the center of their table to the side so that he could look directly into Sierra's eyes. "So . . . as part of Destiny's Divas . . . you're the celibate one." It was a statement and a question.

She lowered her eyes, needing time to come up with the best answer. What would impress him the most? She remembered how he'd blessed the food, how he talked about blessings. But then, he was a man. And what man on earth wanted a celibate woman? After a couple of seconds, she said, "I'm not a virgin," she admitted. "But I have been celibate for a few years. All I can say is that for the right person and the right reason, I can separate my personal life from my professional side."

When his lips stretched from a smile into a grin, Sierra knew she'd given the perfect political response. She hadn't really answered the question.

Sierra wasn't sure what she saw in Jarrod's eyes. Lust? Or perhaps appreciation. But whatever it was, she wanted to increase his temperature. Pushing her chair back, she rose slowly until she was standing tall. As she looked down at Jarrod, he looked up at her, and she knew he was wishing he had X-ray vision. She let his eyes trail over her before she said, "I'm going to run to the restroom."

"It's that way," Jarrod said, sounding like something was stuck in his throat.

Sierra smiled, scooped up her purse, and then turned away from Jarrod, grateful that the bathroom was in the direction where he would be able to watch her walk away.

Inside the restroom, she wanted to laugh out loud, clap her hands, jump up and down. This night couldn't have been any more perfect. He was even better than his résumé: he was kind and gentle, funny and smart. And the fact that he was fine as all get-out and came from a family of means only added to what she already knew—Jarrod Cannon was going to be her perfect husband.

Now all she had to do was convince him that she was going to be his perfect wife.

# CHAPTER 18

## *Liza*

For the first time in their twenty-eight years of marriage, Mann had carried his attitude beyond a few hours. For days now, he mumbled his hellos and good-byes and hardly said a word to Liza in between. It was only in church on Sunday that he'd made any effort, giving their congregants the full act. He'd greeted the church the way he did every Sunday, talked about his beautiful bride the way he did before every sermon, and stood by Liza's side the way he did after every service.

But once they returned home, Mann's tantrum continued. He locked himself inside the office, leaving her alone with her thoughts.

Even Buddy, though speaking to her, was distant. As if he was afraid to get too close.

Their silence, which was supposed to be a deterrent, was actually an accelerant, propelling her to seek and find.

But she had no clues. Even hanging around the church more than she usually did yielded nothing. There was no talk, not even whispers. It seemed like only Mann and Buddy knew what was going on.

Liza guessed that was a good thing; at least the potential

scandal was contained. But it still loomed, and yesterday she'd decided to go straight to the men who were handling the issue—the attorneys. She'd googled their contact information and for the last two days had called their offices. But neither Tom Brody nor Stan Weitzman answered any of her dozens of messages.

As if an unreturned phone call could stop her. Since the telephone wasn't working, her plan for tomorrow was to march right down to lower Manhattan. She'd have a sit-in at their offices. She'd stay until they came in or walked out, but by tomorrow's end, somebody was going to tell her something more.

Her mind was on her plan as she pulled into her garage and slid out of the car, and before she could even insert the key in the door, it swung open.

It shocked her, at first. Yes, she knew that Mann was home. Even in his anger, he still shared his schedule with her. But she'd expected him to be upstairs in the office, still hiding out.

Now, though, he stood in front of her as if he wanted to talk.

"Hi," she said tentatively as she stepped past him.

"Hey."

His voice didn't sound as hard or as cold as it'd been, but still she moved as if she was tiptoeing around a land mine. She held her breath as she moved into the foyer, dropped her bag onto the settee, then began to unbutton her coat.

"Here." He grabbed the collar of her fur and slid it over her shoulders. "I got you."

It wasn't his manners that surprised her, it was just that he was coming to her with any kind of grace. "O-kay."

Liza watched Mann as he hung the coat in the closet, then faced her. "Can we talk?" he asked in a tone filled with the love that she was used to.

Even though he spoke softly, gently, inside, Liza still sighed. She was too tired to go a round with Mann and that's where this conversation would surely lead.

But she followed him into the living room and waited until he sat on the sofa before she sat on the opposite end, crossing her arms and her legs at the same time.

"Tom Brody called me today," Mann began.

*Oh, Lawd.*

"He said you called their offices a couple of times."

"Is that what he said?" Her tone was filled with her attitude. "'Cause it was far more than a couple of times." She paused. "Did he ask you to give me a message? Like an explanation for why he hasn't returned my calls?"

He looked down at his clasped hands, shook his head. "Liza, you really have to drop this."

"If this is what you want to talk about, then we should drop *this*. 'Cause I'm not dropping anything."

He blew out a long breath. "Okay." He paused. "I'll tell you what I can. But after that, if you don't drop it we're gonna lose these attorneys, and we need them."

She nodded.

"The reason I didn't want to say anything is because what's going on affects far more than just Buddy." Liza's eyes narrowed as she listened. "Something happened . . . with one of the girls. . . ." He paused, and his mouth closed, then opened, then closed again, as if he was struggling to say the rest.

Liza pressed her hand against her chest. A girl? She was thinking a woman, a married woman, a deacon's wife. "One of the girls from Deliver Our Daughters?"

He glanced at her for a second, then returned to looking at his clasped hands.

"Oh, my God," Liza gasped. "Buddy—did he"—her voice lowered when she finished with—"did he molest one of our girls?" Even as she asked the question, it was so unbelievable to her. Her cousin would never do anything like that.

"No . . . no! It wasn't like that," Mann said. "Trust me, it wasn't molestation. It's just that one of the girls . . . her mother . . . wants some money, so she's throwing around accusations and seeing if something will stick."

Liza blinked rapidly. "Are you saying that someone is just straight-out lying on Buddy?"

"Yeah."

*Unbelievable.* But then she had to ask, "Are you sure . . . they're lying?"

Now he was the one with wide eyes. "Yes. We're talking about Buddy. You know your cousin."

She nodded. "You're right. I know that."

Of course Buddy would never do anything like this. Getting a woman pregnant—yes. A married woman—maybe. Being involved with a young girl—no. Definitely not.

This would be a major scandal. Thank God it wasn't true.

"Who is it? Who's the girl accusing Buddy?"

"It's not her, it's her mother." He paused as if he didn't want to tell her, but knew that if he didn't she would never leave it alone. "It's Qianna's mother."

Liza blinked fast. "Oh, my God, Mann, remember when I told you about what she said at the dinner? About Qianna spending too much time at the church?"

"I remember. I think that's when she began setting this whole thing up."

"But why? Why would she lie on Buddy this way?"

Mann made a sound, a half grunt, half chuckle. "Liza, there're so many people who look at us, who are jealous, who want what we have. They will accuse us of anything."

"She's not accusing us, she's accusing Buddy."

"To her it's the same thing. But it doesn't matter because it's not true. And Tom and Stan just need some time to work on this without it getting out."

"Okay. I get it." She nodded. "I won't say anything."

"And I don't need you looking at Buddy any differently because he didn't do anything."

"I know." She paused. "Thank you for believing in him."

"Of course. I know Buddy; he's innocent." Mann slid closer to her on the couch. "But, sweetheart, to protect Buddy, to protect Deliver Our Daughters, to protect our church, we've got to play this the way the attorneys want."

"I wish we could just stand up and call Qianna's mother a liar."

"Liza . . ."

"I know."

He moved even closer. "We've got to leave everything to the attorneys. We've got to play this their way because they've dealt with issues like this before, we haven't."

"You're right."

"And if you talk . . . and if we mess it up . . . there's so much at stake." He took her hand. "I need you to believe in me."

"I do."

He shifted once again and now he was so close to her that their legs were pressed together. "And though all of my faith is in God, I know that Tom and Stan are the ones who can fix this, with our cooperation."

She nodded as he squeezed her hand.

"So," he continued, "no more phone calls, no more questions. We'll let those guys just do their job, okay?"

He didn't give her a chance to answer. Before she could make a move, he pressed his lips onto hers. What she expected was just the perfunctory kiss. The one he gave her every day. The one that made her feel like his sister. But today he stayed right there. And parted his lips. And gently pushed his tongue inside.

Her moan was involuntary as he nudged her back against the arm of the couch and pressed his body on top of hers. He kissed her deeply, as if he never planned to stop, and Liza wanted to scream that she never wanted this moment to end.

When he pulled away, she cried out, but he was gone for only seconds. Just enough time to slip her sweater over her head. Just enough time to undress her so that she was naked from the waist up. Then his lips were back on hers, and together they released her from her skirt and everything she wore below.

She was totally naked, though he was not, when he lifted her into his arms. Their lips were still connected as he carried her through the living room.

"Where're we going?" she breathed.

"To the bedroom. I'm dying to make love to my beautiful bride."

All she wanted to do was kiss him again, but she had to say, "You can't carry me up the stairs!"

"Watch me."

They giggled like teenagers as he struggled, wobbling with every step. But at the top, where Mann became steady, their lips met again, and inside the bedroom, he stripped within seconds.

For hours, he loved her as he used to, taking her back to the days when they first got married. He caressed her as if he worshipped her, taking his time as his fingers traveled over the womanly curves of her body. Then his lips followed as well. He kissed her, stroked her, sang to her, made her cry out over and over again.

Afterward, he held her, and in the dark of their bedroom, he sang more songs as she rested in his arms. At the end of every song, he told her again just how much he loved her.

"You'll always be my beautiful bride," he said.

All Liza could do was smile, thank God for this time, and pray that they would unite like this again . . . soon.

A moment before her eyes closed for sleep, he told her again, "Don't say anything to anyone about what I told you today. Let's end the discussion right here in bed."

"Okay," she moaned.

"You promise?"

"I do."

And then he whispered/sang "Endless Love" until she fell asleep.


With the stainless steel whisk, Liza scrambled the eggs, hard . . . just the way Mann liked them.

"What's that I smell?"

Liza jumped a little, hearing Mann's voice. The sound of his steps had been muted in the carpet.

"Are you making me breakfast?" Mann asked as he embraced her from behind and loosened the belt on her robe.

"Mann!" she shrieked with glee when he opened her bath-robe. Her skin felt cool against the sudden air, then heated up quick as the tips of his fingers traveled from her stomach up, up, up. "Stop!" She giggled.

"All right," he said, and backed away.

As he grabbed the newspaper on the table, Mann missed the disappointment that washed over Liza's face. She didn't really mean for him to stop. She would've let these eggs burn—hell, the whole house could've burnt down if it meant that she could have a little bit more of her husband.

She wasn't about to complain, though. The memories of the trip she'd taken to heaven last night would last her for weeks.

As she scooped the eggs onto a plate, her body still tingled in the places where he'd done things that she thought he'd forgotten.

Smiling, and with her robe still open, she sauntered to the table with his plate in her hand. When she placed it in front of him, he lowered the newspaper and grinned. But his eyes were on her eyes, not her body. "You're not eating?"

She shook her head. "You know how it is when I cook," she said, "I'm not hungry."

"Well, do you have a few minutes? I just want you to sit down here with me." He patted his leg.

"Really?" She grinned. "You really want me to sit on your lap?"

He nodded.

This was something he had done all the time in the early days of their marriage. The two couldn't sit in a room together without him wanting Liza on his lap, holding her, caressing her.

Then she'd gotten pregnant and those days were over.

But now he wanted to take her back to that time. Liza almost jumped over the table, eager to be close to her husband again.

"Last night, I broke your back. Now, you want me to break your knee?" she asked, even as she lowered her hips onto his leg.

He laughed. "Do you really think my back was broken?" He nuzzled her neck and she giggled. "See? You're fine, trust me."

Liza hugged Mann as she thought about their talk and the love they'd made last night. Yes, she would trust Mann because that's what she was called to do. And the truth of it all? Liza was glad to give up the fight.

Mann told her the truth of what was going on and now she could leave it up to him, the attorneys, and God to handle it all.

# CHAPTER 19

## *Sierra*

*It* had only been two weeks since they first met, and three days since their first date. But Sierra had no doubt. Jarrod's nose—as her mother used to say—was wide open.

Actually, it started on their date on Tuesday. When she'd returned to the table at Masa, Jarrod was sitting on the edge of his chair.

"There's still so much I want to know about you," he began as he signed the check. "I wish I didn't have to go back to Washington."

She lowered her eyes slightly when she whispered, "Do you really have to?"

His smile told her that he was pleased with her words, and so was she. That was one of her mother's lessons—let the man know how much you've enjoyed him.

"If I didn't have a vote tomorrow, I'd stay in New York for one more day."

Inside, her stomach had fluttered, but on the outside, she said, "Oh, well."

Yes, she wanted him to know that she'd enjoyed him and that

she would love to see him again, but . . . he had to also feel like if it didn't happen, her life would certainly go on.

"So what are we going to do about this, Ms. Dixon?" he'd asked as he helped her rise from her chair.

She shrugged as if it was no big deal. "Guess we'll just have to wait till next time."

"Definitely. Next time."

On the ride home, Sierra and Jarrod had chatted as if they'd known each other for a few years rather than just days. He told her about his hopes to sponsor a major urban jobs bill in Congress that could catapult his career to the next level. She told him about her excitement with her dreams finally coming true with Destiny's Divas.

When the car had stopped in front of her apartment, Jarrod had accompanied her to the front of the brownstone, and she held the door to the vestibule open, but didn't step inside. "Thank you for being such a gentleman, but I can get upstairs. I'll be just fine."

"I'm gonna walk you all the way to your door, Golden Lady."

She looked away from him as if she were shy. Then she shook her head.

He'd chuckled as he leaned against the glass door. "I really like your style, but one thing you've got to know—I always make sure that the lady is safely behind her closed and locked door."

"I'm already safe," she said.

"Why don't we do this?" He pulled his cell phone from his pocket. "I'll stand right here, and as soon as you get inside, call me. Then I'll leave." He had kissed her cheek, said, "Good night, Golden Lady," and then watched as she climbed the first flight of stairs.

She had called the moment she was in her apartment and that was when he asked, "What are you doing tomorrow? Maybe you could fly down to Washington with me?"

She had pumped her fist in the air, but all he heard was her laughter as if his words had to be a joke. "Good night, Congressman," she'd said. She'd heard him sigh before he hung up, and she went to sleep with the ecstasy of victory on her mind.

The next morning, Sierra was awakened by a thunderous knock on her front door that shocked her out of her dreams. She'd trudged into the front room and peeked through the peephole. She saw no one.

"Yes?" she yelled out.

No answer.

"Who is it?"

Still no response.

She wasn't about to open the door since anyone coming up to her apartment had to ring the intercom. Unless, of course, it was the snooping super trying to sneak a peek at her in her nightgown.

But after a few minutes, curiosity made her open the door, cautiously. She peered into the hallway. Nothing. Until she looked down and saw the one dozen lavender roses. The flowers rested on the floor, left alone with only a lavender-colored envelope centered in the middle of the arrangement.

The flowers' fragrance filled her small apartment the moment she brought them inside, and she couldn't tug the card from the envelope fast enough.

*Thank you for a wonderful evening. Looking forward to many more.*

There was no signature, but no signature was needed. She'd called to thank Jarrod, and once again he'd asked, "You're sure you don't want to take a trip down here to Washington just for the day . . . and night?"

His question had made Sierra shiver, but she'd snickered as she had the night before. "Now, Congressman, what would you really think of me if I did that?"

"You're right," he said, sounding like a chastened child. "I'm feeling you just the way you are."

"I like you, too," she said.

"So, what about Friday? Can I see you then?"

"You'll be back in New York?"

"Yeah, but it'll be late. Think you'll be able to come out and play?"

She laughed. "I can't wait."

From that moment until now, it had been difficult for Sierra to not think about Jarrod. From work at the bookstore, through conferences with Yvonne, Jarrod stayed on her mind. He was even affecting the way she watched TV. At five every night, she rushed home from work to catch whichever show was on MSNBC hoping to get a glimpse of Jarrod and, in the process, trying to learn everything she could about his world.

While she was pining for him, she knew that he was doing the same. For the last three mornings, his voice was the first she heard when he called to wake her up.

"I'm looking forward to Friday," he said every time they spoke.

Now, as she stood in the vestibule of her brownstone waiting for him, she peeked at every car that turned onto 123rd Street. She'd been worried for a moment tonight. He hadn't called at eight as he said he would. She'd paced her apartment, dialed his number at least fifty times, and cursed him every time her call went to voice mail. Was he trying to get away from her already?

It was almost eleven when he finally called. "There was a storm in DC. I just landed and I'm on my way, Golden Lady."

"Great," she'd told him, thankful that she hadn't left him any crazy messages.

His car rolled to a stop in front of her building and she darted down the stairs in her jeans and bomber jacket just as Jarrod slipped out of the back of the car.

"Hey," he said as he held his arms out to hug her. "You didn't have to come down; I would've buzzed you."

"I know, but I didn't want you to have to wait." She embraced him and then, for extra measure, gave him a soft kiss, though it was nothing but lips.

Inside the car, he held her hand. "I'm glad to see you."

"Me too," she said, "though for a moment, I wasn't sure if you were going to make it."

He squeezed her hand. "I'm sorry, but there was nothing I could do about the storm." He leaned closer to her. "I'm leaving all that stuff about storms stopping and waters parting to God."

She laughed. "So, what are we gonna do?"

"Well, I've arranged to have a light dinner delivered—to my place, if you don't mind."

The ends of her lips quivered as she tried her best not to break out in a smile. "I don't mind," she said. "Just dinner, right?"

He stared at her for a moment, as if that was the last thing he'd expected her to say.

"Right."

With a nod, she turned her head the other way and studied the familiar buildings on Eighth Avenue. From the moment he'd asked her on this date, she'd debated whether she'd give herself to him tonight. In the past, this wouldn't have even been a question. She would've been planning to lay it on him so thick that by morning he would've been asking her to move in.

But that's what a woman did when she wanted a boyfriend; she was going for the gusto.

Still, the questions played in her mind as Jarrod chatted: Should I or shouldn't I? Will I or won't I?

"People have no idea how Washington works," he said. "I've only been there a few weeks, but I can already tell it's not about governing, it's about winning. It has nothing to do with the people who voted us in."

Sierra had watched enough MSNBC to respond, "It seems that way. The Republicans want to do anything to make sure President Obama is a one-term president," she said, repeating something she'd heard Melissa Harris-Perry say.

"That's true, but don't be fooled. There're a few Democrats who can't believe they're calling a black man Mr. President, either," he said as the car slowed in front of one of the older buildings on 110th Street. "It's just that the GOP is more vocal about their racism."

Sierra was glad the car came to stop because she didn't have a comeback for that. What was the GOP? She'd have to google it as soon as she had a moment.

This time Sierra didn't try to get out of the car. She waited until Harold opened Jarrod's door and then she slid across the seat, taking his hand. He held her as he led her into the lobby of the building that gave the feeling of a loft, with it's brick walls and exposed shiny steel pipes.

The doorman grinned. "Welcome home, Congressman," he said before he nodded to Sierra. "Miss."

The two stayed silent as they rode the elevator to the top floor and Jarrod didn't say another word until he pushed opened the door to his apartment. "Welcome to my home."

This building had smelled of money the moment she'd entered the lobby, but she still wasn't ready for this. She couldn't help but gasp the moment she stepped inside. It was the expansive floor-to-ceiling windows that took her breath away. A front-row view of Central Park was sprawled in front of them.

She strode across the apartment until she stood right in front of the windows. "This is amazing," she whispered, taking in the sights of the park and Central Park West.

It wasn't until Jarrod came up behind her that she remembered she wasn't alone.

"You like?" he said softly into her ear.

She turned and faced him, and with their lips just inches apart, she said, "I do."

In that instant, she made her decision. She would not get into bed with Jarrod tonight.

This was going to be a battle, though, because even in the darkened apartment she could see, could feel his bedroom eyes drawing her in. And against her will, she leaned forward, expecting their lips to meet.

But then he stepped back, and flicked on the light, brightening the room.

Her eyes did a quick survey of the wide-open loft-style apartment. Like the lobby, every wall here was red brick, and above, steel pipes framed the perimeter of the grand room, which comprised a living room, library area, kitchen, and dining room in a space that was twice the size of her 600-square-foot apartment. The room was furnished with ultramodern pieces and stainless steel accents.

She nodded in approval. "This is really nice," she said. "I need to hire your decorator."

He followed her glance around the room. "Sure. What do you need? But, I have to warn you, I don't come cheap."

"You decorated yourself?"

He nodded.

"Wow."

This time, when he stepped back over to her, their lips were even closer than before. All she wanted to do was reach out and kiss him.

He said, "I hope to get a lot more wows from you." Then he surprised her, stepping away once again. The heels of his shoes clicked against the mahogany floor as he walked. "I'm going to get out of this suit. Make yourself at home."

When she heard the bedroom door close, she released a quiet squeal. She wanted to get down on her knees right there and thank Andre for setting her free and thank God for setting her up.

She strolled through the grand room, taking in every part of it. The soft leather of the chocolate sofa and two matching love seats, the Bose stereo system on the stainless steel stand, and the flat-screen TV framed against the wall. It was all so urban, so chic.

In front of the window again, Sierra inhaled as if she could become a part of this life just by taking it in. She could not believe this blessing.

But didn't she deserve every bit of this? She'd had a hard life, and now God had opened the door with this grand prize behind it. Her heart was thumping as she offered up a quiet prayer, "Thank you, Lord. Thank you for making this man my husband."

On cue the bedroom door opened, but this time she didn't

hear his steps. He was barefoot, now in jeans and a tailored white shirt. Just looking at him in all of his fineness made Sierra want to . . .

*No!*

She had to stick with her plan.

"Sorry, I was on the phone with Harold," he explained. "He'll pick up our dinner once we decide what we want."

That's what she needed. Food. Not that she was hungry—at least not for anything to eat. But food would keep her mind off of other things and help her to remember her ultimate goal.

"So, what would you like, Golden Lady?"

*Just you.* "Why don't you order?"

"I'm not that hungry . . . except for . . ." He looked at her.

*Please, Lord. Help me!*

He said, "Except for maybe a salad. Something we could share?"

"That's cool," she said, turning back to the window.

As Jarrod made his call, Sierra watched his reflection in the window as he paced and talked. She took in every part of him: his six-foot frame that always looked like he was standing at attention, his hands that cut through the air as he spoke as if he was conducting a symphony, and his eyes—even from across the room she could see his eyes, which were always smiling when he looked at her. She folded her arms across her chest and shivered. She could see it already, easily. She could see herself in this apartment, in that kitchen, whipping together his favorite meals—after she'd had a few cooking lessons.

"Okay, Harold's on his way."

"What?" She had to blink a couple of times to drag herself back from her fantasy.

"Harold. He'll be back with our salads in about ten minutes.

But in the meantime . . ." He strolled over to her. "Are you going to stay like that all night?"

"Like what?"

She didn't realize that her arms were crossed until he reached for one of her hands and then the other. "Are you going to keep on your jacket all night?"

"Oh." She hadn't realized that she still had on her bomber, but before she could shrug it from her shoulders, he was behind her. She could feel his breath on her neck, as he slipped the jacket down her arms. And even once it was off, he stayed close.

*Lord, hear my cry!*

She closed her eyes as he wrapped his arms around her. Her heart pounded, but then she realized she felt his heart beat, too.

All she wanted to do was spin around and kiss him. But if she did, her plan would be over. She'd have him in bed in ten seconds flat.

Then his lips grazed her neck, and she almost fainted when she felt his tongue right behind her ear. That was it, she lost the battle. There was nothing else she could do. She was ready to sex him up!

Turning, she wrapped her arms around his neck, and for the first time, their lips met intimately. Their kiss was slow, soft, and long. Even though she felt as if she hadn't been kissed in years, Sierra held her passion back and let the kiss just be a kiss.

When he finally pulled away, she was ready to drop her panties, right then, right there.

"Wow!" he said. "I haven't had a kiss like that in . . ."

"Me neither."

Taking her hand, he led her away from the window. "I'm going to ask that you sit"—he surprised her when they stopped in front of the couch—"right here. Or else you might end up in another room in this apartment, which is really where I want to take you."

She wanted to tell him that she was ready to follow him, but she just settled onto the sofa, waiting to see how this would play out. Across from her, Jarrod pressed a button on the wall and she was surrounded by the soothing sounds of jazz.

She was more into hip-hop and rap, or at least that's what the boys she'd been with were into. Right now, if she had been at Andre's apartment, the volume of the bass would have had the walls vibrating.

Sierra sank into the comfort of the couch and the music as Jarrod left her alone and ventured into the kitchen. He returned with two wineglasses filled with Chardonnay. He held one out to her.

"I should've asked. I hope you like white wine."

"I do," she said, and wondered how many more times she would say those two words tonight.

He sat on the other end of the sofa, far away from her, and held up his glass. "Here's to a wonderful evening."

She held her glass up, too, then took a sip. Her hands trembled slightly as she wrapped her fingers around the stem. How was she supposed to do this? Get through a night with wine, and jazz, and him . . . and keep her clothes on at the same time?

But then the doorbell rang, saving her at least for the moment, and after he answered, Jarrod returned with a shopping bag. "Dinner is served."

"Great! Can I help you?"

"Sure." He grinned. "We'll just be casual and eat here at the bar."

She flowed through his kitchen, finding everything they needed; Sierra arranged the place settings while Jarrod opened the aluminum containers. It was just a few minutes, but she loved the feeling of standing side by side with him, preparing their dinner together as if they'd done this before, as if they'd do this again.

When they finally sat at the bar, he held her hand as he blessed the food. Then, as the music still played, they took their time over their dinner. They sipped wine, shared the salad, chatted about Destiny's Divas and Congress.

It was after midnight by the time they finished, and she offered to clean up, but he left the few dishes that they'd used in the sink. Filling their glasses once again, Jarrod led Sierra back to the couch. As before, she sat on one end and he was at the other.

But after he took one sip, he said, "I have a question for you, Golden Lady."

Her heart pounded. Was he ready to tell her that he wanted a relationship? Had he already fallen in love with her?

He leaned against the back of the couch. She rocked forward, waiting to hear every one of his words.

Jarrod said, "Why aren't you married? As intelligent and sweet and . . . look at you." He shook his head. "I don't get it."

"Well, I'm not going to lie," she said, looking down at her hands. "I've had several proposals." She looked up and into his eyes. "But after what my mother went through with my father . . . or should I say what she didn't go through . . ."

"Your mother never married?"

Sierra shook her head. "She held out hope that my father would come back, but . . ." She stopped and looked away when she added, "I take marriage seriously. I want something that will be real, that will last."

He nodded, letting her words sink in.

When he didn't say anything, she said, "I could ask you the same question: Why aren't you married?"

He shrugged. "I had this great plan for my life. I was going to finish law school by the time I was twenty-three, be married by the time I was twenty-five, have children, run for local office, then head down to Washington. I was going to do all of that before I was thirty." He placed his glass on the table. "I'm thirty-one." He shook his head. "Some of my plans worked out and some didn't. It's like you said, I want something real. My parents are still married . . . thirty-five years. That's what I want with the woman who'll be my wife."

"Sounds like we want the same things, but I guess neither one of us has found the right person."

He kept his eyes right on hers when he lifted his glass. "Here's to finding the right person."

As he brought his glass to his lips, she just held on to hers. She wanted to discuss this further. She knew he was talking about her—she was the right person for him. But she bit the side of her bottom lip and kept quiet.

He put his glass down and motioned for her to do the same. Then he held his arms open and slowly she fell into his embrace.

They stayed that way as song after song played until Jarrod whispered, "All I want to do is take you to bed right now and make love to you all night long."

She shuddered. *Let's go.*

"But, I like who you are. I like that you aren't ready to fall into bed with me. I like that you're a woman who knows that she's worth more than her sexuality."

*Oh, my God!*

"And since I really want to see how things grow with us, I'm with you. We'll take this slow, all right?"

She didn't look up at him. Only nodded, then kicked her shoes off before she curled her legs onto the couch.

"I want you to stay with me tonight," he said. "I promise, I'm not going to do anything more than hold you like this."

She held him even tighter, and wondered why she felt like she was going to cry. Maybe it was because she could finally believe in fairy tales. Because right now it felt like every dream she'd ever had was coming true.

She released a deep breath, a cleansing breath. She closed her eyes and in his arms she fell into the deepest, most peaceful sleep.

# CHAPTER 20

## *Raine*

Raine glanced at her watch as she stepped into the sanctuary. She had at least an hour before the others arrived.

Her steps were silent as she moved across the thick carpet toward the altar. Pausing at the second row, she slipped inside, thinking that it was best not to sit in the front pew. Even though the pastor's wife wouldn't be there until the show began, the front row was reserved at all times for Lady Jasmine.

Raine shrugged her coat from her shoulders, blew on the tips of her fingers to warm them, then sat in the peace of the quiet. She wanted this time to offer up a prayer of thanksgiving for all that God had done with her family—especially Beerlulu.

She'd told everyone that Beerlulu having her own apartment was going to work out—and it had. Ten days had passed since she'd moved and even though the relationship between Raine and Beerlulu wasn't warm, it was thawing.

Raine had made every effort, beginning the morning after Beerlulu had spent her first night alone. She had knocked on her mother-in-law's door a little after seven.

Beerlulu had greeted her with a grunt and a frown, and after Raine said, "Good morning," she presented her with a gift.

"What is this?" Beerlulu had asked gruffly.

"It's a Lamborghini coffeemaker, just like the one Dayo uses. I knew you liked it and so I ordered it for you, and it came last night."

Beerlulu's lips looked like they were cemented together, but she'd grabbed the gift from Raine's hands.

Right before she closed the door, Raine asked, "Are you all right? Is everything okay?"

Her mother-in-law had arched a single eyebrow, then, without another word, closed the door in Raine's face.

The next morning, Raine showed up—again, right before seven—and even though she had a key, she knocked, and when Beerlulu answered, she gave her two plants. On the third day, Beerlulu was at the door waiting for Raine when she handed her a handmade black, red, and green afghan so that Beerlulu could proudly display the colors of the Kenyan flag over the sofa in her living room, and the next day she gifted her the rainsticks that had been in Beerlulu's bedroom when she was living with them.

By this morning, when Raine arrived with a lectern Bible that could be propped up on a table, Beerlulu had said, "Thank you."

Just thinking about those two words now made Raine smile. Made her look up at that giant golden cross behind the altar. Made her thank God once again.

It was official—it looked like one day she and Dayo and Nadia . . . and Beerlulu would all have their happy ending. For that Raine was grateful and she wanted God to know it.


City of Lights at Riverside was a different kind of church.

Over the last year, a production wing had been added so

that the pastor, Hosea Bush, could tape some of his cable shows directly from the church. Sierra, Raine, and Liza waited in the green room in the production annex.

In the corner, the grandfather clock ticked the minutes by, but the three sat in the oversized chairs in their separate corners, studying their notes.

Raine smiled when Liza put down her note cards, closed her eyes, and bowed her head. But Raine's smile turned upside down when she turned to Sierra just as she tossed her note cards aside and picked up her cell phone.

Now Sierra was texting so furiously that if she hadn't been grinning, Raine would have been sure that something was wrong.

Clearly, though, all was well in Sierra's world. She typed, then stopped, then laughed. Typed, then stopped, then laughed.

"You got everything together, Sierra?" Raine asked. "You ready for this?"

Sierra didn't even look at her when she shrugged. "Sure," she said as she texted and talked at the same time. "I mean, what could I possibly do now to be more ready? It is what it is."

"Well, you could be studying your notes. Or going over the words to the songs in your head."

Sierra looked up. "I know what I'm going to say. And if the words to the songs haven't changed since yesterday, then I'm good there, too." She paused and added, "I don't have a problem memorizing anything. I'm twenty-five."

Raine squinted and wondered if her words were meant to be an insult. "I know how old you are. I'm just trying to pass on wisdom. I know what it takes to get onstage and perform. You have to be focused, you have to be ready."

Liza jumped up as if she knew this conversation would not

come to a good end. "You know what? I think the best way to prepare is to pray." She took Sierra's hand, then reached for Raine's. As they stood in their purple gowns, Liza led them before the Lord.

The moment Liza said, "Amen," Yvonne knocked on the door.

Peeking inside, she said, "Divas, are you ready?"

The three nodded, and held hands as they followed Yvonne to the stage.

# CHAPTER 21

## Destiny's Divas

Pastor Hosea Bush's voice boomed into the hallway where they waited now. "Saints, this is a very special night."

"Amen," many shouted.

"Destiny's Divas . . ." was all Pastor Bush had a chance to say and the sanctuary erupted with applause.

Liza smiled as she stood between Sierra and Raine. But though she tingled with joy, her singing sisters wore no smiles. Both had their heads bowed as if they were still in prayer.

So Liza bowed her head, too, and prayed that the three testimonies they were about to give would go forth in truth and reach the ears of those who needed to hear. She was still praying when she heard the thunderous applause once again and Yvonne said, "You're on, Divas!" handing each a cordless microphone.

The members of City of Lights were on their feet cheering, especially for Sierra and Raine, who were their own.

"What's going on, City of Lights?" Raine asked, sending the sanctuary into more of a frenzy.

She stood in the center of the stage while Sierra and Liza flanked her on opposite sides.

"Thank you," all three said over and over. They waved at their fans, who cheered as if they never planned to stop.

After long minutes, Raine said, "Please be seated. We want to start singing for y'all."

Now laughter filled the sanctuary, and it still took moments for the thousands to quiet down.

"Thank you," they all said, and then Raine spoke. "What a welcome. And we thank you for being here. This is the first stop on our upcoming national tour."

Again, applause.

"As always, we must first give glory and honor to God. . . ." Raine said as Sierra and Liza nodded.

"And next, we have to thank our very own pastor and first lady—Pastor and Mrs. Bush, or Lady Jasmine, as we all call her."

The congregants were back on their feet as Jasmine and Hosea stood. And Lady Jasmine waved as if she was Miss America.

Once they settled down, Raine said, "We are so glad to be here because for me and Sierra, City of Lights is our home. This is where the idea of Destiny's Divas was birthed inside of me."

More cheers.

"And even though First Lady Liza Washington isn't a member, she is our sister in Christ. Amen?"

"Amen!"

"So tonight we're going to give you a preview of our new CD!" She held her fist in the air and received another round of applause. "And we're gonna have some real talk about the wonders and love of the Lord and how He plays out in every minute of our lives. Amen?"

"Amen!"

"So let's begin with a song that I wrote about how we should just lay our sorrows at the altar, and after we get off our knees, let's stand up with joy. That's the name of this song—'Joy.'"

With a nod of her head, the track began filling the sanctuary with the sweet sounds of a saxophone, and the three began, "Enter into the joy of the Lord . . ."

That was all they were able to get out before the cheering started again, but then the crowd settled and sang along, thousands of backup singers. They sang and swayed to the familiar words that Raine had written and performed at many Sunday services.

The choreography was simple since this first performance was in a church rather than on the massive stage of an arena, but there was enough room for the Divas to saunter across the stage, passing one another, pausing and posing in the positions that they'd practiced.

At the end of "Joy," Raine led them straight into the second song, "Love Unlimited," and this time the praise dancers of City of Lights joined Destiny's Divas on the stage. The dancers swayed with each note, their bodies their instruments, and they all worshipped together.

The sanctuary was humming as Destiny's Divas brought the second song to an end. The congregants held their hands high as they prayed and praised and Sierra, Raine, and Liza joined them. For long minutes the thousands were together in one accord, one message. In those moments it was just about worshipping God.

Finally, the three held hands and bowed to a standing ovation. Then Raine and Liza stepped back to be seated on the stools that had been set out for them. Sierra stood in the center of the stage and waited until they were both seated.

"I'm so happy to be here to share with you what God has

done for me. How He's led me through life and how He's been my father because I never knew my biological dad." She paused and took a breath. "Maybe that's why God's so important to me." With her forefinger, she pointed toward the heavens. "He's my daddy. Although I know that God wanted my biological father to take care of me, when he didn't, God did. God taught me what I needed to know. He loved me when I needed to be loved. He held me when I needed to be held. And He even disciplined me when I needed that."

Sierra looked out at the thousands, grateful that she was wearing a gown that hid her knocking knees.

She kept on. "To be honest with you, all I've ever wanted, all I've ever needed I got from God. My mother . . . she did the best she could. But the best thing she did for me was send me to church with a neighbor when I was just seven years old. That was where I learned about God. I learned to talk to Him and to listen when He talked to me. And the best thing I learned was about His love.

"It's because of how He's loved me that I want to please Him. That's why I stand on First Samuel chapter fifteen every day of my life. I know that God wants us to obey Him. He says that obedience is better than sacrifice. To me that means that even though God wants our sacrifice in terms of time and money and effort, what He wants more is for us to just do what He asks. And how can I not after all He's done?"

Sierra paused, closed her eyes, and sent up a quick, silent prayer. *Forgive me.* "That's why I know that with God true love waits. I'm waiting for the love God has chosen for me. That's why I'm saved . . . single . . . and celibate!"

Thousands cheered, and while she paused during the ovation, Sierra wondered how many of those applauding were in the same exact bed she was in. Because there couldn't possibly be this many celibate people in the church. There were too many little ones running around in Sunday school for this much celibacy.

When the clapping stopped, she continued, "I can't say that I *want* to be celibate, but what I want more than sex is for God to be pleased with me. I'm doing this because in the end all I want to hear are the words that we all pray the Lord will say to us: 'Well done!'"

The masses stood to their feet and once again the applause was loud and long.

Raine and Liza came to Sierra's side, and as each hugged her, she closed her eyes and once again asked God to forgive her. Then she thanked Him for making it impossible for Jarrod to be here tonight. Her plan was to keep him away from all of her concerts—at least until after she had him in bed. She didn't want him hearing too much about how she wanted to be celibate.

While the crowd was still standing, the musical track began, and this time they performed a song by another artist.

With her eyes closed, Sierra began, "I will lift up my eyes to the hills from which cometh my help. . . ."

Again, the audience sang with her and swayed with her and praised with her. At the chorus, Raine and Liza joined in, and thousands sang the words, "All of my help cometh from the Lord."

This time the audience was more subdued when Sierra and Liza walked toward the stools at the back of the stage and left Raine up front and center.

Through the thousands, Raine searched for Dayo and Nadia. She smiled when she saw them, sitting in their usual Sunday seats. First row, the center of the balcony. Her eyes stayed on them a few moments too long. Where was Beerlulu?

Nadia waved, but Raine turned away. When she first became a performer, she'd been taught never to focus on anyone she knew—and this was exactly why. It was a distraction. Now she would have that image of Dayo and Nadia, without Beerlulu, in her head.

After all she had done, after the effort she had made. Beerlulu hadn't even come to support her on one of her biggest nights? What happened to the progress she felt they'd been making?

*That's okay,* she told herself. The people who she loved the most were here.

She pasted on the smile that she'd worn the hundreds of times before when she'd graced the stage. It was her performance smile, which had nothing to do with who she really was or what was really going on in her life. It was all about entertainment.

"People look at my life and say that I have it all," she began with a slight shrug. "And I do. I have a husband whose love for me is unconditional, and my love for him is the same. And truly, we both love our daughter the same way." She fought hard to keep her eyes on the masses and not let her gaze wander up once again to the balcony.

"On top of all that God has blessed me with in my home life, I have been given this fabulous career. Looking out, looking in, I do have it all. My life is possible because my husband and I are in one accord. We do this together. We do this with unconditional love."

Now she couldn't help it. Raine glanced up at the balcony, and many in the audience knew that she was looking at her husband. When the applause started, she smiled. And this time she did wave to Dayo and Nadia.

"I couldn't do this," she began again, "I couldn't have this life, without my husband's approval. Now, some of you may find the word *approval* offensive, but I'm not talking about my husband letting me do something or not letting me do something. I'm talking about my husband being in agreement with me that we always help each other to be all that we can be. But there's a catch—God has to be in the mix.

"We don't do anything in our house without taking it first to God," Raine said. "Because with God in the mix, even with disagreements, you can be in agreement. Even your discord can lead to harmony. Even when you're hurt, you can love unconditionally."

As the audience clapped and said, "Amen," Raine thought about how this was where Yvonne wanted her to say a few words about the love she had for her mother-in-law. But she didn't have anything to say about the woman who didn't support her.

Inside her head, Raine pressed the delete button, erasing the words she'd planned to say about Beerlulu.

"Having this understanding allows you to walk in the love that God has for you and wants for you. His love for us is unconditional and He has asked us to pass that same love along to others. But do you know where that love starts?" She didn't wait for anyone to respond. "At home," she said. "When you give unconditional love to the man or woman that God has chosen for you, when you pass that love to the children He's gifted to you, it comes back to you in the form of abundant blessings because God is pleased.

"Now, I'm not saying that giving this kind of love is easy, but it is expected. It's the only way to experience the fullness of love, the same love that He's given to us. Trust and believe your love will always be tested. But if you keep God in the mix, your love will always be true."

When she nodded her head twice, the music began, and

behind her, Sierra and Liza began singing, this time the upbeat song "Blessings" that Raine had actually recorded when she was still an R & B star.

This was the perfect time to get people on their feet, clapping, dancing, laughing, singing about all of God's blessings. As with every other song, the audience sang, not missing a word. And a few even took to the aisles and busted a couple of moves that Raine had done in the original video back in the day.

On the stage, Sierra, Raine, and Liza danced as if they were at a party, egging the crowd on even more. At the end, the audience collapsed into their seats, ready to hear the final testimony.

"Glory to God!" Liza shouted, out of breath just like everyone else.

"Amen!" "Hallelujah!" "Glory!"

"I'm so happy to be here at City of Lights, singing with my sisters"—she paused and pointed to Sierra and Raine, sitting behind her—"and sharing with you. I bring you greetings from Ridgewood Macedonia."

Cheers rose from the balcony, and Liza smiled. "Yeah, Ridgewood Macedonia's in the house, though unfortunately, the Reverend Mann Washington, my husband, couldn't be here because of a prior engagement. But he sent those folks," she said, pointing up at the balcony. "Those are some of my peeps." With her palms out, Liza pumped her hands as if she was raising the roof.

The audience roared with laughter and cheers at the oldest member of Destiny's Divas's old-school dance move.

"It's so wonderful to be with folks who love the Lord, to be in a place, in a church, in a country where we can praise the Lord without ceasing, without fear."

She held up one hand in praise and the congregation followed.

"It is because of the Lord and His goodness and grace that I've been able to experience love everlasting. That's what I want to talk to you about, saints. A love with my husband, the Reverend Mann Washington, that has lasted"—she paused—"twenty-five years," she said, shaving off the three years as she always did.

As the crowd applauded, Liza said a silent *Forgive me, Lord.*

"Can you imagine how it was for me? I left Mississippi when I was just . . . nineteen years old, a young married woman. And not just young and married. Not just leaving Mississippi to come to the big city, but I was also going to be a pastor's wife. Can I get a shout-out?"

The congregation laughed.

"'Cause you know it ain't easy"—Liza strutted across the stage—"to be a pastor's anything. But to be the first lady . . ." She held up her hand. "Whew! That is more than a notion 'cause y'all know how you saints can be sometimes."

Pastor Bush's wife took to her feet, and when she did a little dance, the audience rocked with more laughter.

Liza laughed, too. "I know you feel me, Lady Jasmine." A beat, and then: "But you know what"—her voice lowered—"I wouldn't have my life any other way. I am blessed to be the Reverend Mann Washington's wife." She held up her hand again, this time stopping the audience from applauding. "But we don't deserve the credit—it all belongs to God. Because He showed us the way, the road map to having an everlasting love. When you have someone who cherishes you, when you have someone who loves you like Christ loves the church, you know that love can only come from God.

"Our marriage has lasted all of these years, and will be everlasting because my husband has it right. He's centered on me and I am on him. Have there been any temptations? Well, I can only answer for me. No! Because with my eyes on the Lord, I'm able to remember all of my blessings with Reverend Washington. And maybe I should answer for him . . . *heck no!*"

She had to pause again for the laughter.

"Okay, you know that's a joke, because, ladies, we need to understand that Satan is after our men."

"That's right!"

"Especially after the men who love the Lord."

"Preach!"

"So yes, there are temptations out there. But if you have honesty and loyalty in your marriage, no one and nothing will be able to interfere in your marriage. There cannot be secrets, there cannot be lies, your heart has to be open to your spouse in every way.

"It's a decision you have to make. To have this kind of love, your eyes must be on each other and the Lord. And speaking of eyes, let me close with this. First, let me talk to the ladies." She strolled to the edge of the stage. "Whether we like it or not, men are visual creatures. So yes, the years may add some weight, but we don't have to be sloppy with it."

"Tell it," a male yelled out, making more laughter rumble through the sanctuary.

"And I will tell it," Liza said as she strutted to the other side of the stage. "Because the same is true for men. Who told you that we find man boobs attractive?"

The congregation roared, and a few women stood on their feet waving their hands, shouting their own messages.

Liza laughed. "The thing is, everlasting love is possible when you think about your husband, you think about your wife, and you go to God with everything." She paused and peered into the crowd. "A love that lasts forever, for always, is the kind of love that God meant for us to have. And it can be yours." She pointed toward the heavens. "Ask Him."

The crowd was on their feet and the cheers roared like thunder.

Sierra and Raine sashayed to the center of the stage to join Liza and the crowd quieted when the track began.

Over the music, Raine said, "We decided that every CD we ever do will have the same song as the final track. My hope, my prayer, is that we will have one hundred CDs. That means one hundred times you will hear this as the last song.

"So, we will end with this tonight, and we hope that you will join us as we close with the Lord's Prayer."

After the introductory interlude, they began, "Our Father . . ."

Each of them sang with their eyes closed and their hearts both light and heavy. They'd made it through this first concert— they were ready for the road. With their songs, their testimonies . . . and with their lies.

# CHAPTER 22

## *Sierra*

The sanctuary was still buzzing with church members and Yvonne was gushing.

"You ladies were wonderful," Yvonne said as she led Sierra, Raine, and Liza off the stage and toward the green room.

As they followed, Sierra prepared her story. With just a little over an hour, there would not even be a second to waste.

Once they were alone, Yvonne hugged Raine, then Liza. But Sierra stepped back when Yvonne faced her.

"My throat," Sierra squeaked. She held her hand up to her neck.

"What?" Yvonne frowned.

"I . . . don't know . . . what's wrong." She pretended to struggle to speak.

"Is your throat sore?" Liza asked.

Sierra nodded and shook her head at the same time.

Raine piped in, "How could this happen so fast? You were fine two seconds ago."

Sierra had known that Raine was going to be the hardest to fool, not that it mattered. She was getting up out of this place within the next minute.

"I . . . was . . . struggling. But I knew . . . I had to be professional . . . and keep it moving."

"Why don't you sit down?" Liza offered.

She shook her head. "I feel too bad. I can hardly breathe. I have to get out of here." She waved her hands, fanning her face as if she was overheated.

Raine said, "You can stay for at least a few minutes to talk to Pastor Bush and Lady Jasmine. We have to thank them."

"No. I'm so sick, I don't want to do anything except"—she grabbed her coat, then tried to stuff her hair under her hat— "get out of here."

"At least change your clothes," Yvonne said. And then; "I'll get you a ride home."

"I'll catch a cab and change at home." She dashed out of the room before anyone could protest anymore.

"Don't forget tomorrow," Yvonne said, reminding her of their meeting.

"It'll depend on how I feel," Sierra gasped back, making it sound like she was still struggling, but making sure that Yvonne heard her.

Sierra pushed the side door open and darted into the church parking lot just a moment before the hallway filled with City of Lights members who had paid extra for the reception with Destiny's Divas.

The darkness of the night along with Sierra's long black coat and hat shrouded her, hiding her identity from those rushing to their cars. She kept her head down, praying that Denise wasn't out here. Her friend had bought a ticket, but had told Sierra that she'd have to leave right after the concert. Sierra hadn't told her that she'd be leaving, too, and if her friend saw her, there would be nothing but questions. And she didn't have time for that.

Sierra trudged to the front of the church, and on the corner of Riverside Drive, she spotted the Town Car. She waved and the lights blinked twice as the engine started and the car eased over to her.

The car had hardly stopped before Sierra jumped into the back, not even waiting for Harold to get out.

"I was going to get the door for you," Jarrod's driver said.

"That's okay," she said as she pushed her coat from her shoulders. "We don't have much time."

"You're going to be fine. Once I hit the Triborough, you'll be there in ten minutes. You should have about forty-five minutes to spare."

"Okay," she said as she kicked off her shoes. "I'm going to change my clothes back here."

"That's fine." He pushed a button, closing the privacy window.

As she slipped the gown off her shoulders and then scooted out of it, her only concern was making it to the airport on time.

"Thank you so much for this, Harold," she shouted as she yanked on her jeans. She wasn't sure if Harold could hear her, but then the window opened halfway.

"It's no problem. I don't have much to do when the congressman is in DC," he said.

She slipped the sweater over her head, and by the time Harold stopped the car in front of the US Airways terminal, Sierra looked like she'd been wearing a sweater with jeans and boots all day long.

"I owe you, and thanks for holding this stuff for me." She pointed to the black bag that held her folded gown and shoes.

"It's all good. Just go and make that plane." He grinned.

With her ticket in hand, she dashed through the airport,

getting her boarding pass, maneuvering through security, and making it to the gate within ten minutes. Another ten minutes, and she was sitting in seat 3A, settling back for the short flight to Reagan National Airport.

Looking out the window at the workers who loaded the final bags, Sierra couldn't believe all that she'd done in one day. From the rehearsal this morning to the concert tonight . . . and now she was on her way to visit Congressman Cannon. There was no doubt that the end of her day was going to be the best part.

This was only the fourth time that the two were going to be together, but ever since last Friday, when she'd spent the night at his loft, she knew she was already in love. They'd finally fallen asleep in his oversized bed and she'd awakened fully clothed and feeling totally loved.

Their Saturday was slow and easy. Sierra had changed into one of Jarrod's shirts and, together, in the kitchen, they'd made blueberry pancakes. She never got dressed as they spent the day sharing the newspaper, then watching a marathon of *The Game*. When he moved over to the study to read some legislative proposals, Sierra went to work on her testimony for the concert. They had sat together, slept together, spent the day together. Even without sex, it felt so familiar.

She'd been cool, relaxed, not a bit of anger within her.

Then came Sunday morning.

They'd slept the way they had the night before, in each other's arms. She'd awakened first, and as she rested on Jarrod's chest, she wondered what it was going to be like to wake next to him every morning? Would they continue to live here or find another place in Manhattan? Or would DC become their home?

Her head filled with dreams until Jarrod woke up and kissed her on her forehead.

"Good morning," she said, and before he could say anything, she asked, "What are we going to do today?"

He pushed himself from the bed and wrapped himself in his bathrobe. "My parents are coming by for brunch."

Sierra had tried to keep her excitement inside. He'd said it so casually; was he really ready to introduce her to his folks? Her mother had always told her that when a man lets you meet his parents, he was ready to make you his wife.

Then he added, "So, Harold's gonna take you home when you're ready, okay?"

It was a good thing that his back was turned and he was headed to the bathroom. Or else he would have seen her face, and next her words would have come. Angry words.

Why was he kicking her out? Was he ashamed of her? Was she not good enough?

By the time Jarrod stepped out of the bathroom, Sierra was dressed . . . and pissed.

"Wow," he said as he wrapped his arms around her. "I didn't expect you to get ready so fast."

"Well, you want me out before your parents get here, right?"

He leaned away from her and frowned. "Are you upset?"

She looked down, focused on her boots, and inhaled deep breaths. "No," she said, once she could speak without her voice shaking. "Disappointed."

With two fingers, he'd lifted her chin and made her look into his eyes. "When you meet my parents, you're going to meet them right. Not here in my place, early in the morning, only wearing one of my shirts."

She had thrown her arms around him. He *wasn't* ashamed of her. She had kissed him good-bye, begrudgingly but not unhappily.

Jarrod returned to DC that evening, but Sierra felt like he was still with her. All week long, her days started and her nights ended with his voice. And during the in-between hours, they texted.

But then on Wednesday, he called with news that could have spoiled her week.

"I'm not going to be able to come home this weekend. I have some meetings on Saturday."

"I can't believe it. I was really looking forward to seeing you," Sierra said.

"Me too. That's why I want you to come to DC, baby." When she stayed quiet, he added, "I'll take care of everything. You just have to show up, but if it's too soon for that, I'll understand."

He'd mistaken her silence, thinking that she was contemplating. But that wasn't it. He had just called her "baby"!

She knew it—he loved her! Just as she loved him.

"I'd love to come to DC," she'd finally told him.

"Okay, you and Harold can arrange the pickup and everything else."

Sierra hadn't told Jarrod about the concert at City of Lights, so it had all worked out beyond perfectly.

Today she'd fulfilled her Diva responsibilities and now she was on the plane to see her man. Because there was no doubt that by the time she left DC on Sunday, Jarrod was going to be her man in every way. But the best part was, she was going to be—really be—his woman.

# CHAPTER 23

## *Raine*

"Mom!"

Raine twirled around, her smile already on her face when she heard her daughter's voice. Even in the midst of the two hundred people who crowded the entertainment room of City of Lights for the private reception, Raine still zoomed in on her daughter as she pressed through the crowd. And her smile widened when Dayo came into her view.

Nadia swung her arms around her mother. "Mom, you were ridiculous."

Raine laughed. "That's good, right?"

"It's better than good."

Dayo said, "She's right, you were wonderful."

His lips were warm against her skin as he kissed her cheek and Raine wanted to reach out and hold him right there. But then her eyes widened when she saw Beerlulu walk up behind Dayo.

Beerlulu said, "Nadia is correct. The concert was very good."

"You were here?" Raine asked. Then, realizing how crazy her question sounded, she added, "I mean, I didn't see you when I looked up in the balcony."

"I was there," she said, "except for when I stepped away to go to the restroom, but I enjoyed it all, especially the way you sang the Lord's Prayer. I've always loved hearing you sing that."

Raine couldn't remember another time when Beerlulu had been so kind. As she reached for her mother-in-law's hand, she thought about the words she'd taken from her testimony. How could she have been so petty? Especially when she was talking about unconditional love. *Forgive me, Lord.* And then she prayed that Beerlulu would get the chance one day to hear her name as part of Raine's testimony.

"Dayo!" Pastor Bush came over to where the Omaris stood. The two men did the universal brother-handshake-pat-on-the-back before Pastor Bush said, "So, I know you're proud of your wife. We are."

Dayo took Raine's hand and squeezed it. "You know it," he said. "Very proud."

"And, Beerlulu, it's always good to see you," the pastor said before he kissed her cheek, then stepped away.

"So how long is this reception going on?" Dayo asked.

"I'm not sure, but I'm exhausted and ready to go. Let me just greet a few more guests and then we can get out of here."

Dayo nodded. "I'll just hang out over here with my mother and Nadia," he said before he embraced her again.

Raine worked the room, along with Liza, thanking everyone for their well-wishes and passing on Sierra's regrets. But the whole time her thoughts were on Beerlulu and how far the two of them had come.

When Raine glanced over at her husband, it was Beerlulu who smiled back as Dayo chatted with one of the church deacons. It was Beerlulu who followed her with her eyes as Raine greeted one guest and then another. And it was Beerlulu who finally came up to her and said, "You're tired; you've stayed long enough."

Beerlulu's words felt like a mother's concern, like a mother's love.

Even after Raine said good-bye to Pastor and Lady Jasmine, it still took minutes for the Omaris to push through the crowd. So many wanted to give Raine just one more hug or offer one more word of encouragement.

But finally they were inside their car, and Nadia said, "Mom, I don't know how you do it. Everybody wants to speak to you and tell you their life story!"

Dayo chuckled. "It's a blessing, *Binti*. Most people will never have the chance to impact anyone the way your mother has."

"I know. It's just that sometimes I don't think they see her like I do. I don't think her fans know that she's a real person and a real mom and a real lady."

"That's the price of fame," Dayo said as he and Raine shared a laugh.

When Raine glanced over her shoulder, Beerlulu was smiling, too.

Raine leaned against the headrest as Dayo guided their SUV east across Manhattan to the FDR Drive. There was no way she could have imagined this night when the morning began. But here they were as a family, Beerlulu included.

Only Nadia chatted as they rambled along the drive, passing the Queensboro Bridge on the left and then Gracie Mansion on the right. Raine rested in the normalcy of this feeling, the normalcy of family.

When they sped past South Street, Dayo eased to the right and took the next exit. Minutes later, they were home.

He handed the keys to the doorman, helped Raine from the SUV, then tended to his mother.

Inside the elevator, Raine asked, "Do you want to join us, Beerlulu? I know it's late, but maybe for a cup of tea?"

She shook her head. "No, I'm fine. I'm going to call my sisters and then go to bed."

When the elevator stopped on the eighth floor, Dayo whispered to Raine, "I'm going to walk my mother to her door."

But Beerlulu stopped him. With her hand on the elevator doors, she said, "No. Go home with your wife, *Mwana*. I'll be fine."

"I just want to walk you . . ."

She shook her head and then looked into Raine's eyes. "Go home. I will see you tomorrow." And then she smiled her good night to Raine.

The moment they entered their apartment, Nadia shouted, "I'm going to bed," as she dashed to her room.

Raine rolled her eyes, though there was a smile on her face. Only a twelve-year-old would think that her parents would believe she was really rushing off to bed. She shouted, "Only an hour on the computer."

"Okay, Mom!" she said before the door of her room closed.

As Raine followed Dayo into their bedroom, she put her hand on his shoulder. "Call your mother. Just to make sure that she's inside and settled."

He nodded and she slipped into her closet. As she slid the straps of her dress from her shoulders, she listened to Dayo ask his mother if she was okay. There was silence as she stepped out of her dress, then hung it up. Next, he asked Beerlulu if she needed anything. More silence on Dayo's end as she pulled a T-shirt over her head.

He hung up right when she came out of the closet and their eyes met.

He said, "My mother said to tell you good night."

Those were simple words that meant a lot, that almost brought tears to her eyes.

*Good night.*

Dayo pulled Raine into his arms. "You were right," he whispered. "Thank you for doing what was best for all of us. Thank you for caring for my mother."

She didn't have words, so she just held him and kissed him. And thought that Beerlulu was certainly right. This was truly a good night.

# CHAPTER 24

## *Sierra*

There were lots of reasons why Sierra had to get Jarrod into bed—number one was that by the time she went on tour, she wanted no doubts as to where she stood. She'd learned a lot from losing; she was going after a real commitment this time.

But this wasn't just about strategy. This was also about needing it. Four weeks had passed since she'd been with Andre, and while celibacy was her testimony, it definitely wasn't her gift. She needed to be in Jarrod's arms, and not in the way they'd slept last night.

Once again, they'd shared a bed, but not each other. There just hadn't been any time. From the moment Jarrod picked her up at the airport to the moment he brought her back to his one-bedroom apartment, he had been on the telephone, then the computer, talking about some speech that was taking place on Monday.

It had been frustrating when Jarrod had simply pointed to the bedroom, kissed her on the cheek, then stayed on the phone in his living room. She'd fallen asleep in the center of his bed, still in her clothes, with the TV on Mute.

Sometime in the middle of the night, he'd crawled onto the

bed, and when Sierra woke up this morning, she was wrapped inside his arms, just as she'd been the weekend before.

Only this was not the way the video had played in her mind. Lifting up her head, she glanced at the clock on the nightstand. It wasn't even seven o'clock and there had never been a time in her life when she'd been an early riser. But she was going to be one today, just so she could get back into bed.

Carefully shifting from under Jarrod's embrace, she rolled off the bed, then stood for a moment to make sure she hadn't awakened him. Tiptoeing through the bedroom, she grabbed her overnight bag in the living room and dragged it into the bathroom.

She eyed the shower stall for a moment: Should she or shouldn't she? She wanted Jarrod to stay asleep until she was ready. On the other hand, she wanted him to never forget what was about to happen. She wanted him to always remember the way she felt, she smelled, she tasted. . . .

Decision made.

She stripped, secured her hair under her shower cap, grabbed her Victoria's Secret products, and jumped into the shower. It wasn't until the warm water washed over her that Sierra realized just how tired she was. But there was no time to relax under the shower's massage. She didn't want Jarrod to get up and start working before she had a chance to implement her plan.

The bathroom was filled with the fragrance of her shower gel when she turned off the water. Jarrod was probably awake now, so she only had a few minutes. Quickly, she lotioned all over, fluffed her hair, then slipped into the negligee that she'd packed for this trip.

She studied herself in the mirror as she secured the straps of the sheer mesh baby-doll set that barely covered her butt. There wasn't much that was going to be left to Jarrod's imagination, but that's the way she wanted it. This was flirty, flattering, and barely there. Picking up the matching G-string, she twirled it on her fingers, then tossed it back into the suitcase.

She glanced one last time in the mirror, moistened her lips with her tongue, then used the door that connected the bathroom to the bedroom.

She'd been right—Jarrod was up, sitting with his back against the headboard as he scrolled through his BlackBerry.

For an instant, Sierra wondered if she had made the wrong decision with the shower. Jarrod was already into his day and there would be no room for her.

But then he looked up. And his eyes slowly widened. And his BlackBerry slipped from his hands.

"Good morning," she said as she posed in the doorway.

"Good"—Jarrod paused and swallowed—"morning."

She sauntered toward him, her eyes never leaving his. His eyes roamed over her body.

"What?"

By the time he got that word out, she was already at the edge of the bed. She took his hand, then scooted onto the bed and straddled him.

"Sierra."

"What?" she said before she kissed his forehead, then his nose, then his cheek, finally his lips.

Their tongues did a slow waltz before Jarrod pulled back. "What are we getting ready to do?"

She smiled. "Well, at least you know my intentions."

He pushed her away when she tried to kiss his neck.

"What's wrong?" she asked.

"It's you . . . it's this." He took her hands into his. "Are you sure?"

She leaned back a bit so that he could get a better view of the gift she was about to give him. "Don't I look like I'm sure?"

His eyes slowly roamed over the parts of her that he could see and he sighed. "But what about . . . I know you've been celibate."

She bit the corner of her lip. "I have been, but, Jarrod"—she squeezed his hands—"I know this is right with you. I can feel it."

"I can, too, baby, but this isn't why I invited you down here. I wasn't trying to set you up. I just wanted to spend more time with you."

"Well, what better way for us to spend time together than this?" When she nuzzled her lips against his neck, he moaned.

"What about . . . what about . . . Destiny's Divas?"

Her eyes were lowered when she said, "Being in the group means a lot to me." Looking up, she added, "So, this must show you how much you mean to me."

The way he looked at her, Sierra could tell that he was searching, studying, determining, deciding. When he leaned forward and kissed her, his decision was the same as hers.

Now he kissed her as if he was an impatient lover—so ready to get to the good part. His hands glided up and down her body, exploring the new terrain. She shuddered at his touch, he moaned at her response.

Guiding her, they traded places and now, he straddled her. It was her turn to moan as his fingertips teased her and made her shiver. But then in the next instant, he set her skin on fire as his tongue set its own trail.

She ripped off the T-shirt he wore and he slipped out of his boxers and she gasped at the gift that awaited her.

They joined for the first time and Sierra knew this was where she was supposed to be. Their moans sounded like music, a joyful sound. And when they got to the end, they sang again. And after that they sang a new song.

Finally spent, she lay in his arms as she had before, but this time they lay skin to skin, knowing one another. He held her differently—at least that's the way it felt to her. He held her like the woman he'd want to be his wife.

He kissed her forehead as he said, "I could tell with all of that bottled-up passion, it's been a long time for you, hasn't it?"

She nodded her lie. "I've been celibate for a while."

"Thank you for trusting me, Sierra." He held her tighter. "I wouldn't have done this, I wouldn't have let you do this if I didn't know we were ready."

With the tip of her forefinger, Sierra made heart signs through the hairs on his chest. "I wouldn't have done it, either, because I don't take being intimate lightly."

She could feel his nod before he said, "I'm going to ask you something, but you don't have to answer if you don't want to."

"Okay." In the silent seconds that followed, she imagined his question. Could this be it?

He asked, "How many men have you been with?"

Her body stiffened.

"You don't have to answer."

No more than two ticks passed on the clock as she calculated what would be the best, the proper, answer for a woman who was about to become the wife of a rising congressman. "I don't mind telling you. I've only been with two men," she said, grateful that she didn't have to look into his eyes.

"Wow." He held her tighter.

She continued her tale. "The first was my boyfriend in high school, and then about a . . . well, two years ago . . . I ended a three-year relationship."

"Why did it end?"

The story unfolded in her mind. If she was going to lie, it had to serve a purpose. "He didn't want a commitment and I didn't want to keep having sex without marriage. It had been three years and . . ." She stopped.

But she didn't need to say anymore. Both of his arms were around her when he said, "I understand."

Rolling onto his side, Jarrod sat up on his elbow and looked into her eyes. "I'm not going to play with you, Sierra." His eyes bore into hers. "You can trust me with your heart."

Tears that were not part of her lie filled her eyes. "I know I can."

He said, "I understand commitment."

She hoped his eyes would stay on hers and not wander to her chest, where her heart was trying to pound its way out.

"I don't know what's in store for us," Jarrod continued, "but I'm so excited that you're in my life and I can't wait to see where we're going to go."

She didn't want to cry, but she did as she hugged him close. And then they kissed once again, but this time it wasn't a kiss of lust; this time it was a kiss of love.

# CHAPTER 25

## *Liza*

*M*arch had truly roared in, not giving any break from the winds of February.

So the moment Liza pressed the remote for the garage door, she shivered and wished that she could run back into the house, crawl under the covers, and just relax this Saturday away.

"Why in the world did I let Yvonne talk us into a meeting this early?" she fussed as she fumbled with her house keys.

She locked the door, spun around, then gasped.

"Excuse me, miss, we didn't mean to scare you."

Her eyes scanned the two suited men standing at the edge of her garage. "May I help you?" She pressed her shoulder bag a bit closer to her chest.

"I'm Detective White and this is Officer Haley. We're looking for Reverend Washington. Is he home?"

Liza's eyes moved from one man to the other. "No. What do you want with my husband?"

"We just have some questions. Do you know where we can find him?"

She crossed her arms and frowned. "I'm not sure," she said. "I can give him a message."

It was the one who'd done all the talking who pulled the card from his coat pocket, then took a few steps toward her. "No message, but you can give him this."

Liza took the card without glancing at it.

"Thank you."

She stayed in place, not moving until they jumped into their white Taurus and backed their car from her driveway.

She didn't move until they were out of her sight. Then she ran to her car as if she was being chased. Her hands were shaking as she locked the doors, then pressed the number 1 to speed-dial Mann on her cell.

He answered as he always did before the second ring. "What's up?" he asked.

"Are you at the church?" Her voice was shaking.

"Yeah. I'm still meeting with the deacon board for the Men's Celebration. What's up?"

"Two policemen just left the house looking for you."

There was silence and then: "Hold on a sec."

Liza heard the muffled sounds of whispers, then footsteps.

Then: "Policemen? What did they say?" He whispered, but she knew for sure that he was alone.

"Nothing. They just asked if you were home and left their card. Does this have anything to do with Buddy and Qianna?"

"I don't know, Liza, but don't start worrying. It could be they were looking for the church to buy tickets to the Policeman's Ball or something. Don't worry. I'll take care of it."

"They're probably on their way to the church right now."

A beat and then: "I'll handle it. I'll talk to you later." He hung up before she could ask any more questions.

Liza tossed her cell onto the passenger's seat, twisted the key in the ignition, but didn't move the car. All she wanted to do was go down to the church, to see what this was all about. But if she did that, Mann would be upset and she'd miss the meeting with Yvonne.

In her head, she went back and forth, over and over, until she made her decision. She had to get to her meeting with Yvonne, but she'd rush straight to the church afterward. In the meantime, all she would do was pray, and pray, and pray.


"I'm sorry I'm late," Liza said, bursting into Yvonne's office.

"That's okay, you're not the only one." Yvonne shook her head.

Liza hugged Yvonne, then turned her attention to Raine. "Where's Sierra?"

"That's what I'm trying to figure out," Yvonne said as she pounded her hand on the conference table. "I've been calling her for two hours."

"Two hours? I'm only twenty minutes late. Didn't you say ten?"

"Yes, but with Sierra I start calling her as soon as I wake up in the morning." She grabbed her cell, dialed the number again, then: "Ugh! It keeps going to voice mail."

"Well, she was sick last night," Raine said.

"Oh, please. Did you really believe that story?" Yvonne asked.

Raine shrugged. "I like to take people at their word."

"And she did look a little flushed," Liza said as she eyed the breakfast spread that Yvonne had laid out on the table. But she knew she wouldn't be able to eat a thing. Not the way her stomach rumbled—and it wasn't from hunger.

"Flushed? Yeah, right." Yvonne shook her head. "I'm telling you . . . I just hope we didn't make a mistake with that one."

"What do you mean?" Raine and Liza asked at the same time.

"I don't know." Yvonne squinted. "I just have a bad feeling. I'm not buying her whole good-girl routine. I mean, come on. Twenty-five and celibate?"

"I know you're not saying there's no one out there who's twenty-five and celibate," Liza said.

"I'm not saying that. I'm saying . . . I don't know."

Raine said, "Okay, you're gonna have to really explain this to me 'cause I don't get it. Sierra's never done anything, you don't see her with anybody, she's always at our church or over at Abyssinian."

"Exactly. She's just a little too perfect for me. I mean, really? She doesn't even have a boyfriend, really? Look at her. Guys have got to be after her all the time."

"Well, maybe she just knows her worth," Raine said.

Liza nodded as she reached for a bagel. She had to eat something.

"I hope you're right," Yvonne said, "because this is our platform. It's just like being a pastor, and you know what happens to churches when scandals break out."

Liza pushed her bagel back.

Raine laughed at Yvonne. "You're kidding, right? First of all, Sierra hasn't done anything except not show up this morning and you have her in the middle of a scandal. And we're certainly not pastors."

"Trust me, remember, I used to be a celebrity publicist. I know the image you need to project and what it's going to take to get to the top and stay there."

"You're worrying way too much," Raine said. "Don't you think so, Liza?"

"Huh?" She glanced from Raine to Yvonne. "Sorry, I didn't hear what you said."

Raine waved her hand at Liza and said to Yvonne, "I say give Sierra a break. Nothing's gonna happen and she really is perfect to be the young one of this group."

"I hope you're right." Yvonne shook her head as if she doubted it. "I hope I never have to say I told you so."

"Dang!" Raine pushed her chair back from the table and stood up. "What's with all of this negative energy? I'm in too good a mood after what happened with me and Dayo last night. . . ." She giggled.

"TMI." Yvonne rolled her eyes. "No wonder you think the world is so wonderful right now."

"It is. Have you seen the gorgeous man I go to bed with every night?"

"Ugh!" Yvonne said. "Let me give Sierra one more try, and then we'll get started."

As Yvonne dialed, Raine leaned over to Liza. "What do you think got into her this morning?" Raine whispered. "Talking about pastors and scandals. Geez. Maybe we need to put some vodka in her orange juice. Get her to lighten up a little."

Raine laughed.

Liza didn't.

# CHAPTER 26

*Sierra*

There was no way that she was going to let Yvonne ruin her day.

"Yes," Sierra said again. She'd been saying yes for what felt like forever. Well, at least ever since she'd gotten off the plane a few minutes before.

"So you've been sick all this time?" Yvonne asked again.

Sierra rolled her eyes. "Yes."

"For three days, Sierra?"

"Yes!"

Then the overhead speakers announcing the departure of flight 727 to Memphis screamed through the terminal.

"What's that?" Yvonne asked.

Sierra pressed her face into her cell to muffle the surrounding sounds of the airport terminal. "The TV," she said as she ducked inside a women's room to get away from the announcement. "Anyway"—now her voice echoed inside the bathroom— "I'm sorry I didn't call you, but I was so sick, I hardly got out of bed." *At least that last part was close to the truth.*

"I just need to know that you're serious about Destiny's Divas, Sierra."

Sierra stood in front of the bathroom mirror and smoothed the hair that she'd pulled back into a ponytail since she hadn't had a chance to do a thing with it in the last three days. "Of course I'm serious. Because I miss one little meeting you think I'm not?"

"It wasn't a little meeting. We needed to discuss what went right on that stage and if you wanted or needed anything changed. You're not getting another shot at this. The next time we do this, it will be on tour, for real."

"Well, it was all good to me. I had a great time, even though I was sick."

Yvonne sighed. "I'm going to need you to bring me your gown. I need to have it cleaned and then all the dresses will be packed together."

"Fine. I'll do it this afternoon."

"What time?"

"I'll be there by noon," Sierra huffed.

"Please! Be on time."

Sierra shook her head as she heard the click of the call ending. Yvonne hadn't even said good-bye, as if she was supposed to care. Sierra wasn't about to let that hater take away her joy.

And joy was what she had for real.

Her boots tapped out her steps as she rushed through the terminal to the escalator where Harold waited for her at the bottom.

"Good morning," he said, taking her bag from her. "So, you had a little extra vacation, huh?"

The warmth rose from her neck to her face and she knew she was blushing. That was exactly the way she felt—like a blushing bride who'd just had three hella-wonderful days on her honeymoon.

"I'll get you right home," Harold said as he rolled the bag outside of the terminal.

"Okay," she said, though she doubted Jarrod's driver heard her as a jet's engine roared overhead. But she didn't feel like talking anyway. All she wanted to do was think. And bask in the memories.

If Sierra had her way, she would've never left the country's capital, or the apartment in Capitol Hill, or Jarrod's bed. There wasn't even a need for extra clothes once she decided to stay another day, and then another. It was only when Jarrod had come in from the hill yesterday that he decided this morning would be when she had to leave.

"I'm getting addicted to you," he had said when she met him at the door wearing nothing more than her faux Louboutins.

"And me to you," she said before she pushed her tongue down his throat.

They had made love right there in the living room, but before they took their party into the bedroom, he'd told her that she had to go.

"You have a life," he'd said as he gently grasped her wrists, trying to keep her hands from between his legs. "And believe it or not, I do, too."

"I just love being here with you."

"And I love having you here, but we both have to get back to work. What about your job at the bookstore?"

"I called in sick," she lied. She hadn't made a single call—not to her job at the bookstore and not to Yvonne.

"But you can't keep doing that." He gave her a quick kiss. "You should take the first flight back in the morning."

Those words stopped her cold. "Why are you trying to get rid of me?" she snapped. "Who are you trying to see?"

He leaned back a bit. "What?"

She inhaled a deep breath, calmed and softened. "I was just playing. It's just that I want to stay," she said softly. "Just one more day so that we could do more of this." When she leaned in and kissed him, she didn't let go. When her hands finally found their way to his center, he scooped her into his arms and carried her into the bedroom.

Like the nights before, they'd made love long into the early hours of the morning. But that had not changed Jarrod's mind. They'd both risen with the sun and Jarrod had Sierra at the airport in time to catch the eight o'clock flight.

Leaving wasn't what she wanted, but she'd made her mark, staked her claim. Jarrod wasn't going to forget her.

"Here we are," Harold said as he opened the door of the Town Car.

*Girl, don't you know . . . . You're so beautiful . . . I wanna give all my love to you, girl. . . .*

The corners of her lips almost stretched to her ears when she heard her ringtone, knowing for sure it was Jarrod. Inside the car, she rummaged through her purse and grabbed her phone right before it stopped ringing.

"Hey, baby!"

"Golden Lady, I was just checking to make sure you landed safely."

"I did. I'm with Harold now."

"Great. I miss you already."

She smiled, she calculated. Should she tell him the same thing? No! He deserved a little punishment for sending her away. She said, "Well, when are we going to see each other again?"

"As soon as possible. Let me figure out the rest of this week and we'll talk about Friday and Saturday."

"Okay."

"I had a great time, Sierra."

More calculations. "Let's talk later and see what we can do." She was sure her words would make him wonder why she was a little distant. Make him think that he might have some competition, and shouldn't be so quick to send her away next time.

"Okay," he said after a beat. "Let's talk tonight."

"Can't wait," she replied, wanting to throw him something before she clicked off her cell.

The car glided toward the Triborough Bridge and Sierra leaned back, her thoughts churning.

*Make it all about him,* she heard her mother's voice say in her head. She'd already taken this advice. Like with her job at the bookstore—she'd quit so that she could spend more time with Jarrod. Well, she hadn't officially quit; she just hadn't shown up, and since no one had called her, Sierra figured that they'd gotten the message. Marva was probably just tired of giving her chance after chance. That was cool. It worked for Sierra.

Beyond the bookstore, she was even ready to give up the tour if she could figure a way out. But actually, Destiny's Divas would end up being an asset to Jarrod. Her fans would run out and vote for her husband. Because of her, Jarrod could be a senator in the next election, and after that the White House would be just a few years away.

Yes, her thoughts were all about him and now it was time for him to think about her. Now that they'd slept together, she needed that engagement ring.

She wasn't going to come out and ask him, but she was going to give him enough hints. She wanted the ring, she needed it.

Before she left for the tour.

# CHAPTER 27

## *Raine*

*R*aine couldn't believe it.

She was almost excited about taking the elevator down six floors to have dinner with her mother-in-law. This was an all-around celebration, that's what Beerlulu had told her when she extended the invitation.

"I want to have a dinner for my family," Beerlulu had said as she pulled Raine aside after church on Sunday. While Dayo searched for Nadia in the teen church, Beerlulu had led Raine to a corner in the front vestibule to chat while they waited. "I want to bring everyone together so that you can get to know my sisters. I know it hasn't been easy for you with my family."

Raine waited for Beerlulu to give her an excuse for her sisters in Brooklyn. The sisters who had been no more welcoming to Raine than Beerlulu had been. The sisters who'd never offered her a hello or a smile the few times that Dayo had taken her to visit his family. Raine hadn't been back in years—not that she'd been invited.

"And I want us all to start over," Beerlulu continued. "Because they are your family, too."

It took her a moment, but Raine said, "I'd like that," and she meant it.

Beerlulu added, "And this will give me a chance to thank you. Having my apartment is the best thing. You and Dayo needed your space and I needed mine."

Before Raine could say anything more, Beerlulu had pulled her into an embrace. At first, she was so shocked she just stood there stiffly. But then she settled into the warmth of Beerlulu's arms and rested there in a comfort and peace that she'd always imagined.

She was thinking of Beerlulu's embrace even now, as she stood next to Nadia in the elevator on the ride to the eighth floor. Raine didn't even have to look behind her to know that Dayo was beaming—the elevator was bright with the warmth of his smile. She was sure this night had been in her husband's dreams before Beerlulu had even landed in America—it had certainly been in hers.

The moment they exited the elevator, the sweet fragrances of what had to be native dishes of the motherland greeted and escorted them down the hallway toward Beerlulu's apartment. Raine inhaled, relishing the aromas, although she knew there wouldn't be much for her to eat. But that was okay; it was the fellowship, not the food, that she most looked forward to.

As they moved closer, music melded with the scents, and by the time Dayo put his key inside the lock and pushed open the door, Raine felt like she was in Kenya.

"*Hooyo!*" Dayo called out.

Over Dayo's shoulder, Raine saw her mother-in-law in the center of the living room with her arms held up and open wide. Her smile and her stance was welcoming, but it was her clothing that delighted Raine the most.

Beerlulu had cast aside the black and the navy that she always wore for a bold orange and yellow geometric-print skirt that swept the floor. The oversized yellow top was the same as the wrap that loosely covered her head.

She looked like an African queen.

"Wow," Nadia gasped, and Raine had to agree.

Behind her were the two women whom Raine had met the few times she'd been to Brooklyn. But she hardly recognized them with their smiles, which were as wide as their sister's. Their caftans and head wraps were just as bright as the one Beerlulu wore.

Beerlulu's arms were still open when she motioned to Nadia. "Come here, *Mjukuu*."

"You haven't called me that in a long time," Nadia said as she fell into her grandmother's arms.

This moment made Raine want to sing as Beerlulu squeezed Nadia and kissed her over and over. The longer Beerlulu held Nadia, the more the song in Raine's heart turned to tears. This was all that she ever wanted.

Then she had her Hallmark moment, when Beerlulu reached for her.

"Welcome to my home, *Binti*."

Raine had to blink to keep it all together when Beerlulu called her *Binti*. The way Dayo called Nadia *Binti*. Daughter. That single word made this moment even better.

If the evening had ended then, it would've been enough. But that was the beginning.

"You remember my sisters." Beerlulu pulled Raine closer to the women.

One grabbed Raine, and the other swallowed Nadia into her arms. As Raine smiled at her grinning daughter, she thanked God for this feeling—she was one of the Omaris, finally.

Beerlulu moved to the kitchen, but she shooed the others from following her. "This is a party, there's no fun in here. I'm fine and I can watch."

So the celebration began. Dayo cranked the music louder and danced with Raine while his aunts and Nadia shimmied around them.

"I don't understand the words to the song." Nadia laughed.

"It's Swahili," Dayo said before he went back to singing along with the CD.

While Dayo and his aunts sang, Raine and Nadia clapped and swiveled their hips to the beat. There were only five, but it felt like a full-fledged party as music and laughter and chatter bounced through the room.

Soon Beerlulu joined them, wiggling and jiggling, making them all laugh even louder. After one more song, Beerlulu turned down the music.

"It's time to eat." She swept her arms toward the buffet table.

"Wow!" Raine said as she eyed the Kenyan banquet.

Food in brightly colored bowls awaited them: *chana masala*, with garbanzos, millet patties and samosas, and steak and *irio*. Even though there wasn't much on the table that Raine would be able to eat, the feast before her made her mouth water.

But then Beerlulu said, "*Binti*, I made this for you," and she placed a vegetable curry on the table. Raine wanted to reach over and hug Beerlulu again. All of the efforts that she'd made toward her mother-in-law were raining back on her. She smiled as widely as she could to hold back her tears.

After the food was blessed, the eating and stories began. Beerlulu and her sisters shared memories of Dayo's childhood.

"He was just so precocious," Beerlulu said, shaking her head. "I couldn't do a thing with him."

"Ah, you know you loved it, *Hooyo*. I kept the hotel guests entertained and coming back," he said, referring to the business his family owned.

Beerlulu sucked her teeth and waved her hands, but never lost her smile.

Then they shifted, and Beerlulu and her sisters shared stories with Nadia about her grandfather, Dayo's father, who had passed away one month after Dayo had left Kenya to study in London.

"He was finished," Beerlulu explained to Nadia with a small smile that belied the tragedy of her words. "He'd done his job. He raised a great son and so God took him home to rest."

As the tales continued, Raine sat back and imagined that the two years Beerlulu had been in the country had never happened. For her, tonight was the first time they met and sat and shared as a family. This was going to be her new history.

In the middle of their laughter, Justin Bieber sang out.

*Somebody to love . . . I don't need nothing else . . . I promise, girl, I swear . . . I just need somebody to love . . .*

Beerlulu and her sisters were startled into silence as Nadia jumped from the table and dashed into the living room.

"That's my phone," she squealed.

"Say 'Excuse me,'" Raine yelled after her.

But by the time Nadia's pardon came, she'd already answered her call and was charging toward the bathroom for privacy.

Raine shook her head. "Sorry." She took a sip of her tea. "One day, she'll have one of my songs as her ringtone."

But while Raine laughed, Beerlulu and her sisters frowned. She watched them exchange glances, and even when Dayo started talking again, Beerlulu's eyes kept jetting back to the bathroom door.

As the minutes moved on, Beerlulu stayed focused on the bathroom, and the smiles on the sisters' faces had dimmed. Only Dayo was unaffected by Nadia's absence.

"Excuse me," Raine said as she stood. In front of the bathroom, she pushed the door open.

"Mom!" Nadia whined. "I'm talking to Shaquanda."

"This is so rude," Raine hissed. Stepping inside, she added in a whisper, "When you're at someone's house, you don't leave them for someone on the telephone."

"I had to answer. It might have been important."

"You're twelve; you don't even know what's important. Tell her good-bye." Raine crossed her arms and stayed right in front of Nadia.

Into the phone, she whispered, "PIR," then she ended her call with a sigh as if the act took much effort.

Raine frowned. "PIR? What does that mean?"

She twisted her lips. "It doesn't mean anything. I was just letting Shaquanda know that you were standing right there. It just means 'parent in the room.'"

Raine motioned for Nadia to make her move toward the door. Nadia shuffled in front of her back to the dining room table, and when they sat down, Raine apologized for both of them.

Though the stories continued, the smiles had definitely dimmed. Raine held her breath, waiting for Beerlulu to say something, to scold Nadia in some way, to end this night and this dream of a family.

But except for some eye signals that passed between the sisters, the night returned to the way it had started. When it was time to say good night, Beerlulu's good-bye was as warm as her welcome.

"I'll see you tomorrow, *Binti,*" she said as she hugged Raine and then turned to say good-bye to Nadia and Dayo.

Raine left the apartment holding hands with her husband, so grateful to know that God changed hearts.

"Oh, no!" Nadia shrieked just as they stepped into the elevator. She held the door from closing with her hands.

"What's wrong?" Raine and Dayo said together, both looking to see where their child was injured because surely that would be the only reason for such a scream.

"I forgot my phone!"

Raine grabbed the back of Nadia's sweater before she could take off down the hall. "What's wrong with you? Yelling like that? Go upstairs with your father. You don't need to be on the phone anymore tonight."

"But, Mom . . ."

"I'll get it."

Raine shook her head the whole time she walked back to the apartment. It was time to put a few restrictions on Nadia's use of the telephone—maybe only while she was out of the apartment and on weekends.

When Beerlulu opened the door, Raine apologized right away. "I just came back for Nadia's phone."

Beerlulu said, "Oh, yes." Her eyes darted toward her sisters. "The phone. We just found it."

Her sisters sat close, side by side, with their heads bowed as if they had been in a deep conversation. Nadia's phone was cupped inside one of the sisters' hands.

It was their expressions—their wide eyes, as if they were startled, as if they'd been caught—that made Raine frown. What had they been doing with the phone? She wanted to ask them, but all she said was "Thank you" and "Good night."

Inside the hallway, the questions stayed with her. As she waited for the elevator, she scrolled through Nadia's cell phone.

The home screen showed her recent calls made and received. Every single one was to or from Biggie Mack.

Was that what the sisters had been looking at? Did they think Nadia was talking to a boy? No, it couldn't be that. Beerlulu had to remember that Biggie Mack was Shaquanda's nickname.

Raine shook the questions away. Maybe they were just older women who didn't understand the ways of teenagers. They were probably just trying to figure out the smart phone.

In her mind, though, their expressions were what bothered her the most. But she wasn't going to allow her imagination to mess up this chance that she'd been given with her mother-in-law.

No matter what her gut told her.

# CHAPTER 28

## *Liza*

$\mathcal{J}$t had been a long time since Liza had a Saturday free, and this was the day that she'd been looking forward to because she wouldn't have too many more of these lazy days before her tour.

When this Saturday first showed up on her calendar, Liza's plan had been to lounge in bed, flip through old magazines, and catch up on shows on her DVR. She didn't even plan to get up to write her final article for her *Life as a First Lady* magazine before she went on tour. She was going to write it from her bed on her laptop.

And her hope had been that with all of those hours in bed, Mann would have spent a few of them with her.

But this wasn't the day that she'd imagined. The stacks of magazines were on her nightstand and the flat-screen television was on, and her laptop was on her bed. But her head was clogged with so much that she couldn't concentrate on what was supposed to be her fun.

For a week now, the cover-up, the lies continued. They started last Saturday. As soon as she'd finished the meeting with Yvonne, she'd rushed to the church. Mann had still been in the meeting, but she'd called him out and had taken him into the hallway that connected his office to Buddy's.

"Why did those men come up on me like that this morning?" she'd whispered when they were alone.

"Oh, God, Liza. Please don't tell me you pulled me out for this." He held his head in his hands. "I told you, I have no idea who those men were or what they wanted. But I've got to get back into the meeting."

He'd left her standing there and then, when he came home, he made it clear that he was too exhausted to have any kind of discussion. He'd shut her down, that night and into the next week.

But those detectives had spooked her. Made her feel as if her nightmares were coming true.

And then Liza had a thought. Maybe she needed to speak to Qianna's mother—woman to woman. Maybe there was something Qianna's mother needed. Maybe there was a way for Liza and Mann to actually help her and in the process turn her into a friend instead of an enemy.

The idea was too good for her to sit on, and Liza rolled out of bed and rushed into her closet. Without the thought and the care that she normally gave to dressing, she jumped into a jogging suit and sneakers, and within ten minutes flat she'd clicked off the television, grabbed her wallet and keys, wrapped herself in her coat, and pointed her car toward Ridgewood Macedonia.

That's where Mann was, and had been for the last few Saturdays. This was something that he'd started just recently—heading to the church on Saturday mornings to work on his sermon. Buddy had come by to pick him up about two hours ago to drive him, so she was sure that he was there.

As she maneuvered through the streets, she planned her

words to convince Mann. Surely he knew that women could talk to women better than any man could. Certainly better than any attorneys. If Mann really wanted to put this to rest, he'd let Liza take action.

At the church, she parked next to Buddy's SUV. Glancing up at the window to Mann's office, she saw nothing. Good—she didn't want him to be prepared.

But inside, even though she wore sneakers, her footsteps against the parquet floors announced her arrival, and right before she passed her cousin's office, Buddy leapt into the hallway.

"Liza!" he shouted, as if she was one hundred feet away rather than right in front of his face. "What are you doing here?"

She paused and stared. "Why are you yelling like that?"

"You just shocked me, that's all. I didn't know you were coming in."

"I didn't know it either," she said, pushing past him to take the few steps to Mann's office. "I need to see my husband."

"Uh . . . he . . ."

She grabbed the doorknob, then jiggled it. "Why is his door locked? Mann?" She knocked.

"Liza?" Mann called out from the other side.

"I'm trying to get in."

"Oh, okay. Come in."

She stood back on one leg, crossed her arms. "I can't get in," she said, knowing that her husband was aware he was behind locked doors. She turned to her cousin, but he was back in his office.

As she pivoted toward Buddy's office to use the hall that connected the offices, Mann's door opened.

"Hey, what are you doing here?" he asked, as if he was pleasantly surprised to see her.

Her eyes were like slits as she slowly entered. She kept her eyes on him, searched for signs, though she had no idea what she was looking for.

Mann looked the way he had when he'd left this morning: open-collared white shirt, black slacks, polished loafers. But his hands were jammed inside his pockets, and his weight shifted from one leg to the other—those were the signs.

Now her glance wandered around his office. She took in every square foot, from the desk to the chairs to the conference table and sofa. She paused as she glanced at the hall that led to Buddy's office. There was nothing . . . except for the air that felt like it was heavy with trouble.

Suspicion was in her eyes when she turned back to her husband.

His voice was light as he strolled behind his desk. "I was working on my sermon for tomorrow." He pointed to the computer as if that was his proof. "What's going on with you? What brings you by?"

"I came down here to talk," she said.

He held up his hands as if he knew what she was going to say. "Liza"—the frustration was already in his voice—"we're not gonna talk about this anymore. I can't do it."

"It was just that I had an idea. I was thinking that I could talk to Qianna's mother."

"What? No!"

"Just listen to what . . ."

"You're stressing me the hell out."

She jerked back a bit at his words. In the years they'd been married, she could count on one hand the number of times he'd cursed at her.

He kept on. "How am I supposed to run this church and

the ministry when I have to spend all of my time talking to you about the same thing. I'm getting tired, so listen to me—the attorneys are handling everything. It's almost over."

It was because she stood there, stiff with shock, that he gently placed his hands on her shoulders. "Please. No more talk about Qianna's mother, all right?"

She said nothing. Just nodded.

"Great." He stepped away. "I was gonna take a little break. You want to go to lunch with me?"

She took a quick glance at the tracksuit she had on underneath her down coat. "This isn't exactly the way I want to be seen in public."

He chuckled. "Well, you know you always look good to me." Stepping closer to her, he said, "Maybe we'll just go home and have lunch there." He kissed the tip of her nose. "We'll have lunch and you can be my dessert."

She waited for it, the tingling that always came when he spoke to her this way. But she felt nothing, said nothing, and Mann didn't seem to notice.

"I have to drop these files off on Deacon Brown's desk. He'll be here this afternoon, and just in case you have me so tied up that I don't come back . . ." He grinned as he let his voice trail off with innuendo. He picked up a folder, and kissed her again before he left her alone.

He hadn't fooled her, he wouldn't stop her. She glanced again around the office, taking a slow tour, trying to see if anything was out of place. Then she saw something move. Through the miniblinds. At the window. She took slow steps forward to get a better view of the parking lot. And her cousin, Buddy. And a young girl. Qianna.

As her cousin scooted the girl into his SUV, Liza stood at the window and watched Buddy trot around the front of his car as if he were in a hurry. He jumped inside, and when he put the key in the ignition, he looked up. His eyes met hers.

He held her gaze as he backed out his car, and then he sped out of the lot.

Liza stood there for seconds longer and then closed her eyes, as if that would help her forget what she'd just seen.

# CHAPTER 29

## *Sierra*

"I want you to go somewhere with me."

Sierra leaned back on the bed and pressed the phone closer to her ear, wishing that it was Jarrod's lips that she felt and not the cold metal of her smart phone.

"I'll go anywhere with you," she said. "When? This weekend?" she asked, so glad that she no longer had to be concerned about her hours at the bookstore.

"No, tomorrow."

She bounced straight up on her bed. "Tomorrow as in"—she glanced at the clock—"one hour from now?"

He laughed. "Yes, tomorrow as in I'm coming to New York tomorrow afternoon. I've been asked to speak at a dinner. A fund-raiser. A good friend of mine was supposed to do it, but he had a death in his family and I was asked to step in."

"I'm sorry," she said as she stood and paced her bedroom. "I mean about your friend. But I'm thrilled that I'm going to see you."

It was much more than seeing him that made her want to dance. There were so many ramifications of this. They were going public. Not that they hadn't been in public before. But at a fund-raiser—this was work and he wanted her by his side.

This would be like a coming-out—Jarrod Cannon and Sierra Dixon.

"So even though this is last minute, you don't mind?"

*Was he kidding?* "No. I meant what I said, I'd go anywhere with you."

"That's a good thing."

"But you've got to tell me the details because I have to look great as your date."

"Baby, you look good all the time."

"The way I look good to you is not the way I'm going to show up." She laughed with him. "I can't be naked."

"Aww, no. Really? I was hoping to see you completely in your birthday suit."

"Well, that can be arranged, Mr. Congressman. In private."

He chuckled. "Well, you're right about the private thing. Even though I'd love to share you with the world, not a great idea for someone with my ambition."

"I know that's right," she said. "At all times, I have to be a proper congressman's wife—I mean date, date . . . Congressman's date," she stuttered, not believing that had actually slipped out of her mouth.

He laughed. "What's wrong with being a congressman's wife?"

"Nothing. It's just that I don't want you to think that I'm pressing you or anything." Sure, she needed that ring, but she never wanted to hit him directly like that. *Never be obvious*—another something from her mother.

"Well, we'll talk about this again . . . soon," he said.

Anticipation made her tremble with those words. She wanted to talk about this now.

He added, "But for tomorrow, it's not formal, just after-five attire."

Sierra wanted to take him back to where they'd been just seconds before. But she didn't want to push. *Never push.* So she just listened to what he was saying about the event at the Metropolitan Museum of Art for the Youth Foundation. And she wondered what she would wear. Maybe if she looked extra special, he'd want to have that talk now instead of later. She did have a little red number that she'd been saving. This was definitely the time for that one.

"So, my plane lands at about three and I'll pick you up around six, okay?"

"I'll be ready," she said before blowing him a kiss.

She bounced from the bed, tossed the phone aside, and did a couple of high kicks and tucks that she remembered from her high school cheerleading days.

This was a big deal and it couldn't have come at a better time. Just a week before she had to leave. Before she hit the road, Jarrod would see that he could, he should have her on his arm; she couldn't wait to show him how she truly belonged there.

She kicked and cheered her way to her closet, then pulled out the dress that she'd wear. Wiggling out of her T-shirt, she slipped into the silk design that almost felt a size too small. Standing in front of the mirror, she couldn't help but smile. This dress was fire! The red was bright, was hot, and wasn't red the color of love?

She twisted back and forth, checking her reflection from every angle. Her chest was perky, her waist was cinched, and her behind was her pride. The best part of the dress—the long zipper in the back that went from the nape of her neck to the edge of her butt and would make it oh so easy to step out of quickly.

Once Jarrod saw her in this, once he realized how much of an asset she was, he'd be dragging her back to his bed.

Returning the dress to the closet, she checked the bottoms of her home-made Louboutins to see if the red spray paint needed a touch-up. Satisfied, she climbed back into bed, nude this time. She rested her head against the pillow and thought of the words he'd spoken.

*We'll talk about this again . . . soon.*

She felt the tingling all the way down in her toes. This was true . . . this was real . . . this was love.

Sierra's eyes opened slowly, reluctantly. She didn't want to awaken from the magical dreams that had filled her night. Her dreams of life with Jarrod: what their wedding would be like, what their children would look like, what their life would be like.

She focused on the clock and she moaned a groan of pleasure. It was only a little after ten, but the day had already begun. The day when her fantasies became reality—this was the first day of what would be the best of her life.

All she wanted to do was sing and dance and cheer, but she had to stay relaxed so that tonight she'd look as fresh as the morning.

She tarried over a breakfast of one scrambled egg white (which was the only thing she'd eat today so that she'd look extra fabulous in her dress). Then she hung out on Twitter and Facebook. She wanted to announce to the world that she was dating Congressman Jarrod Cannon, but she was smart enough to know the importance of discretion. Plus, after tonight the world would know anyway. That was the part of the evening that excited her the most—the press would be there.

Thinking of the press made her click over to Andre's Face-book page. She hadn't stalked him since she'd traded him in for a better model, and right now she longed to leave him a message. She wanted him to know how grateful she was that he hadn't answered any of her messages, and had just stepped out of her life. She wanted to send him a gift.

Andre's page was loaded with female friends, each leaving one provocative message after another. Messages that a month ago would have sent her into a red rage, but messages that today made her feel sorry for these female desperadoes.

Andre probably thought that he was hot, the way these women were coming at him, and she wanted to cool him off. Clicking on the button for message, she decided that she could tell Andre about tonight. After all, he was an acquaintance, and by morning it would be public anyway.

She typed: *Hey Andre: I hope you're well. I was wondering if you'd be covering the fabulous gala at the Metropolitan tonight. My boyfriend is the keynote speaker, so of course I'll be there. Just wanted to give you a heads-up so you wouldn't be surprised if we run into each other. Okay, be blessed, because I certainly am. SD*

It gave her great pleasure to click the Send icon. Of course, Andre wouldn't be at the museum. He worked for a freaking low-life tabloid. They would never be invited to cover an event as classy as this. While Andre would be chasing extraterrestrial beings, she would be mingling with the rich and powerful. The two of them would never mix in the same worlds again.

How wonderful it was to rub this in Andre's face!

Through the afternoon, she tweeted, posted on Facebook, and then turned her attention to the Internet. She googled everything she'd need to know for tonight: the Metropolitan

Museum, the Youth Foundation, and she even read through more articles about Jarrod and his family.

After she'd had enough of that, she turned on the TV and clicked over to MSNBC to watch all the afternoon news shows.

At three, she soaked in a sea salt bath before spending the next hour on her hair and makeup, imagining the day when she would be sitting in someone's chair, sipping on champagne, while it would be his (because her stylist would definitely be male) job to make her beautiful. But even though she had to do it all herself, by the time she slipped into her dress, she was perfection.

Jarrod agreed when he met her at the door.

"Wow!" he said as he held her hand, guiding her down the stairs.

*And he hasn't even seen the best part yet.* She hated that she had to even wear a coat. The way she looked in this dress, everyone deserved to see her in this glory.

Inside the car, Jarrod's adoration continued. "Do you know how glad I am to have you with me tonight?"

There was no need to hold back anymore. Tonight would be a full-court press. "Do you know how thrilled I am to be going with you?"

He squeezed her hand. "I just hope this isn't too boring for you. First, we're going to meet all the dignitaries—the president of the Youth Foundation . . ."

Jarrod continued, but Sierra found it difficult to hear. How could she focus on his words when her thoughts were at least two hours in the future? She wondered if she would be able to see the moment in his eyes? The moment when he would light up because he realized that she was the one.

At the museum, Harold eased the car into the line for the

VIPs, and then, as the museum's lights glistened, Jarrod held her hand and the two climbed the stairs. As she'd suspected, there was a gaggle of press at the entrance, though she didn't even waste a moment searching for Andre.

"Congressman Cannon," a young man greeted them. "I'm Brandon Holt, the assistant director of the foundation. I'm going to escort you into the reception and the dinner."

Jarrod shook his hand, and then turned to Sierra. "This is my friend, Ms. Dixon."

The young man guided Jarrod and Sierra to the Sackler Wing to leave their coats, and when she took hers off, Jarrod released a low whistle.

"You're going to hurt them tonight," he whispered.

"I hope it's not too much."

"You're too much, baby. But you look wonderful."

At the reception, as a violinist played and tuxedoed waitstaff circled the room with champagne and hors d'oeuvres, Sierra stood by Jarrod's side as he greeted guests and constituents. And every single person who shook his hand was introduced to Sierra Dixon.

"This is my friend, Sierra," he said to them all.

The jealousy that seeped from the women and the envy that burned in the men's eyes let Sierra know that everyone was aware of what the word *friend* meant.

When Jarrod was told that it was time to take his seat at the dais, he led Sierra to the table front and center, kissed her cheek, and said, "I'm gonna keep my eyes on you."

"Please do," she whispered back.

Throughout dinner she chatted with Charlotte and Lovell Hollingsworth, two members of the museum's board, and she impressed them with her knowledge of the Metropolitan, one of the world's largest art museums, founded in the 1870s and now home to more than two million pieces of art.

"My dear," Charlotte said in that old-money lilt, "you must have the congressman call us so that we can give you a private tour of some of the collections."

"I'll certainly do that," Sierra said, trying to emulate the older woman's tone.

When Jarrod stood to give his keynote to the six hundred guests, Sierra beamed as if she already wore his ring. He winked at her before he began and Sierra knew that anyone who doubted who she was in his life before that moment knew then.

Two hours later, the master of ceremonies gave the final good night, and Jarrod strolled to Sierra's table, took her hand, and then whispered into her ear, "I cannot wait to get you back to my place and make mad love to you."

Their good-byes were quick, and as they exited, the press was there once again, snapping shots as they descended the stairs. They found Harold at the curb, slipped into the car, and the privacy window was barely closed before Jarrod was all over Sierra.

"Do you know how sexy you were working that room?" he asked as his tongue tickled her ear.

"I thought you said I was working the dress," she panted.

"That too."

They kissed and caressed, stopping only to get out of the car. Inside the loft, their passion exploded, there was no way to make it to the bedroom. In an instant, Sierra was out of her dress.

Jarrod stepped back and clicked on the lights. His eyes were wide. "Oh, God. You were naked under that the entire night?" he gasped.

All she did was smile and give him a perfect pose.

"Oh, God," he moaned as he lifted her into his arms. "I wouldn't have made it through my speech if I'd known that."

Five times and hours later, they lay in his bed in the dark, holding hands in the silence. Jarrod kissed the top of her head.

"I love you, Sierra," he whispered.

She settled into the wonder of those words and all that they meant. After a few seconds, she said, "I love you, too."

She wanted to get up, do a dance, sing a song, but she did none of the above.

All she did was exhale.

# CHAPTER 30

## *Raine*

Raine gently closed the door to her daughter's room, then checked the front door once more. She clicked off the lights before she headed to the bedroom.

In their room, Dayo sat bare-chested, his back against the bed's headboard. He glanced up from the catalog that rested on his lap. "You checked on Nadia?"

"Yeah," Raine said as Dayo drew back the covers on her side of the bed so that she could climb in. "She was just about asleep. Without her cell, she doesn't know what to do."

"So how long are we going to keep her on this punishment?" he asked before his eyes returned to the African furniture catalog.

Raine shook her head. "I'm not punishing her; I just think she spends too much time on the phone."

They were talking about Nadia, but every time Raine thought about the phone, she remembered the dinner one week ago and the scene she'd walked in on. The image hadn't left her, of the women hovering over the cell, though she hadn't mentioned it to Dayo. What was she supposed to say—that she'd caught his mother playing with their daughter's phone? What was wrong with that?

Nothing.

Except it felt wrong.

"Baby, let me ask you something. Your mom . . ."

He lowered the booklet and turned his attention to her.

Raine asked, "Does she have a problem with Nadia?"

He gave her a blank stare as if he couldn't believe her question. "Why are you asking me that? After all we've been through and the progress we've all made?"

"I think Beerlulu and I have made progress, but I'm just not too sure about how she feels about Nadia." She held up her hand stopping him from saying what he'd told her before. "I know, she loves her. I get that, but—" She stopped, didn't have any more to say.

"Stop looking for what's not there. Nadia's fine, my mother is fine, and anyway"—he tossed the catalog he'd been reading onto the floor—"why am I in bed with the woman I love, talking about my mother?"

She giggled.

"You know there's something wrong with that, right? Especially since you'll be leaving the day after tomorrow."

"Can you believe it? My first tour for Christ."

"I like the way that sounds." He pulled her into his arms. "I'm proud of you, *mchumba*. And I'm really going to work it so that Nadia and I can join you in at least one city."

"And I'm going to come home any chance I get. Even if it's only for a day."

"Or night," he said as he lowered his lips onto hers.

She melted into the softness of his embrace, and when he pulled back, he whispered, *"Nakupenda sana. Nakupenda sana,"* letting her know how much he loved her.

It was when he spoke to her this way, in his language, during these times, that she felt like she'd go mad with pleasure. She had no thoughts of Beerlulu or cell phones. Her mind was wrapped around the man who held her.

She wore one of his pajama tops, but not for much longer. With gentle fingers he freed her from his top and in the next seconds, he was naked, too.

He covered her body with his and then did the same with his lips. Thirteen years had passed, yet they still melded together, the two the same as one.

Dayo was a lover extraordinaire. He was a slow lover, a wonderful lover. Exploring every part of her body, touching every square inch of her skin. Every part of her would be loved.

He began with her hands, pressing them down against the bed, then using his fingers to massage her palms. His tongue followed his fingers and he blazed a trail from her hands to her arms, tickling her at her elbows, then rising up, up, up until he was devouring her neck.

All Raine could do was moan.

Then Dayo's odyssey took him lower, lower, lower, making her pant when he paused and teased her breasts, then continued his passage south. When he worshipped the place that made her a woman, she screamed, crying out in languages that she didn't even speak.

But that was never the best part. It was when he joined with her that she got caught up in the rapture. He loved her as if she was his heaven.

Dayo was never in a hurry. Dayo never tired. Dayo could go all night.

And that's what they did. All night long.

# CHAPTER 31

*Liza*

"*I* just saw Qianna!" Liza told Mann the moment he came back into his office.

"Really?" He walked right past her to his desk, never glancing her way.

"I just saw her leaving with Buddy!"

"Oh, yeah!" he said as if he suddenly remembered. Looking down at his calendar on his desk, Mann continued, "She was supposed to be bringing by a proposal from her school for a program they want the church to sponsor."

"So, you let her drop it off with Buddy?" Liza couldn't believe it. "That doesn't make any sense based on what's going on."

He waved his hands in the air. "The attorneys said it was fine. Our problem is with her mother, not with Qianna." For the first time, he looked up and at her. "It's fine, Liza. Buddy didn't do anything, so it's fine."

She didn't miss that he'd only been able to look into her eyes when he spoke about Buddy.

There was no need to ask Mann anything else. Clearly, they were on a train heading for a major wreck and Mann was driving it all. The only thing she could do was hold on . . .

For the last ten days, Liza had been walking through life like a zombie, reliving that conversation. Even now, as she sat at her desk in her home, her thoughts were back in that place.

Finally, she swiveled around in the chair. For an hour, she'd been trying to write her article for *Life as a First Lady* magazine. She had to get it done since she was leaving tomorrow.

The moment she set her fingers on the keyboard, the phone rang. She glanced at the caller ID, then, without answering, returned to the computer. The ringing stopped, but then started again.

Another glance—it still said PRIVATE NUMBER.

Liza growled. She hated answering before she knew who was on the other end. But when the ringing stopped and then seconds later started again, she picked up the phone.

"Mom?"

"Ingrid!" Liza exclaimed, the joy in her voice instant.

"Is Mann there?"

That question and her tone returned Liza to the darkness where she'd been before the phone rang.

"I'm sorry," Ingrid said as if she could imagine her mother's frown. "But remember the last time I called, he was there and you tried to put him on the phone?" She didn't give her mother time to answer. "I don't want to go through all that drama again. That's why I blocked my number."

"He's not here, but, Ingrid, I wish . . ."

"Please, Mom, don't wish a thing. I called you on your cell first, hoping that you were out."

"My phone is charging."

"Well, I'm glad I got you. How you doin'?"

"I'm good, baby, how about you?"

"I'm hanging. You know, just doing my thing."

Liza had all kinds of questions about what kinds of things her daughter was doing. "Do you need any money?" Even though she was alone, the question came out in a whisper.

A pause and then: "No, Mom, I'm good." Another pause. "Really, I am."

Liza blew out a long breath. She'd been ready to whip out her checkbook just as she had all the times before, even if Mann would get upset the way he always did. But if Ingrid wasn't asking for money, then things must be as she said—good.

"I'm working, Mom. I'm a barista at Starbucks in Santa Monica."

Liza closed her eyes and pushed back all the dreams that she'd had for her daughter before her teenage years. "Do you like it?"

"I do. I mean, there's a chance for advancement and everything. Don't worry. I'm not going to be serving coffee forever."

"I'm not worried," Liza said, shaking her head. "And even if you were to serve coffee for the rest of your life, it's good, honest work. That's all anyone wants from you, baby."

Liza could imagine Ingrid nodding her head in the silence. Then her daughter asked, "So how are you, Mom? You haven't wised up and left Mann yet?"

"Ingrid . . ."

"I know, I know. You love that man, but he doesn't deserve you."

This was her daughter's mantra every time she called, though Liza was sure that Ingrid didn't feel those words in her heart. She couldn't. Mann had doted on Ingrid the way he doted on Liza. There was no reason for Ingrid to speak with such anger against her father.

That's why Liza had decided long ago that the words were not her own, but belonged to her brother. Ingrid and Charlie had been close growing up, and although Charlie now lived on another continent, her children were still in touch, speaking to each other much more frequently than they spoke to her.

"I'm leaving for my tour tomorrow," Liza said, needing to change the subject.

"That's great, Mom! Are you coming to LA?"

"Not this time, but maybe next time we'll get somewhere close in California. Or . . . you can just come home when I get back."

Ingrid sighed. "I was just there," she said, as if the thought of returning to New York was a burden she didn't wish to carry.

"You were here for Christmas. For one day. Not even a night."

"I meant what I said, I'm never sleeping in that house again."

For the millionth time in the six years since Ingrid had been gone, Liza asked, "What is it, Ingrid? Why are you so angry? Why have you shut your father and me out like this?"

"My answer is never going to change. I don't hate you. I just hate the man you live with."

"He's your father, and after the way he treated you, this makes no sense. It never has to me."

"I gotta go."

"No, wait. I'm sorry. Don't hang up."

"Really, Mom, I gotta go. But now that I know you're gonna be on the road, I'll call you more. Okay?"

"Have you heard from your brother?"

A pause. "Yeah, I talked to him yesterday." Before Liza could say anything, Ingrid said, "Please don't ask for his number again. He's cool, Mom. He's really happy. He'll call you for your birthday."

"Okay," Liza said, just grateful for that tidbit. "Next time you speak to him, tell him . . ."

"I will. He knows. And I love you, too." Ingrid ended the call without any more of a good-bye, without giving Liza another chance to ask another question.

She stared at the phone for a long while after she hung up, trying to hold on to Ingrid. She was living a life that she never dreamed of in her young days in Mississippi. Folks in Corinth would never imagine her massive home. No one would be able to picture the cars she drove, or having the money to buy whatever she desired, any designer item she wanted to wear or carry.

It was a fabulous life.

A tortured life.

Because she lived without her children, and now she lived with a secret in her gut that felt like it was ripping her apart.

But she had to push all of her thoughts, her doubts aside. She had to write this article before she got on the plane.

She rested her fingers on the keyboard and then she typed: *Love Unlimited—The Secrets to a Perfect 25-year Marriage.* Her fingers were trembling when she typed the last letter. She stopped, stared at the words on the computer screen.

Then she laid her head down on the desk and cried.

# CHAPTER 32

# Raine

This was a feeling that Raine had forgotten. The overwhelming sadness that washed over her as she placed the last pair of pants into her suitcase, then closed it.

A few years had passed since she'd last left Nadia and Dayo to hit the road. Now she was used to being home just about every night. How was she supposed to do this?

Well, at least she'd finished packing so when Nadia and Dayo came home it would be all about them. She was going to squeeze the joy out of every last minute with her husband and her daughter because she was already on the verge of some serious tears.

Just as she dragged her suitcase from the bed, the doorbell rang and her smile was back. She didn't even have to peek through the peephole to know who was on the other side. All outside visitors had to be announced by the concierge, and since Beerlulu came by on the regular, Raine knew it was her mother-in-law.

"Beerlulu," she greeted her when she opened the door.

While they hugged, Beerlulu said, "One day, you're going to just call me Mama, *Binti*."

Raine's smile was wide. She wasn't there yet, though she hoped to be soon.

Beerlulu said, "I hope it's okay for us to drop by like this." It wasn't until her mother-in-law said that that Raine noticed Beerlulu had not come alone.

"Oh . . . *Shangazi,*" Raine said, hoping that her pronunciation of the Swahili word for "aunt" was close to the way Dayo said it.

Dayo's aunt stepped toward Raine with a blank face, but her hug was as heartfelt as Beerlulu's.

"Come in," she said to them both.

In the seconds that it took for Raine to close the door, then follow the women into her home, her mind was flooded with questions. She had seen Beerlulu just about every day in the month since she'd moved into her own apartment. But this was the first time that any of Dayo's other relatives had ever been in their home.

Raine asked, "Is everything okay?" as the two women lowered themselves onto the sofa side by side, so close they almost looked like one. Her eyes shifted from one to the other.

"Everything is just fine, isn't it, *Dada*?"

Her sister nodded.

Turning back to Raine, Beerlulu asked, "So, you're leaving in the morning?"

"Yeah. I'm excited, but on the other side, I'm gonna miss my baby"—she paused—"both of them." She laughed.

"I will miss you." Beerlulu bowed her head slightly. "I will always be sorry for the way we started and I thank you for forgiving me."

Raine wanted to stand and embrace her mother-in-law again. "There were things that I could've done better, too. Maybe if we had just talked . . ."

"Well, that's what *Dada* and I want to do." She glanced at her sister. "We want to talk to you."

Raine nodded. "Okay." She tried to keep the cheer in her voice, but it was difficult because of the way her heart beat hard against her chest.

Beerlulu sat up a bit straighter, if that was possible, and clasped her hands in her lap. She sat so still that only her lips moved. "This is something I should have talked to you about a long time ago. If I had, all of that . . . trouble would have never happened between us."

Raine sat as still as Beerlulu, just waiting.

Beerlulu continued, "As the matriarch of my family, I am responsible for everyone." She leaned forward slightly. "I am responsible for you, *Binti.*"

That should have made Raine feel wonderful. She'd never had a woman speak those words to her and she wanted to sit back and savor the glow of a mother's love. But she couldn't ignore the pounding, pounding, pounding of her heart. "Thank you for saying that." And then she added, *"Asante."*

Beerlulu and her sister laughed together; Raine's effort to speak their language seemed to put them both at ease. But it did nothing for Raine's heart. It was pounding. Pounding. Pounding.

"I am responsible for you . . . and I am responsible for my granddaughter."

Raine fought to push back the images that rushed to her mind. Beerlulu's responsibility had manifested in horrible words and in the binding of Nadia's feet.

"I want the very best for my granddaughter."

The words were already rising up inside of her. Words that she'd said to Beerlulu so many times. But in the past when she'd told Beerlulu that she and Dayo wanted the best for their daughter, too, she'd spoken those words in anger. She didn't want to speak that way today. So she let her words settle in her throat and stayed silent. And waited.

Beerlulul kept on, "Your daughter, my granddaughter, is Kenyan."

Raine shook her head. She couldn't stay silent about that. "She's half Kenyan." Her voice was sharp with attitude. "Half of her comes from me."

"Of course, I didn't mean anything," Beerlulu said. "It's just that I have to make sure that she knows her Kenyan roots, the side of her father. She needs to know her family. You believe that, don't you?"

This felt like a trick question, so Raine moved her head— half shaking, half nodding.

Beerlulu said, "I want her to know about Kenya and Kenyan women."

Raine chewed on the edge of her lip, still not sure about what all of this meant. "I don't have a problem with that, Beerlulu. If you want Nadia to spend more time with you, to get to know her family better, I'm fine with that. I'll make sure that Dayo and I take her to Brooklyn more often." And then another peace offering. "You can take her with you, too, sometimes."

That made Beerlulu smile. Her shoulders softened and she exchanged a glance with her sister. *Dada* smiled, too.

"That would be great. And then she will come to understand her family, and the pride that comes from being an African woman." She glanced at her sister. "And we will prepare her for womanhood."

Now the pounding marched from Raine's heart to her head. She recalled these words—so similar to the ones Raine had heard Beerlulu say to Dayo. "Nadia's only twelve," Raine said as if Beerlulu had forgotten that fact. "There's nothing to prepare her for yet. I mean, she's had her period and she and I have discussed that."

"She's already menstruating?" Beerlulu said as if that thought put her in shock.

"Yes."

There was another side-eyed glance between the sisters, then: "Well, this is something that must happen right away. We have to make sure that Nadia has the full rights and privileges of being a proud Kenyan woman."

"Beerlulu, maybe you just need to tell me what you're talking about, because I can't figure out what you're trying to say."

"We want to prepare Nadia to become a woman with class, with grace, and with the pride of a Kenyan woman."

"O-kay . . ."

Beerlulu continued, "None of that comes naturally." She glanced at her sister, who nodded. And then Beerlulu said, "There is a procedure . . ."

A beat—and Raine knew!

"There is a ceremony . . ." Beerlulu kept on, unaware of the rumbling inside of Raine.

"You better be talking about a sweet-sixteen *ceremony*. Or a debutante *ceremony*." Her volume rose with each word she spoke.

Beerlulu stared at her for a moment, cognizant now that her daughter-in-law understood. She looked right into Raine's eyes. "It must be done."

Raine jumped off the love seat. "You're talking about *cutting* my daughter?"

"I'm talking about making sure she has everything she needs," she said, as if she was not affected by the outburst.

"You're talking about *cutting* my daughter!" Raine repeated.

"It's necessary. She's already menstruating and that means she's on the verge of being totally out of control. That's why she's friends with that girl and why she's talking to boys. It's her hormones, and if we don't take those away, she'll give in to those desires. We have to take away that desire . . ."

"You actually want to *cut* my daughter," was the only thing Raine could say.

"I want to make sure that she doesn't make a mistake and bring disgrace . . ."

"Get out," Raine said, shocking herself at how calm she sounded. She felt everything except calm, and as she pointed to the door, her shaking hands proved her true rage. "You need to leave, Beerlulu."

Beerlulu and her sister sat still, as if they hadn't heard Raine.

"No matter what you say," Beerlulu continued as if Raine was not stark, raving mad, "I know you see your daughter going down the wrong road. But, we can help because we love her, too."

In three strides, Raine was in front of her mother-in-law. Her sister jumped up, but it was too late. Raine grabbed Beerlulu's arm, dragging her up from the couch, shocking both women. "You will never touch my daughter." Now her words were a warning. "You need to just get out of my house," she said, her hand still latched on to Beerlulu, "and if you ever mention this again, you will never see Nadia."

"Listen to me, *Binti,* listen to me!"

"No, you need to listen to me and you better hear me good. You will never lay your hands on my daughter that way. And if that means she's not good enough for you, then fine. You don't have to have anything to do with her or with me. But you better trust and know and understand that you will never perform that on my daughter. Do you hear me?"

"If you don't allow this, Nadia will be an outcast in our community. Even in our family."

"Call her whatever you want, but you'll also be calling her a child who was never abused or mutilated by you!"

Beerlulu's head snapped back. "What are you talking about? This is not abuse. This is love."

"Then you and your love need to get the hell out of my home." This time Raine led her mother-in-law and Dayo's aunt to the door.

Before she stepped outside, Beerlulu said, "Please."

Raine's glare was like a laser beam, and before the women were fully over the threshold, she slammed the door behind them.

Stumbling into the living room, she grabbed the telephone. She had to call Dayo.

The pounding had left her heart, but it had not moved away from her head.

It was because she couldn't tear her eyes away from the computer. She watched the video—again—of the girls as young as five years old being mutilated. In rooms filled with mothers and aunts and cousins and neighbors who held them down and then cut out the very center that made them women.

"Oh, God."

That's what she said every time she got to the end of video. But then she hit the Play button again, watching, cringing, actually feeling her blood boiling as it pumped through her veins.

Raine never heard the accompanying sounds. She kept the audio on Mute because she didn't think she'd be able to handle it. Not that any volume was needed; the images brought the girl's cries right through the screen.

Then a sound broke through the silence—the key in the front door. She glanced at the clock; Dayo had made it home in less than thirty minutes. Seconds later, she felt him standing at the entrance to the library, and when she looked up, the pain that was in his eyes matched what was in her heart. He moved toward her and her eyes returned to the computer. Behind her, Dayo gasped, and she knew he was looking at what she'd found on the Internet as soon as she'd hung up the phone from him.

"Turn that off," he demanded.

When she made no moves, he reached around and pressed the button to shut down the computer.

She didn't look up when she asked, "Did you know your mother wanted to cut Nadia?"

"She's talked about it."

Slowly, her eyes rose to meet his. "And you were going to let her?" she asked with tears in her voice.

"No!" He shook his head. "No! I . . . don't want to do that and she knows it."

"Then why did she bring that mess to me?" Raine worked hard to stay steady.

"You know my mother. She's strong in her convictions."

"And I'm just as strong in mine." Raine pushed herself up, raised her chin, and stood on her toes. Still she was not eye to eye with her husband, but she was close. "That will never happen to Nadia!"

"Of course not," Dayo said.

After a moment, she nodded and slumped back into the chair. "I should've known, though. I should've seen this coming. The day I overhead you and your mother, and then her suddenly being so nice to me."

"That had nothing to do with it. My mother genuinely loves you and she loves Nadia."

"I told her to keep her love."

Dayo inhaled a long breath. "My mother thinks that is love."

"It's sick and it's illegal. How could you even entertain any discussion of this?"

"Because it's not sick and it's not illegal where I come from. It's a rite of passage into womanhood. It's something to be proud of."

Raine looked at her husband with new eyes. "Just hearing you say that makes me want to scream. There's a reason why it's called female genital mutilation, Dayo. It's mutilation."

"That's not what we call it. That's not the way we see it. You have to understand . . . it's how I grew up. It was done to my mother and my aunts and my cousins. The girls at school would come home after summer holiday and they would be proud."

"It's sick."

"It's part of who we are."

"It's sick."

"It helps . . . For my people it's a wonderful part of our life."

"Wonderful?" she hissed, and pointed to the darkened computer screen. "You show me one second on that video where something wonderful happened!"

"I'm not trying to convince you. I just want you to see that my mother is not some monster. This is what she knows, and she can't wrap her brain around this not happening for her granddaughter."

"I don't get it, Dayo. You know how making love is for me and you—why would you want to take that away from your daughter?"

His chin fell to his chest as if he'd been wounded by her

question. "I don't want to do that." He looked up. "I agree *with you*. I stand *with you*. That will never happen to Nadia." His eyes were filled with emotion when he added, "Never." He pulled her from the chair and into his arms, and for the first time in the hour that had just passed, Raine exhaled.

He said, "I will speak to my mother. The subject is closed."

"Thank you," she whispered, though it wasn't as easy to dismiss her thoughts, her rage.

She needed to calm down, though. She trusted Dayo to handle his mother. Plus, she didn't want to spend her last night at home ranting in her head.

Her last night.

*Dang!* Raine thought. *This is not the time to be leaving.*

# CHAPTER 33

*Sierra*

Sierra rolled her carry-on into the living room and sat it next to her suitcase, then plopped down onto the sofa and yawned. She glanced at her watch once again. Yvonne said the driver would be at her door at eight sharp, so she had a few minutes.

A month ago, she'd been waiting for this day, but now she didn't want to leave. It was because of the last two weeks—after her appearance with Jarrod at the Metropolitan.

Their picture had been in the *New York Post,* though it was small and one of many that went along with coverage of the event. And then there was that footage on MSNBC where for five seconds Congressman Jarrod Cannon was seen holding hands with Sierra Dixon.

She still didn't have the ring, but she wasn't pressed about that anymore. The ring was coming. With the way she and Jarrod had been getting on, she wouldn't be surprised if he met her in one of their first cities and presented her with the diamond. No, she wouldn't be surprised at all—in fact, she expected it.

The only blemish on her fabulous life had come from that shine stealer, Yvonne. Yvonne, who had seen the pictures of her and Jarrod in the *Post.* Yvonne, who had come over unannounced, which is the only way she could trick Sierra into answering the intercom. Yvonne, who stomped into her apartment with the newspaper in hand, demanding an explanation.

"What is this?"

If Sierra hadn't been floating, she would have told Yvonne to lower her voice and never speak to her like that again. But it was hard to say all of that with the grin that was on her face, so she only responded with, "It's a picture of me and Congressman Cannon."

"Are you going out with him?" Yvonne had huffed.

That had taken her smile away. "Not that it's any of your business, but yes."

"Not my business? Are you kidding me?" Yvonne had paced in the small space of the living room. "We're about to go on tour!" she shouted. "What are we going to do now with this picture all over the place?"

"What does this picture have to do with the tour?"

"Don't play dumb with me. You're supposed to be celibate, and now that you've hooked up with the most eligible man in New York, are we supposed to believe that?"

Sierra's mouth had opened wide. "I cannot believe you're getting in my business like this."

"And I keep telling you, anything that affects Destiny's Divas makes your business my business. So, are you sleeping with him?"

Sierra waited for a moment before she picked up her cell phone.

"What are you doing?" Yvonne asked as she watched Sierra press numbers into her phone.

"I'm calling Jarrod so that you can ask him because I know you won't believe me. So I want him to answer your questions."

When Sierra pressed the phone to her ear, Yvonne said, "Hang up, Sierra. I don't need to talk to him."

She waited a moment before she did what Yvonne asked.

Yvonne said, "So, you're *not* sleeping with him?"

"No, I'm dating him, and I didn't know that dating was against the rules."

"It's not, but people won't believe that you're not sleeping with him."

"I don't care what people believe, but I'll tell you this—he knew who I was when he met me and he knew that I was celibate. We talked about it, we talked about why I'm celibate, and he's fine with all of it. In fact, he celebrates it. He respects me, he respects what we're doing, and him going out with me is an awesome addition to his résumé."

Yvonne frowned. "So, this is just a publicity stunt?"

"No! We're very serious. I'm just saying that having a Christian woman on his arm who has the same values and morals that he has is not a bad thing. Jarrod plans on moving up politically—way up—so he would never do anything to jeopardize his career or mine."

Sierra wasn't sure if Yvonne had bought her story, though she didn't have much to say after that explanation. But right before Yvonne walked out the door, she added, "There's a lot riding on this group, Sierra. We all need to be on the same page."

Sierra had looked straight into Yvonne's face and said, "You will never have to worry about me."

Yvonne had left Sierra's apartment seemingly satisfied, though Sierra was sure that she wouldn't have been if Yvonne had known that she never planned on calling Jarrod. Her phone had been off the whole time.

But at least Yvonne had been taken care of and that left Sierra to delight in the two weeks that followed. Out of the fourteen days that had passed, they had spent ten of those days together. He was an extension of her now, so how was she supposed to leave him behind?

And it was all the more difficult since Jarrod's plans had changed and he hadn't been able to come to New York last night.

"I'm so sorry, babe," he said after he told her he wouldn't be able to spend her last night with her.

"What happened?"

"A special meeting was called and . . ."

"So, you're saying I'm not important to you?" she snapped.

"What?"

"It's my last night, Jarrod," she yelled. "How can you do this to me?"

"Look, Sierra, I didn't call you for this. I don't do drama, and if you can't understand that my work, then . . ."

"No, no, no . . . please," she begged. "I'm sorry. It's just that I wanted to see you so badly. It's going to be weeks before . . ."

He paused for a long moment. "I understand. Listen, I have to go. I've got to get to this meeting, and I'll call you later."

She'd hung up and tossed the frame that held the picture that she'd cut out from the *Post* across the room and screamed for ten minutes. But then she was calmer after she'd packed, after he called back and told her that he loved her and would miss her and couldn't wait to see her again. He'd tried to make up for his time with his words. It was a valiant effort, but she was not happy.

The buzz of the intercom pulled her away from her reflections and she pressed the button to let the driver in. Opening her door, she yelled down, "I'm on the fifth floor," in case Yvonne hadn't told him.

She gathered her purse, slipped on her coat, and then stood

in the silence for a moment. Her life wouldn't be the same when she returned to this apartment. She had no doubt she'd be a bona fide star after five weeks on the road, but even better, she'd be engaged. This was the end of her life as she'd known it and she couldn't say good-bye fast enough.

Sierra turned around at the soft knock on her opened door and gasped.

"Good morning, Golden Lady." Jarrod leaned casually against the door.

Sierra stood, stunned with surprise, and then leapt into his arms. "What are you doing here?"

He held her for a moment before he grabbed the handle of her roller bag, then reached for the carry-on that she held. "I'm here to make sure you get to the airport on time."

"Oh, my God! I thought I was never going to see you again."

He laughed. "Never?"

"Well, it was going to feel like never. But you can't take me. There's a car service on its way."

"Not on his way; he was here, but Harold . . . and a couple of hundred dollars . . . made him disappear." With the bag on his shoulder and the other in his hand, he paused. "So, is it okay for me to take my woman to the airport?"

*My woman.* "Are you kidding me? Yes, yes, yes!"

Harold met them in the vestibule, and after greeting Sierra, took the bags from Jarrod.

"LaGuardia, right?" Harold asked as Sierra and Jarrod followed him down the brownstone's steps.

"Yes."

Inside the car, Jarrod said, "I had only one goal for today. To hold your hand"—he wrapped his fingers around hers—"and then give you a hug before you leave me for all of these weeks."

"Just a hug?" she asked, leaning toward him.

"If I could've gotten here any earlier, I would have, but this is best anyway. Because you know how we do, we might have never gotten out of bed."

She laughed. "Well, I can't wait for my first day off because I'm gonna take the earliest plane to DC and I'm not going to let you get up, no matter how many meetings you have."

The corners of his smile dipped just a little. "About that. My meetings yesterday. Young lady, you have quite a temper."

"No I don't," she snapped, not able to help herself.

His eyebrow arched. "Well, when we spoke yesterday afternoon, it started to get a bit heated."

"I thought I apologized. I thought you understood that all I wanted was to be with you one last time."

"First of all, it's not going to be the last time. And secondly, these kinds of things are gonna happen, baby. We have fabulous, wonderful careers where sometimes we have to put the other off to take care of business."

She wanted to tell him it wasn't that way for her. She would walk away from Destiny's Divas if that's what he wanted her to do. Anything for him.

He squeezed her hand. "Sierra, I care about you more than I've cared for anyone. I love you and you've got to trust that and trust me."

She turned away from him for a moment and took in her favorite view—the New York City skyline from the Triborough Bridge. Without looking back at him, she said, "I'm sorry," so softly he barely heard her.

With a smile, he leaned over and kissed her, a long, soulful kiss that she felt deep inside her bones. And then she rested her head on his shoulder. No more words were spoken, no more words were needed. For the first time in her life, Sierra felt it for real—she was loved, really loved.

At the airport, Harold took her license and checked her in at the curb. Sierra and Jarrod stood together, inside each other's arms.

"I just realized," Jarrod said as he squeezed her tighter, "that in all the time we've spent together, you've never sung for me."

"Really?" She laughed. "So you don't count all that singing that you have me doing when we . . ."

He chuckled. "I'm talking about you singing in English. And I want to hear you sing. In fact, I think you should write a song for me, about us."

"I'm not a writer."

"But, you could do this for me."

Harold returned with her boarding pass and then slipped into the front seat of the car. Around them, the airport bustled with energy as vans pulled up beside them, cars honked behind them, travelers rolled suitcases by them. But Jarrod and Sierra stood in the center as if they were all that mattered.

"I'm going to miss you so much," he said.

"That's good to hear."

"My mom told me last night that she's a big fan of Destiny's Divas. She and my father can't wait to meet you." He paused and looked right into her eyes when he added, "It's definitely time."

His words made her want to sit down on the curb and just cry. She'd found her prince and now she was leaving?

"I can't wait," she said, glad that her voice held up and wasn't trembling the way she was inside.

Jarrod pressed his lips against hers, but then he pulled back so quickly, he gave her no time to taste him.

"Have a good trip, Golden Lady. Call me tonight." He blew her a kiss before he disappeared into the car.

Sierra stood at the curb as Harold maneuvered around double-parked shuttles and taxis. She stayed and watched until she couldn't see Jarrod's car anymore.

She sighed. *Dang!* This was not the time to be leaving.

# CHAPTER 34

## Liza

$\mathcal{B}$ehind her, Mann snored as if he was in a deep and restful sleep. But for the three hours since she'd been in bed, Liza had not closed her eyes. How could she? In just hours, she'd be leaving home. Leaving her husband to do God knows what.

For over a week, she'd been in such a dilemma. For over a week, her head had hurt because she just couldn't leave it alone. She hadn't even tried to talk to Mann again, but she was sure that she could go to Buddy.

Her Buddy, her cousin, her ace, her first and only best friend. But her cousin had transferred his allegiance, though she couldn't be mad about that. Mann had given him a new life, too. Because of Mann, Buddy was a college-educated, six-figure-income, key staff member of a prominent church. Buddy wasn't about to give up anything on the man who turned him from a country bumpkin to a city slicker.

There was no place for her to go for answers.

Except . . .

For a moment, Liza listened to Mann's snore, and then she rolled out of the bed. Not that she had to worry about her husband, he'd sleep through a fire. Grabbing her robe, she tip-toed from their bedroom.

As she moved toward the office, she wondered how what she was about to do would help. But it was something that had been on her mind—had never left her thoughts for weeks.

By the time she sat behind the desk in their office, her hands were shaking, her heart was pounding, her head was hurting. Still, she powered up the computer. Her fingertips felt cold as she typed *www.* into the browser, and just like last time, *www.females4men.com* came up.

She scrolled past the User Name and Password until she found the Join Now button. She typed in a fake profile as fast as her trembling would allow. It was too simple. In an instant, she was in.

Her jaw dropped so fast, she was sure she'd injured herself. But what hurt more were her eyes. She'd never seen anything like this.

On the first page, there were nothing but photos. Of girls. Young girls. Doing all kinds of things to each other and themselves.

These were girls. Not women.

*Girls!*

Liza's eyes scanned the photographs. Black girls. White girls. Brown girls. All around the same age, maybe fourteen, maybe fifteen, not one of them looking even sixteen.

"Oh, God," she moaned as the dots in her head began to connect.

She stared for minutes, not even able to move. Just stared. Until her emotions began to rise from her center and she rushed from the office into the hall to the bathroom. She made it just in time to regurgitate her disgust.

"Oh, my God," she whispered once she was empty. She fell onto the floor and hugged the commode. "What am I supposed to do?"

Liza sat there, in that bathroom, on the floor, asking herself that question until the sun began to peek over the horizon. But even in the brightness of the first morning light, Liza had no more clarity.

Liza was grateful for God's amazing timing. It was God's timing that allowed her to leave without having to look straight into Mann's eyes. Mann had to be at the church this morning at seven for an online video interview he was doing with a church in London. So she'd snuck back into the bedroom just minutes before the alarm clock rang, and as Mann showered, she lay preparing for the performance she'd have to give once he returned to the bedroom.

When Mann jumped out of the shower, she stayed stiff in their bed, as if she was dead. He dressed, then only kissed her on the cheek. "I'll miss you; call me tonight. And, oh, I'll take your bags downstairs for you, okay?"

He didn't even notice that she didn't respond.

Even after he left, she waited for minutes—just in case he returned. Because there was no way she could face him. She didn't know if she'd be able to look into his eyes ever again.

When she felt safe, she showered as if her life wasn't over. As if all was normal. But she had to act this way because if she didn't, she'd have to admit that her husband was . . . was what? A pedophile?

As she waited downstairs for the car that Yvonne had sent, her eyes traveled around the living room. It amazed her that there was no sign of the sin from the sinner who lived in this house. Not that she was a saint, but . . .

What was she supposed to do? Go to the police?

No! How could she? What would she say? She saw a web-site—would that be enough? Plus, he was still her husband.

The sound of a slamming car door rescued her and Liza rushed to the door before the bell rang.

"Mrs. Washington?" the driver said.

She nodded, pointed to her bags, then stepped out of her home without taking a single glance back.

As the driver loaded her suitcases, Liza settled into the back-seat and closed her eyes. Moments later, the car edged away from the curb, and then: "Mrs. Washington, I think that woman is try-ing to get your attention."

Liza spun her body around. Through the back window, she saw her. A woman running, waving her hands wildly. She recog-nized her right away. Mrs. Tucker. Qianna's mother.

Her mouth was moving like she had lots to say, but Liza couldn't decipher her words through the closed window.

The driver said, "Do you want me to turn around?"

Mrs. Tucker was closer now, and Liza could see her eyes. Mad eyes that darted around like her hands.

"No," she said. "I don't know her. Just go. Quickly, please!"

As the car sped up and exited the cul-de-sac, Liza didn't turn back. She'd wanted to talk to Mrs. Tucker before, but there was no need to talk to her now.

She closed her eyes and considered it all.

*Dang!* Liza knew this was not the time to be leaving, but what else could she do?

# CHAPTER 35

# *Destiny's Divas*

The moment the airplane leveled and the seat belt sign clicked off, Yvonne released such a loud sigh that all three of Destiny's Divas stared at her.

"What?" she asked, looking first at Liza, who sat next to her, then across the first class aisle to Raine and Sierra. "I know y'all aren't looking at me, not the way I was stressed out this morning."

"You're our manager." Raine waved her hand. "Stressed out is part of your job description."

"Not stressed out like that, thinking that one of my Divas wasn't going to make the plane." Yvonne snatched a magazine from the seat pocket in front of her, crossed her legs, and began to flip through the pages. But after only about three seconds, she shut the magazine. "And anyway," she started again, "*why* did you have me all stressed out? I can't believe that I was standing out there waiting for you." She pointed to Raine. "I expected that from Sierra . . ."

"Hey," Sierra yelled out.

". . . but not from you, Raine. You're the professional."

"That's what you get for not believing in me," Sierra said.

But then, with a smile, she curled up in her seat and returned to typing on her cell phone.

Yvonne could tell that Sierra had tuned her out, but she still wanted to know what was up with Raine. "So . . . are you okay?" she asked her.

"Yeah," she said. "Sorry I was late, but Nadia wasn't feeling well this morning, and I had a hard time pulling away. I didn't want to leave."

"Okay, so now I feel really bad," Yvonne said. "So, is she really sick?"

Raine shook her head. "Just a little cough, but it still wasn't easy walking out the door."

Yvonne reached across the aisle and patted her hand. "I understand. Well, maybe this summer she'll be able to travel a little with you."

"Maybe," she said as she reclined in her seat and closed her eyes.

Yvonne sat back, a bit surprised at being dismissed, but when it didn't look like Raine was going to say another word, she turned her attention to Liza. She watched the matriarch of the group as Liza stared out the window. Even though she couldn't see Liza's face, she imagined that it was stiff and serious just by the way she sat.

"So," Yvonne began. "Are you going to finally tell me what happened? Why were you crying when you got to the gate?"

Liza took her time turning to face Yvonne. "It was nothing. I'm just a little emotional about all of this."

"You know I have to ask—everything okay at home?"

"Of course," she said, turning back to the window.

"Okay, well, at least we're all on the plane. We're all headed to Houston and it's all gonna be fine now, right?"

Liza only nodded, hoping that would be a clue for Yvonne to just shut up. She didn't want to talk. All she wanted to do was take in the white cover of the clouds below. And just imagine that she was in heaven. At that moment, she almost wished that she was. Then, at least, she wouldn't have to deal with the pot-pourri of emotions that swirled inside of her. For weeks she'd been living inside a mystery, but it had been solved. Every dot connected.

And the first dot started back in 1982, when she was fifteen and the big-city preacher came to town. Back in those days, he couldn't keep his hands off of her. Not until she became pregnant at twenty, and then again a few years later. Liza would swear right now that she'd be able to count the number of times they'd had sex since.

When Mann had not been able to do anything more than hold her, she thought it was the weight she'd gained during pregnancy that had turned him off. She knew now that it was . . . and much more. It was the way her breasts had filled out and the curves that came from having a baby that made her unattractive to her husband.

That's when his ministry had been born. Deliver Our Daughters had been a gold mine of young girls. How many had there been?

"Oh, my God!"

"Liza?"

She hadn't meant to moan like that out loud. "I'm sorry," she said, facing Yvonne with what she hoped was a good enough fake smile. "I'm still thinking about this morning."

"I know. And some of what you're feeling might be a little bit of nerves, too."

"Yes"—she nodded—"nerves."

*Nerves* was the perfect word. Because how was she supposed to have the nerve to go on—with Mann and Destiny's Divas?

She really had no choice with the Divas. Financial commitments had been made, people had purchased tickets, Sierra, Raine, and Yvonne depended on her, not to mention the forty, fifty people who were employed with the tour. Too much would happen, too many would be affected if she dropped out.

She had to stay with the Divas. But the question was, did she have to stay with Mann?

# CHAPTER 36

## Sierra

The limousine was waiting right at the curb of the Houston airport, and as the three Divas, plus Yvonne, rushed out of the terminal, Sierra still wondered about their luggage.

Yvonne had given them the drill: the limousine would take them to the radio station, then to a two-hour run-through at the arena before they would go to the hotel. By the time they got there, their bags would be, too, Yvonne had assured them.

Sierra wasn't sure how much she liked that, but this was the beginning of her celebrity life. She had to get used to not having to worry about trivial things.

What was important to her right now was Jarrod. All she wanted to do was speak to him, hear his voice, and tell him that she'd arrived. But there was no privacy in the car and even though Yvonne knew about Jarrod, she really didn't want the others in her business. No use inviting unnecessary drama.

So, as the car rolled toward the radio station, Sierra texted Jarrod, then focused on the song that she'd typed into her smart phone. Jarrod was right—she had been able to do this.

She read over some of the words that she'd written:

*Love without you . . . is like a song without words, a beginning without an end, a day without night. . . .*

This was so much better than anything she'd ever expected, and now that she read the words again, she knew exactly what she was going to do with this song. She was going to sing it to Jarrod . . . at their wedding. Yes! Right as they stood at the altar, she would surprise him, make him break down and cry in front of their three hundred or so guests.

"Okay," Yvonne said as the car came to a stop. "I told the show's producer that we wouldn't be here for more than twenty minutes 'cause my focus is to get you to the hotel as soon as I can. Y'all need to rest up. Especially after the mornings you had."

"Not me," Sierra sang. "I'm fine."

She laughed as both Raine and Liza rolled their eyes. If they had just half of her joy, they'd be singing and dancing, too.

There weren't many nice things Sierra had to say about Yvonne, but she couldn't hate on the fact that this lady was on her job. She whisked the three of them into the studio as if they were the president or something, and just a few minutes passed before they were sitting inside the studio.

The DJ, a young woman who reminded Sierra of Yolanda Adams, greeted them. "I'm so happy to have you ladies here," she said, hugging each of them. "I'm Debbie."

Once they were all seated with their headphones and mics, she told them that after the song that was playing, they would be on.

A couple of seconds later and Debbie nodded. Into her mic, she said, "Everybody knows that song. Marvin Sapp's 'Never Would Have Made It.' Y'all know what he's singing about?"

"Yes!" the Divas said in unison.

"Well, in case y'all don't recognize those voices, you just

heard the sound of the hottest gospel group in America, ladies and gentlemen. They are right here in the studio with me. Right here in Houston for the first stop on their twenty-city tour. Ladies and gentlemen, I give you Destiny's Divas. How you ladies doing?"

"Fine," they said together again.

"We are so happy to have you here. Thank you for kicking it off in Houston."

This time only Raine spoke. "We are so excited to begin our tour deep in the heart of Texas."

The DJ laughed. "I know that's right. So, ladies, tell us a little bit about yourselves." She turned first to Sierra. "Let's start with you, the one everyone calls 'the young one.'"

They all laughed and Sierra said, "Well, I've done a little bit of modeling and I've worked in a bookstore in Harlem, New York, but singing has always been my dream, and I was blessed when I sang with Raine in the choir at our church. The next thing I knew, she scooped me up. I'm here because of Raine."

"Yes, Raine," the DJ said. "Also known as Rainebow, one of the hottest singers of the nineties. What's up with you, girl?"

"Everything," Raine said. "But before we move on to me, I just want to say that it wasn't just Sierra's singing that impressed me. One Sunday, she stood up and gave her testimony of how she was still a virgin. And I just thought that was so amazing on so many levels, because in today's times, you're treated like a pariah if you're not sleeping with every man you meet. Especially someone as young and as beautiful as Sierra."

"I know that's right," the DJ said. Turning back to Sierra, she added, "There are so many young woman who need to hear what you have to say."

Sierra's smile was stiff as she nodded. She wished that Raine and everyone else would just shut up about that celibacy thing. What were they going to do when she got married? What were they going to say about her story then?

The DJ said, "Now back to you, Rainebow. I remember when the announcement was made that you were going gospel. Now, you know how much I love the Lord, but I'm telling you, I was one of the ones from the sidelines yelling, 'No! No! Don't give up all that cash money.' "

Raine laughed. "Well, as you can see, I didn't give up anything. I took it all straight to the Lord and He blessed me not only with a new career, but with sisters that I could share all of this with. Plus, the idea of giving our testimonies . . . there's nothing out here like Destiny's Divas."

"That's right," the DJ affirmed. "And you're still married to that sexy African," the DJ growled, and they all laughed. "That's a heavenly blessing in itself." Turning to Liza, she said, "So now let's hear from First Lady Liza Washington. How are you?"

"I'm fine," Liza said. "Thank you for having us."

"So, on the tour you're going to be talking about having that long marriage. How long?" The DJ looked down at her notes. "Twenty-eight years?"

The question startled Liza. "No, no. It's only been twenty-five," she said. "We're heading toward twenty-eight."

"Oh, sorry about that. One of our producers got the number mixed up. Twenty-five, twenty-eight—it's still a long time and that's what you'll be sharing with the crowd tonight, right?"

"Yes," she said simply, and when she didn't add another word, Raine and Sierra frowned.

Liza's testimony was always the longest, so what was up with the one-word answer?

"Well, we're glad to have all of you ladies in Houston. And

you're going to have a little bit of our Texas hospitality because all three shows here are sold out already."

They all clapped.

The DJ continued, "And I'm going to be the guest DJ tonight for the opener. I can't wait to be there with all of you as we jam for the Lord. And you know what I'm most excited about?" She paused, and when she started again, it sounded like her voice had gone down an octave as she spoke more seriously. "There are a lot of people who can sing, but what we all need— men and women—is to hear the testimonies, the real stories of real life, so that everyone knows that no matter what they're facing, they can make it. So thank you, Destiny's Divas, for getting onstage and telling your truths."

Their voices were softer now when they said, "Thank you."

"Now, I'm gonna spin one of the songs that you'll hear tonight from Destiny's Divas. This song just dropped today and it's on their new CD. Let's give it up for Destiny's Divas and their new single, 'There's Nothing But Truth in the Lord.' Nuff said, right, ladies?"

The DJ laughed, but she didn't seem to notice that she laughed alone.

## CHAPTER 37

~∞~

# *Destiny's Divas*

"Sierra! Give me your phone!" Yvonne barked.

Sucking her teeth, she slammed her cell into Yvonne's hand. This was what she hated about being in Destiny's Divas— Yvonne often spoke to her as if she was her mother. She needed to tell Yvonne that her mother had passed away a long time ago and she wasn't in the market for a new one.

But she pushed aside thoughts of Yvonne and went back to where her mind had been all day—on Jarrod. She was about to go on a real stage for the first time in her life and she hadn't been able to speak to him.

She'd tried to call him all day, from the moment she was finally alone in her hotel room. They weren't in the Ritz, but the four-star hotel was luxurious enough, and as she lounged around for the few hours she'd had, she imagined Jarrod by her side. They could have made mad love all day and all night in that place. But she couldn't even get him on her cell for some good old-fashioned phone sex. Not that they'd ever done that before, but her plan had been to introduce Jarrod to it and have plenty of it while she was on the road.

Well, phone sex was out of the question because she couldn't even catch him long enough to say, "I love you."

Now she'd have to go onstage for the first time without speaking to the man she loved. *Loved.* That word swept away her angst and now she felt nothing but joy. Because Sierra wasn't just saying it or thinking it—this time she could trust her heart to really believe it.

"Okay, ladies," Yvonne whispered. "Get ready, get ready."

From the side of the stage, Sierra heard the DJ that they'd met this morning riling the crowd.

"Y'all ready to rock this house for the Lord?" the DJ's voice screamed through the arena.

Twenty thousand cheers came back to her and Sierra shivered. All of those folks were waiting for them.

"In five, four, three, two, one," Yvonne counted. "All right. Go!" she shouted.

Liza, Raine, and then Sierra stepped onto the stage, following the same path that they'd practiced this afternoon.

The crowd's cheers rocked the arena. The applause and screams mixed together and bounced back to the stage like thunder. It was a continuous roar that went on and on and on.

As she stood in front of the adoring fans, Sierra felt a thrill that she'd never before felt. She was front and center when she raised her hands and waved, the way Liza and Raine were doing on the other sides of the stage.

"How you doing, Houston?" Raine shouted out.

That sent them into a greater frenzy, and the hysteria didn't stop until the saxophonist behind them blew his first note.

"Love the Lord . . ." they sang in three-part harmony, the words to their number one song.

The fans stayed on their feet. They raised their hands and swayed and sang, twenty thousand backup singers. The audience stayed that way, with them through the next song and the next, and as time moved on, Sierra's excitement inched higher.

When the music stopped for the first testimony, her testimony, she glanced out into the darkness, not able to see many faces beyond the first few rows.

But she could feel their excitement and their expectation for what she was about to say. They knew what was coming, and for a moment, Sierra felt a tinge of guilt. Then she pressed her shoulders back and spoke the words they'd all been waiting for.

"I'm saved . . . I'm single . . . and I'm celibate!"

The applause was loud and long and Sierra felt just fine. There was nothing wrong with what she was telling these women. Her story was one that needed to be told, needed to be shared, needed to be heard. She was telling them the truth; it wasn't her truth, but that didn't diminish the testimony.

So she strutted across the stage with a confidence that she had never felt, so sure that this newfound authority was because of Jarrod. She told the story that was as fake as the Louboutins she often wore, but the crowd stayed with her. They were silent, though, as she spoke, and Sierra even imagined a few tears being shed as she went on about God being the only father she knew, but the only one she needed.

When Raine and Liza joined her at the center of the stage, they sang "Blessings," and the aisles filled with fans dancing up and down, praising in a new kind of way. Song after song, they sang, until it was Raine's turn to stand alone in the center.

Like Sierra, Raine breathed deeply before she uttered a word.

She glanced into the crowd and told herself that no matter what she was feeling toward her mother-in-law, she could still talk about unconditional love. That's what she had for Nadia and Dayo. She just didn't extend that kind of love to people who didn't deserve it—like Beerlulu.

"It seems so impossible to live up to the standards of the love that God wants us to have for one another," Raine said. "But you can do it as long as you understand that it's the same love that He gives to us."

Once her testimony was complete, Sierra and Liza joined Raine, and this time they took it down a notch. They sang the song that the DJ had played on the radio this morning, "There's Nothing But Truth in the Lord." As they sang, the crowd swayed, but with the release of the song just today, only the Divas knew all the words.

So they sang by themselves, and as they sauntered across the stage, crisscrossing each other as the choreographer had planned, none of them realized they shared the same thought—they all wished this song had been taken out of the show.

Liza began her testimony without a hint of hesitation. "I've been married for twenty-eight years. I mean, twenty-five years." Her hands shook nervously. How did she let the truth slip out like that?

"I guess it's been so long that it doesn't matter. The point is, twenty-five or twenty-eight, either way you still have to have the same ingredients to have longevity in your marriage. It's like baking a cake. You can be known for making the best seven-layer, double-chocolate fudge cake in the world, but if there is one ingredient missing, you will not bake your masterpiece.

"The same is true with marriage. You need all the ingredients. You need truth. You need honesty. You need loyalty. The

husband and the wife must communicate. There can be no secrets and there can certainly be no lies. The best part of my marriage is that my husband and I share everything, even the things
that we think may hurt each other. It doesn't matter—we lay it
all out, then work it out together. That's the only way to have a
long, fruitful, wonderful marriage."

Behind her, Sierra and Raine held hands as they moved to
meet Liza at the center of the stage. Then together they sang the
finale "The Lord's Prayer."

They sang the prayer and again they shared more than the
words to the song. As they harmonized, Sierra, Raine, and Liza
offered up the same requests to God—they sent up prayers asking Him to forgive the secrets they kept and the lies they'd just
told to the twenty thousand people who had paid good money
to come and hear nothing except the truth.

# CHAPTER 38

⁓

## *Liza*

Destiny's Divas had two ovations, and when the curtains draped down for the third and final time, the three women huddled and hugged.

"Oh, my God, that was wonderful," Liza sang.

"Right?" Sierra piped in. "Now I know why you were doing this all these years," she said to Raine. "Forget about modeling, give me a stage!"

They laughed and held hands as a production assistant escorted them off to stage left. At the bottom of the steps, Yvonne waited.

They were all filled with so much glee that none of them noticed Yvonne's stance. They missed the way her arms were crossed, the way one leg trembled, the way her eyes were on fire.

"So, what did you think?" Raine said.

It wasn't until Yvonne opened her mouth, but then closed it so hard her teeth clicked, that they noticed her fury.

"What's wrong?" Raine asked. "I know you can't be upset about anything that we did out there. Did you see those people? Did you hear them?"

Yvonne shook her head. "The show is the last thing we need to talk about. We have a major problem; I need to talk to all of you now!"

With deep frowns the three followed as she marched toward the dressing area where they'd prepared before the show. Once inside, Yvonne slammed the door, shocking them, and sending Liza's heart into a panic pounding.

*Oh, my God.* Liza watched as Yvonne roamed from one corner of the long room to the other as if she was checking to make sure they were alone.

"I don't even know where to begin," Yvonne finally said with such a quivering in her voice that it left the three Divas trembling.

"Okay, you're gonna need to start explaining," Raine said, "because now you're scaring me."

"You should be scared. Very scared. Because unless we get some kind of miracle, after tonight Destiny's Divas may be over."

"What!" The exclamation came only from Raine and Sierra.

Liza said nothing; she didn't have to imagine what Yvonne was talking about. She knew. Mann had been exposed. And now she was costing everyone everything.

"Come on, Yvonne," Raine said. "Just tell us what's going on."

Yvonne blew out a breath that came out as a growl. "Look at this." She pointed to her opened laptop on the vanity. As the three stood up behind her, Yvonne clicked just a few keys and Liza closed her eyes.

All kinds of thoughts were going through her mind. Had Qianna's mother gone to the police? Had Mann been arrested? Was it on the news or had the story broken in a newspaper?

She could actually see it—her husband being led away from their church in shackles. The picture in her mind made her moan, and at the same time, Raine gasped.

"Oh, my God!"

Slowly, Liza opened her eyes, expecting the absolute worse, but then her mouth fell open as wide as her eyes.

On the computer screen was a split image, but it had nothing to do with her.

It was Sierra.

One side of the picture was Sierra and a man that Liza recognized as the new congressman from Harlem leaving some sort of formal event. And right beside that photo was an image of Sierra holding a camera in front of a mirror and showing the world every single inch of her glory. There was nothing blacked out, nothing hidden from anyone's eyes.

It was Liza's turn to declare her shock. "Oh, my God. What is this?"

"That's what I want to know," Yvonne said, whipping her head around and facing Sierra.

All of their eyes were on her, but Sierra's were still stuck on the screen. Suddenly, she grabbed the laptop as if she needed to get a closer view just to be sure of what she was seeing.

"Where did you get this?" she cried.

"You don't need to be asking me that," Yvonne grumbled through clenched teeth. "You need to be asking where did our tour promoter, Kevin, get it. And where did the *New York Post* get it. And where did the hundreds of newspapers I'm sure have this now—where did they all get this?"

Sierra shook her head. "I don't know."

"Well, I can tell you. Kevin said it first showed up on

MediaTakeOut.com, but according to him, it's all over the Internet now."

"Oh, God," Sierra cried.

"And because you're dating the congressman, Kevin said, it was one of *Access Hollywood*'s lead stories, so it's all over TV, too."

"Well, what does this mean?" Liza asked, her heart still pounding, even though she wasn't the center of this disaster.

"I don't know!" Yvonne exclaimed. "But I know it doesn't mean anything good." Turning to Sierra, she asked, "What is this?"

"It was just a picture that I sent to my boyfriend."

"The congressman?"

"No," Sierra whispered. "The one before him."

"Oh, Lawd!" Yvonne exclaimed.

"It was only a picture and it was supposed to be just between us."

"You just got off the stage telling an arena full of people that you are celibate."

"This doesn't mean that I'm not celibate," Sierra protested.

"You're right. It doesn't. It just says that you're some kind of exhibitionist freak who might as well be sleeping with the world."

"Whoa! Hold on," Raine interceded when tears sprang into Sierra's eyes. "Come on, Yvonne. Lots of young people send these kinds of pictures."

"And it's bad enough if they're not in the public eye. But these kinds of pictures have cost people their careers. Politicians have lost their offices, teachers have lost their jobs, pastors have lost their churches. If you think this is not going to affect us, you are so wrong."

"Well, I don't know a lot about it," Liza piped in, wanting badly to come to Sierra's defense. Their young friend deserved their grace because, the Lord knew, she would need the same grace soon. She continued, "But entertainers have these kinds of things going on all the time. What about all those celebrities who make sex tapes?"

Yvonne looked at Liza as if she couldn't believe her naïveté. "They make their living off of scandal, Liza. We don't. We make our money by living our lives a certain way and then getting onstage and telling everyone about it."

"Well, I'm not willing to give up," Liza said. "Surely something can be done. We can say that someone doctored the picture."

Yvonne grunted before she swiveled her head to Sierra. "Can we say that?"

Sierra stayed silent.

So Yvonne turned right back to Liza. "I don't think the way to fix this is to tell more lies, *First Lady.*"

Liza pressed her lips together, clearly hurt by Yvonne's tone.

"Okay, this is getting out of hand." Raine jumped up. "You're right, Yvonne. This is bad. But this is when we need to be coming together, not beating each other up."

"Fine." Yvonne snatched the computer from Sierra's hands. "I have to meet Kevin back at the hotel. He's waiting for me, and as the promoter of this tour, he's not happy." She shook her head as she stuffed her laptop into its case. "I'm leaving, but a car will be waiting outside for you ladies." She paused and looked at each of them, her eyes finally settling on Sierra. "Can you do me a favor?" she asked. "For once, can you just listen to me? Just change your clothes, get dressed, and together get into that car. Don't stop to talk to anyone. Not here, not in the hotel. Just call me when you get there." With a roll of her eyes, she stomped toward the door, but then stopped and turned around.

From her pocket, Yvonne scooped out a cell phone. "Here," she said, tossing Sierra's phone to her. "And see if you can stay away from taking any more nasty pictures." She swung around and slammed the door behind her.

# CHAPTER 39

## *Sierra*

There was no need to hide now.

From the moment Yvonne had thrown the phone at her, Sierra had been calling Jarrod. She had changed her clothes and called. Slipped into the waiting limousine and called. Walked through the lobby of the grand hotel and called.

And not once did Jarrod pick up.

By the time she stood outside of Yvonne's room with Raine and Liza in front of her, she was shaking—and not just because of the photograph. All she could think about was whether Jarrod had seen it.

Of course he had! If the rant that Yvonne had just had was true, not only had Jarrod seen it, but Harold had seen it, and half of Congress had probably seen it.

And oh, God! His parents had seen it, too.

She had to get to Jarrod.

But the moment Yvonne opened the door, Sierra tucked her cell into her purse. The last thing she wanted was for Yvonne to see her with that.

Sierra would never admit it to anyone, but she'd been so hurt by Yvonne's words. Maybe she was hurt because everything

Yvonne said was true. How could she have been so stupid? And stupid enough to send that photo to Andre.

Andre.

This was the first time since the blow-up backstage that she'd allowed his name to seep into her consciousness.

Andre.

The one who had obviously sent the photograph.

Andre.

She had to push the thought of him and his name aside, because if she didn't, she would see his face. And if she saw his face, she would see a knife. And if she saw a knife, she would see herself stabbing and cutting and slicing until there were only the smallest pieces of him left.

So she took a calming breath as she stepped inside the room behind Raine and Liza. She let them enter first, two bodies of protection in front of her as she faced Yvonne and Kevin.

Kevin, who reminded Sierra of Heavy D, was leaning back against the desk. His arms were crossed until he pushed himself up. "Ladies," he greeted them, though he sounded as if he were just talking to a wall. He hugged Yvonne, then Raine, and nodded as he passed Sierra and Liza.

They all watched him amble his three hundred pounds to the door before he turned back.

"I'll call you first thing, Yvonne. We'll see how this goes."

"Okay," she said, sounding completely worn out.

Once they were alone, she motioned for the three of them to sit down. They fanned out across the bedroom. To the sofa and the chairs.

"So . . ." She paused. "We do have major problems." She dropped that bomb with a much calmer voice than she had at the arena. Then: "One of the three sponsors just called Kevin and pulled out." They all exhaled long breaths.

"He wasn't surprised at losing that one. It was the radio group that has all those family-oriented shows."

"Christ and the Family?" Liza asked.

Yvonne nodded. "But Kevin actually thinks that the tour may still be salvageable. He thinks that in some ways it may sell more tickets—at least that's how he's trying to spin this." She shrugged. "We just have to wait and see."

"Any challenges with tickets already sold?" Raine asked.

Yvonne nodded. "Ticket cancellations are coming in. Someone from TicketMaster called Kevin and asked how cancellations should be handled."

"That means that they have a substantial number of folks wanting their money back," Raine concluded, sounding like the veteran of the music business that she was.

"All of this because of one photo." Sierra shook her head.

Yvonne looked at Sierra as if she didn't get it. "It's more than the photo. It's everything that you stand for, Sierra. And not just you—all of us. If one-third of this group is a lie, then we're all liars. Destiny's Divas is a complete lie."

Raine and Liza bowed their heads as if they were being chastised, too.

"Is there really a chance that the entire tour will be canceled?" Sierra asked.

Yvonne shrugged. "I'm hoping not, but you did hear me say that one of the sponsors is out. And without them, and if tickets get canceled, who do you think is going to pay for this tour? Who's going to pay for the airline tickets, and the tour bus on the East Coast, and the hotels?" She looked from one to the other. "I know you understand this Raine, but, Liza, Sierra, this is a big deal."

"I'm sorry," Sierra whispered. Her eyes were lowered, and the room was filled with silence before she repeated, "I'm sorry. I'm just so sorry."

Her shoulders shook as tears spilled from her eyes. Liza rushed to Sierra's side and held her in her arms. "It's okay, baby. Any one of us could have made the same mistake."

Yvonne's eyebrows rose.

"Well, maybe not the same mistake," Liza said, correcting what she'd just said, "but we could have all done something to mess up everything."

Yvonne shook her head.

Liza said, "I mean it. It always gets me when we look at other people and think what they've done is so bad. We all need to look at ourselves and our hearts. And if you've never done anything wrong, if you've never said anything wrong, if you've never hurt anybody, then step right up there with Jesus. But if you've ever made a mistake, then show some compassion when someone else makes a mistake."

Now it was Yvonne's head that was bowed.

"I just didn't know . . . I just didn't think . . . I just didn't—" Sierra stopped. Was she about to say that she just didn't care? Because the truth was, at the time she didn't. To her, the relationship with Andre had nothing to do with Destiny's Divas. Just like her relationship with Jarrod had nothing to do with the group.

So many people had tried to warn her—Denise, even Andre and Jarrod had asked her about it. But she'd waved away all of their words. To Sierra, her life was completely compartmentalized. One part had nothing to do with the other. *Not!*

"Okay, okay. I'm sorry," Yvonne said as she took Sierra's hands into hers. "Look. We won't know what's going on until morning, so let's not speculate. Let's just wait to get the call from Kevin and we'll regroup from there. Okay?"

Sierra nodded.

"Let's get a good night's sleep and be ready for the world—whatever it looks like—tomorrow."

Yvonne walked them to the door, and before Sierra stepped outside, the manager hugged her, too. "Liza was right. I've made some mistakes in my life when I needed forgiveness, and sometimes I forget that. So, again, I'm sorry."

"Thank you," Sierra said.

In the hallway, Sierra was met with more hugs.

"Keep your head up," Raine told her.

Liza added, "I'll be praying for you, for all of us, all night."

Then all three went in different directions to their rooms to wait this disaster out, alone.

# CHAPTER 40

## *Raine*

Raine patted the space next to her on the bed until she felt her cell. Without opening her eyes, she clicked the Accept Call key and pressed the phone to her ear. As soon as she heard Dayo's voice, her eyes fluttered opened.

*"Mchumba,"* Dayo said softly, knowing that he'd awakened her. "How's it going?"

She stretched her limbs the way she did every morning. "Nothing much has changed since we hung up, what"—she peeked at the clock on the nightstand—"five hours ago?"

"I know," he said, as if she'd given him the answer he expected.

"But truly, Dayo, I don't think too much is going to happen. There are celebrities who've done much worse, and with Sierra this was just a photo."

"Yeah," Dayo said, "but have you seen the photo?" He chuckled. "And before you ask what I was doing looking at it, let me tell you it's all over the place."

"Really?"

"Yup, the newspapers, on the entertainment shows on TV, everywhere."

Raine shook her head. "I just never suspected."

"Well, how could you? Sierra sold us all."

"It's just that when she spoke about how she lived her life, I always felt that she spoke from her heart."

"Well, she likes to email pictures that show way more than her heart."

"Ha-ha! Okay, enough of you," she said. "I think we're going to make it through all of this, though. We'll at least stay here in Houston for the next two shows and then we'll see. But I'll keep you posted, all right?"

"Definitely. I'm just worried."

"Don't be. Is Nadia up?"

"You must've forgotten; today is an administrative day, so she's out of school. She's asleep, but I can wake her."

"No, don't do that. I just wanted to check on her since she had that little cough yesterday."

"She's fine. It's just a change-of-weather cold. Don't worry. I'll take care of our daughter."

"Are you taking her to the store?"

"Yup, she'll spend the day with me."

"Okay, then. I'll speak to both of you later. I love you."

*"Nakupenda sana."*

The moment she ended her call, the phone on the nightstand rang, and though she knew who it was, she still said, "Hello."

Yvonne said, "Just got the call. We're rolling out in two hours."

Raine's heart fluttered. "Really? They're canceling the tour?"

"Yeah, there's been sufficient financial damage. Kevin just wants us to go home and regroup. See what we can do," she said, though there didn't seem to be much hope in Yvonne's tone.

"I just didn't think it was gonna go down like this."

"Well, here we are," Yvonne sighed.

"Okay, okay," Raine said, wanting to shut Yvonne down before she got started. She didn't need this negativity. Jumping from the bed, she asked, "Have you called Sierra?"

"Nope, first you, then I was going to call Liza . . . and Sierra last."

"Call Liza. Let me handle Sierra."

"Gladly."

"Yvonne . . ."

"I know, I know. Just make sure that both of you are in the lobby in two hours. And tell Sierra that she'd better not be late."

After hanging up, Raine stood, reflecting for a moment. Yvonne was telling her that this was the end, but she knew in her heart that it wasn't.

Hurriedly, she brushed her teeth, then threw on the sweat suit she'd worn from the arena last night. Within ten minutes, she stood in front of Sierra's room.

She tapped lightly on the door, wondering if she was waking her up. When she heard the sounds of movement, Raine said a quick prayer, knowing this news was going to be toughest on Sierra.

"Wow," Raine said, taking in Sierra's face when she opened the door. "You look like you haven't slept all night."

"Good morning to you, too." Sierra's voice was deep, a mixture of exhaustion and pain. Her eyes were red from what Raine suspected was a night filled with tears. Sierra dragged herself back across the hotel room and bounced onto the bed. "I guess this isn't just a friendly visit," she said, looking down at her cell phone.

Raine took a moment to study Sierra with her hair pulled back in a messy ponytail and dressed in a pair of pajamas that made her look like she was thirteen. This wasn't at all what Raine expected from the sex kitten whose photograph had just ended their tour. But she knew she was probably sitting with the real Sierra, the vulnerable Sierra, and that made Raine hate what she had to say even more.

Before she spoke, she joined Sierra on the bed and, keeping her voice as light as she could, she said, "Well, the tour has been canceled."

Sierra's tears were instant, as if they hadn't been far away, and Raine took her hand.

"Listen," Raine began, "this doesn't mean that the tour is canceled forever. Kevin and Yvonne just want to go back to New York to regroup."

"I can't believe that I did this to myself, to everybody, especially you," Sierra sobbed. "You gave me a chance and I ruined it for everyone."

"Well, you can sit back and feel sorry for yourself or you can learn from it." She squeezed her hand. "Girl, I did lots of dumb things in my twenties that I would never do in my thirties, and truth be told, I'm looking forward to my forties 'cause I think then you have real wisdom. Look at Liza, she don't take no mess," she said, trying to bring just a bit of a smile to Sierra's face. But when she got nothing more than tears, she continued, "This is just a lesson. Now that you know better, you got to keep it moving and do better."

Sierra sniffed back her tears and sat stiffly as Raine hugged her.

"Something inside of me tells me that we still have much, much more to do as a group. Destiny's Divas is very much alive. Trust me, okay?"

Sierra nodded, though her eyes were filled with doubt—as if

she knew Raine's words were spoken just to make her feel better.

Raine stood and pulled Sierra up with her. "So here's the thing. Yvonne said we're rolling out in two hours, so get yourself together, sweetie."

Outside in the hallway, Raine leaned against Sierra's door. She thought about the words she'd just spoken to Sierra and, truly, everything she said came from her heart. Destiny's Divas would be back. God had given her the idea for this group and He wouldn't have brought it this far just to have it end before it even began.

She didn't know exactly how it was going to work out, but it would. Of that she was sure.

# CHAPTER 41

## *Destiny's Divas*

$\mathcal{Y}$vonne couldn't believe that twenty-four hours later, she was back in the same place. The same seats (she had no idea how Kevin had worked that out), this time heading east instead of west. Her eyes wandered over to Sierra, then Raine, and turning to her left, she took in Liza. Each seat was reclined and every eye was closed.

But Yvonne suspected that not one of them slept. As she flipped through her magazine, she wished that she could see inside their minds, hear what they were thinking. Were their thoughts like hers? Were they wondering where they were going from here?

With a sigh, she closed her magazine. How was she supposed to read when she couldn't concentrate? So Yvonne sat back and did what the others were doing. She closed her eyes and wondered.

If she had been able to see into Sierra . . .

Sierra wasn't anywhere close to sleep. Through deep breaths, she was suppressing the rage that was rising in her. Not that she wanted it to stay deep inside forever. She wanted this rage; she needed it. She just couldn't let it explode right now. It had to come out at the right time. It had to come out when it could save her and Jarrod.

She still had not spoken to him, and with each call she had made between last night and this morning, a piece of her heart had been chipped away. But she understood his refusal to acknowledge her. He was a rising congressman with a heart full of ambition. And if he had seen the picture, then there would be no way he could imagine taking her on his journey.

So she decided that she wouldn't call him anymore—at least for now. Because the next time she spoke to him—and she would speak to him—she would convince him that they could still do this together. But she couldn't talk to him until she could assure him that there were no more pictures.

She was going to take care of that right away. As soon as she landed, she wasn't even thinking about going home to Harlem. She was going downtown to Andre's apartment to get all the other pictures.

The main challenge was that every picture he had of her was digital—so how was she going to retrieve them all? She wasn't sure how, but she was going to do it. Because there was no way she was going to lose the best man who'd ever come into her life.

She'd rather die before she'd accept that.

Next to Sierra, Raine was awake as well. . . .

Raine's thoughts were beyond what was happening right now. She was thinking about something that Yvonne had said last night—that Destiny's Divas was a lie. Yvonne had spoken the truth and she didn't even know it. Because Sierra wasn't the only one living a lie. Raine had stood on that stage and lied to those people about how she loved unconditionally. Certainly most would say that her lie wasn't a big deal, especially when compared to Sierra's. But Raine had a feeling that a lie was a lie in God's eyes. She was never going to stand onstage and lie that way again.

However she had to do it, she had to find a way to do that unconditional love thing with Beerlulu. Of course, her mother-in-law would have to get rid of that crazy ceremony idea. Just the thought of that made Raine want to pick up a gun.

But if Beerlulu was willing to walk away from that, never mention it again, Raine could get back to that place where Beerlulu called her *"Binti."* Now that would definitely be pleasing to God and would definitely be the unconditional love that He so desired.

Across the aisle, Liza didn't sleep either. . . .

Her thoughts were wild the way they galloped from one side of her brain to the other. Should she say something to Yvonne or not?

She wanted to sit up right now and tell Yvonne everything. It was the scenario that was playing out in her mind that made Liza want to confess—she could see it: the way Kevin and Yvonne would spin Sierra's photo in just the right way and Destiny's Divas would be back on the road.

But then Mann's news would drop, sending them all into a blackened abyss from which they would never recover. So she had to tell . . . but how? . . .

Yvonne had no idea what was in anyone's head. And it was a good thing, because as bad as it all was, it was about to get much worse.

# CHAPTER 42

*Liza*

There had been so much excitement about arriving in Houston, but it was just the opposite when they landed back in New York.

Together, Sierra, Raine, Liza, and Yvonne marched through the terminal, passing the same shops and stores they'd rushed by yesterday. But this time their heads were down, as if they didn't want to be noticed. Only Yvonne talked into her cell, checking on the cars for each of them.

At baggage claim, they huddled together, still silent, each in her own world. Liza pulled her phone from her purse and powered it back on. For a second, she thought about calling Mann—she'd only spoken to him one time since she'd arrived in Houston and that was right before their performance last night. But she hadn't called him at all today and he hadn't called her.

"Okay," Yvonne said, breaking into their circle and their thoughts, "your drivers are here. Do you want to just go get in the cars and let me take care of your luggage?"

"No," the three said together.

"We're fine," Raine added.

The light on the luggage carousel blinked, and moments

later, their bags were the first to slide down the conveyor belt, the priority tags working.

Right as they rolled their bags outside of the terminal, four Town Cars lined up behind one another at the curb.

"Great," Yvonne said. "Let's all just get home, rest up, and we'll convene in a day or two. I'll give you a call when I know more about what's going on. But here's the thing. No one"—she paused and looked straight at Sierra—"not one of you, should talk to anyone. Not the press, not your friends, not your neighbors—no one. We don't want to give this story any more legs, you hear?"

They nodded.

"And I'm really serious about the press. If you get any of those calls, refer them to me."

"We got it," Raine said, her voice filled with enough agitation for all of them.

They formed a hug circle and embraced, holding each other longer than normal, whispering in each other's ears that everything would be all right.

Yvonne made sure that they each got into their cars: Sierra, then Raine, and finally Liza. But just as the driver rolled Liza's bag to her car, Yvonne's phone beeped, indicating a waiting message. She scrolled through her phone, read the entire text, and groaned.

"Liza, wait!" she yelled out before Liza slid inside.

Yvonne dashed to the car and handed her bag to the driver. "I'm going with you," she said. When Liza frowned, Yvonne said, "Get in; I'll explain as we go." To the driver, she said, "Get us to Ridgewood, New Jersey, as fast as you can!"

&#x224B;

Liza didn't know much, just what Yvonne had told her. But it was enough to have her shaking. She'd been this way ever since Yvonne jumped into the car and told her there was trouble at her house.

"I don't know much," she'd said. "But one of my contacts just texted me. There was a 9-1-1 call made from your home. The police are on their way."

"Oh, my God!" Liza had exclaimed. "Mann?"

"I don't know."

"Did he have a heart attack or something?" Liza asked as if Yvonne hadn't just spoken.

Yvonne folded Liza's hand into hers and held her the rest of the way. Over and over, she told Liza to stay calm. That there was no need to get worked up—at least not until they knew something.

She didn't want to before, but now Liza wanted to talk to Mann. But there was no answer on his cell phone, no answer on their home phone. And there was no answer from Buddy, either. So she texted Mann, texted Buddy, and then sat and shook. And waited. And shook.

These were the longest forty minutes she'd ever lived, and when they finally turned onto the cul-de-sac, Liza scooted to the edge of the seat. She craned her neck, trying to get the best view of the scene that looked like something straight out of *Law & Order*. Spectators and police and flashing lights . . . and an ambulance.

The car was still rolling slowly when Liza jumped out. She pushed through the small crowd, then dashed across the lawn to her front door.

"Ma'am, you have to stay back."

"My name is Liza Washington," she said quickly. "I live here."

"Oh." The policeman at the door motioned to someone else—and Liza recognized him. Officer Haley, the detective who'd given her his card for Mann a few weeks back. But there was no time to ask him any questions. Because of the gurney the EMTs were rolling her way.

Liza pressed her hand against her chest. "Is this my husband?"

No one had to respond: it was Mann. His torso was covered with a white sheet, and his eyes were shut. But he was breathing—through the oxygen mask that covered most of his face.

"Oh, my God!" was all that Liza could get out because in the next seconds, the scene played out in front of her. Behind the gurney, a girl—Qianna—sobbing as a policeman led her from the house. And behind Qianna . . . a woman . . . her mother. There were no tears in Mrs. Tucker's eyes, just a black stare, a cold stare as she glared at Liza.

"I tried to tell you," she said before the female officer led her away.

Liza covered her mouth with her hand. Her other hand was still over her heart, just to make sure it was still beating.

"She tried to tell you what?" Yvonne whispered.

Liza had forgotten that her manager was with her. "I don't know," Liza said, although that wasn't the truth.

"Oh, no!" Yvonne groaned.

For a moment, Liza allowed her eyes to break away from the scene unfolding in front of her and she turned to her manager as Yvonne scrolled through her phone as if she were reading an email or a text.

Liza wanted to ask Yvonne what happened? What was wrong? Was there anything she could do to help? But she needed her energy to breathe.

"Liza, I have to go," Yvonne said, her tone filled with urgency, "but I don't want to leave you alone." Yvonne searched the mass of people who had gathered at the edge of the Washingtons' home. "Is there anyone I can get to stay with you?"

"I'm fine." Liza finally pulled her hand from her heart to wave Yvonne away. "Go on, take care of whatever you need to."

"What are you going to do?"

She shook her head. "I don't know."

Yvonne glanced down at her cell again. "I'll call you in thirty minutes," she said, already moving. "Make sure you answer your phone," she yelled over her shoulder as she waved down the driver who'd just brought them from the airport.

As the car with Yvonne sped off, Liza's eyes moved from the ambulance that carried her husband, whom she had loved down to her soul, to the police car that carried the woman who'd tried to end his life.

Which way should she go?

In the next instant, she said, "I want to go to the hospital with my husband," to Officer Haley. "Please!"

The policeman nodded and rushed her to the ambulance just a moment before the EMTs slammed the door and then sped away from the cul-de-sac.

# CHAPTER 43

## *Sierra*

The spark had been ignited last night, when Sierra first saw the email, and now, with those photographs forever rooted in her mind, the spark had burst into flames.

She was fire hot as she sat in the center of the car's back-seat so that she could glance in the side-view mirror. There was Yvonne, still standing at the curb, looking down at her cell phone. As Sierra's car squeezed between the traffic that crowded the front of the airport terminal, she kept her eyes on her manager as Yvonne got smaller, smaller, and smaller, until she could be seen no more.

That's when Sierra said to the driver, "Change of plans. I'm going downtown. To Fourteenth Street." She gave him Andre's exact address.

His grin was wide when he asked, "Going to see your boy-friend?"

She remembered when Andre had the privilege of that title, but now he was her enemy. Her response to the driver was simply a grunt and the driver turned his attention to the road.

Sierra could hardly breathe as she closed her eyes and inhaled to the count of ten, then released it. It was a reminder that had come from Denise. Her best friend had called, left messages, texted, but Sierra hadn't answered. Not that she was ignoring Denise. It was because of her last text—*Remember to breathe, remember Vanessa Williams was fine*—that Sierra was even trying to calm down.

But the breathing did nothing to smother her emotional flames even as she knew she had to control herself. As much as she wanted to march into Andre's apartment, push a gun to his head, and give him the ultimate punishment for what he'd done, she couldn't. Because he still had photographs, and videos, and she had to get all of that.

She mulled over her options. She could force Andre to delete any photos that he'd saved, but really, how could she make him do that? And how would she ever know if he was deleting them all? That wouldn't work.

So what else? She could bribe him . . . but with what? Another time in bed? Just the thought made her gag. There was always money, but the three hundred or so dollars that she had in her purse wouldn't move Andre. Not even the ten thousand dollars she had left from her first advance would do anything for a man who could get that amount for one photograph.

What she needed was full brute force. She needed a Pookie kind of guy who would beat Andre down until she was out of this situation.

But she had nothing to bribe him with and she had no Pookie.

She was going to have to take care of Andre herself.

"Okay, we're here," the man said.

Sierra opened her eyes, shocked that they had traveled so fast. She wasn't ready to be at her destination; she didn't yet have her plan.

"So, how long are you going to be? Should I wait or is this your final stop?" the driver asked.

"My final stop," Sierra said, and wondered why her voice sounded like she was a zombie.

"Okay, let me get your luggage."

*Luggage!* She hadn't thought about that. She wasn't sure what was about to go down, but whatever, how could she be inconspicuous running through streets dragging suitcases behind her?

"Is there any way you can keep my luggage for me?"

He frowned and shook his head. "We can't be responsible for your items, sorry."

She thought about just taking the suitcases and dumping them behind the building. But not only did she have some of her best clothes inside, if the suitcases were found, that would be evidence that she'd been here.

"Okay," she said. This driver was already a witness. Already knew that he'd taken her to this address. She'd handle him later . . . if she had to. "Just come back in . . . an hour."

He shrugged like he wasn't sure. But his shrug turned to a grin when she handed him four fifty-dollar bills. "I'll be back," he told her as she got out of the car.

At the building's entrance, Sierra pressed the buttons to every apartment. And just like on TV, someone buzzed back. She ran up the stairs to the second floor and took a deep breath before she banged on Andre's door.

For the first time, she wondered if he would be here. But then he did do most of his dirty writing from home. So unless he was hanging out at some local bar trolling for women, she was sure this was where she would find him.

And she was right.

Andre's face was stretched with surprise when he opened the door.

"Hey," he said casually, as if they were still friends. "What're you doing here?"

She marched by him, ignoring the fact that he hadn't extended an invitation. And ignoring the fact that he wore nothing more than plaid pajama bottoms—this late in the day.

"Uh, excuse me if I don't bother to close the door all the way considering what happened to me the last time we were alone." His chuckle, as if this was funny, as if what he'd done was just a little joke, made her temperature rise.

"Why did you do it?" she whispered.

"Do what?"

She stuffed her hands inside her coat pocket to hide her shaking fists. "I'm not going to play this game with you, Andre. I've never done anything to you." Her voice elevated with each word.

"Never done anything to me? Remember this?" He pointed to the scar on his forehead. "The last time I saw you, you knocked me upside my head. For no reason."

If her stomach hadn't been burning, if her blood hadn't been boiling, if her thoughts hadn't been smoldering, she would've laughed. She would've reminded him that he deserved it.

She said, "I need to know what you're going to do. With the other pictures."

His eyes were steady on her as he strolled away from the door. He sat on the sofa, stretched out his legs on the coffee table, crossing his bare feet at his ankles. "What do you want me to do with them?"

"Delete them. Every one that I ever sent you. Delete them."

"I thought you'd love having the world see you in all your

magnificence. 'Cause"—he paused as his eyes roamed over her, as if he remembered every inch of her body—"you are magnificent."

She growled inside and wondered if he could hear it. But he didn't move; he just watched her as if she was his evening entertainment. "Those pictures were just for you, Andre."

"Exactly! That's what I'm saying. The pictures belong to me and I can do whatever I want with them."

She wasn't sure if it was tears or rage that burned behind her eyes.

He kept on. "And what I want is to get paid. I never imagined it, sweetheart, but your pretty . . . face is worth a whole lot of money."

"Why can't you just leave me alone?"

He shrugged. "Don't take it personal, this is all business. And what's so beautiful about the way this went down is that you gave me the whole idea."

She blinked.

He explained, "I wasn't even thinking about you, and one day I open my Facebook page and there was this gift from you."

She wanted to cry right now. Thinking about the message she'd sent just to get revenge.

"So, figured I'd check out the fund-raiser, and do you know how surprised I was to see that your boyfriend was the congressman?" Andre shook his head as if for days he'd been marveling at his luck. "I knew right away that I was sitting on a boatload of cash."

"People are going to find out that you leaked the pictures."

"Leaked? Who said a doggone thing about leaking? Baby, you must not have looked at that photograph too closely. My name is right there. I got credit, I got fifteen thousand dollars and I got media attention." Leaning forward, he added, "Do you know how many people have called to interview me?" Again, he shook his head, amazed at the fortune that was at his feet. "You're bigger than I think you even know. The young one in that Christian group, preaching celibacy and dating the congressman that people are already calling the second coming of a black president." He laughed out loud. "It was a gift, I tell you, a gift."

It took everything inside of her to hold back the rage that was burning to burst out. But she had to hold it because she still had to get this done. If she was ever going to get Jarrod back, she had to convince Andre. Convince him or . . .

She said, "Now that you've been paid, I hope this can end here."

He arched his eyebrows as if her statement was a joke. "Are you kidding? I've already told my paper that I'll have a new photo for them every week. I have so many pictures that this could last me a year." He paused and grinned. "Maybe two."

She couldn't help the sob that came through her lips. "Andre." She said his name as if she was begging. And she was. "Please. Don't do this to me and Jarrod."

He frowned. "Are you telling me that the congressman is still with you?"

With the back of her hand, she wiped away the tears crawling down her cheeks. She nodded. "And Jarrod and I can work this out if you . . ."

He was already shaking his head. "Nah. Nah. I'm going through with it. Not only because I need to fatten my bank account, but the congressman needs to know about you. Shoot, I'm doing him a favor, saving him from your crazy ass."

It was the word *crazy* . . . or maybe it was the realization that she would never get Jarrod back now. Or maybe it was the way Andre sat in front of her, teasing, taunting, tormenting her.

The jury would call it self-defense. All she was trying to do was save her mind. But even if she'd be declared a murderer, did it matter? Nothing mattered if she couldn't be with Jarrod.

Her eyes searched the space, and right on the counter that separated the living room from the kitchen was a knife block. This was her sign, probably from God, that she had to exact justice.

This *was* justice.

She snatched her weapon—it wasn't the biggest, but it wasn't the smallest. She charged at Andre with the fury of a bull, reaching him before his brain had a chance to process the scene.

"What the hell!" He jumped up just as she slashed his bare stomach. "Ah!" He tried to dodge her fury and grab the knife at the same time. But madness propelled her and she sliced his wrist. "Argh!" he screamed.

His back was pressed against the wall, his hands covered his wounds, his eyes were wide with his fear.

He looked like a coward to her. A jealous, hateful coward who needed to be put out of his misery.

"Sierra!"

The call came from behind her, but she was smart enough not to turn around. No one was there. It was her mind trying to trick her out of what she had to do.

"Sierra! Don't do this."

This time she recognized the voice. Yvonne! What the hell was she doing here?

Still, Sierra wasn't going to turn away, not until she finished. There would be a witness now, but so what? She'd lost Jarrod and Destiny's Divas was finished. What else was there?

So she focused her eyes on where she'd cut Andre's stomach and then her gaze rose to the center of his chest. She wondered if it was appropriate to pray. To pray that when she cut out his heart, his soul would go straight to hell.

She decided no prayers were necessary. She just lunged forward to the sound of screams: hers, Yvonne's, and Andre's.

# CHAPTER 44

## Raine

*It* wasn't the best of circumstances, but Raine couldn't say she was sorry that she was home. She still believed what she'd told Sierra—Destiny's Divas was going to survive. Just look at their name—Destiny. They would be back, probably even stronger. All that was needed was a little time for this to die down, and Sierra would have quite a testimony to tell young women now.

As she rolled her suitcase off the elevator, she shook her head. That sexting stuff was crazy, and soon as she could, she was going to talk to Nadia about it—even though she was only twelve.

She couldn't wait to see her baby. When she'd called Dayo after they'd landed and told him that she was back, he'd told her that he'd left Nadia at home this morning.

"She still isn't feeling well," he'd said. "I figured she would be good as long as I kept checking on her. And I let my mother know that she was home alone."

Well, she was here now to take care of her child. The moment she pushed the door open, she yelled out, "Surprise!"

Her joy was met with silence.

Now she knew that Nadia really wasn't feeling well. Her daughter always greeted her at the door whenever she came home. And with Nadia not knowing that she was even coming back, Raine expected her daughter to come tearing out of her room, sickness and all.

She strolled down the hall toward Nadia's bedroom and pushed the door open.

"Nadia?"

The covers on Nadia's bed were tossed aside as if she'd just gotten up.

Raine stepped inside, grabbed a pillow from the floor, and checked her daughter's bathroom. "Nadia?"

The lines in her forehead creased with concern and then she saw the paper on top of Nadia's pillow. It was a single sheet, torn from her school notebook.

*Dad: I'm down at Grandma's.*

Raine's heart began to thump.

*She said she had something to make me feel better.*

And her hands began to shake.

*Come and get me when you get home. Love you.*

The note slipped from Raine's hand the moment she read the last word and she dashed through her apartment. Grabbing her keys, she darted through the door and then sprinted toward the staircase. She jumped the steps, two, three at a time, until she came to the eighth floor.

She was breathing hard, but fear propelled her and she ran to Beerlulu's door. She banged and called out her mother-in-law's name.

And then.

The scream.

A soul-ripping screech.

*"Nadia!"*

Raine's hands trembled as she fumbled with her keys, then she burst through the door. Her eyes were wide and wild as she searched the empty living room.

Another scream.

"Nadia."

"Mommy!" her daughter shrieked.

Raine tore into the bedroom and took only a second to survey the scene. It was exactly like the video she'd watched on her computer. A young girl held down by women as another woman stood over her. All Raine could see was the razor and the blood.

"Get away from my daughter!"

She pushed Beerlulu, but the woman was as strong and sturdy as Raine always thought; she hardly budged. "We're just about finished," Beerlulu said as if she was proud.

There was not enough time to think, to reason, to talk. She only had time to save her daughter. Next to the bed was the rainstick. And in just one second, she lifted the gift that she'd given Beerlulu, raised it above her head, and swung as hard as she could, knocking Beerlulu halfway across the room.

The woman fell with a thud and her sisters cried out, now leaving Nadia to rush to their sister's side.

"Mom," Nadia cried, and Raine grabbed her.

"I can't . . . I can't . . . sit up. It hurts."

"That's okay, baby. Just rest here for a moment," she said as she held her.

The two cried together and Raine closed her eyes. Because there was no way she could bear to glance down. No way she could look and see what had been done to her daughter.

# *Epilogue*

## NEW YORK CITY, MADISON SQUARE GARDEN
## OCTOBER 1, 2011

*Y*vonne stood stage left and spoke into the walkie-talkie. "Are the ladies' microphones in place?"

The walkie-talkie cackled, and then "Yes" came through. "We'll be ready to start in three minutes.

Even though she stood alone, Yvonne nodded. She couldn't believe they were back where they started. Destiny's Divas, only they were very different now. But just like these ladies, Yvonne was grateful for this journey. She had never seen three women rally together this way, and if Yvonne thought the group was special before, she knew they'd have a real impact this time around.

They'd had lots of debates about how to relaunch the group, but they'd all agreed right away to use this as the venue.

In her headphone, Yvonne heard the countdown. "In five, four, three, two, one . . ."

Cued music started and then the audience applauded.

"Welcome to Bring It On! I'm Pastor Hosea Bush, and today we have a special show for you. Let's get right to it.

"By now, everyone has heard the story of Destiny's Divas, the gospel singing group that was a hit the moment their first song was released."

In the background, "Love Unlimited" played softly.

Pastor Bush continued, "But then a photograph was released that changed the destiny of each of these divas. Today, the ladies are here, all three of them. . . ."

The audience gasped.

"Yes," Pastor Bush continued, "all three are here to tell their stories. Please welcome, first, Sierra Dixon."

The audience clapped as Sierra strolled onto the stage waving to the studio, which was, as usual, packed to capacity.

"Sierra, welcome," the pastor said.

"Thank you for having me."

"Well, we started with you because the entire wave of events began with you, isn't that true?"

She nodded. "It was horrible," Sierra said, folding her hands in her lap. "Not just having my photograph splashed everywhere, but the fact that our tour was canceled because of me."

The pastor said, "So tell us, how did the photos get out there?"

Sierra took a breath. She hated whenever she heard the word *photos*—yes, in the plural. There had been one more after the first full frontal that Andre had released. Another one of her posing for him in his apartment, this time she was covered by only a cowboy hat on top of her head.

"They were pictures for my boyfriend," she explained. "One I'd sent to him through my cell phone, and the other I'd posed for."

"That's one of the points that you make now, a message to young ladies, as Destiny's Divas returns to the road, correct?"

"Yes! The point I want to make, Pastor, is that it is not just young women doing this. It's all ages and it's men and women. The thing that no one thinks about is that in today's times, digital photos never go away. It's not like film, where you can destroy negatives. Not only do the photos not go away, but they can be sent to everyone."

"Like yours. It went viral, right?"

She nodded again, and for at least the one-millionth time she thought about how close she'd come to killing the man who had caused all of this.

There were times when she wished she had actually stabbed that knife through Andre's heart. Times when she wished that Yvonne hadn't run up behind her and wrestled her to the ground, leaving Andre bleeding from his stomach. . . .

"Sierra!" Yvonne had not stopped calling her name. Even as Sierra fought to break away from the hold of Yvonne's arms.

"Are you crazy?" Andre kept saying over and over.

Each time he said that word, energy surged through her. She wanted just a single chance to stab him in his heart and take away his life the way he had taken hers.

"Sierra, you don't want to do this." Yvonne's arms were still around her, holding her hostage, not letting her move and hardly letting her breathe.

Finally, Sierra gave up the fight, and in the middle of that living room floor, she balled up as if she was in her mother's womb and cried from her soul.

Once he took the knife away, Andre backed up and glared down. "I'm calling the police. Your crazy ass is going to jail."

"And if you call the police, I will testify that I walked in on you attacking her."

"What? Are you crazy, too?"

"Call me whatever you want,"Yvonne said."But, I can guarantee that you won't win." As she helped Sierra stand, she told Andre, "Just call this even. You've ruined her life. Just move on with yours or else you're gonna have to deal with me."

"Two crazy asses," Sierra heard him mumble as she stumbled out the door.

Yvonne took her home, helped her into bed, fed her, and told her how lucky she was the paparazzi had followed her to Andre's place, how lucky she was that one of them was a friend of hers, how lucky she was that he had texted her. Yvonne had stayed and held her hand . . . until she got that phone call. . . .

Pastor Bush asked, "So, what can young girls—excuse me, everyone—do to protect themselves? What's your advice?"

"Never send the pictures in the first place. And what I'd like to tell young people is to really listen to what older people are telling you. Because I actually had a few people telling me to be careful, that what I was doing was wrong. And if I had just been smart enough to listen . . ." She glanced at her best friend. Denise was sitting in the front row, her face glowing with her proud smile.

"So when you return to the road," said Pastor Bush, "I understand that you will still be talking about celibacy."

She nodded. "First, I will be honest and tell everyone that celibacy is what God wants, but it isn't my gift."

The audience laughed and even Pastor Bush smiled at her honesty.

She continued, "I'll talk about the struggle that I had in the past and I'll tell the truth about where I am now. I guess it's because the biggest lesson I've learned from all of this is that no matter where you are, there is no shame in God. Not if your heart's in the right place and you take it all to Him."

"That's beautiful, Sierra," the pastor said as the audience applauded more. He continued, "Now, after this break, we will have the next member of Destiny's Divas join us. We'll be right back."

Again music played and the makeup artist that Yvonne had hired came onstage to freshen Sierra's powder.

"Are you doing okay?" Pastor Bush said.

"I'm good."

"I really liked how you ended that segment."

"Thank you," she said, hoping that the words reached the man for whom they were intended. In all the months that had passed, she had never spoken to Jarrod. Not a call, not an email, not a text.

She couldn't believe that she didn't rate even one phone call. Not even one chance to explain. It was hard to understand how he could just brush her off like that. Yes, she had hurt him, but she didn't mean to. Shouldn't she have been given a chance?

There were many days when she wanted to run past his office or stake out his apartment. But Sierra was concerned about paparazzi; she didn't want Jarrod to be caught off guard in a picture with her. He didn't deserve that and apparently he thought that she didn't deserve him.

So all of this time had gone by, and at least now, six months later, she didn't go to bed thinking about him every night and she didn't wake up with him on her mind every morning.

"Okay," the cameraman cued them all. "In five, four, three, two, one . . ."

This time "Joy," another Destiny's Divas song, played, starting loud and then fading.

Pastor Bush said, "Our next guest is First Lady Liza Washington."

Liza entered, waving at the applauding audience, looking fresh in her winter-white ankle-length dress. She hugged Sierra, who was standing, too, then took her seat on the stool in the center of the stage, next to Sierra.

"Welcome, Mrs. Washington." Pastor Bush beamed at the woman who'd been a friend for many years.

"Thank you for having me." Liza crossed her right leg over her left, then switched.

"I know this is not easy for you because you also went through quite a transformation upon your return home after the tour was canceled," said Pastor Bush. "Tell the audience what happened."

"Actually, my life changed even before the tour began, before I got on that plane to Houston. Because I knew for a while that something was wrong. I suspected that my husband was having an affair and I was right."

The crowd groaned and Liza wondered why. It was hard for her to believe that there was a soul in the country who hadn't heard her story. At least that's the way she felt whenever she went into the grocery store or went for a walk in the park. She'd even had someone honk at her when she was sitting at a red light a month ago. She thought they were going to ask her for directions, but when she rolled down the window, they said, "Aren't you Reverend Washington's wife?"

"The worst part of it all," said Liza now, "is that the affair he was having was with an underaged girl."

The rumble in the studio audience was a little louder this time, and again Liza wondered why. Had the women who sat staring at her with pity in their eyes been cued to do that?

"Allegedly, she's underage," Pastor Bush said, as if he'd been warned by his legal department.

Liza nodded, though she wondered how someone could be allegedly underage: either you were eighteen or you were not. But she wasn't about to say anything that would add to the time she had to speak. She just wanted this to be over.

"So, what is that status now?" he asked.

"With my husband or me?"

"Both," Pastor Bush said with what Liza thought was a grimace. As if he didn't want to really ask the question.

"Well, my husband and I are separated." She paused as the audience emitted a perfunctory moan. "I haven't spoken to him at all since the incident, but I understand that he's temporarily stepped down from his position as senior pastor." She paused, not giving the name of their church in case there were a few people who hadn't heard their story.

This was the second worst part of it all for her. After the fact that her heart had been crushed by the man she'd loved forever, her soul had cried at the way their ministry crumbled. Ridgewood Macedonia still stood, but with only half of its members.

"As a pastor who's worked to build my own ministry, I was sorry to hear about Reverend Washington stepping down."

"It was best for the church," she said. "Especially since the DA says there will definitely be charges against my . . . against the reverend."

"Do you know what the charges will be?"

"Well, I don't understand all the legalities of it, and since we've been separated, I'm not privy to everything, but I think he and his lawyers are working it out with the prosecutors."

She stopped. That was all the information she was going to give because that was what she had agreed to with Mann's attorneys. She wouldn't say that the prosecutors were looking for other girls. Nor would she say the worst part—that her own daughter couldn't wait to get on a plane so that she could testify against her father.

That was the part—Ingrid's story—that hurt her the most. That was the part that still kept her up at night. That was the part that made her wish that she'd had a gun. . . .

Liza picked up the phone the moment it rang, knowing that she wasn't supposed to have her cell in the hospital. But this time she recognized the number.

"Mom! Are you okay?"

"I'm fine, Ingrid," Liza said as she stepped out of the waiting room and into the hallway.

"I just saw it on CNN."

"What?" Liza asked, only because she was so shocked that the news was out already.

"That Mann's been shot."

"He was. I'm at the hospital now."

"Get away from there, Mom."

"What?"

"The news said that a girl's mother shot him because he was messing with her daughter."

"Ingrid . . . I don't know anything yet. . . ."

"It's true, Mom," Ingrid cried. "You can know that it's true 'cause he did it to me."

Liza fell against the wall at her daughter's words.

"I'm sorry, Mom, but it's true. He molested me!"

It was hard for Liza to listen to all the details that Ingrid gave her in the ten-minute call. But her daughter answered the questions that Liza had had for years. She now understood what had happened to her daughter at thirteen. She now understood what all the daddy and daughter time was about. And she now understood a little about her son.

"Mann hated Charlie because he wasn't a girl. That's why he beat him so much."

Liza couldn't believe that was the only reason. "Ingrid," she'd begun, then stopped as the question stuck in her throat. "Did your father . . . did Mann ever do anything to . . . your brother?"

"No, Mom. He didn't. But Charlie knew what was going on with me."

"Why didn't you tell me?" Liza cried. "Why didn't he?"

"Because I never wanted you to hate me!" Ingrid sobbed. "Please, Mama. Just get out of there."

Liza hung up the phone with promises to call Ingrid back. Then she purchased a bottle of water from the vending machine, called a cab, and then directed the driver to take her to her home.

Liza knew that she had some time—the doctors had already told her that Mann would be there for a night or two. He'd been blessed that Qianna's mother had never learned how to shoot a moving target and she'd only hit him in his leg and his shoulder. So that night, Liza packed everything that she wanted: her clothes and the photographs of her children. And she left.

She might have been living in an Extended Stay hotel, but Liza still found herself in the middle of this drama. The whole sordid situation made for wonderful news fodder.

First there was Qianna's mother. Right on the scene, she'd told the police that she wasn't trying to kill Mann; she'd been trying to castrate him, like that Reverend up in Harlem had done to the man who'd raped his daughter. She wanted to do the same thing to the man who'd raped hers. Her case had yet to come to trial, but most agreed that she would probably get just a year or two, if that.

The Reverend Mann Washington's case was different, though. So much of it had turned into a joke, especially when Mann's attorneys actually had the audacity to stand in front of cameras and try to convince the world that Mann, a fifty-eight-year-old man, actually thought Qianna was eighteen. It was ridiculous—the child barely looked her real age, fifteen. But the media was eating up every salacious moment. . . .

"So, First Lady, what is going to be your message when you go back on tour with Destiny's Divas?"

Liza breathed, she was glad to get to this part. Because now this wasn't about what she'd rehearsed. Now she could speak from her heart.

"The first thing I want to say is that my husband has not yet gone to trial, and in this country we are all innocent until proven guilty," she said, even though she knew he was as guilty as O.J. But still, she waited for the applause to end before she continued. "I think it's important to remember that he's declared his innocence." She paused for a moment as she remembered that moment, that Sunday when he stood at the podium before his congregation and declared that he would fight the false charges. She hadn't been there on that Sunday, or any Sunday since. But the moment had played again and again on the news.

"But what I will be talking about when we go back on tour is what I've been saying all this time. In any marriage, in any relationship, you need complete honesty. And it wasn't just my husband who was being dishonest; I stood on the stage many times, even at your church, and told people that I'd been married for twenty-five years because I was embarrassed to let people know the truth—I'd been married twenty-eight years; I met my husband when I was fifteen and we were married when I was sixteen."

The silence was so loud at first that Liza almost laughed. Even Pastor Bush stood, shocked. And then came the muttering—yes, they were all drawing the same conclusion. Mann Washington had had this affinity for young girls for a long time, probably even before he'd met Liza. She was just the one he'd chosen to marry.

"There were parts of what I'd been saying that were the truth," Liza said, pulling the crowd back in, "and I will continue to speak of these things." She paused and held up her fingers. "Honesty, loyalty, and integrity in every relationship, in every marriage. I'll still be talking about how to have that. I'll still be talking about the wonders of being a wife because, Pastor Bush"—she crossed her ankles as if she was demure—"I plan on being a wonderful wife again to some very blessed man."

The audience laughed and applauded, and Pastor Bush said, "On that note, we'll be right back."

Sierra was the first to stand up when the music cued and the audience was still applauding.

"You were fierce, girl!"

"So were you!"

"This is all going so much better than I thought," Sierra said as she sat down so the makeup artist could check her again. "I thought I was gonna be scared and shaking, having to face all these folks."

"Me too, but I guess whoever said that confession is great for the soul was telling the truth," Liza said, though she hadn't confessed everything. She hadn't said a word about her cousin who had fled to Corinth as if Mississippi was far enough to stop officers from coming after him. It wasn't. The police wanted to charge Buddy, too, though his sin wasn't molestation. His sin was participation, harboring a pedophile. Liza prayed that the district attorney would find a way to throw her cousin into a cell right next to her husband.

One of the stage assistants broke through Liza's thoughts. "We're gonna move your stools for this segment, all right?"

They both nodded, and as Sierra sat on stage left and Liza on the other side, the countdown began. "Five, four, three, two, one . . ."

This time there was no music to lead the show back in. The studio was silent until Pastor Bush began to speak.

"Our next guest is one that we've all known for over fifteen years. Rainebow was a star in the nineties and then, just a few years ago, she decided to become a star for the Lord. Destiny's Divas was her idea, and even what the group is doing now is her brainchild."

The camera moved in for a close-up as Pastor Bush continued, "Here, with the most tragic of all the events that happened on that day, is Rainebow."

Raine's image suddenly filled the fifty-inch video screen in the center of the stage. Her hair had been cut very short, still natural, and the blue prison uniform she wore almost looked fashionable on her.

The studio audience was on their feet; Sierra and Liza joined them, both wiping back tears.

It took more than a minute for the ovation to die down and for Pastor Bush to say, "Well, Raine, I think you can see that you're still very much loved."

Raine grinned. "Thank you, Pastor Bush." And then she waved. "Hey, Sierra, hey, Liza."

The two in the studio waved and laughed, even though tears were still in their eyes.

Pastor Bush said, "Your sisters are sitting here a little choked up, Raine."

Her laughter was full of joy when she said, "They do that all the time when they come to visit me, Pastor."

"So, Raine, tell the audience how you're doing."

"I'm good." She nodded. "I'm so excited that we're going back on the road and really excited, Pastor, that you once again have come through for us and you're letting us do our debut with you."

"Well, you know that I'd do anything for Destiny's Divas, especially you," he said. "So why don't we start at the beginning. What happened when you returned home from the tour?"

"Well, like Liza's, my story doesn't begin that day. It began when I met my husband. Dayo is from Kenya, and about two years ago, his mother came to live with us. From the beginning we had challenges. She had issues primarily with how we were raising our daughter."

"Your twelve-year-old daughter, Nadia."

Raine nodded. "Yes," she said, taking a breath. "She's thirteen now; her birthday was last week."

A sigh rose through the audience as everyone realized the meaning of her words—Nadia had become a teenager while Raine was behind bars.

Raine continued, "To make this story short, my mother-in-law believed in female genital mutilation."

"Without getting too graphic, can you describe what that is."

"Definitely. But first, I want to emphasize that this is cultural, not religious. This is not an Islamic custom. This is practiced by Muslims, Christians, and other religions as well. With that said, in many cultures it's believed that women aren't supposed to experience sexual pleasure. It's believed that if the opportunity for sexual pleasure exists, a girl will become promiscuous, will lose her virginity. Then there's the concern that a woman will stray after marriage. So that's the context of this." She took a deep breath. "The procedure is performed with nothing more than a pair of scissors, a knife, or a razor, and the external female genitalia is removed."

Through the video section that was on the screen in front of her, Raine could see women in the studio cringe, shift, cross and uncross their legs. But no matter how uncomfortable, this was a message that she was going to tell, because it needed to be told.

"This is actually considered a rite of passage into womanhood. Without this procedure, the girl will bring disgrace to her family."

"So," Pastor Bush began, "this was an issue between you and your mother-in-law."

"Yes. She wanted to perform it"—Raine paused for a few seconds—"on my daughter. And I told her, absolutely no way . . . but . . . but . . . ."

With a quick intake of breath, Pastor Bush said, "When you came home, you found her."

Raine sighed, grateful that her pastor was helping her through this part. The hardest part. She nodded. "I found her in my mother-in-law's apartment. She and her sisters were performing . . . they had performed . . . the mutilation on my daughter."

The gasps were loud, and then the chatter. Like Liza, she was surprised at their reaction. This had been on the news all over the country. So why the shock?

Maybe it was because this was the first time they'd heard it from her. Because to this point, Raine had said nothing in public, and had spoken very few words about this in private. . . .

Though she heard the sisters' cries, Raine never looked down at her mother-in-law. Instead, with a strength she didn't know she had, she lifted Nadia from the bed.

"Mom, it hurts. It really hurts!"

"I know, sweetie. But, you're gonna have to help me. I need to get you downstairs so that I can get you to the hospital, okay?"

She nodded and Raine scooped her into her arms. She stumbled through the apartment, down the hall, and into the elevator.

In the lobby, she still cradled her sobbing twelve-year-old as if she were an infant.

"Stanley," Raine screamed, "please get me a cab."

"Oh, my God. Do you want me to call an ambulance?" the doorman said, eyeing the blood on Nadia's legs.

"There's no time."

In less than a minute, she was in the back of a taxi, with Nadia still crying in her arms. At the hospital, the cabdriver helped her carry Nadia into the emergency room.

"Help me," she wailed.

It wasn't until Nadia was taken from her arms and settled on a gurney that Raine broke down.

While Nadia was behind curtains with two doctors, Raine called Dayo from an emergency room telephone.

"My God! My God!" he exclaimed. "I'll be right there."

That was when she told Dayo not to be concerned about their daughter. "I think I killed your mother." She told him to go instead to Beerlulu's apartment.

She was right. The autopsy revealed that Raine had killed Beerlulu with a single blow to her nose with such force that it was driven into her brain.

Dayo had found his mother, still in her apartment, still with her sisters crying over her body. To this day, Raine didn't know why they hadn't called 9-1-1; she didn't care—not really. Her concern was only for her daughter, who had been halfway through the mutilation procedure.

"Your daughter's clitoris has been cut away," the doctor told her.

Raine had screamed until her throat was sore.

The doctor added, "Right now, we're just trying to stop the bleeding. We've sewn her up, but she's lost quite a bit of blood."

Raine had sat by Nadia's bedside, holding her hand, even though she was sedated and asleep. She sat there with tears flowing until Dayo arrived, his eyes reddened with his own sorrow.

Right behind him were two police officers, who dragged her away from her daughter and stuffed her into the backseat of a police cruiser. . . .

"So," Pastor Bush said, "your mother-in-law performed the procedure on your daughter. And . . ." He paused, leaving the opening for Raine.

"And . . . I stopped her, but not before she had cut my daughter."

Moans rose through the studio.

"I didn't mean to hurt her . . . I was just protecting my daughter."

"But you were charged with her murder, correct?"

"Yes. At first, I was charged with first-degree murder, but I took a plea."

"Why did you take a plea? Why didn't you let the people decide your case, because I'm sure there are plenty of mothers here who would have done exactly the same thing."

The applause was as loud as it had been when she first appeared, but Raine held up her hands.

"I don't think I should be applauded in any way for this," she said. "I'm sick about my mother-in-law. I did not mean to kill her—and now there are so many people who've been hurt. My husband, especially. Can you imagine what it's like for him? His mother mutilated his child. And his wife killed his mother. He and I will never be the same."

"How are you and Dayo?"

She hunched her shoulders just a little bit. "Well, this may be one place where prison is helping us. We're separated, but still together, you know. But right now, we're not talking or thinking about us. Our focus is on our daughter."

"So don't you think it would've been better if you had gone to trial? For your daughter?"

"I didn't go to trial *because* of my daughter. First, I wanted her to see that when you do something wrong, you should take responsibility. But the second reason I took the plea—and it was my idea because I didn't want my family dragged through court—but I took the plea because sixty-four months was much better than what I could've received, and that was as little as ten years and probably upwards of twenty."

"Ah," "Oh," "Yes," rang out through the studio.

"Plus, I'm in a minimum-security prison, an experimental prison where offenders are given privileges such as my being able to do this video."

"That makes sense."

Raine said, "That's why I knew we had to make something out of all this tragedy."

The studio erupted once again in applause.

"So, tell us, what will Destiny's Divas be doing?"

"Well, with your help, I was able to petition the court and I can do these video programs. It will allow me, Sierra, and Liza to continue to perform, and even though I can't earn any money from this until I get out of prison, that's okay with me.

"You already know what Sierra and Liza are going to bring to the tour. My focus will completely change. I'll be bringing attention to female genitalia mutilation. To the fact that not only is it performed in Africa, the Middle East, and Southeast Asia, but right here in the United States. It's all underground, of course; women mutilating girls most of the time without anesthesia."

More groans.

"This has already affected more than two hundred million girls worldwide. And it has to be stopped!"

The crowd was on their feet again, and this time even Pastor Bush applauded.

"Well, ladies, this has been quite a show. And I thank you, Sierra Dixon . . ."—the studio audience was still clapping so, Pastor Bush spoke over the sound—"Liza Washington"—the applause grew louder—"and Rainebow!"

This time cheers accompanied the clapping, and from her seat in the prison room where the mini studio had been set up, Raine took a bow, and then laughed.

She said, "Pastor, can I say one last thing?"

When the crowd died down again, Pastor Bush said, "Go ahead."

Raine said, "There are probably people who look at me and Sierra and Liza and think, 'Wow, such horrible things happened.' That's true, but I believe there are no coincidences in Christ. And though I know the Lord isn't happy with some of our decisions, He's turned all of this horror around so that something good can be gained. This is our destiny.

"That's why from this point forward, we're dropping the Divas. We're gonna get down and dirty as we share our tragedies so that someone else can triumph. And with that as our mission, the name Destiny is enough."

The music cued in the background, Pastor Bush said, "On that note, let me introduce to you . . . Destiny . . . singing their hit song, 'Blessings.'"

Cheers rose as Sierra and Liza stood, held hands, and sang to the track. Behind them, Raine sang into her mic, and the three sounded like they were back on the stage.

With the people in the audience clapping and swaying with them, Destiny sang, letting the world know that in spite of it all, there was always a way to hold up your head, look toward heaven, and receive the blessings that God has in store for you.

# Acknowledgments

First and foremost there is no way that I could do this, no way that I could still be writing, without the gifts and blessings that I've been given from my Heavenly Father. Thank you, Lord, for the gift. It is because of you that I have the discipline, that I have the stories, that I have the contract and the readers to keep doing this. My prayer is that I'll be able to do this a while longer.

To the people in my life whom I love. My mother, my sisters, the rest of my family, and my friends—I hate to begin the list because I may leave someone out. And since my goal is never to hurt anyone, it is best that I do it this way. Thank you all for supporting me in all ways and always. I truly do love my family and friends.

I do have to give two special shout-outs: one to ReShonda Tate Billingsley, my writing twin who helped to bring the fun and excitement back to writing after being in this business for so many years. If I could write every book and tour every city with you, that would be such a blessing. Thank you for your friendship and for your love of the craft that challenged me.

The next shout-out is for my pastor, Apostle Beverly "BAM" Crawford. What can I say about you? Thank you for your love, your prayers, your guidance, your teaching. If it were not for you, I wouldn't have written the very first novel back in 1997. It was your teachings that nudged me then and continue to encourage me now. The readers love Pastor Ford and I can't wait until your own story is ready to be told.

To my new editor, Heather Lazare. I have had a wonderful career because I've had the very best editors. That has amazed me, so I just knew my editorial experience couldn't get any better. And then . . . it got better! Heather, you did the doggone thing with this book. It is so much better because of you and I thank you so much for your time, your effort, the lessons, and for helping me take it up a notch.

I was blessed to have one agent for my entire career, and when Elaine Koster passed away, I wasn't sure what would happen to me. In walked Liza Dawson. Liza, you have been a joy. Thank you for jumping in so quickly, for believing in me, and for letting me know that I could and would and should continue doing this. This is our first book together, and I have a feeling there are lots more in our future.

Everyone who's ever heard me speak about my writing career knows how I feel about my publicist, Shida Carr. Shida, I've never been able to capture just how grateful I am for everything you've done. This is our tenth novel together! Can you believe it? You are just simply the very, very best!

To the rest of the team at Touchstone—whenever I call, I feel as if the focus is totally on me, like I'm the only author there. For all of these years your support has meant so much and it continues to get better and better.

And finally, to the people who really should come first because without you, the readers, none of this is even possible. So many of you have been with me through the years, through all twelve adult novels and four young adult novels. Many of you have come along the way and, for some, this novel may be your very first. I am so grateful for your support and I promise that I will continue to bring you the very best novels that I can. Let's make a deal . . . if you keep reading, I'll keep writing!

Whew! Now that this is done, I can press Send and get to work on my 2013 novel. See you then!

Blessings to you all,
*Victoria*

# *Destiny's Divas*

The hot new gospel group Destiny's Divas has gained a following for its special blend of multi-generational singing and sharing testimonials. But its three members are each hiding a secret behind the stories they share on stage. Sierra says she's "saved, single, and celibate," yet her frequent bed-hopping belies her claims. Former pop star Raine advises fans to put family first, but her meddling mother-in-law is driving a wedge between her and her husband. And grand dame Liza is hiding a dark secret about her seemingly perfect marriage—even from herself. As their popularity grows and their first national tour begins, the faith and fate of Destiny's Divas is put to the ultimate test.

## FOR DISCUSSION

1. Sierra, Raine, and Liza each have premonitions about the drama that will later unfold, but they choose to ignore their own intuition. Why are the three main characters so afraid to face the truth? What does the truth ultimately teach them?

2. How could the three members of Destiny's Divas have better used the sisterhood of their group to handle the challenges they faced, before problems escalated? Who do you turn to for support in your own life?

3. Of Sierra, Raine, and Liza, who do you think has the strongest moral center? Whose faith was most tested?

4. Sierra appears to feel no remorse that she lies to the world about being "saved, single, and celibate." Discuss how Sierra is seduced by the idea of fame, and what factors in her life contribute to her attitude.

5. How did the flashbacks to Liza's teen years and her first meeting with Mann add to the narrative and to your understanding of Liza?

6. Mann, the seemingly perfect husband, turned out to be the greatest villain of *Destiny's Divas*. What were some of the clues Liza ignored, and what personality traits did Mann possess that allowed him to mislead her so easily? Did you ever suspect Mann's true nature?

7. Raine had premonitions of the problems Beerlulu would bring to her family. Is there anything she could have done to prevent the tragedy with Nadia? Why or why not?

8. Sierra's ultimate message centers around the pitfalls of sexting and emailing provocative photos. What other lessons does she learn? When it comes to relationships, what does she need to do to temper her sometimes outlandish behavior?

9. Do you believe Sierra's relationship with Jarrod was the real thing? After the pictures were released, is there anything she could do to win him back?

10. Do you think Raine's marriage to Dayo will survive after the fatal incident with Nadia and Beerlulu? Can love between husband and wife truly be unconditional, as Raine says?

11. Yvonne was skeptical of Sierra's past, yet she never fully investigates the singer's background. How could a more thorough vetting of all three divas have saved them from public humiliation?

12. Discuss the main themes of *Destiny's Divas*, like sisterhood, honesty, family, and faith. What other universal messages did you take away?

## A CONVERSATION WITH
## VICTORIA CHRISTOPHER MURRAY

**What first inspired you to write Christian fiction? Are there any universal messages you hope to communicate through your writing?**

You know, I was never inspired to write Christian fiction. I wanted to write fiction about characters that I knew and that meant that some of them would be Christian. While I am not religious, being a Christian is who I am to my core, so no matter what I would've done in my life, my faith was going to go with me. My faith was going to show up.

As far as universal messages, I don't ever plan to put a message in my books. I write and then when a message shows up, I'm pleased. I think the universal message is what the center of the Christian doctrine is all about—forgiveness. Forgiveness of yourself and others. It is the hardest thing to do, but it is what Christ commands.

**Why did you decide to focus on the inner workings of a gospel group for this novel? Were you inspired by the popularity of any real-life group?**

I had this idea for this novel for at least ten years. The seed of the story was inside of me all of that time, but it was just ready to come out now. I wasn't motivated to do the story by any singing group. I was just intrigued by the idea of three women keeping such secrets. I wasn't even really sure about what the secrets would be until I began writing the book.

**Do you think the three divas' testimonies were in any way self-righteous? What message were you hoping to convey?**

No, I didn't think their testimonies were self-righteous at all. I think these are all messages that are being given at conferences around the world even as we speak. Their messages were all great messages. They just weren't living that way; their walk wasn't as strong as their talk.

**In what ways do you think readers will relate to Sierra, Raine, and Liza? How would you have handled each of the situations these divas face in the novel?**

You know, while readers may not find themselves in these exact situations, I think many of us have found ourselves giving advice to others, advice that we know is good, advice that we know is right. But, we may not be walking our talk for lots of reasons. As far as how I would've handled these situations, I just can't imagine myself in any of these situations. I guess the best way to answer that is that I just try to walk my talk, though even I fall short of that sometimes.

**Why did you choose to include the subject of modern-day female genital mutilation in *Destiny's Divas*? Did you find that this is currently practiced in the United States?**
I found out not long ago that this procedure was performed in this country. I could not believe it! Of course, it's illegal and therefore underground, but it is a cultural practice. I decided to study this procedure more, and the more I found out about it, the more I wanted to write about it. I found it fascinating—not in a good way—but fascinating, nonetheless.

**Was the drama in *Destiny's Divas* inspired by any real, ripped-from-the-headlines events?**
Hmmm, no, not really. I did want to address the dangers of sexting. I think young women don't realize the problems with that. Young people in general don't realize that what ends up on the Internet will be there forever; there is no way to erase it. And decisions they're making today are the foundation for their future. So Sierra's story was very important to me. Raine's story has not been in the headlines, though it needs to be. I chose that story because I wanted to let people know female genital mutilation is happening today, it's happening in this country, but it's not something we can change until we understand why it's done. Liza was just my exploration of what happens when we live with long-term lies.

**As a Christian author, how does your own faith reflect or differ from that of your characters? Have you ever had a "divine intervention" while writing?**

Not sure that I've had divine intervention, but I know I'm divinely inspired. My prayer is that my books will not only entertain, but will teach and inspire. I really want God to show up in all of my books, but I don't sit down and figure out how that's going to happen. I just let Him flow in the pages. I hope that my faith is reflected in the characters. I hope that I show that I'm not perfect, but I can lean on God, who is. I would like readers to see that—to see what happens when someone depends on their faith and what happens when someone doesn't.

**Music plays an important role in Sierra, Raine, and Liza's lives. Do you ever listen to music while you write? What songs would readers find on your favorite playlist?**

Ha! I've tried to listen to music while writing and the only thing that happens is that I'll get up and start dancing . . . and will get no work done. So, no, I don't listen to music. I usually have the TV on . . . on mute! I guess I like the feeling of someone there, but I need quiet to "hear the scenes" coming alive in my head.

**Where do you see the future of *Destiny's Divas* headed? Any chance of a sequel?**

There's always a chance for a sequel, but I don't see it. As far as I'm concerned, their story is over.

If you weren't writing, what do you think you'd be doing instead? Do you have another "dream" profession?

If I weren't writing, I'd be a political journalist/pundit or writing teacher. Those are both my dream professions! I'm still dreaming. . . .

## ENHANCE YOUR BOOK CLUB

1. Author Victoria Christopher Murray has written a number of popular books. If you've read any of her previous novels, discuss some of the universal themes and how *Destiny's Divas* differs from her previous books. Browse the author's website at www.victoriachristophermurray.com.

2. Set the mood at your book club meeting by creating a playlist of songs by popular gospel artists like CeCe Winans, Donnie McClurkin, Mary Mary, or the Blind Boys of Alabama. Do you and your book club members have a favorite song? Why do you think these singers have such loyal followings?

3. While you may never be a famous artist or performer, you can still pretend! Arrange a karaoke night with your book club members and let your inner diva shine through. For a collection of lists ranking the best karaoke songs to belt your heart out to, visit: www.karaokepartymachine.com/top_karaoke_songs.

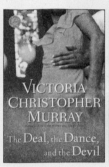

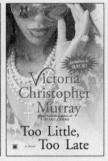

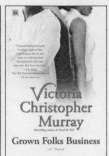